The

To r
or go
and select "Renew/Request Items"

	DATE DUE	

The Lair

The Lair

NORMAN MANEA

TRANSLATED FROM THE ROMANIAN

BY OANA SÂNZIANA MARIAN

YALE UNIVERSITY PRESS ■ NEW HAVEN & LONDON

A MARGELLOS
WORLD REPUBLIC OF LETTERS BOOK

Copyright © 2009 by Norman Manea.

Translation copyright © 2012 by Oana Sânziana Marian.

All rights reserved.

This book may not be reproduced, in whole or in part, including illustrations, in any form (beyond that copying permitted by Sections 107 and 108 of the U.S. Copyright Law and except by reviewers for the public press), without written permission from the publishers.

Yale University Press books may be purchased in quantity for educational, business, or promotional use. For information, please e-mail sales.press@yale.edu (U.S. office) or sales@yaleup.co.uk
(U.K. office).

Set in Electra and Nobel types by Keystone Typesetting, Inc.

Printed in the United States of America.

Library of Congress Cataloging-in-Publication Data

Manea, Norman.

[Vizuina. English]

The lair / Norman Manea ; translated from the Romanian by Oana Sânziana Marian.

    p.   cm.—(Margellos world republic of letters)

ISBN 978-0-300-17994-1 (cloth : alk. paper)

I. Marian, Oana Sânziana. II. Title.

PC840.23.A47V5813 2012

859'.334—dc23

2011042645

A catalogue record for this book is available from the British Library.

This paper meets the requirements of ANSI/NISO Z39.48-1992 (Permanence of Paper).

10 9 8 7 6 5 4 3 2 1

CONTENTS

The Lair

Part I

A new morning, not yet opened. The long and powerful arm of a magician sets in motion the trick of the day. The yellow box stops at the curb's edge.

"Penn Station."

Above the steering wheel, the mug shot and name of the driver: Lev Boltanski.

"Are you Russian?"

"I was."

A hoarse voice. A wide face, small eyes.

"Where from?"

"Odessa."

"I thought Odessa was in Ukraine."

"The Soviet Union! Like me, Odessa is from the Soviet Union. Few people know the difference between Russia and Ukraine. You're not American."

"I am now. Just like you."

No, it's not exactly the beginning of the day . . . The day had started with the stranger whose small, white hand handed him an immaculately white card with gold letters.

"I wonder if you'd agree to appear in a television commercial. The pay is very good."

And before him, the diminutive Dr. Koch. And before him, the thought of Lu, the failed attempt to see her.

The present! The present, mumbled the pedestrian. The new

motto of his life: THE PRESENT. That was all: THE PRESENT! In his past life, there was the guilty past and the gleaming future forever deferred. Now, however . . . he stood bewildered in front of the stranger who was reaching out a small, white hand to him.

"Don't be alarmed. One question, that's all. Just a question."

It was a sudden confrontation. The approach gentle, but guarded.

The intruder is about forty years old. Long, beige mohair overcoat. Immaculately white shirt. No jacket. Short, black hair; black, reckless eyes. Rounded movements, like those of a dancer or a jester. He pulls a black leather wallet out of his jeans. He unfastens the magnet clasp and pulls out the business cards. He extends an immaculately white card, with an address in gold letters: the code of happenstance.

The pedestrian isn't paying attention, entranced by the aggressor's footwear. Cowboy boots! The elegant gentleman is wearing cowboy boots under expensive, slim-cut jeans.

"I'm a producer. Curtis. James Curtis."

That's what it says on the business card: James Curtis, producer.

"I wonder if you'd like to appear in a television commercial. The pay is very good."

"Me, in a commercial? What kind of commercial?"

"For Coca-Cola."

"Me? Coca-Cola?"

"As a chess player."

"Chess and Coca-Cola?"

"Yes, something like that. A man concentrating on the game. At a certain point, he reaches for the glass on the table. Coca-Cola."

"Aha," says the chess player, smiling. "No, I'm sorry. I'm no good for something like that."

"The pay is very good, as I've said. The ads go into syndication and the royalties come automatically. When you least expect it."

"No, that's not my kind of thing."

"Think it over. You have my card. Call me. If you change your mind, give me a call."

"Thank you. I told you, I don't . . . "

"Never say never, as we say here. You're not American, isn't that right?"

"Why wouldn't I be? Do Americans not play chess? They drink Coca-Cola, in any case. And Pepsi. I don't, but I've played my share of chess games. When I was younger."

"See? I knew it. You look the part. Think about it. You have my number, call me. What's your name?"

"Peter."

"Peter what?"

"Peter."

"Okay, Peter, I'll remember. Give me a call."

"You look the part!" Peter the pedestrian mutters, abandoned on the corner of Broadway and 63rd Street.

That's what the producer thinks, if he's even a producer. A nice day, isn't it, Dr. Koch? James Curtis, commercial producer, offered me the ad of the day, Doctor! And so, I looked into the Curtis mirror.

A step to the left, and another step. Once off the curb, he raises his hand. Taxi! The yellow cab stops at the curb's edge.

"Penn Station."

Above the steering wheel, the mug shot and name of the driver: Lev Boltanski.

"Are you Russian?"

"I was."

A smoker's voice. A wide, soft face, small eyes, large teeth, weathered brow.

"Where from?"

"Odessa."

"I thought Odessa was in Ukraine."

"The Soviet Union! Like me, Odessa is from the Soviet Union. Few people know the difference between Russia and Ukraine. You're not American."

"I am now. Just like you . . . Do you like it here on the Moon? The capital of the wanderers, lunatics, and sleepwalkers. Do you like it? A real wonder! One of 777 wonders of the world."

Lyova is silent, but seems attentive.

"Manhattan Island, bought for a song in 1626 by a Frenchman, Minuit. For twenty-four dollars! He paid the Indians in glass beads. They were growing wild strawberries and grapes here, corn, to-bacco. All around there were wolves and bears and rattlesnakes."

Lev or Lyova listens, silently. He doesn't ask anything, seemingly uninterested in the gregarious passenger. He drives slowly, relaxed, atypical for the New York taxi driver. He stops at 34th Street in front of the station, simultaneously turning off the engine and the meter.

"How much?"

"Eight dollars."

The passenger rummages through his pants pockets: first the one, then the other. Next, his jacket. The two pockets of his pants, four of his jacket. He stammers; he doesn't stammer.

"Two dollars! That's all I've got."

"What's that? What are you talking about?"

The mirror above the steering wheel. Look at that, we have a mirror, Doctor. Fate gave me a real mirror.

"Did you say something?" the Soviet-Ukrainian Russian asks.

"No, nothing. But I have no money. Two dollars! That's all I've got. Let's go to the bank. I'm sorry. I didn't realize it. Don't worry, I'll pay for the trip to the bank. There's an ATM on 28th, right there on the corner. A couple of minutes from here."

Lyova peers at his passenger in the mirror, mumbles something in Russian, or Ukrainian. The taxi takes off. The bank is close by, on the corner of 28th Street. The passenger says nothing and waits. Lyova turns around, taking a closer look at the lunatic in the back seat. The mirror's not enough; he wants to see the crook's face.

"What're you doing? Not getting out?"

"I really screwed up. What a mess. My ATM card is in my wallet. I've only just realized that I left my wallet at the library. The cafe-teria. Or maybe at the doctor's. I went to see a doctor."

"You lost your wallet, with your ATM card in it. Is that what you're trying to tell me?"

"I haven't lost it. I left it somewhere. At the doctor's or at the library."

"Should we go there, then? Are you going to pay for this trip, too, with money you don't have? Is that what you're trying to do? Do we go to the library, or the doctor's?"

The customer doesn't answer.

"Was the doctor a psychiatrist? Actually, it doesn't matter. Here they don't ask you what your trouble is, just if you have insurance. That's what they ask. Do you have insurance? Not what hurts or what you think hurts. He was a psychiatrist, wasn't he?"

"He wasn't a psychiatrist. I don't know where I forgot the wallet. Maybe at the library. Let's go back to the station. I'm going to miss my train."

"And the train ride is free, huh?"

"I've got a ticket already. I bought a round-trip ticket."

"Aha, so we're going back to the station. A free ride, eh?" He mumbled something in Russian, or Ukrainian. "Ah, no, I forgot; you've got two bucks. You'll give me your last two bucks to get me going. The rest in colored beads."

"I'm really sorry. Please forgive me. Look, here's my MetroCard, with twenty dollars on it. Take it. I only just bought it today."

"When? When did you buy it? Before the doctor or before the library?"

"I got it when I arrived at the station."

"What am I supposed to do with a MetroCard? I don't ride the subway."

"Maybe someone in your family can use it?"

"Ah, so now you're subsidizing my family! It's probably used up. Or there are only two dollars left on it. So I'd be better off taking the two dollars in cash. Is that what you're saying?"

"I'm not saying anything. I'm just asking you to forgive me. Believe me, I am ashamed. But things like this happen. They can happen to anyone."

"And what do we do when they happen?"

"Look, let's go to the subway station. Right here, near the bank. We can check the card on the machine. It'll show that it's not used up. Twenty dollars left on it. It'll only take a minute."

"And who's going to do that?"

"Well, I . . . or no, better you. You check it. I'll wait here in the cab."

"Sure, I go check it, and you take off!"

He whistles out a short phrase in Russian, or Ukrainian.

"Take my bag with you. Believe me, I won't leave without my bag. It's too important. Here, I'll give it to you. I'll wait here."

The passenger struggles to get the bag over the divider. Lyova takes it and groans at its weight.

"What've you got inside, granite? Mercury? Mercury is heavier, isn't it?"

"Books, stuff. Personal things."

"Personal things! That's why they're so heavy!"

Lyova heads toward the subway station, with the bag in tow. He waddles like a potbellied duck. He comes back, slouching to the left, because of the bagful of mercury.

"Okay. It's unused. Twenty dollars. I'll take it."

He goes to get back into the car but his door is blocked by a cheerful Italian. Jacket, pants, hat, all made of black leather.

"I have to get out to Westchester, fast. It's very urgent. I'll give you a hundred."

"Westchester! I can't. I'm in enough of a mess as it is. This jerk doesn't have the money to pay for his ride."

"How much is it?"

"Eight dollars. Actually, twelve. Now it's twelve."

"I'll give you eight bucks, twelve, whatever. I'll give you twenty. A hundred and twenty bucks to Westchester. Let's go. Right now."

Lyova measures up the mobster, takes a step toward the car, raising his hands up in the air like a heavyweight.

"Look buddy, I'm not going to any Westchester! I'm taking this passenger to Penn Station. Penn Station! He's going to miss his train."

"Penn Station! Let the guy walk, it's close enough! I'm offering you a hundred and twenty bucks!"

"I'm not going! I already told you."

"You're an idiot! An idiot!" yells the mobster.

Lyova doesn't seem offended. He agrees, "Yes, sir, I'm an idiot." He returns the bag to the passenger in the back, slams the door, spits some words in Russian, or Ukrainian, and sits behind the wheel. He doesn't start the engine. He wants to calm himself. Distracted, he looks at the passenger in the mirror.

"Why were you at the doctor's? Are you sick?"

The patient doesn't answer.

"Is it serious?"

"There's nothing wrong with me."

"Why did you go to the doctor? A checkup, as Americans call it? But you're not American. What's the matter with you?"

"Nothing, I told you."

"Here, we're just numbers. Nothing more. Insurance, accounts, credit. Numbers. Why see a doctor? The wife? Is your wife sick?"

"My wife?"

"Your significant other, as they say here? Wife, friend, partner, *significant other*. Is she sick?"

"No, she works at that doctor's office. I go there to see her from time to time. She finds out when my appointments are and makes sure she's not around. She knew this time, too, I'd bet on it. No sign of her."

"Divorced? I mean, are you separated? You go to see her even though she doesn't want to see you? Is that how it is?"

"We're not divorced."

"Okay. Let's go to the station."

Lyova turns the key, the cab sputters, and then they are at the station. The customer descends; the bag descends.

"Wait, mister! Take your goddamn MetroCard. Take it with you."

"What's that? I thought we agreed . . ."

"Beat it! Go on, get out of here!" Lyova shouts, swearing in Russian, or Ukrainian.

Crowd. Hubbub, commotion. The traveler eventually finds the timetables, then gets lost. Then finds track 9. Then the train.

THE PRESENT, nothing else. Not too bad, not too bad, the train repeats in rhythm as it slowly leaves the metropolis behind.

It's not bad, it could be worse, the exhausted passenger thinks, once in his seat. The bag next to him in the empty seat by the window. He considers the brand new MetroCard. Lyova's gift. A good man, that Russian. Or, rather, that Ukrainian, er, Soviet. Solid. A solid, good man, that's the conclusion of the day, Doctor. Lu wasn't there, but it was better that way. I need to get used to it. She's already gotten used to it, probably. No, she hasn't gotten used to it. Otherwise, she'd be there. She wouldn't care. She's avoiding the past. As well as the present, of late. The present is the past; that's why she wasn't there. So that I'd have no mirror. She's sparing me the mirror, the old as well as the new. She's protecting me, the sweetheart.

No, that wasn't how the morning had started . . . The irreversible chronometer of the day had been set off earlier in Dr. Koch's office.

"Look in the mirror," the doctor ordered.

The patient looked at his shoes. Giant. Surly. Mummies, prehistoric animals!

"Have you looked in the mirror recently? I've told you before, exercise. Exercise, diet, rest! In the old days, the plowman didn't have neuroses. And neither did the forester, who worked in the woods whole days on end. The body is our home. If we don't take care of the body, life becomes miserable. Have you looked in the mirror?"

Leaden back of the neck. Pain in his arm. Shivers, cold sweats, panic.

"Lose some weight! Get some exercise, avoid stress. Your head aches? Take an aspirin. Confusion? Apathy? This time, it wasn't a crisis. Tics. Nervous tics. Neuro-vegetative, as we used to call them in the Old Country. Lazy stomach. The sedentary life."

The doctor stares at the patient, the patient stares, thoughtfully, at his shoes.

"Ulcer? Maybe. Pressure 140 over 92. That's not too bad. Pain in the back of your neck? From sitting still too much. Movement, man! Have you looked in the mirror? Have you looked in the mirror, recently? Electrocardiogram? Money in the garbage. Your heart's not the problem. Exercise, diet, fresh air! That's the prescription. Lifestyle. Did you look in the mirror? Did you look? An elephant!"

The patient abandons the doctor's office, stumbling. He sits on a bench, in a nearby park.

Friday, after lunch. The rush before the break. The nine-to-fivers hurrying across the week's river, toward the weekend. Before anyone is aware of what's happening, another seven days and nights blow by. Spring's uncertain sky; the doctor is there. Avicenna-Koch! A mirror, what do you know! The patient waves the image away. The trio of puppeteers in the park juggles burlesque marionettes on the ends of long, delicate fingers. Thundering music. Alleys to the left and right. Passersby of all ages and ethnicities. The doctor among them. The kaleidoscope of the city spins, with little Koch in the center of it all.

The river moves gently to the left of the train. You never step twice in the same primordial water. This is what the passenger sees out the window, along the length of the train tracks: water that doesn't grow old and is never the same water. Nor the air. Nor the fluid, therapeutic horizon.

Past, present, future, time at one with itself, was that the horizon? Mild waters, moments aging, rot and dejection. The water grows slowly, quietly, comfortingly, over the sleeping passenger. The conductor taps him gingerly on the shoulder. The train is stopped in the station.

He quickly gathers his bag, his jacket. He descends; he's on the platform; look at him, poor lost sucker, in the station, gazing at the wide and quiet river in front of him.

Oof, he's arrived! The empty platform, the mountains in the distance, the river only a stone's throw away. A clear, cold afternoon.

The beginning of the world. He doesn't yet have a clue how close the end is. The end of his world.

The chronometer swallows the seconds of the armistice.

■

Peter appeared suddenly, as though in a dream, or in a nightmare.

"Peter. Gaşpar. Mynheer. Mynheer Peter Gaşpar here."

A voice from the void. Professor Gora was no longer sure where he was. He took note of the walls lined with books and remained silent. He was in no mood to answer; it was an aggressive surprise.

Peter! Was it *Mynheer Pieter Peeperkorn*, the popular protagonist from the great novel he'd read decades ago, once the novel of his world? Or Peter Gaşpar, dubbed *Mynheer*, from the socialist literary café in the Balkans?

Nothing was certain, except for the bookshelves, those in front of him and the ones in his mind.

Young Gaşpar's only publication from the years of "legalized bliss," as he used to call his former utopia, was titled *Mynheer*. The story behind the nickname was thin and bizarre; chance had conspired with the library.

How had Peter Gaşpar found the phone number of Professor Augustin Gora, who had vanished into the great United States of America?

"Where are you? Have you also made it to the other world?"

The ghost confirmed that, yes, he'd come some time ago, as a doctorate fellow at New York University.

"A doctorate? In architecture? Weren't you . . . ?"

"No, I wasn't an architect. Just a technician-architect. A junior in college when they arrested my father again; they expelled me. Three years of architecture were equivalent to a midrange school."

"There's such a thing as a doctorate here . . . "

"In art, Professor. History of art. Even in our tranquil Homeland, there were night classes. Art history classes. You couldn't have known this."

"No."

Not true, but he wasn't in the mood for a long conversation.

Gaşpar explained that he had no intention of becoming an expert in German abstract expressionism, as his scholarship promised. He simply wanted to remain in the New World.

Right now, when hope was being reborn in Eastern Europe? He wasn't a young man anymore; nor had he come for the future of his nonexistent children. And so, then? Was he alone? No, Lu had come with him. She'd finished university with an English degree, as Professor Gora knew all too well. English would dull her in this land, where she'd moored, or run aground. Yes, she had initiated Peter in the New World's native language, with underwhelming results; he couldn't decipher the station names as they were announced in the subway. For the time being, he had no work permit.

Laconic answers to Professor Gora's spare and weary questions.

"I'd had enough, that's all. I'm not the adventurous type, and I'm not interested in tourism. But I'd never left my country even once. Not once! Forty years of legalized bliss, in the same place! But now I've left! *For good*, as you say here. I have an absolute, urgent need for irresponsibility. At least now, before the funeral processions. Ir-re-spon-si-bil-i-ty."

He accentuated this word, heavily, twice, as if he were talking to an idiot, or simply to himself. Ir-re-spon-si-bil-i-ty.

He was speaking of an end, not a beginning, about getting out of a situation, not of entering another. About a departure, not an arrival.

"You're right. I'm not staking my claim to a new place; I'm freeing myself of the old one. The same hide-and-seek game with death, somewhere new, outside of the old cage. For the time being, I need a job. A salary. It would be both dishonest and wearisome to keep up the charade of the scholarship. Lu's a babysitter now. She's always liked the children she never had."

So, the adventurer had, in fact, come for the adventure . . . Gloomily, Professor Gora smiled, measuring with his eyes the shelves full of adventure.

"You've come for adventure."

"I didn't say adventure. Ir-re-spon-si-bil-i-ty."

Peter Gaşpar made sure to specify that Professor Gora wasn't to send him money. He just wanted advice from time to time, or, at least, to be able to talk to someone familiar, that was all.

Familiar? Yes, they'd gotten to know each other when Gora was Ludmila's husband.

"We'll be in touch," and that was all that the newcomer wanted to say.

■

Some time had elapsed since that nebulous conversation with Peter. Or had it been nebulous only in Gora's mind? Peter maintained that though he'd arrived in America resolved not to look for Gora, he'd changed his mind without knowing why. Time passed between his arrival and this decision, and some more time passed after this first conversation, as well. Peter disappeared but continued to haunt Gora. The professor asked himself how he should define reality. He closed and reopened his eyes, looked at the bookshelves, the large and lustrous desk, the computer, the pair of red gloves on the edge of the table, the telephone, the big, open folder spilling a pile of blank pages.

Peter Gaşpar evoked memories about which he was no longer—and didn't want to be—sure. He had increasingly more faith in books than in memories he didn't want anything to do with. He believed in what survived in writing. The mind and soul of the interlocutor. The interlocutor that he was now belonged to the past.

A stranger among strangers, one may still reencounter friends from a previous life. In books! The books from his previous life were waiting for him. Hopeful comrades, they welcomed him in other languages. Loyal conversationalists, ready to restore his familiar habits, to humanize his wandering.

He wasn't at all in the mood for Peter Gaşpar. Pieter Peeperkorn, yes. He was happy to encounter Mynheer Peeperkorn again, and immediately following the telephone conversation, he reread those three chapters about the Dutchman in the massive novel of the 1920s.

In the sanatorium of *The Magic Mountain*, Hans Castorp is waiting wistfully for Clavdia Chauchat. The woman of his dreams appears on the arm of a fabulous companion. Tall and rosy brow, dense lines. Long, thin, white hair, thin goatee. Large mouth and nose, mangled lips. Wide, spotted hands, long, sharp nails. With his stature and accent, the Dutchman dominated the society of the sanatorium. Jerky, elliptical, incoherent discourse.

That set-tles it. And you must keep in mind and never—not for a moment—lose sight of the fact that—but enough on that topic . . . So then, Emchen my child, listen well: a little bread, my dear.

That's what Peeperkorn called the booze that enlivened him: bread.

Bread, Renzchen, but not baked bread, of that we have a sufficiency, in all shapes and sizes. Not baked, but distilled, my angel. The bread of God, clear as crystal, my little Nickname, that we may be regaled . . . in light of our duty, our holy obligation—for example, the debt of honor incumbent upon me to turn with a most cordial heart to you, so small but full of character—a gin, my love!

The wide-breasted stranger with the tall brow, dingy eyes, and the strong head enveloped in the white flames of his hair was an imposing man. Seized at alternately by chills and by fever. An imposing force, a magnificent incoherence.

Life is short, whereas our ability to meet its challenges is but— those are facts, my child. Laws. In-ex-or-a-bilities.

Telegraphic, fractured missives, confused understandings. A personality! With the greatness of a tribal chief, his countenance and dingy gaze subdue his audience. The large hand of a captain, a clutched fist pounding the table.

Whatever is simple! Whatever is holy! Fine, you understand me. A bottle of wine, a steaming dish of eggs, pure grain spirits—let us first measure up to and enjoy such things before we—absolutely, my dear sir. Settled.

An offbeat burlesque. Powerlessness, just like strength, devastated him.

It may be a sin—and a token of our inadequacies—to indulge in refined tastes without having given the simple, natural gifts of life, the great and holy gifts, their due . . . the defeat of feeling in the face of life, that is the inadequacy for which there is no pardon, no pity, no honor . . . It is the end, the despair of hell itself, doomsday . . .

The face and silhouette of Peter Gaşpar, whom he hadn't seen for over twenty years, and not often even before that, remained obscure. Gora remembered only that he didn't resemble Pieter Peeperkorn. This he remembered for certain.

There was another motivation behind that nickname. A story that Peter Gaşpar wrote, *Mynheer*, caused some ripples among the socialist literati. Slaves forced to praise their slavery are happily receptive even to the most furtive winks of complicity, or a fraction of mockery. Was there some secret gunpowder hidden within the story that spurred Peter Gaşpar's notoriety among the socialist underground? It was just a story! Published in a provincial journal, what's more. Forty years after the celebrated novel of the celebrated Thomas of Lübeck! Was there some codified allusion that escaped the censor's eye? Such oddities did happen, quickly to be forgotten. Not long after the publication, the author was branded with the name of his protagonist. Not even a name, a formal address-become-name. Mister, Monsieur, Monsignor. Mynheer! The nickname circulated in the literary café, and then beyond it. The name fueled the rumors that surrounded Peter Gaşpar; the author never published anything again, but the halo wouldn't be shattered. In the country that invented rumors, it was rumored that Peter had authored other literary charades, unknown to anyone. It was whispered that he worked, in secret, on a masterpiece. Rumors were the garlicky black bread of the dictatorship.

Nothing but a petty technician in a petty, socialist enterprise, Gaşpar contributed to cultural journals with short, ironic texts, eschewing the wooden, official language. Casual little columns on theater and art exhibitions, even on the races, or philately. He could be spotted at shows and gallery openings and cocktail parties. Embarrassed (but not embarrassed enough) by his phantom and persistent prestige, obsessed with the spies that teemed all around.

Tall, lean, and ill at ease as a result of a lanky body, as if he'd borrowed it for too long and forgotten to return it.

Shaved head with a black moustache and goatee, he resembled a hussar employed by a musical theater producer. His intense, black gaze under his thick eyebrows of crude oil. Small hands, smooth brow. Straight nose, in defiance of his heredity.

The way he looked, his name could have been Hungarian or German. It was rumored, however, that he might be circumcised. So he was. The rumor proved sovereign, in keeping with tradition. Some even alleged that his biography contained certain dramatic details, though the facts were vague, just like those concerning his supposed masterpiece. He seemed like any other, though maybe he wasn't. His comradely casualness, left over from when he played hockey and basketball and football in youth leagues, inspired sympathy.

His post-Habsburgian-Transylvanian education conflicted with the Balkan and Parisian mannerisms characteristic of metropolitan Bucharest. Could Transylvania be considered occidental? Mynheer Peeperkorn also conferred on his successor a second, convenient ennoblement, "The Dutchman." His company took to calling him by that nickname; you could hear them yell loudly, "Hey, Dutchman!"

Gaşpar's text defied the distorted "debates" of the Authority, the great words and the humanist catchphrases.

Incoherence was subversive. Is that what Gaşpar was suggesting? He appeared sometimes, donning Peeperkorn's felt hat, and, after a few shots of vodka, recited his namesake's lines, with an outstretched, imploring hand.

We're cheating, my good men. This wind, this tender, fresh fragrance . . . presentiments and memories. Liquidated, my good men. I'll stop. Li-qui-da-ted. The summit, a black and rotating point and a grand bird of prey. An eagle of the great solitudes. The bird of Jupiter, the lion of the air.

Was the story *Mynheer*, somehow, a codified plea in favor of the New World? A *self-made man*, the international Peeperkorn! The King of Coffee, a Dutchman with a residence in Java, near his lover with the Caucasian eyes. A plea for freedom and for the Statue on the Hudson? Liberty, vitality!

How well can you know a person lost among the consumers of illusions, along the meridian where the Orient meets the Occident? Professor Gora would not have had the courage to respond. Pieter Peeperkorn brought the page to life, while Gora waited in vain; Gaşpar would not appear.

In the book the giant Dutchman commits suicide, injecting himself with animal venom and plant poisons. The tropical fevers drain his power. "The failure to perceive life intensely is a cosmic catastrophe," the letter says. Shame before God.

Gora hoped to understand, gradually, what he couldn't understand previously. Could Mynheer Gaşpar become in America what everyone had said he was, after all?

■

Some years back, Peter, who was then a senior in high school, suddenly found himself on a visit to relatives in the capital.

Tall, pale, furrowed, and burdened with a mission disproportionately heavy for his age. He had only a few hours to go before the return train. He'd traveled overnight from the western corner of the country, for this bizarre family reunion, to relate what had happened to his father, or to warn his relatives about the consequences that could befall them.

The prosecutor David Gaşpar was entirely unaware of his wife's initiative to send the adolescent—who was, at that moment, generally more preoccupied with basketball than with the shadows of politics—on such a mission. Eva Gaşpar arranged for the boy's absence not to produce any suspicion. The son sometimes used to sleep at the house of a fellow student, Tibor, whose parents kept the secret.

Augustin Gora instantly registered the concern on the faces of Lu's parents. They already knew, it seemed, about David Gaşpar's dismissal and about similar cases. Comrade Serafim and Comrade Gaşpar were merely cousins, but fear was transmitted quickly, like a virus. Worried about their own situation, they didn't discuss the news with their son-in-law, who was also asking himself, then—and continued to ask himself afterward—if they had confided in friends, and who these friends could have been. He preferred to believe that, if these friends existed, they would have counted him among them.

On that dusty July afternoon Peter was invited to sit in the large, red leather armchair in the living room, to relate the details of his message. Gora felt the danger migrating from the western borders of the country toward his new family.

The young athlete became instantly contaminated with the unease of those listening while he described the absurd and sudden raid of his parents' house. The former watchmaker David Gaşpar was inexplicably dismissed from his function as a prosecutor of socialist justice! If the Party wants to, it sends a watchmaker to a one-year school and turns him into a prosecutor overnight; and if the Party wants to, the prosecutor, overnight, is no longer a prosecutor. He couldn't be accused of dishonesty or politically iconoclastic actions, just for the excessive intransigence with which he served the Cause. The pretext of the dismissal remained obscure; the disgrace could have consequences just as absurd as the motivation. This was the message with which Eva Gaşpar entrusted her young son.

The silence was soon followed by the assurances with which the hosts overwhelmed the guest: it was nothing but a mistake or misunderstanding; David wasn't the kind to take such an injustice sitting down; he'll contest it, demand recourse and be exonerated in the end. Rivalries and intrigues exist everywhere people exist; the indignities and mistakes couldn't go on forever; the young student will find out, and soon, because justice always prevails, after all. The guest was served with sweets. Lu showed him the family library and took him on a long walk through the capital. On the way back, the traveler was advised to rest, as he faced a sleepless night on the way home.

That night, on the way back from taking his guest to the train, Gora learned the story of Peter's birth.

The watchmaker David Gaşpar had succeeded in hiding during the first year of the war, and then the second year, as well, together with his wife and daughter; but in the spring of 1944, they were discovered and sent to Auschwitz by the Hungarian authorities who presided over Transylvania. His wife and daughter were gassed immediately after arrival. David survived, working first in a little workshop where the gold taken from the living and the dead was turned into jewelry. He was transferred to hard—brutal—labor. He was lucky to possess a vigorous constitution. After the death of his loved ones, he put aside sentiments, worries, and became alone and strong. Indifferent, calculated, determined to survive.

Liberated by the Soviets, he met his future wife in the triage hospital for former detainees. They were married on the long way back home.

Eva, ten years younger than he, didn't want to return to the place from which she was sent to her death. She dreamed of the Promised Land, the land set aside for survivors. David proved unyielding, however. Determined to come home, to look into the eyes of his former friends and neighbors, the former policemen and politicians who'd erased his name from the roster of the living.

They returned in the fall of 1946, after detours through devastated Europe. David and Eva, his new wife, and the infant Peter, born in Belgrade, along the complicated detours of the return. Otilia Serafim, Ludmila's mother, contended that Peter might not even be David's son. "In the chaos of the liberation, copulation was general. Anyone with anyone. A great orgy to enliven the dead."

"The story disturbed us all," Lu confessed. "Even today the family is uncomfortable with it. We weren't that well off either during the war. Filth, humiliation, danger, labor camps, daily panic. But David's story is still something else entirely."

Once back in his native town, the watchmaker David Gaşpar

didn't look into the eyes of former neighbors or policemen or politicians, as he'd sworn he would. He simply refused to remember the concentration camp. He called on his friends and family to do the same.

Lu's face had become slender, as in old biblical images. His Madonna had paled. Gora was shocked at the effect those very words had had on her. Vulnerable to emotive excesses, she herself intensified them. Her fragility seemed like the visible face of a presentiment, suddenly alerted. She intercepted, or allowed herself to be intercepted by, vague signs; her incertitude prompted her unease.

She stopped, to calm her pulse. She looked increasingly pale.

"I can feel what you're thinking. No, there was never any room in my family for religion, as you well know. Not in the past, and even less so now, when atheism has become opportunism. My parents were freethinkers before becoming Communists. They instilled in me their rationalism, and solidarity with the humiliated and oppressed. I had no access to mystical books or people, and I didn't attend debates about the transcendent. And still, again and again, moments come when something obscure slips by me, or derails me. Something leaves me vulnerable. Susceptible to I don't know what. Something unknown lives here, hidden, inside me."

All of a sudden, she shook her rich, black hair. Her face remained white; her eyes burned like a fever. In the course of a brief and nervous spasm, she seemed to have shaken her burden loose, along with her hair.

"I was thinking of Peter. When the boy was born, David Gaşpar said to his wife, 'He's going to live in another world, and we, with him.' And Eva told him, 'He was born to marked parents. The New World contains the Old World, the past will live in him, as well.' They never revealed to Peter that his father had been married before, and that he'd had another daughter, a sister who was never to be a sister. My mother doubts that David is actually Peter's father. Only he and Eva know, maybe not even they."

Lu's voice and gaze had fallen.

And now that he was in the New World, how much had Peter brought from the past, and how much had Lu? Gora asked himself. What else did they bring?

Later, Professor Gora learned that Peter had refused the "survivor" status that the well-intentioned Americans were prepared to give him, just as he'd always refused any allusion to the tragedy out of which he was born. He distanced himself abruptly from any discussion about the horror that was responsible for his parents' union.

Between the teenager who found himself unexpectedly in his relatives' house and the exile who awoke like a phantom, twenty years later, at the sound of the phone (and in the mind of Professor Gora), was Lu, the wife of Augustin Gora, seen on a summer's evening, on an abandoned sidewalk.

Old anxieties assaulted Professor Gora's solitude once again. He would have liked to delay them, to remain in Lu's story. It pained him and pleased him; it invigorated him; it retrieved him from the void.

He'd closed his eyes, to remain this way with Lu, suspended in the impossible.

After the adolescent's return home, there was no more than the rare news from the Gaşpar family.

Lu had started to speak more and more about Eva Gaşpar. She didn't know her personally, but she described her with a mix of admiration and apprehension. She called her on the phone. Eva's anxiety was probably tied to Peter, not to her husband, or so it appeared to Lu. Some kind of maternal fervor. Eva seemed at last to have found, not through her husband, but through her son, some relief from the past. An obsession with Peter's future had taken hold of her.

"Eva is possessive," Gora decided, annoyed. "She's uncertain about the resolution of her own life. And all too certain about the lives of others."

Lu shuddered, shocked. She watched him. Frowning, hurt. Frightened, it seemed. The silence had grown, and Gora never brought up the subject of Eva Gaşpar again. He resigned himself to listen to the subsequent short bits of information, all of them selected, it seemed, with the aim of contradicting his interpretation.

Peter had been neither a predictable nor a natural choice for Lu. Was he the modest acceptance of the familiar? Lu didn't value modesty, and didn't accept psychoanalytical speculations. She considered them frivolous forays devoid of intimacy. She preferred to judge and to be judged on the basis of facts. Though, actually, she didn't like at all to be judged.

Familiarity, then?

"I'm leaving for a few days, to see the Gaşpars. I want to meet Eva. To understand what's happening over there. Especially, what happened. In that past that wasn't mine . . . "

Her husband didn't hide his perplexity.

"Don't you see? I live in an aquarium. I can't, just like that, become a bricklayer on a construction site. Just to see what a wonderful existence our wonderful working class leads, an existence about which I know nothing, except the fairytales I read in the papers. But I can go to the Gaşpars. Not to find out why the prosecutor is no longer a prosecutor, even though the effort would be worth it. But to find out something else, something more painful, probably."

She wanted out of the aquarium! The family-aquarium? Marriage-aquarium? She'd dreamed of refuge in marriage and family; the familiar had both balanced and stimulated her. So, why this sudden other impulse?

She returned from the Gaşpars with horrific stories of the concentration camps. She was white, pale, as if she had returned from another world. Something essential seemed to have changed. She'd acquired something painful and powerful. She'd decoded, perhaps, mysteries of her own, which had been closed off from her until then. It could be a transfer of one premise to another, thought Gora.

Or had she absorbed something of which she wasn't conscious, a premise not originally her own? Was she now convinced that it had always been there?

■

Gora didn't hear about the bizarre union between Lu and her young cousin Peter until his friend Palade returned from a visit to the faraway country, then just barely out of dictatorship. Palade, called Portland in his adored America, had departed in order to present his fiancée to his family. He returned disgusted by the chaos, the corruption and demagogy that marked the transition from nowhere toward nowhere.

Gora had met Mihnea Palade a long time before that, at the beginning of his time at university, when he was a student. During the period of Eastern totalitarian "liberalization," when the days and nights of the amphitheater were bloating from the yeast of hope. Exaltation and suspicion competed for supremacy. The mere mathematics student Palade, with his enormous lenses slipping down his fine nose, was quiet for a long time, and then spoke for a long time. No one knew who'd brought him to the attic of simmering controversies. He listened attentively, answered excessively. He was widely read, seemed to know everything, and conscious that he didn't really know anything. Through the large windows of the university, he measured the horizon in the distance. He worked fastidiously, complained that the library hours were too short.

Having descended from the provinces like a conquistador, he immediately stood out among the students and professors, and was therefore immediately suspect. He was proud of that dubious honor. He wasn't the only intruder in the group of humanists. The students from the medical and polytechnic schools, some still in high school, and even some former students, who now worked as laborers, or unemployed graduates, were experimenting with a salon of readings and open dialogue.

In that small circle of friends, they discussed books gotten through complicated subterfuges. A feverish, subterranean trade of inaccessible volumes, an interloping, bookish world. The dark magic of the forbidden and the unknown.

Expatriate authors took on a mythical aura. After the war, some made a name for themselves in the West. The great scholar Cosmin Dima had become the cult model. Palade managed to find his old books, and even some that had been published after the war, in the Occident.

News, books, rumors, debates. The urgency of days and nights. All of it was a mere respite. At any moment, illusions could become prohibitions, or crimes. The sense of the provisional and of impatience kindled the dialogue; no one could withstand impatience.

The French assistant professor Augustin Gora would often mingle with the students. The meetings took place in an attic, in the home of one of the members. An ample loft furnished with old couches and odd chairs. The immense window gave the impression that they were outdoors, on the roof.

Gora attended the discussion of Kafka's *The Trial*. The groundless arrest of K. was loaded with connotations; anyone could be arrested, without justification; terror was a juggler of absurd games. Arrested without fault, K. didn't pretend to be innocent. He seemed burdened by an obscure, metaphysical guilt.

The young tried to liberate themselves from the compromises of the aged, but they also understood their own cowardice in the face of the Authority. They learned to manipulate the official slogans to justify controversy. In shadow themselves, they prowled for spies; there was no shortage of informants disguised as rebels. You could readily identify intelligence, but not character.

Mihnea Palade asked Gora at the end of one night if he could accompany him on his walk home. Along ambling detours through the park by the lakes, Gora allowed himself to be both conquered by friendship and liberated from his own caution. And in the frenzy of this covetous torment, he let slip the fact that he'd received an invitation from an American university. In risking a real conversation, he was recovering his dignity.

The student grew quiet. Not just in response to the confidence that was being entrusted to him, on a first meeting, no less, but also to the news itself. In those years and in that place, isolation was the thing that unified them. The captives of the reading room had a double pretext for their alliance to one another.

At the following meeting, they read Borges, translated by a student of Spanish among them. The fictional planet of Tlon, imagined places, the cosmos revealed through a cerebral game. In 1942 in France, in the apartment of a princess, a real artifact was supposedly found bearing an inscription in the Tlon alphabet (also the name of the fictitious planet). Some time later an unknown metal, also from Tlon, was found in the pocket of a dead man in South America. Then, just as unexpectedly, in 1944 in Memphis, Tennessee, forty volumes of the *Tlon Encyclopedia* surfaced.

Gora followed these captivating charades, watching the young man seated on the floor; he was quiet, ecstatic, at times opaque to the influence of controversy, absorbed in the pages he'd received from the translator after the reading. In the next Borgesian story, the enigma in question was an investigation, a series of entangled crimes. The detective, obsessed with the killer's logic, comprehends too late that he has been ensnared by reason; he becomes aware that he himself will be the next victim. He submits nonetheless to the fatality and shows up at the established rendezvous. Before emptying his revolver, the killer pronounces the sentence and the explanation, "The world is a labyrinth from which it's impossible to escape." Victim and killer are caught in the logic of the same dark, codified past.

No sooner had the reading ended that Palade rose, electrified, in the middle of the room.

"It's a complicated symbolism. Actually, the text focuses on a certain evasion. Is freedom the escape from the labyrinth, or the dissolution of the labyrinth altogether? And what's the meaning of the word *labyrinth* when found in the context of an invisible and murderous trajectory? A single and eternal labyrinthine stroke . . . why labyrinthine? If it's a single stroke, it should be rectilinear, and swift. Like a mathematician, I should be able to understand the labyrinth of a straight line, the shortest distance between two points, even if situated at an infinite distance between them."

The student's voice was shaking. A thin, timid voice, in opposition to the vitality of his argument and gesticulations.

"Do you remember the words of the blind man from Buenos Aires? 'I know something that the Greeks didn't know—uncertainty,' says Borges. Should I repeat the quotation? I won't repeat it, but it would be good not to forget it. Freedom is escape from the tyranny of a singular and rational system of thought, that's what freedom is, an open, incomplete thought; it's antidogmatic, the uncertainty, the nebulous nature of probabilities."

His glasses had slipped down his nose, as often happened in agitated moments. He was mumbling, "Uncertainty! The imperfect allows for dispute and revelation."

Gora was shocked. Palade's words reminded him of something he'd read or heard, but he couldn't locate it. He hoped that the student would repeat the idea.

On the way to Gora's home, young Mihnea Palade's glasses slipped down his nose again and again. In that neighborhood near the lakes, the more elegant periphery of the city, the spring evening conspired with mystery and enchantment.

Augustin Gora had now not only the invitation, but something even more improbable—a passport.

"Yes, people are talking about this," the student muttered, sheepishly staring at the pavement. "You have relatives in high places."

"My wife's relatives," Gora hurried to specify.

A naïve reply. Despite the mild relaxation of things during that time, if you could come by a passport, you couldn't exactly be trusted. Even children knew this for a fact.

"Are you leaving with your wife?"

The question was actually, "Are you leaving for good?" One passport alone was a dubious privilege; a couple with passports fueled more doubt.

"I hope. I don't know yet."

Gora didn't feel like talking anymore. The silence lengthened and grew thick. It wasn't easy to confess that Dr. Feldman, Ludmila's uncle, had been held captive in the same cell with the great Party and state leader when he was a young Communist. Or that Dr. Feldman had obtained the passports for the Gora couple.

"I was asked to join the Party," whispered the now agitated student, the comment bearing an ambiguous relevance to the subject.

"I was, too," said the professor after a while.

"The price of the passport?"

"I didn't accept."

With this, the already suspect Gora became, evidently, more suspect. Palade didn't hesitate to raise the stakes.

"I was visited by an officer from the secret police."

This time, the student was staring the professor directly in the eyes, looking to see what couldn't be seen.

"Routine. Standard recruiting procedure. But this, you can't do; don't do this! Anything but this. Not at any price, whatever happens. You don't need the red card. They're no longer Stalinists; they won't arrest you. All they can do is heckle you."

"And never give me a passport."

"Yes, this may be true. Let me tell you something . . ."

Gora was ready to offer a new proof of his trust, just to ease the tension.

"Today you were talking about evasion. Freedom as an escape from a singular, rational system of thought. Should we call it an incarcerating system of thought? The detainees are isolated from other people; that's the punishment. At the cell window, however, at a certain moment, a cat appears. It passes from one window to another, from one detainee to another, curiously and playfully. The captives call it over, offering some of their food through the grates; they invent decoys; the feline slips through the bars sometimes, lets itself be petted. One of the detainees can't stand these frivolities, the ease with which the comrades allow themselves to be won over by such stupid distractions. 'Assholes, idiots, morons!' screams the prisoner. He fights with them; he's strong-headed, cruel, arrogant, vindictive. As he is well situated in the hierarchy of the party, they have no way of ignoring him. And they're not up to contradicting him, either. In the end, the prisoner catches the cat and kills it, right there in the cell. And you know who the cat killer is?"

"The prisoner? It's a true story?"

"Yes, it's true. The hero is our great leader, the most beloved son of the people."

"How do you know?"

"From a relative of my wife. He was imprisoned with that fanatic, who, by all accounts, was forever scowling, incurably serious. Without vice, deeply offended by any deviation from the supreme, final goal."

The last conversation. In the end, Gora left, alone. He'd left his country and his wife, to whom he was more attached than to anyone or anything. To his surprise and despair, Lu had refused to accompany him!

A year after he arrived in the New World, he received a long, affectionate letter from Mihnea Palade, in which he mentioned the difficulties of finding his address, and in which he reported (as much as he could in a censored letter) on his academic projects. He intended to give up mathematics! For the time being, he was stalling, poring over mathematics, too, even though he was already preoccupied with medieval judicial systems of torture, the persecution of Joan of Arc, alchemy and astronomy. He'd already published some exegeses, had read the entire works of the erudite scholar Cosmin Dima, and he was wondering who might be able to act as an intermediary, who might be able to write to Dima on his behalf. Gora didn't respond to the request, but tried to help him secure a fellowship in America. And just as he'd anticipated, his passport was refused. After two years, before graduating magna cum laude from the university, Palade received a new American fellowship, this time through the intervention of the great Dima himself. His passport was approved. Had the pressure of the Party subsided, or the secret police? The matter was never addressed, not even on the night of the American reunion between Gora and his former student.

The new immigrant spoke about one subject only, the evasion. The miraculous opportunity, negotiated by the gods and obscure forces.

After the first months of euphoria, Palade was overwhelmed by depression. Estrangement, solitude. The refuge of the library no longer seemed to help him. He lingered in bed for hours, days, waiting for the miracle that would revitalize him.

"I'm desperate, but not lost. Despair is a sign of vitality, I hope. In the wilderness, free to be anything or nothing, I'm not going to try to decipher the confusion of my destiny. I haven't been given the key code yet. I'm waiting in apathy and decay. I hear the steps of the former gatekeepers on the stairs, always nearby."

They spoke daily on the phone. Meanwhile, Gora had grown closer to Dima. Generous and affable with all compatriots, the Maestro agreed to meet Mihnea Palade, his admirer who had freshly arrived from the Homeland. When Gora later asked about his impressions of the young scholar, Dima confirmed that he'd found his apprentice in Palade.

The meeting had lifted Palade's black cloud. The Maestro had sketched out a series of lectures related to his doctorate, promised him collaborations based on common exegetics. Even though he'd been forced to leave one university for another, Palade published intensely under Dima's guidance, on myth and mysticism, the Renaissance and the Inquisition. He was following the encyclopedic model of his master.

Palade also first met his wife in Dima's spectacular house. Gora knew her. Kira Varlam had been his student, and, as it would seem, something more. They'd also been colleagues, when Kira became an assistant professor in the Spanish department. In her junior year as a student, she had the lead in a film, no thanks to her relatively mediocre acting talent, but on account of her peculiar features, her slim, green eyes. She braided her long, flaxen hair into a braid that reached down to her waist and exposed her superb legs with short dresses. She'd married a sports star soon after the film's premiere, divorced him after a year, was left with a little boy, with whom she'd emigrated to an aunt in Cleveland, immediately after finishing university.

Immediately, in fact, on their first night together, Palade put his love under the spell of ritual. In front of the bed, each of the lovers signed the eternal pact with their index fingers dipped in their own blood. "The traitor will die quickly and shamefully," it said in a deep red at the bottom of the parchment placed in view near the bottle of red wine waiting to be sacrificed. A September night. On every anniversary, unto death, Kira would receive nineteen roses as red as the pyre that burns the promises. Kitschy little details, Peter Gaşpar and Professor Gora would both agree.

Maestro Dima evidently had a kind of hypnotic power over his apprentice, who was, anyway, already susceptible to magic and mystery.

The years after the separation from Kira didn't slow Palade's productivity, nor diminish his oddness. However, at a certain point, his relationship with Dima started to focus on a question without an answer. In those days, one would have been hard pressed to find factual information about the Homeland in its own (the Homeland's, that is) libraries. It was only once they'd arrived in their new country, across the ocean, in the American Library of Congress, that Gora and Palade discovered their Homeland's old newspapers, and in them, the bizarre political episodes from the 1930s. And, as it turned out, it was thus revealed that, as a young scholar, the Maestro was once particularly fascinated by a sort of fundamentalist Christian Orthodox terrorism.

Palade staggered from the blow. Dima wasn't just an extraordinary scholar, a true library unto himself, but also a generous, altruistic conversationalist. His flaws were difficult to locate.

Gora tried, in vain, to provoke a dialogue with Dima on the subject. "He's knitting! He's knitting a little nightcap. If I ask him about that period and about what I found in those old newspapers, he picks up his knitting needles. He begins to knit, tacitly and absently, a little black nightcap, to warm him against the cold and against memories. That's how I interpret the silence with which he honors me," Gora told the former student during a phone conversation.

Utterly confused and desperate for new evidence to the contrary, Palade couldn't work, divided as he was between adoration for his schoolmaster and the unanswered questions that sprang one from the other.

"Every lover is a cretin, that's what he is!" he'd exploded over the phone. "On top of which, a disciple! My whole life I've dreamed about this meeting with the Teacher. Do I have to give up my critical sense at the schoolhouse gate, so that I can remain in love? The critical spirit is outlawed at the entrance to the Temple of Love."

Exploding with attacks of self-indictment, Palade decided, gradually, to forget about the whole dilemma. Dima was the protector, in fact, and his friendship was invaluable. He couldn't renounce him. Slips of intelligence and morality from half a century ago? They're not the present. If the past wasn't clear, the present was; the scholar was a man of books, not street disputes.

Gora wondered if Palade had joined the Party, which he hated, and which he would have needed, nonetheless, to be able to leave. He would have had some experience with compromise.

These irritations would reappear, cyclically. Despite everything, the Old Man and his apprentice continued to publish books together.

At the funeral service for the dearly departed Cosmin Dima, his successor bid him a heartrending farewell. The fervor of affection, as well as a public affirmation of his liberation. In just a few phrases, Palade announced that he had a different vision of the world, as well as of the field of study to which he and his illustrious predecessor had dedicated themselves. "My Master believed in organicism; I prefer the medieval *ars combinatoria*. I believe in today's theories of information and cognition, where we begin from a point in a vacuum and move toward variations that dispute their own messages and logic. I believe in the idea of imperfection and I'm obsessed with the dynamism of the mind."

Dima's political blind spots, and even his arrogance in ignoring or denying them, couldn't compete with the love of his apprentice. Palade himself confirmed this, publicly declaring his affection and admiration for his lost master once more. It was probably a form of therapy for his inability to forget or forgive those political deviations and the silence that surrounded them.

"After death, Dima continues to send me messages. I reject most of his ideas, I contradict him, but we continue the polemic."

Palade aspired to influence cosmic as well as terrestrial events, after deciphering their codes. Obsessed with social prophecies, personal cataclysms, and sexual charades, he interrogated the heavens. He'd estranged himself from the community of exiles, publishing antinationalist texts in the exile press. He made weekly attacks on the ideologies of the Nazi and Communist patriots of post-Nazism and post-Communism.

That was when the threats started, phone calls, letters, assaults on the street. He knew he was being followed, but he didn't know how to take precautionary measures, and he didn't inform the police. The strange packages multiplied, and he refused to open them, throwing them away in the garbage bin in the backyard. He made public his wish to abandon Christianity for any other religion, or, even more, for the religion of the nonreligious.

There was a moment when Palade decided to return for a short visit to the Homeland, to see with his own eyes whether post-Communism looked like the year 2000 or 1930. He returned to America dejected and depressed. The news intended for Professor Gora wasn't all too calming, as much as it was communicated with gaps and a kind of homeopathy.

One evening, he saw Lu at the theater, accompanied by a young man, who, as it turned out, was her cousin.

■

Peter. He was Lu's only cousin. There could be no other. A youth, now grown up, good looking and loquacious? What, in fact, did he look like, cousin Gaşpar? Had he graduated from college? Had he become a great athlete? Was he still passionate about basketball, as he was in the old days? Did he write gallery and racetrack reviews? Had he been Lu's companion on other occasions, as well?

Lucian Palade (Mihnea's brother) and his wife had maintained an amicable relationship with the former Mrs. Gora. They'd seen her around at family gatherings and social occasions. Was anyone with her?

At the theater, with Peter! And so? They were cousins, weren't they? Peter had probably come from the far corner of the country for a few days, and his cousin invited him to the theater. A simple courtesy. Lu couldn't stand going to the theater or to the cinema alone, nor to concerts or on excursions, for that matter. It was no surprise that she used young Gaşpar as a companion.

Or, did Peter Gaşpar have a car, by any chance? On a visit to Bucharest, years back when he was only a high school student, Peter had been fascinated by the cars on the boulevard, few and pitiable as they were. Had he gotten hold of one of those famous Trabants, that plastic, socialist toy with the motorcycle motor? Prr-prr, pic-pic, smoke, the holy little spark plug that needs frequent replacing, the efficient and economic cocktail of diesel and gas, the low mileage, the poor man's car—and despite all that, it was a five-year wait-list till it was your turn for this social advancement. Maybe Prosecutor Gaşpar was able to procure one such machine from his dear Party, to indulge his son? Had he become Prosecutor David Gaşpar again, or did he spend many years in prison, as had been rumored?

The past. Fragments appear and disappear when you least expect them. Look, for example; Lu was rejoining Gusti Gora, even though she'd previously said she wouldn't. Even now, she was playing the role of his one and only wife! No, their marriage hadn't been an illusion—their separation was the illusion.

"When I first met her, I didn't just simply meet her; I found her again. She'd been inside of me for a long time," Professor Gora whispered into the mute receiver.

She hadn't agreed to accompany Gora to the wastelands of liberty and well-being, but she couldn't let him go off on his own either. She joins him, unaware—or perhaps aware—that this is how she defies their separation.

The couple proceeded silently on the sidewalk in front of the station. Bound to each other. All of a sudden, Lu shook her black hair, looking at her husband.

"I don't think that Peter knows the story of his parents. His father, once married to Liza, who was burned away, along with their little girl Miry . . . Peter represents Eva's new beginning, not David's. The basketball player can't stand her maternal excesses, I'm sure."

They were coming back, after accompanying the guest to the station. Gora had been surprised by the ardor with which Lu invested the subject.

In the months that followed, Lu seemed to be uncovering the mysteries of her own being. David and Eva Gaşpar's biographies provided the lost code. Through them she was beginning to come out of the unknown inside of herself.

"It isn't certain that Peter is David's son. The delirium of liberation triggered . . . let's say impulses, as the former detainees would say. The orgy of liberation, the orgy of pent-up senses. They say that everyone coupled with whoever was around. David might have seen his momentary partner only afterward. Peter was born in Belgrade, on their way home. Eva didn't want to return, but David insisted on reestablishing the facts. To reinstate justice! It was among parents such as these that Peter grew up to play basketball."

Fragmentary information, gleaned from others, tied up in presumptions. It wasn't mere gossip occasioned by the—till then—unknown cousin's visit, but the reawakening of a dormant question. Warning signs, interferences, expectations. Lu seemed consumed.

Gora felt excluded, relegated to the role of a spectator who had only part of the puzzle in front of him. Lu had had similar lapses previously, swift, imperceptible slips; all of a sudden, you could no longer reach her. It was like an affectionate and reversible kind of autism. An opportune touch was enough to call her back; a lethargic rippling movement would follow, and she was lifted out of the trance, reconnected to reality, with a heightened vitality. She instantly electrified her partner. Her abandon had the same ardor as her absence; you weren't sure whether the intense communion wasn't just another form of estrangement. The dark embers in her eyes deepened, her hands trembled, her lips quivered, her mouth dilated, a voracious leech sucking the blood and pus of her prey.

The magic of desire spurred his memory and brought him close to her. And the memory of desire never faded. An initiation, ever the same, and different every time. A lasting black void, murmurs of enchantment and melancholy.

He'd tried, more than once, to stifle those memories, but they returned in waves, like the tides. The distance in which Lu had hidden herself made the obsession more acute and permanent, intolerable at the start, then magical and longed for.

He'd accepted the highly improbable news, that Lu was Peter's partner! The young cousin represented an unspeakably shrewd ruse, but also an exercise in humility. And a test, reinvented by the Gora couple—that was what the former and actual husband Augustin Gora believed.

The beautiful Lu had no reason to pair up with Peter! There must surely have been more formidable suitors. To choose the young cousin was to show a dubious resignation, and a suspicious defiance of public opinion. While Lu didn't necessarily champion social conventions, she wasn't impervious to their implications either.

Was it the masochism of humility? Gora was as happy to fantasize about Lu's humility as he was to dream about the complicity between them.

■

The castaway Augustin Gora had also found himself alone and free in the New and Free World, some years back. After a few days, he'd written to Professor Cosmin Dima. He'd gotten a prompt response, repeated phone calls and questions about their common Homeland. Dima offered immediately to help him; he invited Gora to see him and paid for the plane ticket. One of several similar trips over the course of the following months.

Right away Gora was fascinated by the lucidity the Old Man (as he would call him) exhibited. The scholar experienced exile as a sort of adventure and initiation; he even succeeded in opening the world of the new arrival, who'd already wandered around in books and the worlds of books. An essential experience. "Pushed into an extreme situation, you reinvent the strategy of renewal," the feeble voice was saying.

He considered his relationship to his native country—full of so much collapse and nostalgia—with the same detachment, or apparent detachment. And lately, it was apparent, indeed. If you were up to date with the newspapers of the Library of Congress, you understood that it was only *apparent*.

He would say, ad nauseam, "Existence is a privilege! Immense and fleeting," the timid voice repeated.

As if to amplify the enfeebled sonority of the voice, his small hands, which were stained by ink and disease, animated the words, vibrating above the piles of manuscripts.

And death? Gora asked himself. He'd read Dima's celebrated texts about Death and the morbid labyrinths; he knew the slogans of Dima's acolytes, who were armed for the Apocalypse of Purification. Just like his former comrades, the Old Man had made many pious bows to Death, with studies and exegeses.

After a short pause, Dima added melancholically and without having been solicited, "Supreme Death! Reigning over all, absolute Queen, and God Himself. It's only through Death that we get to embrace Him." He advised the newcomer to remain in touch with people back home, not to disavow anything, good or bad, from the past. "Our graves are there, in the past. More lasting than we are."

Dima drew his pipe from the edge of the desk, embarrassed, and began to twirl it between his fingers. "I'm not allowed even this pleasure anymore," he whispered, still turning his pipe. There was no tobacco in sight.

"Don't forget the privileges of the past, and take advantage of the present!"

Empty rhetoric, thought Gora. After a few days, in a letter to Lu, he mentioned the conversation with the idol of those lost souls in the attic where they'd first met. The famous Dima seemed amenable to taking legal steps with the American authorities in order to secure a passport for the young Mrs. Gora, left behind on the other side of the Iron Curtain.

The situation in the faraway country had worsened; Gora hoped that Lu had reconsidered her initial refusal. Her stupefying decision hung heavily. Without qualifying it, he evoked that night so long ago, that attic room full of tempestuous and juvenile debates, when one of the students victoriously put on the table three French volumes by Cosmin Dima.

The discussion surrounding the famous and exiled scholar ignited instantly, but, to everyone's surprise, Gora was quiet and unengaged, answering the students' questions with curt, paradoxical remarks. He didn't need to remind Lu why he hadn't managed to pay attention to those earnest and heady speculations—he was convinced that she hadn't forgotten their first meeting, either, and that she'd understood, then, just like the others, the reason for his uncustomary silence. He wasn't simply retreating into himself. He was distancing himself from the loquaciousness of the audience, which he generally dominated, in order to attract—through his sudden silence—the attention of the unknown newcomer.

No one knew who had brought Lu into their midst. But everyone noted the person who accompanied her out at the end of the night.

The following nights they came and left together, and then they were absent for a long time. When they returned, they no longer seemed very interested in subversive controversies. They appeared unexpectedly, disappeared for weeks on end, until they disappeared altogether. After a year, they were married. After the wedding, Lu looked more beautiful than ever. Now, she was also happy, voluble. Even while his marital responsibilities seemed to mature him, Gora infantilized himself. He intently followed his wife's every gesture. A happy time, devoid of history.

Her refusal to follow him to the majestic United States of America represented for Gora an unfathomable enigma, even after so many years. In the public eye, the fissure was indiscernible. Intimacy, however, revealed strange constrictions. The rational and pragmatic partner was being undermined by a sleepy double, loosed from a dark place. He no longer recognized the stranger who crouched in the corner as if she were being punished, who thrashed, unseen, among contaminated lianas. Her pride persisted, however. Lu had been taught not to complain, to avoid showing weakness or sorrow. She never lamented, except to herself, in solitude.

These regressive reprises took a grave toll on the enchantment of their first years of living together. Gradually, that enchantment was replaced by the fascination of seemingly living with more than one person at once, each persona asserting its supremacy. He deciphered his wife's codes slowly and never fully. Ever on the ready, he waited for the shocks, in cycles of shock.

Looking back made him anxious even now, after so many years.

The finery had evaporated, no one knew when or how; Lu would wake suddenly in the morning, robbed of her security, shattered, submerged in gloom. Suspicion would quickly reclaim her; the happy past would recede and cease to exist. There was no longer anything solid around her, just a dubious trap for what might still be. The captive felt herself flung into the void of the anonymous and the rejected, frightened by adverse winds, pushed toward a precipice that had in fact been waiting for her for a long time.

She no longer knew how much love her past had contained, and she couldn't name the enigma that separated that Lu from the present one. Everything seemed diluted and obscure. And still the confusion of this fraternization, this incest with the sister who didn't resemble him, persisted.

Was domestic love undermining actual love?

The idea of exile, the humility of wandering, had always frightened her. Was her union with her younger, aloof cousin a kind of orphan's shelter? Or was she looking for the familiarity of the tribe?

The Dutchman's Balkan successor was nothing but a simulacrum. And the age in which she lived was just a parody without posterity.

Posterity? Here it was, a step away and all around. Camps of gossip and goods, the citizen plagued by publicity, an earthbound jumble. Mynheer's laughter in the grave of the farce that celebrity had made of him.

That was a venomous thought, one with which he could go to bed, our good friend Gora. This night was certain to be a garrulous one.

■

Lu wasn't yet employed at Dr. Koch's office when Peter quit his fellowship at New York University. Was that the irresponsibility invoked in his first conversation with Gora?!

An Italian colleague of Gaşpar's was touched by the ease with which the eastern refugee renounced the income of the fellowship, as modest as it was to begin with, and by his readiness to hurl himself into the unknown. She was a colleague with a legendary name, Beatrice, a doctoral candidate in the Department of Art History, married to an elderly, wealthy American. She'd come up with a sensational solution; Peter would have breakfast with her husband every morning! After which, they'd discuss the headlines. The public service would be decently remunerated.

To Mr. Artwein the name Peter Gaşpar inspired trust immediately. Peter was to bring and discuss the day's newspaper. Only, not the current year's. Mr. Artwein wanted the newspapers of the year in which he himself was born. January 5 became January 5 of 1920; June 22 was June 22, 1920, and so on. The world came into being on the same day that Mr. Artwein did, on February 24, 1920.

Peter seemed excited by the bizarre preoccupation. He didn't care that he was, evidently, the object of an act of charity. "Now that's what I call an idea! Everyone says that Americans are *workaholics*, physically addicted to work; they can't stop working and they can't stop thinking about money—look, here's one who's made enough, who gives up working, who is ready to throw his money out the window. Unconventional pleasures! As for his wife's being too young and available, that doesn't bother him. He's not obsessed with supervising or lording over her; he leaves her to the will of her unlimited appetite, hires a Balkan vagabond to conduct his morning conversations about the past among men, just like in the old days!"

He'd begun the gig with great enthusiasm. Every afternoon he went to the city's central library and photocopied the old newspaper that he would present the following morning at work.

Breakfast would sometimes lengthen, but Mr. Artwein never exaggerated his courtesy; he never invited him to lunch. Not that he'd have had time, anyway. He had other things to do in the afternoons.

But destiny wasn't to allow a long life to these meetings, unfortunately. Two months after the birth of Mr. Artwein, Beatrice appeared—elegant and distinguished, as ever—to inform her former colleague that her husband had suffered a stroke and was now semi-paralyzed.

"Semi? What does semi mean?"

The young Mrs. Artwein didn't appear shocked by Gaşpar's quick blunder and apparent lack of compassion for his patron's state; she stared the lank Peter Gaşpar directly in the eyes, as she'd done many times.

"It would do him good, I think, if someone continued to read to him from the newspaper, in the morning, at lunchtime, and in the evenings. However, in his case, semi-paralysis means absence. His body isn't entirely paralyzed, but his mind is blocked, at least, for now. He may return, with time. In fact, now that I'm really thinking about it, I don't see any problem with continuing to pay, a few months, a year, whatever, for the service from which you were so unexpectedly suspended. Seriously, not a problem at all. You could come every day. Read the paper, just as you've been doing until now, even without anyone to read it to. At whatever time suits you."

Again she stared the hussar directly in the eye.

Peter declined the offer again and again.

After that, he found small paying gigs here and there. He even worked with a group that translated menus for transatlantic airline companies, domestic and international; and so, he was among Russians, Arabs, Chinese, Spanish, all sorts of Africans, Indonesians, Greeks, Turks, French, Japanese, the whole Babel brigade. The universal ingredients of feud and fraternization bored him; the pay was small and temporary.

By the time Gora heard her voice again after a long pause, he was on the threshold of a more extravagant endeavor.

Lu and Peter Gaşpar used to amuse themselves in the evening in the tiny, miserable hotel room where they lived by reading the phone book.

Find the rabbit hole—that was their game. They would try to guess from where the next rabbit would jump, so to speak.

And out of the forest of unknown names, a true surprise leaped out at them when they least expected it. Not from the phonebook, but from the illustrated magazine that Peter had bought on his way home, a long article about the Eastern European Mafia in New York. The central figure was someone named Mike Mark, described in biographic details that were none too banal: his studies in chemistry in Bucharest, his complicated emigration to America, with just one suitcase, his infiltration into the oil business. "No business like the oil business," the sharp reporter had specified. Then there was the perfecting of the taxicab meter, selling the invention to the city clerk's office, sensational alliances with the Russian and Albanian mobs, the growth of their wealth. Seen from the street in Queens, the two-story Mark house didn't seem at all imposing, but it had three subterranean levels, a swimming pool, security cameras galore, six luxurious bedrooms, walls and ceilings made of glass. On the doors of the numerous rooms, in gold, were engraved the words: *I love America.* An FBI informant and counterinformant, the master embezzler had been captured countless times, and released just as many, due to lack of evidence. Mike Mark was the proprietor of two hundred gas stations and some large apartment buildings.

He'd refused the FBI's protection against the threats of his former accomplices. "I don't need the FBI, I'm better than they are. I'm not moving my family from my home, as I've been advised to do by the idiots who claim they want to protect me. My family is sacred and my house is sacred," the reporter quoted. An exemplary father and husband, and the fanatically devoted son of Holocaust survivors, who had arrived in the Dreamland not too long ago. The magnate upheld the honor of the family above anything else.

Among those mentioned in the fabulous history of the immigrant Mike Mark there was a friend of this man, a neighbor from the street in the modest suburb of Bucharest where he'd grown up. Lu recognized the name of a former university classmate. Peter smiled. In the jungle of the unknown, here at last was the name of a real person. Professor Gora, the name they avoided mentioning, he was also real; you could call him on the phone; but he remained a ghost hidden among the literary ghosts.

"There's no end to trying," cried Lu. She was feverishly looking in the phonebook. There could be no other; it had to be Mişu Stolz, or rather, the one and only Michael Stolz.

Peter was smiling; Lu was picking up the phone and, hop, there he was Mişu-Michael, out of the woodwork, reporting for duty. It seemed as if it were only yesterday that he was tailing the beautiful brunette like a rabid dog. He didn't explode with surprise. Phlegmatic but polite, Michael Stolz invited the couple to visit him in Forest Hills. A long way on the subway, then by foot, up to the doorbell to the right of the massive oak door.

The Chinese doorman welcomed them in with a bow.

Mişu Stolz was waiting for them in the vast and elegant foyer. He himself was vast and elegant. Tall, massive, black suit, white shirt, it seemed as if he were just coming out of a business meeting, and he'd hardly had time to loosen his tie. He introduced himself to Peter, bowing ceremoniously, without directing any of his erstwhile charm toward the beauty.

The former colleagues looked at each other sympathetically. Mişu, happy to find himself in a superior social position, and Lu, amused by the American incarnation of her admirer.

"I live alone. I'm celibate."

He stared intensely and defiantly at the couple of cousins, if they were actually cousins, which he evidently did not believe they were.

"The Chinaman is my cook, butler, housekeeper, errand boy, everything. I'm not a wealthy man. I never accepted Mike's offers; I smelled trouble and didn't want to be mixed up in it. He helped me enormously at the start. Even with money. He's merciless with his competitors, but generous with friends. A heart of gold. Gold wrapped in shit."

While Mişu interviewed the adventurers, the Chinese man arranged the sandwiches and bottles with a mastered condescendence.

At the end of the visit, with a glass of French cognac, he admitted that he also owned three gas stations, a few limo-taxis and an income a little larger than was entirely honorable. Of course, there was a lot of work, he'd never worked so hard in his life, with so much stress, *of course*, but money doesn't come from hard work. He smiled, proud of the horse sense of his remark; the pronunciation of the remark, however, completed his smile with a short laugh completely devoid of cordiality, "In fact, money is never made through work. It's not the workers or the drivers who make money, but the owners. I make it."

At the end, the host gave the guests his card, saying to Lu, "If you need me, call. The third number on the card is less busy."

The visit didn't indicate there might be a sequel. But there was one. After a few months of unemployment and short, transitory gigs, Peter called Stolz, without warning Lu, and obtained an interview and a job. A dangerous move, as Professor Gora was about to find out.

He didn't need a name to recognize her voice, which was inside of him, beyond good and evil, beyond space and time. He grew silent. Embarrassment on both sides. Lu had certainly arrived with great difficulty at this decision, he knew too well. Despair had provoked the call.

"Chauf . . . chauffeur! Chauffeur . . . listen. The great Stolz. He . . . hired him! Chauffeur. I didn't know that Peter . . . that Peter had wanted to commit su . . . su . . . suicide. He doesn't admit it. Or he does, but only as a joke," the suave voice from long ago said.

"Suicide. It's no longer about walking ten dogs in the park at five dollars an hour. Or triage at the post office. This is something else altogether."

Lu paused to gather her strength. The couple had obtained drivers' licenses, before leaving for America. They didn't have a car, but they knew that it would be impossible to get by in America without driving. They took driving lessons; they took the test, theoretical and practical, and there was also, of course, the inevitable Balkan socialist bribe. Nothing was possible without it. Gora knew this well, as he'd gone through the same ritual himself. The examining officer took home a private bonus for every license obtained. Conscientiously, Lu took the exam and received the license that had already been paid for. Peter didn't even show up. He received the license in an envelope, in the mail. For the same fee, of course. Yes, Gora remembered the procedure well.

"He doesn't know what he's doing. At all. He has no driving experience, at all. But he says he's fascinated by the Lunar City. As a chauffeur, he'll scour the cosmos. 'The lunar monster is made for us somnambulist wanderers,' he keeps saying."

Silence. She seemed as frightened by her own words as by the potential digression into another subject. Silence. Gora didn't feel capable of deviating, either.

So as not to prolong the danger, Lu began to string together the wonders to which Peter aspired, quickly, like a labored recitation from a touristic guide: the Brighton Beach's Moscow, Little Italy's Naples, Queens' Balkans, Pakistan and India, Chinatown, Harlem's Senegal, Hasidic Brooklyn.

The iceberg of silence that spanned two decades wouldn't thaw. Gora promised to talk to the potential suicide. To no effect, of course.

He was left only with the echo of Lu's voice. That wasn't nothing.

On his first day of work, Peter was to present himself at the house of a certain celebrity, driving one of Stolz's limousines. A top-level university personality, a politician, a diplomat, it wasn't too clear. A VIP, that was all, and the rest didn't matter. He was to take the celebrity to the airport. After that, the taxi-limousine was to arrive at another address, and another, the schedule established by Stolz's dispatcher.

The novices had trained for two days, three hours per day, in a car that belonged to the porter of the small hotel where they lived.

"Key in the ignition, foot on the gas. Brake. Left, brake. Mirror! Mirror, watch the mirror," warned the Mexican, sweating in panic. "Slow. Not that slow. Not enough gas. Back! That's it, left. Your foot, your foot, yes, on the brake. Foot on the brake! Gas, yes. Left. Mirror! Right, mirror on the right. Check the mirror. Always check the mirror."

The Mexican's hair was greasy now from perspiration and fright; his small, grimy hands were trembling, his eyes popping; he was crossing himself; he was gripping his small head between his small hands, covering his face so as not to see the next moment. Peter, on the other hand, was perfectly calm, grateful for the training; he liked the wheeled dragon.

He muttered the same word over and over, "Slow, slow . . . " He'd found his prayer and motto: SLOW. That was all he needed to keep saying; the mantra would mollify the gods. Slow, go slow, you have time to correct your mistakes. The death race, the burlesque horror movie.

The car engaged, but the driver didn't. Slow commands, demonic, left, slow, stop, foot, brake, like that, gas, brake, foot, slow, left, too much, too much, now right, slow, mirror, watch the mirror, left, that's it, stop. Red light, stop.

The prehistoric driver at the wheel of the modern car remained calm and absent. Slow bouts, short commands, the prayer SLOW. He didn't hear the apocalyptic uproar of the road; the prayer was protecting him. Slow, slow, as the prayer says.

"The suicidal syndrome," whispered Lu at one point, in the back seat and in Gusti Gora's dream.

That's it, left. Foot! Foot on the brake. Gas, that's it. Right, the right-side mirror. Slow, stop. Red light! Stop! Collision, stop. A miracle! Arrival! SLOW, SLOW, easy curbs, calm changes of direction, the blare of horns, the despair of drivers who passed alongside like comets, their fists raised to the sky. Happy ending: stoplight.

The gods had spared him; the stoplights had spared him; he believed in salvation. Slowly, terror-stricken, he'd arrived! When, how, who knew but here he was downtown. Little Italy, the celebrity's residence.

He'd closed his eyes, exhausted, bent his head over the steering wheel, to sleep forever, to pass long minutes of dizziness and elation. Should you kill yourself? Dance every second, in front of the sacrificial altar. The pagan altar. The unknown around you and within you. Above the eagle of destiny, around, life, the primordial wedding. Fear, too, he felt fear, a gothic, luxurious horror. Gas, brake, mirror, horn. Left, right. Slow. Red. Stop. Saved! Short, unpredictable. Liquidated! Saved.

He woke up, smiling, in the mirror, over the wheel, kissing the complicit wheel; enlivened, he looked again at the wheeled monster. It was as if he were perceiving the magical machinery of death for the first time.

He climbed out of the car, rang the bell at the celebrity's door. A short, agile gentleman. White moustache, a brush of white hair on his calabash of a head, blue bow tie, large hands, large nostrils, hurried, well disposed. He introduced himself quickly, threw the small valise on the backseat, and sat in the front passenger's seat, near the hussar.

"How . . . what did you say your name was? Kaspar? Kaspar Hauser? The famous character? Is that it, Kaspar Hauser?"

The driver stared at him, lost at sea. He'd hit on a talker! He was ready for any conversation, if only it could be long, long, so that he'd never need to start that engine. He'll talk about Kaspar Hauser until nighttime with this fabulous client, and he'll forget all about the death race.

"My name isn't Kaspar Hauser. That was a joke. Karl, that's my name."

"Karl? Marx? Karl Marx?"

"No. Rossmann. Mynheer Karl Rossmann."

Peeperkorn would have been too much, Rossmann seemed all right.

"Mynheer? As in, *mister*? *Monsieur* Rossmann, *Herr* Rossmann?"

The passenger stared at him for a long time. Smiling. Ready to burst into laughter, smiling; he liked the game; he liked his playing partner. He was no longer hurrying to the airport. He'd found himself a talker, too!

"Rossmann, you say? Karl Rossmann? Kafka? The American novel? America seen from Prague?"

The driver smiled, too, convinced that the voluble gentleman could even have talked to Peeperkorn. It wasn't easy to interrupt him, he was jumping out of his seat to find out the immigrant's biography, his country, his profession, the languages he spoke. He knew a few languages, wasn't that right? That was the fate of little countries, many languages, wasn't that right?

"And your name? What's your name, in fact?"

"RA 0298."

"What's that you say?"

"My name has become a number. It's engraved on my arm, just like . . . would you like to see?"

The passenger's eyes widened.

"You mean to say . . . no, no, you're too young. That's a bad joke. Auschwitz is a bad joke."

"Okay, okay. It's a bad joke, I'll give you that."

"So then, what is it? Your driver's ID?"

"Resident Alien. RA 02987896. RA 0298, for short."

They spoke endlessly, that is, for five minutes. Little Italy, like America, was hurried, pragmatic, energetic, hurried. The engine needed starting.

The driver started the engine. He stepped on the gas, repeated the magic formula of the devil that had brought him to Little Italy and that will take him further. SLOW, slow . . . Gas, and so on. Foot, yes, foot on the brake, left, mirror.

He stopped. No more than a few meters, and he stopped. Happily, he stopped. A stoplight. A divine, red light. The talkative passenger had stopped talking. Stupefied, he watched the taxi driver. The driver waited a second, the light turned green, he waited another second, "SLOW, SLOW." Another one-two-three seconds. He could hear the horns behind him, but he had the magic formula. SLOW. There was no other solution. That was how he'd gotten to Little Italy, and that was how he'd get to the cemetery of the airport. SLOW, this was the only password the devil understood.

He started again, cautiously, was just about going.

"No, no!" The mustached gentleman yelled. "Enough. This isn't working. No, no, it's not working," the VIP was screaming, exasperated. "This isn't working," or, "this isn't working anymore," or whatever he was jabbering. Red in the face, on the brink of apoplexy.

"Stop! I'm getting out."

The driver stopped, waited for the elegant gentleman to ask for his valise and for the scandal to start. The celebrity forgot about the bag, however; he didn't even look in the backseat.

"Get out! You get out, too!"

The driver didn't understand. He watched the client in a daze; he didn't understand; he lacked the courage to understand.

"Get out. We'll change places."

He got behind the wheel, and by the time they arrived at the airport, they were friends.

Before heading over to the departure corridor, Larry forced Peter Gaşpar to call Stolz, to say that he'd gotten sick at the airport and he'd left the car in the parking garage, and someone should come and get it.

"Here's my card. I run a college. It's small, bizarre, but vibrant; I don't have open positions right now; I can't offer you anything. If you can't get by, call me and we'll figure something out. Give up driving. Choose poison or a bullet. Death at the wheel is trivial, and you're a sensible man."

Peter stared, bewildered, at the card. Bedros Avakian! Professor Bedros Avakian. That was all it said. It meant that he was famous, there was no need of other details. Bedros Avakian. So then,

Larry! Peter the Driver, alias Kaspar, alias Karl, had decided to call him Larry.

That's how he'd met Larry. In later retellings, the immigrant Peter would identify through the same generic name, Larry, all the harbingers of his American destiny.

After the failed meeting with Death, the improvised taxi driver was hired by Stolz at one of his gas stations. Lu became the assistant to Dr. Koch. The couple's situation improved somewhat.

Peter never forgot the first Larry's advice. Any other kind of death is better than death at the wheel. Even falling off a trampoline.

■

He'd become friends with the manager at the gas station, a Syrian with his own network of schemes and shady earnings. Cars came and went; it was the sexual hum and hub of the city. A city with no equal, muttered Peter, in love with the Lunar City, unique and unifying.

A seasonal observer of the sky, Peter Gaşpar observed, without actually taking in, the red sky. The Hamletian clouds, astral and archaic symbols, birds of every color, elephant bodies riding the improbable batons of their legs. A drizzly twilight. The new Babylon was brashly raising the arrows of its buildings. Pylons stuck into the sordid subterranean depths, where rats, vagabonds, roaches, beggars, moles, and murderers—the fauna of the metropolis—teemed. "A marvelous city," the wanderer murmured, dumbfounded in the face of the impassable Syrian. A mountainous cheek made of clay, secular whetstones, wilderness in full view.

"Change those bulbs," a hoarse voice said.

He found the bulbs, grabbed the ladder and went out. He'd been putting off changing them for a few days. One step, and another, hands on the ladder, a rung, then another, left hand holding the side, the right hand outstretched toward the post to unscrew the burned bulb. Hand in the air—boom! Explosion. Not the bulb, but the ground. The mammoth mass hits the earth like a meteor, shaking the pavement.

In the ambulance, the dead hallucinated, "Hauser. Finished,

liquidated. Airways. Kennedy." Kennedy and Airways were easy to distinguish. "Hauser. So little. Liquidated."

The dead tossed around over the steering wheel in his dream. Those dear, red lights. "Irres . . . ir-re-sponsible. Liquidated."

He leaned the evening up against the wall. The burned bulb on the post in the front of the station. The new bulb in his right pants pocket. He'd gotten to the top, and the rain was hammering down. His hand extended toward the post, his hand and his mind up in the air. Wet pavement. Twisted ladder, the elephant toppled to the ground that once bore him. Boom! The cadaver on the pavement.

Emergency visits don't require insurance, the hospital has to receive anyone who arrives in an ambulance, this much the Syrian knew, as well as Stolz the proprietor, who didn't offer the immigrants he employed any health insurance. The doctors woke the victim from his blackout to inform him that he'd crushed the bones in both of his legs. He urgently needed surgery, the soldering of crushed bones, implantation of metal rods to make them straight again. The Pakistani surgeon relayed the miracle: Stolz paid a spectacular sum out of the pocket of his former friend Mike Mark, the sensitive shark.

Once revived, Peter Gaşpar was spared all further medical costs, but the incident aggravated the misunderstanding between the cousins, it would seem.

After his return from London, Dr. Avakian inquired about the chauffer Gaşpar. Professor Augustin Gora, once given an honorary title by Avakian's institution, received a call from the president's secretary. She was asking if he knew anything about that bizarre compatriot of his.

"So then you know Gaşpar," the historian exclaimed after a second. "Gaşpar! RA 0298! Peter Gaşpar."

"Yes," Gora responded, stammering. "I know the name . . . and more, believe me, much more!"

"No, no, we're not just joking around. There's more, believe me. Death is the matter at hand. The paradoxical messenger of death."

Gora was silent, suddenly overwhelmed.

"Death! That's the institution your compatriot represents. At first I thought he didn't know the city, that he was mixing up addresses, that he'd gotten confused. I was trying to divert his attention from the madness of driving, I talked about Little Italy, the neighborhood where he was hunting for death, who was hunting for him, and about Kaspar Hauser, about Brecht, the troupe from Vilna, Kafka, anything. I'm a historian, but I'm also a reader, of course, and not only that. How to distract his attention from driving? No one else could do a better job of this than he himself. His eyes opened wide to the chaos through which he was navigating, but his mind somewhere else, in hell, in heaven. Intangible! He groped around blindly, slowly, extremely slowly, meticulously, horrified. His feet fumbled for the pedal, his eyes electrified, in prayer. Pure terror. Pure, my good man!"

Gora was preparing his questions, in his mind, but Avakian didn't allow any pause.

"Should I keep him talking about things that he knows? Should I try to steel him up? This wasn't a time for conventional solutions."

President Avakian was laughing heartily, happy that he'd beaten Death.

"You know that Gaşpar, as a man, is quite . . . "

"Miraculous! You mean miraculous? He's a miracle, no more, no less. I escaped with my life only through a miracle. He didn't care at all. About me, about himself, about the car, New York, it was all just a spectacle, that's all. The spectacle before the catastrophe, and the spectacle of the catastrophe."

The historian couldn't forget that experiment, and wouldn't allow himself to be interrupted from recounting the morbid screenplay, which he'd probably already recounted many times over.

"The business card he gave you represented . . . "

"A letter of thanks! A reward. He was about to hand it over, the next occasion, to his boss: Death. A cash reward, no matter how big, would have been merely trivial."

"You'd be disposed to see him again, then? To . . . "

"To see him again? As a pedestrian . . . as a pedestrian, Mr. Gora! As a pedestrian, anytime! Disposed? Obligated! That's how I see it. A matter of conscience, I can't forget that. A miracle can't be repaid in any other way."

No one could have pleaded Peter's cause better than Bedros Avakian himself. There was nothing to add; you simply had to let him exhaust his inexhaustible discourse.

"I was, you understand, in the heart of Experimental Theater . . . Experimental History. The great experiment of the other world. Martyr and guinea pig. In less than a half an hour, death had kissed me everywhere. I was powerless. But I escaped, after all! The madman at the wheel has no escape, however, that's for sure! Now or in an hour or tomorrow, the holocaust, an atomic bomb, a worldwide earthquake, or a cosmic hurricane will meet him. That's certain! Should I call the police or the taxi company, or should I hire him instantly at the university? You know how people are, always in a hurry—I was in a hurry to arrive in London, at a conference about the Armenian genocide in Turkey, I was presiding over the conference. Not even after I eluded death did I forget that I didn't have time to spare, I needed to get to London. And I did."

"So, then, Gaşpar could . . . I wonder if he might call you," Gora ventured to say. "He kept your card, this I know. I could, eventually . . . "

"If he's alive! If he's still alive. If the miracle revalidated itself. It would be beyond my understanding, as well as the understanding of any rational being. I'd do anything, Professor, for such an intangible being, anything. I'll hire him to teach the occult! Spells and magic and astrology?"

Dr. Avakian was laughing, quite pleased with himself. At the height of his frenzied monologue, probably to perfect the dark humor of the incident, he asked for a letter of recommendation for Peter Gaşpar.

In the folder on Gora's desk, there was a heap of documents related to Peter. Yellow, white, blue sheets; Gora liked to jot notes quickly, on colored paper, details, whether real or imagined, thoughts, information that might someday be useful to him. He collaborated, under a pen name, with the journals of the exiles; he also wrote brief, ironic obituaries. He prepared them carefully, while the dead were still alive. Then he would thin out the compositions, without giving them up all together. The passages seemed too short, as the results of such extended research. How to make a simple, ephemeral inscription out of a biography that accumulates and burns through so much? A cynical frivolity, a bow in the face of unavoidable ferocity.

The deceased deserved more than the bureaucratic summary of visible existence! One should capture not just what was, but also what could have been, the potentialities that dissipate at once with the deceased. What he endeavored only in his mind, what he sketched out only in thought but never brought to fruition or had the courage to admit, even to himself. The secret life, often unconscious, surrounding and stemming from the heart of the ephemeral, time and space extended beyond the immediate present.

This was the start of Professor Gora's gradual dedication to a laborious project.

The file on Peter Gaşpar RA 0298 didn't begin immediately following the conversation with Avakian. Gora preferred small deferments: if in two weeks Peter is still alive, then, yes, he will be honored with the yellow folder that he very much deserved.

The first notes were older accounts, then the conversation with the historian Avakian. There was also, already, the copy of the letter of recommendation that he sent to Avakian.

It didn't suffice to say that Peter Gaşpar had been, in a superrealist country, the author of a minor work (because it was a parody) and an unknown masterpiece (because he never wrote it) adored by a gallery of admirers. The work existed while the literary café intelligentsia said it existed, but couldn't be proven to exist, and perhaps this wasn't even necessary. Gaşpar's bylines about sports and shows and philatelic exhibits and horseraces were worth mentioning only in the obituary, but not in the letter. Gora underscored Peter's lucidity in hard times and even slipped in a wave of sympathy for Ludmila's bewildered cousin, referring to that first encounter when the chauffeur had attempted to bring Avakian to the Other World instead of to John F. Kennedy airport. He didn't forget to include a paragraph about Gaşpar's parents, survivors of the most infamous of all the Nazi concentration camps, a chapter that the son—a survivor of socialism—refused to discuss. As president of the Conference on the Armenian Genocide, Avakian was certain to be sensitive to such a detail. He mentioned, finally, the intellectual and pedagogic potential of the immigrant.

Once out of the hospital, Peter found himself unemployed. He inspected the business card of his partner in the race of death. There was no point in calling, he wouldn't be able to access the celebrity. He consulted the train timetables; he'd arrived in the idyllic mountain setting and the college run by the ancient European historian.

While he waited to be received, the secretary informed him that the president wasn't just a historian but also an authority called to testify in scandalous human rights violations cases, and a translator of ancient Greek.

"America!" Peter bumbled ecstatically. Universities hidden in the woods, like in the Middle Ages. University professors ready for adventure! Historians who plead in famous cases, musician chemists, psychologist bankers, athlete film directors, mathematicians blocking the mise-en-scène, actors turned senators, governors, presidents.

"The baroque? The baroque was your thesis? The baroque and the Dadaist derivation, you say? *Fine, just fine.* I'd like to hire you on this subject. But I can't. Be a little more modest. Something else. Something else?"

The candidate was silent; his imagination balked.

"Something else. Something more exotic. Less academic. We have a lot of American literature doctors. As historians, I admit. Something more exotic, another subject?"

The candidate was silent; he couldn't think of what might be exotic enough for such an exotic country.

"Communism? Could you talk about Communism?"

"No. Not exactly. But if there's no other way . . . "

"The Holocaust?"

After the letter from Augustin Gora, President Avakian wasn't surprised that Gaşpar wasn't answering the question.

"You know what this is about. You come from damaged territory. You have a lot to say, I imagine."

"I don't. I prefer not to. No."

Larry gave him a long look and shrugged, dejected.

"Anything else? Another subject. Something unusual."

"Circus," muttered Peter to himself, considering the meeting in which he was participating.

"The circus, you say? Did you run a circus?" Gaşpar's former passenger became more animated.

"Not exactly. Somehow, out of curiosity. I've read a lot. I was passionate about the subject. I planned a scholarly work, but I never finished it."

"The history of the circus? The baroque in the circus, the Dadaism of the circus! Bread and circuses? That's what the ancients said, right? *Panem et circenses.* The people need bread and circuses. We're a popular democracy, we need circus, too, not just bread. And we have it. Circus after circus. Maybe you have another idea."

Larry hired Peter Gaşpar as a visiting assistant professor after evaluating the needs of the college and establishing the subject of the new colleague's first course.

■

Peter Gaşpar responded to the prospect of his picaresque American debut without too much astonishment. He expected such unexpected adventures. For those who knew him in his faraway country, the indulgence with which he received the extraordinary and the detachment with which he assimilated intermittent shocks were not at all surprising.

Still, Gora suspected something irregular in this fatalistic submission to chance. Was this the irresponsibility to which he aspired? He'd also dreamed of a similar emancipation, more than once. To be able to be anything, to simulate anything. The freedom of improvisation, metamorphosis and availability. At a certain age, and with an Eastern European background, it seems preferable to confront just about anything, rather than have nothing else happen to you ever again.

Peter reappeared at unexpected moments. Long monologues followed by long absences. Gora's silences didn't discourage him. He didn't limit himself to practical questions—quite natural for a newcomer—he offered intimate and sometimes embarrassing details.

Exile brings together people who previously moved in different circles; Gora was well aware of this state of emergency and indulgence; now it seemed like a substitution, the progressions and surprises of which he measured with some embarrassment.

Reasonably social in his home country, a good comrade and friend in a time of need, Peter seemed to codify his exuberance in small, incidental passages. Some thought him brash. Now he was punishing the listener through aggressive questions and revelations. Was it a suicidal vitality? A kind of trance that defies the normality; it was hard to know anymore whether it was benign or malignant. Was he finally experimenting now, in the American wilderness, with his own narration? Was he accepting his reeducation, the simplifications called for by the pragmatism of his new residence?

"Peter on the phone. I hope the name still means something to you."

And voilà, the ghost returned. Urgency granted it a victorious and superior air.

"Larry was lying in bed. He'd fractured his leg. His apartment was relatively banal, but in the wealthy neighborhood. A long body, in a long bed, the harsh face of a martyr. White plaits, tied in the back like a rat's tail."

"You said that Larry was short, with bristly hair, a mustache and exotic goatee."

"Ah, no, that's Larry One. We're talking about the newsman Larry Two. Larry One brought me to Larry Two. A real celebrity, this man! I had no idea. I was seeing him for the first time, and his name didn't mean anything to me yet."

Enchanted by what he had to share, Peter allowed himself vast pauses in between sentences, mastering the rhythm of provocation.

"Friday. I was at Dr. Koch's office again. I was hoping, of course, to run into Lu. And, of course, in vain."

There was no need for a pause. It was enough that he'd mentioned Lu, their game of cat and mouse, or dog and cat. No, there was no need for such an aggressive silence, no need at all. The silence only emphasized the aggression with which he assaulted the husband.

"On the street, I ran head to head into Larry. Larry One, the president, the historian. I'm used to it. Coincidences hunt me here; they could never find me in my former life. And so, then, Larry, Larry One, the president, the client from the taxi. 'How are you? Where are you headed? How are things? I haven't seen you in ages. Are you busy? On your way to meet someone?' 'No,' I say. 'Come with me, I'm going to see a friend who's bedridden.' We arrive. It's Larry Two. The famous newsman. The famous intellectual. 'The Phosphorescent,' as Avakian calls him."

Silence. He was waiting for a reaction from Gora, who savored his silences.

"I had the *Times Literary Supplement* in my hand. I still bother with this nonsense; I haven't found a cure yet. In the paper, a review of our great Dima."

This didn't elicit amazement, either; Gora just gazed at the folder in front of him, the computer and the white gloves on the edge of the table.

"Who could have guessed that Cosmin Dima was Larry Two's professor! At the same university frequented by the historian Larry One."

Pauses, breathing, shock; Gora accumulated shocks.

"The beginning of a passionate discussion. Enlightened by the devil, Larry One suddenly proposes that I review the last volume of Dima's memoirs. Me? Me! I'm speechless. I refuse. No, not me! He feels that he's pressed a tender point. He'd read the *TLS* review that scorches Dima. Fascist, Nazi, reactionary, hypocrite beneath the mask of a man of culture. He looks askance at Larry One and insists. I make excuses, I stammer. I find my way out: I can't write in English. 'No problem, we'll find a translator.' 'Dima's biography is complicated,' I say, 'the review needs a historian of complicated times.' I look desperately at the historian, for his confirmation, his help, his salvation. My boss is silent. 'My man,' says the invalid, 'there's no better historian than life itself, and you have the best qualifications.' Again he looks at Larry One, who remains silent. 'Careful, Bedros, make sure your man sends me the review next month, not later than next month.' Done! Liquidated!"

Gora should have muttered something, at least after this scene, something to himself, should have hummed a song, something, *anything*. Nothing. *Niente*.

"And there you have it, Professor Gora; it's a disaster. Will you save me? Will you write this review instead? It's great for your curriculum! Larry Two's journal is important. Plus, you know Dima's life and work better than I do. I'll call the journalist and tell him that I found the perfect replacement. The distinguished Professor Augustin Gora will write a better review than I could. Out-stand-ing, that's Saint Augustin."

Gora was looking at the lustrous table, full of papers. He rifled through the scribblings and, yes, finally found what he was looking for, pulled the document closer, inspecting it ecstatically, as if it were the transcript of the conversation he was just having with Peter.

"It's you they asked. I can't see why you won't write it."

"Yes you can; it's impossible not to. You know the Old Man's life better than I do. You know what I'm getting into."

Old Man Dima had died a few years back, at a venerable age, but only Gora had used such familiarity before and after his death.

In the end, the newcomer started to prepare the review. He referred often to Gora's acquaintances and to the bibliography that Gora recommended. Soon he would change his mind, he didn't want to write it anymore; then, he would change it back. Gora advised him to ignore the details and periods that would provoke unpleasant reactions on the part of many, including the Gaşpar family.

But this was exactly the impulse that mobilized Peter! Like a masochist, he solicited ever new information, maintaining all along that Gora was better suited to write the text, deploring his dubious caution in long, furious phrases. Even coming to America, despite real risks, seemed more cautious than remaining in the socialist underground, wasn't that right, Professor Gora? Prudence was just an elegant term for cowardice, wasn't it?

Gaşpar knew that kind of prudence himself; he wasn't so different among the underground socialist duplicities. And he was still the same now while experimenting with a different metabolism for survival. Evidently, he avoided conflicts with his former country. Just like Gora. Caution prevailed in Gora's refusal to make a public statement about Dima, but also in his acknowledgement of the Old Man. Ever ready to help a compatriot, Dima had recommended him to some universities. He also couldn't forget the Old Man's encyclopedic culture, his books, books, books, his extraordinarily prolific intellect, his kindness. After the scholar's death, he'd remained in contact with the widow who sanctified his memory. The unsavory episodes of his past would surely have shaken her.

He encouraged the neophyte to confront the risk, guiding him toward an accessible bibliography. Uncomfortable conversations, Peter increasingly more aggressive.

"Who's writing this review? Am I? Am I to reveal—or rereveal, to be exact—Polichinelle's secret? Am I to be the one who turns the distinguished deceased over to the public's vengeance?"

He asked, really asking himself. He wasn't waiting for an answer, but the interrogated became an accomplice to the interrogation. An indirect complicity.

"Wasn't this what our ancestors taught us? An eye for an eye. I crucify Saint Dima, the way they crucified the Savior. You recognize this language, sir Gora, you've heard it so many times. Did you recoil? You did, I know it, there was a reason you were suspicious.

You're the sinners' and pagans' accomplice, just as I am. Did you know? Of course you knew . . . what you didn't know is that Judas, precisely Judas, understood the need for martyrdom in the beginning of any new religion! So then, the sinful Judas is a hero. Marriage outside of religion is no blessing, nor is it charitable, but you're a Christian hero, Saint Judas. You had that nickname long before you met Lu. But I'm not interested in Judas. I'm interested in hearing you tell me why I, specifically I, should be the one to write Saint Dima's indictment."

The speaker was exposing himself frenetically; one moment he directed his aggression toward Lu, then toward her parents, her former husband, the whole world.

"And why should I be the one to sympathize with him, to show tenderness toward the great Dima? Because I, too, am exiled, crucified; so I should stand by him in solidarity, no? I should understand what it means to be dispossessed of your country, right? A country like the sun in the sky, right? Or like the moon? You remember? Dima's comrades glorified collective death. 'Sweet deliverance,' they cried. The nation is a compact alliance of believers and martyrs. Democracy means corruption, demagogy, decadence, impurity and disorder and disaster, you remember? Then came the Teutonic defeat, the superior race turned to shit, while their Balkan allies were living their own apocalypse. The revolution of the crooked cross started an industry of death, on the pavement and in the furnaces, underground and in water and in the air, millions of dead. Then followed exile, loneliness, the terror of the moralizers who could unmask the Master's past. And I'm the one who's supposed to understand all this? I understand, without effort, Professor."

He stopped, but only to take a breath of air.

"Yes, the great scholar is worthy of admiration. The work, yes! Without the biography. Why, then, did he publish his memoirs and journals? He couldn't put down the mirror, not even when it was cracked and dishonest. Of course, I know what the Old Man felt when his library burned. Trembling, isolated, he watched the flames from the street. The ashes of a life about to be swept away forever. Believe me, I know what fire and ash mean, what burning and ash mean."

He addressed his virtual audience; he couldn't stand to be his own and only listener.

"Do you know, Professor Gora, how much I hoped to be nothing, finally? I'm a wanderer. A happy and ir-re-spon-si-ble wanderer in the land of wanderers."

He wasn't drunk, and there was no sign of any other distress except the frenzy of his tortured mind. He'd rifled through his memory, finding wounds he'd never shared with anyone and which, obviously, he was still sickened to share. He was sickened by the vehemence into which he'd sunk.

A whimper of powerlessness. Self-pity was the less than honorable mark of powerlessness.

It was harder and harder for Gora to accept the punishment to which he was being subjugated.

"You should meet Palade."

"Portland? I heard he changed his name. Out of anger toward his former country as well as devotion to the new one."

"Yes, Palade-Portland. He was close to Dima. His admirer. He came to America for him. He knows many things about his Maestro, he could tell you a few things. In fact, I think . . . "

Professor Gora wiped the sweat off his brow and throat with his palm.

Gaşpar refused to widen the circle of listeners. After another two phone calls, however, he suddenly became obsessed with the idea of visiting the apprentice wizard. Until then, he'd known the eminent Palade only from his books.

A week of conversations, not so different from the one with Gora some years back.

"The case of Dima has implications that go beyond Dima, that's why it's important. Can we ask anyone to admit his own sins in public? We can't. Especially in death and rebirth and the imposture named exile. You don't introduce yourself in your new residence by exposing your former filth, you want a clean start, you present your-self clean and new, isn't that right? Is that imposture? Maybe. You own it, you embody it, until you can't tell it apart from your former impostures or those to come in the future. It's the routine of life itself, isn't that right, Professor? Did you ever imagine such banality? In love and cheated, poor Palade . . . he can't let go of that disenchantment. Angry and envenomed. Still, we've arrived at the same conclusion. Dima is merely a man, like so many men. The context, the history, the mentality that he represents, yes, it's worthwhile to aim for this. In the past and in the present. The griping and confusion and crimes of the Nation. Nation, with a capital N. With all the letters large and black. There and anywhere. Yes, yes, he told me about the little hat, as well. About the knitting, as you say.

"Dima hadn't spoken to Palade about his former comrades, and he couldn't attack his Communist adversaries. He was in their hands, they could at any point pull out the old documents from the archives . . . The good Granny hears and sees and says nothing, Palade would say, just like you. The Old Man responded to any difficult question by cracking his boney knuckles and taking up the knitting of his little hat, that's what your friend Palade, the unrequited lover, would say."

Days and nights of controversy. Gora anticipated a harsh review. Would Peter Gaşpar verbalize his hesitations, or the rhetoric of justice?

And what if it's an admirable text, muttered Gora to himself. It would revive the rumors that had circulated after Peter published *Mynheer*, when people began to regard him as the author of who knew what masterpiece. That's all we need!

■

That's all we need, not just a poor story or a poor review, but a masterpiece, babbled Gora to himself, assaulted by another attack of Peter's loquaciousness.

"Should I write in the name of truth, or memory? Do you have any other clichés to offer me?"

Gora held his head in his palms and scrutinized the matte surface of the table, on which the yellow folder entitled RA 0298 was left visible and open.

He didn't want to listen and couldn't escape the voice of the phantom. He already knew the variations in the score.

"The Maestro refuses to judge himself, but what about us? What do we know about the Old Man? That he wrote some idiotic articles, after he was enraptured by the vitality and piousness of idiots determined to change the world. Why should that interest me? Because those idiots gassed a sister of mine or because I wouldn't have been born if she hadn't died first?"

Ach, Peter's long lamentations! The listener felt that something was slipping past him in this interrogative fervor.

"I know, I should have written it," babbled Professor Gora, gripping his head with his hands; he wanted to smash it, to release the worms from his gelatinous brain. "I couldn't do it! Dima showed me some of his highly improbable generosity, you can be sure. Nor could I harm his wife, that innocent Englishwoman; Merrie would have been devastated if my name were to appear with that review. Yes, Dima is guilty; even Palade confirmed it. He would have been forgiven if he'd asked for forgiveness, I agree with you. Was it a definitive, ideological guilt, a lapse in intelligence? Indirect evil, yes, he could have asked to be forgiven for that, too. But he believed himself to be brilliant, it didn't matter if he admitted his guilt or asked for amnesty, for his sins to be forgotten. But to ask forgiveness, he'd have had to believe in something. And he only believed in himself! In his supreme endowment, his supreme eminence. The genius, comparable only with other geniuses, but incomparable! Intangible, generous, above everything, in the ether. It would have meant to ask forgiveness of himself. The drunkenness of vanity. The amoral, above the profane! In the stratosphere of the occult, in the illusory Olympic realms."

"So was he an idiot, a child, an affable monster? That would all be fine, but why also militant?"

This time, Professor Gora sighed, tired of Peter's wailings.

"Why do I feel pity for him?" cried the newly exiled. "Pity, pure and simple! He lived his life among books and produced books. The idiot, that's what he believed was essential. It was the game of an aged child. Posterity, immortality, all of that nonsense. I wonder what he felt when his library burned? As if he himself were burning, piece by piece, book by book. The books, arranged so carefully, for Judgment Day. Yes, I'm sorry for him. The idiot that I am is sympathetic and will write sympathetically about your and Palade's idiot."

The ghostly guest stopped, but not really. Gora was listening to him but heard himself.

"Was the Utopian joke innocent? Was he getting bored in his lonely cell? Was he tired of isolation, of the futility of words? Was he vitalized by the staging of the vitalists who sing, convert, and kill in the name of God, dreaming of Death's embrace? And why should I, specifically, understand that? The cannibal beast is waiting for me, too, in the corner of the room, unseen. Cancer, stroke, at your command, ladies and gentlemen. The stateless exile found his revenge, that's what they'll say . . . He wrote the indictment in the blood of the sister that was never to be his sister. That's what both my detractors and defenders will say."

He was panting, poor Peter, suffocating with the passion and joy of listening to himself.

"With the blood of his sister, no? Good publicity title. I'm not a magistrate, Professor, I'm not writing in anyone's name, not even to avenge those who deserve much more than vengeance. Don't worry, Professor, I'll be moderate, and careful. I'm a former relative of yours, isn't that right? By association, of course, by alliance, semi-alliance, discrepancy. Relation by alliance . . . what kind of alliances can exist between us? Are you afraid, maybe, that I might compromise your position? Don't worry. The obituary must be honest; it's enough that the life was protected by lies."

The word *obituary* had been uttered with a well-disposed sarcasm. Peter Gaşpar seemed to intuit more than he knew and to know more than he let on about the obituary dedicated, by Gora, to Maestro Dima.

Gora was gripping his head in his hands once more. "You don't even know the whole story, my boy. You haven't heard of Marga Stern, the love of the scholar's youth. During the war, the Maestro lived in a neutral country, where rumors and spies intersected. He had access to newspapers and information. He knew about the horrors being committed by the Germans and their acolytes, but he was working, day and night, on his Magnum Opus. The shaking brothels allowed him to forget that Germany was losing and that the world was falling into the hands of the Russian beasts and the idiots in the West."

The phantom continued to yell while Gora continued his own mute monologue. Neither heard the other anymore.

"I read his private journals. I understood his duplicity, his loneliness, his drugs, his lectures, his fascination with death. His literary experiments and his political bedevilment. I also know about Marga Stern."

A long pause, just like last time. Gora was groaning; Peter Gaşpar had exhausted the evening's discourse. Quietly, Peter had disappeared, while Gora continued his own lamentation, "You don't know everything, my boy, you don't know. Marga remained in her native country, and the Maestro forgot her name. He was taking a special substance, similar to morphine. A drug he'd gotten from German Nazi soldiers from the front."

The pause had been a mere illusion, just as last time. A cheap trick for catching his breath and reclaiming his audience. Peter found his rhythm once again and his sonority, and Gora recovered his hearing.

The fury of the phantom gradually covered a whole world, but the world it covered was incomplete.

"Nonsense! The Party editorials that comrade prosecutor Gaşpar, my loyal father, used to read us in the evenings, at the table, weren't any better; they were merely promoting opposing clichés. On the one hand, there was the Party of comrade Gaşpar, and Dima's saintly bodyguards, on the other! Sure, comrade Gaşpar paid in advance, at Auschwitz, so he was entitled to error, to foolishness. Was he, I wonder? Did he have the right to believe in commissars who promised paradise?"

Another pause for air, his voice lowered, a sigh.

"And what about us, in this tiresome democracy? Are we following the script? What do you say, Professor? Do we get a new car every few years, a new wife, a new look? Do we renew our organs and our cheek, go daily to the gym and the bank, to our modern temples? Do we buy a vacuum, a hairpiece, spare kidneys, new hearts, second homes? We're joking, right? Here, any funereal discourse begins with a joke, isn't that right? That's what you told me; you were trying to explain the New World to me, *Mynheer*'s world, isn't that right?"

Gora didn't answer. Even his groaning had grown quiet, he seemed to have dozed off.

"Could I revive my unknown sister, I wonder? Or will I obtain immortality from the Great Assassin in the sky? Do you think the Almighty forgot about me, somehow, among his post-Auschwitz projects?"

Gora unclasped his palms from his cheek, pressed them on the edge of the table, strained to raise himself up, pressed the switch on the desk lamp.

The light found him upright, stiff. The glass in the window reflected his wrinkled face and grizzled hair.

The moon was retreating from the sky, defiantly. The dawn was coming, the fires of a new day.

Gora's face had frozen in the mirror of the window.

■

The American papers barely mentioned Professor Palade's assassination. Some articles in the local press, but echoes and rumors continued only within the university.

The stir in his native country was incomparable. In the chaos of post-Communism and the crush of the capitalist emissaries, the East writhed with bitterness and resentment. The wonder that had toppled the dictatorship, and the less wonderful wonders that followed, intensified the disorienting transition toward something indefinable. The crime happened somewhere far away, in a multi-colored gangster's America; even in his death, the victim mobilized contentious opinions.

A crime with a bizarre aim, perfectly executed, by a professional. Those who'd planned the execution couldn't have had more than an ideological motive. It was said that Palade's publications were increasingly critical of the nationalism that Dima had served, and of the ever-active Communist secret police. A Sicilian execution, though not for money; he was an ideological adversary. Was there a connection between extreme right-wing expatriates in America and his native country's former Communist secret police, which infiltrated everywhere? Palade represented a disturbing voice for both camps.

While he was rewriting the review of Dima's memoirs for the tenth time, Peter feverishly followed the university news, the police investigations, and speculations drawn from coffee cups and stars by friends of the parapsychologist Palade. He never withdrew the review sent to Larry Two; neither did he supply an addendum about the assassination of Dima's infidel apprentice.

By the time the text appeared, nearly a year after the assassination, the American police had long given up the investigation due to lack of funds. And yet Larry Two didn't hesitate to mention the sensational slaying on the cover of the magazine. It would be hard to say whether or how much it helped sales. It certainly perpetuated the rumors in the faraway country. The guilt of the traitor Palade had been connected to the conspiracy against Dima. Gaşpar had become associated with Palade. Who is hiding behind the name of this Peter and who is this Gaşpar? Were they code names of the Masons of wherever and everywhere? Or, a strung-out fugitive traitor serving obscure antinationalist interests!

His audience didn't seem to remember his story *Mynheer* from long ago, nor the nickname, nor its motivation, nor the old rumors of a mysterious masterpiece hidden in his mind or in his cupboards.

Larry One, alias Avakian, the president of the college where the traitor was operating, had found out about the hysteria in the press across the sea. He'd found the headline under the American review very provocative. The college informed the FBI about the potential danger to the reviewer, and about his relationship with the assassinated.

Gaşpar turned sleepless and irritated, and Gora felt guilty for opting out of writing the text about Dima himself. One of the epithets with which Gaşpar had been overwhelmed would not have been there. Ashamed, he tried to forget.

In the meantime, Peter was receiving letters from American readers who were shocked by the ambiguities of the review. So much attention and so much scruple afforded to an extremist who sided, along with his country, with Nazi Germany? The reviewer seemed to excuse him—or worse, in fact—to actually admire the Nazi, one professor of ethnic studies from California said. A young poet posed the question, "How do you separate one being into two separate ones? You maintain that the political writings should be held apart from the scientific and literary works. Do they belong to another person? Wouldn't it be worthwhile to find this other person? To see what he has to say? Aren't you implying a kind of censorship, somehow? Where do we stand on the unity of the contraries mentioned by the illustrious deceased?"

Gaşpar didn't appear affected by this kind of correspondence. The good, the true, and the beautiful? His new compatriots ignored the beautiful, the good had to be evident and canonical, and the truth without stain. Always this need for coherence and for churches! They don't care at all about aesthetics. Scared of contradictions, they don't understand that incoherence is their greatest realization, the triumph of their democracy.

How had he let himself be "cheaply bought" by the glory of a "disgusting, fascist library rat?" asked a political science student from Kansas.

The wryness with which he took in the calumnies of his own country showed, however, that he had failed to emigrate. The past was still alive in the present. His wounds coexisted with the illusions that provoked wounds. He was dragging his native terrain with him everywhere he went.

"I have in front of me one of our respectable cultural journals. From some time around Easter. Christian iconography. The Savior on the cross. The title is: *The Crucifixion of Dima.*"

"Where did you get that journal? Who sent it to you?"

"Palade's brother. Lucian. It would seem that I'm the one who upholds the vigilance and good humor of the Nation, week to week. The spy across the ocean, *c'est moi.*"

After this intermezzo, Gora didn't want to hear anymore. When some new information came, he refused to comment, accepting Gaşpar's aggression mutely.

"Lu forced our coming to America. They'd taken the cap off the bucket of slops. Freedom. Poisoned, daily, *poisoned.* Filth that had been hidden for decades on end exploded at every step, just like the day when Lu had parked the car belonging to the driving school. She was just getting out of the car, when the angry man yelled, 'Why don't you all leave and go back to your Arab cousins!' The unknown man had tried, probably, to find a parking spot and the car with the big DRIVING SCHOOL sign was in the way. Surprised, Lu turned around to see whom he was addressing. She'd never seen that brawler before. There was no one else around, as you might guess."

Gora listened, silent.

"Was it her Oriental beauty? Yes, but not the one praised by King Solomon. Romanian, Hungarian, Armenian, one as good as the other. Russian, German, Italian, Peruvian, it didn't matter. No, Lu is no typical Sulamite beauty. Is that important? It is. Not to mention the fact that she was raised on the lullabies of humanism. Indiscriminate citizens of the world. Universalism, humanism. Colored tags on jars of expired preserves. The guy had probably followed her, he could recognize a beautiful woman who wasn't ashamed to go out at a particular time in an old, beat-up car, while putting on the mask of a common receptionist. 'You brought us Communism! The comedy is over, get out of here!' The guy was yelling at her, 'Invent another mission, another Messiah, somewhere else.' Lu gave up on going inside the building. She returned home, overexcited."

Heated discussions followed. The one who'd previously refused the departure now wanted it. We're getting out of here! We should have done it long ago, we could have done it long ago. "I'm a joker in love with the baroque," cousin Gaşpar had replied. "Does anyone need me there? Will anyone feed me?"

Surprisingly, Lu replied, "I will." She spoke English and was willing to do any kind of work. A juvenile impulse, wanderlust and change. It was hard to imagine Lu doing "just any kind of work." It was just her impatience to abandon the place that she'd refused until then to abandon. She'd separated from her husband, turned down the great adventure and the unknown. Liberation had come, the Communist morass was receding, reasons to leave seemed to be disappearing. Why push into the unknown *now*? The curses of a Mercedes owner seemed providential.

Professor Augustin Gora hadn't forgotten his own embroilments with Lu; destiny's new joke didn't amaze him one bit.

"Larry One is on his third wife. They're all subalterns of his at the college. Larry Two, though younger, is on his third, too. The energy of renewing oneself! Infantility? Humor? Imposture? Courage? The right to happiness! The constitutional right to happiness! Here, no speech starts without a joke. Even a funereal speech. Was Mynheer Dutchman a forerunner of all this?"

He'd changed the direction of the dialogue. The author of obituaries Augustin Gora had become pensive. The question was addressed, as usual, to no one in particular.

■

"Palade found himself a new wife . . . You're the only one left without one. You've got plenty of choices here. Chinese, Irish, Arab, whatever your heart desires. Even immigrants from our former country, if you can't break away from the native cuisine."

Gora was no longer sure if this was Gaşpar's final account of

Palade. After Palade's death, he returned often to the subject of the Palade-Gaşpar meeting. The way you reminisce about friends while keeping vigil by their coffins, when only the imagination can modify everything that was never meant to be.

Palade knew too much, and it bored him to take up the tortuous enigma of Cosmin Dima once again. For years on end, he'd struggled on his own, agitated, down the serpentine and darkened roads of the Maestro; he never fully recovered. But Peter's own life, in turn, was curious. Here was a survivor! The survivor child in the belly of survival. And then there was his rejection of the Communism upheld by his prosecutor father. Curiosity probably overcame the hangover.

"Did he make you tell him the story of his life?"

"He proposed something like that, without saying it, a kind of exchange. I offer him my story, he gives me Dima's. In spite of all his bitterness, he'd been, and still was at the time, fascinated by Dima, his attraction to modernism, then myth, transcendence, mystic nationalism, extremist politics, defeat, his refuge in mystery and masks, then his academic career. Was it all Dima's inability to examine himself? His narcissism empowered his evasions. He couldn't admit his guilt or his mistakes; he didn't have time; his great projects were subjugating posterity. Though often at the pulpit of spirituality, he declined to debate on moral themes and condescended to the babbling mob."

"The Dima capsule contains modernism, nationalism, mysticism, diplomacy, and brothels. Narcissism, exile, isolation, esoteric evasions, academic excellence."

Gora was listening, absolutely unconvinced that Gaşpar was relating the meeting honestly.

"And the refusal of a naïve democracy, naturally! The Anglo-Saxon world won't ever accept him, Dima said, right before taking advantage of the New World's freedom. Narrow-minded to the rhetoric of progress. Democracy and debate were for the masses' consumption. It was hard for Palade to move from the unlimited admiration he had for the Guru to suspicion. He'd uncovered documents, he'd scrutinized the gaps in his biography, the coded allusions in his work. He still adored him. An extraordinary spirit, a lucid conversationalist, erudite, childlike, adorable. I didn't have the unrequited lover's disappointment to contend with, as he did. I only had to decide if I would write the review."

"Have you decided?"

"Yes. We're not going to untie these knots that are so tightly tangled! That's what Palade yelled. Freedom and spectacle? To hell with that. The sacred and the profane, narcissism and hypocrisy and so on? He was no less fascinated than Dima himself had been fascinated by his esoteric adventure. The revolt was against himself; he was suspicious of himself, suspicious of his own revolt, just as he was suspicious of his admiration for Dima."

Did the voice of the intruder come from the void or from inside of Gora himself? He himself knew the whole story all too well, and then Palade had told him the same things, as well, and more than once. Dima's widow had entrusted him with access to the *Green Notebooks* of the deceased. Him, Gora, but not Palade. In the yellowed pages of a school notebook, an isolated man was struggling with erotic frustration and the frenzy of writing, furious that Germany was incapable of defeating the Communist beast and the democratic chameleon.

"I recalled the novella about the comrades who were tried for terrorism in 1938; I imagined the night when the Movement mobilized; I saw the photograph of the virile Leader, the moral and mystic guide. Was the sacred hidden inside the profane? Did the Maestro still believe that secrets remain confined in the soul's memory of previous lives? Was it a camouflaged message? Camouflaged in writing, in fiction? These things nagged him to the point of intoxication. There was always ample intoxication of words and alcohol among us. There was no end to questions. What need did Dima have, after the war, for his old obsessions? Why did he continue to see an old, fanatic doctor who still endorsed the slogans of the Movement? Was it the intensity of idolatry, its magic? Drugs, bordello, Utopia, even writing . . . He would smile like a baby, no longer seeing."

Gora remembered Palade's smile. It was no longer clear whether Gaşpar was quoting Palade or had moved on to his own questions.

He recognized Palade's discourse, but also Gaşpar's seasoning.

"At some point I mentioned to him a former lover of Dima's, one who stayed behind in the country, in danger," replied Gora, apropos of nothing. Deported to Transnistria, she'd survived and returned to the village where she'd been hidden for a while, until the authorities found her. After her return, she committed suicide, in the same village. Dima never even looked into her fate.

Gaşpar wasn't asking questions any longer, and Gora couldn't guess if Palade had talked to him about Marga Stern.

"When Palade grew enraptured again with the great Dima, I would intervene. When he would dissect esoteric mysteries or dubious incidents, I would let him be. I watched Ayesha, his Indian fiancée and former student. They both wanted to become Buddhists. 'Any disorientation was better than orthodoxy,' Palade cried. 'Better than any orthodoxy.' And he gazed, adoringly, at his fiancée. 'We're both looking for a religion that's not a religion. We'll be Buddhists or Martians or polytheist pagans.' The girl was laughing; we were all laughing. Those were long days and even longer nights. I didn't know I'd be representing him postmortem. 'Write the review,' he said, 'it will be useful for the book I'm writing. If our countrymen don't kill us.' That's what he said. He'd received threatening letters, phone calls. He was assaulted on the street by an unknown man who told him that the hour of judgment was near. Bad signs in his horoscope. He was anxious, obsessed. He was living out his destiny intensely. He was working on three books at once, unloading. Students swarmed around him."

"Had he won them over?"

"He exalted the juvenile imagination with extravagant lectures. An encyclopedic mind and memory, just like Dima's. He'd enchanted the Indian girl. 'We're all searching for Ithaca, exiled just like Odysseus,' that was his leitmotif. We discussed exile often, Dima's exile, Palade's exile, yours, mine. Lu's . . . "

Gora lay in wait, as usual, for the moment when the phantom would utter the explosive name. He was silent, waiting.

"Often, often we talked about exile, the second chance that becomes the only one. Was it an imposture? We're the same and we're different, we rid ourselves of ourselves, we change without changing. Palade was head over heels in love, vitalized. The right to change, to happiness! The opportunity wasn't about truth, but about love."

Love, happiness, the pathetic words were preparing the attack, and Gora waited.

"Palade had found a new wife; you're the only one left without one. Here you can choose. Whatever your heart desires. Choose your heart. That's all."

■

Palade had also spoken with Gora about threats and stalkers. The professor didn't diminish the gravity of the danger, only its mystique. "You receive the results from some medical tests. You have cancer, an incurable kind. Everything changes around you. You're condemned! You look behind you with bitterness and ahead with terror. This I understand. Terror of death provoked by a medical test, not by some vague premonition."

Palade had called him the night before the assassination.

"This time, it's serious. I can feel it. Don't ask me what or how."

Gora advised him to tell the police. He refused, as he'd refused many times before; he didn't trust the police.

"She's not here. Ayesha isn't here. When she leaves, I'm vulnerable. She went to see her mother who isn't well. She'll be gone for two days. They know. This time it's for real. I can feel it."

He was quiet, but not for long. He wanted to add something.

"Dima asked me at one point to recommend a student to help him rearrange his library and archives. I suggested a student of mine, Philip Mendel. You could distinguish his ethnicity by his name and his nose. 'I don't want this young man to be going through our papers,' said Mrs. Dima. 'I don't know why, but I don't feel comfortable with him,' she said. An adorable woman, as you know. Refined, cultured, aristocratic. They were worried about indiscretions."

Gora wasn't interested in these asides; he kept repeating that the police needed to be alerted. He suspected that Palade hadn't revealed all the ins and outs of the danger, but the police should be alerted. Something needed to be done.

"A kitsch farce," retorted Gaşpar. Death is no farce, it has a doomed compass and no sense of humor. Palade had no way of being sure that destiny was drawing out the fatal circle. How could he be sure? No one can be sure. Premonitions, that's all.

Climbed up on the toilet seat in the bathroom, the mercenary leaned toward the victim, over the top of the short and thin wall that separated them, with a small weapon, like a toy. A victim on a toilet seat!

The face of the deceased aged unexpectedly in the moment when the game abruptly stopped time.

Gaşpar ignored Dima's and Palade's obsession for the occult. "I don't have an organ for perceiving the invisible. The occult is a comic subject. A farce," Peter would say, with the firmness belonging to a man of conviction.

The occult occupied a central place in Dima's and Palade's lives.

Palade's death remained sealed with mystery; this couldn't be ignored. Even if you refused to tie the assassin to the coded games of fatality.

■

From the sociable and charming immigrant defined by confused, first attempts to adapt to a new place and time, Gora had turned into a sullen and bizarre hermit. Just when he'd gotten past the initial hardships and regained the social status to which he was entitled.

At the start, everything had enchanted him. The inhibitions long exercised in his old byzantine socialism were dissolving effortlessly, as if through magic. He was rapidly liberating himself from the self that had inhabited him in the closed and perverted society of compulsory bliss. He was fascinated by the contrasts and the expansiveness of America, the joviality and innocence, simplicity, the indiscriminate cordiality. He was hopeful, waiting for news that his wife had decided, finally, to follow him.

At the end of the Fulbright scholarship, he promptly asked for political asylum. He was hired at the Voice of America. His intellectual prestige was an advantage over other collaborators, and he'd found himself the head of the department that dealt with his far-off country. Those who worked with him then recalled his curiosity and competence. His lack of any overbearing managerial tendencies, his luminous camaraderie. The collective harmony was shattered, however, by the arrival of an arrogant and rigid dissident.

"The Jap," as they called him, incited tension. He was abrupt, full of himself and full of the frustrations of a timid employee who wants to be Boss. He would defy the rules and the work schedule, would go missing for days on end, reappearing serenely and sarcastically, wearing the armor of a celebrity. Gora's efforts to temper the conflicts failed; the pedagogy of moderation couldn't subdue the rancor and volatility of the newcomer. In desperation, he called on Dima, who could facilitate his temporary engagement at a state university. Readily welcome and quickly distinguished as a widely read polyglot, Gora was hired permanently. He transferred afterward to Avakian's college, and from there, to a big university. He frequented circles of immigrants; he seemed to have some vague, budding, amicable (or downright amorous) ties; as an experiment, he began the column "Necrology" in a journal for exiles. He wrote only about the deceased, whether these were deceased ideas or books or ideological or religious movements.

Those who knew him knew him as the brilliant scholar, the former participant in secret debates in an attic refashioned as intellectual redoubt; they expected more from him. It seemed that he himself hadn't forgotten the large attic with the enormous skylight, where we'd met for the first time.

Mihnea had brought me there, curious to watch my reaction to the heated discussions. I was silent and attentive among the participants; I didn't comment and I didn't inform anyone, not even Mihnea, before taking leave of that feverish company. Bookish discussions with long lines of dialogue, like essays read out loud. I was intrigued by those people, their way of speaking as if they were writing, instead of the other way around, which is a much more common occurrence. In the end, their tirades bored me, though I never forgot them. They were excessive and bizarre, not just for the promiscuous intellectual that I was then; but I never again frequented troublesome attics.

Neither Mihnea Palade, nor Augustin Gora, nor Lu, suspected that they would meet me again, sometime. As for Peter Gaşpar, he wasn't there. At that time he was still a teenager in the province.

None of us suspected, then, that we'd see each other again in exile, across decades and meridians.

Part II

The old trees, the uncertain sky of spring: Dr. Koch is there. The narrow waiting room, the diplomas arranged on the office walls, the doctor among them. In the park, a trio of black puppeteers juggling the strings of the marionettes in the bombardment of music. The doctor among them. The playground, the swimming pool. Alleys to the left and right. Passersby of all ages and races. Dr. Koch cloned in dozens of hurried impersonators.

The kaleidoscope of the citadel and little Dr. Koch in the center.

The vise was squeezing his forehead and temples. Two expired sedatives from the old Gomorrah and a fresh, perfect aspirin from fresh, perfect Babylon. Night after night, gathered into one night.

Peter Gaşpar, thrown on the banks of a new morning. In the mirror. The little gnome Koch repeated the sentence, "Have you looked in the mirror? An elephant! An elephant. The scale doesn't lie. An elephant."

Soon the elephant finds himself on a bench, in the nearby park. He leaves the park; he looks at his watch. His gaze floats up, to the sky. The present, the motto of his new life: THE PRESENT. That's all. The unknown extends a small, white hand.

"A TV commercial. It pays well. The chess player concentrating on the match will slowly extend a hand toward the glass of Coke."

The corner of Broadway and 63rd Street. One step to the left, then another. Taxi! The yellow cab brakes at the curb's edge.

Above the steering wheel, the photo and the name of the driver. Russian accent. The hoarse voice of a smoker. A wide, gentle face, small eyes, large teeth, a brow furrowed with wrinkles. Lyova drives calmly, slowly. In front of the train station, he gently stops the motor and, simultaneously, the meter.

"Eight dollars."

The passenger stammers, doesn't stammer.

"Two dollars! That's all I have, two dollars. My credit card is in my wallet, which I forgot at the library. In the cafeteria of the library. Or, maybe, at Dr. Koch's office. Forgive me. I have a new MetroCard, worth twenty dollars. I will give you that. I bought it today."

"Get out of here with your MetroCard! Get out, get out!" yells Lyova, swearing in Russian, or in Ukrainian.

The madman doesn't move.

"Give me your address."

"What address?"

"Your address. Your phone number. Your bank account."

"You want my email, too? You can't do anything without an email address these days."

"Anything, just so I can find you and send you the money. The debt I owe you."

Lyova looks the crazy man in the eyes, like those ophthalmologists who examine the retinas of paralytics. He pulls out the pad of receipts from the right of the steering wheel, tears a sheet and extends it to the passenger.

"Okay. I hope you won't be back."

"No danger of that."

The crowd. The hubbub, the haze. After a while, after looking at the departure schedule, the traveler discovers platform number 9.

THE PRESENT, that's all there is. The city on the Moon. It's not so bad, it could be worse, thinks the passenger. The Russian, that is the Ukrainian, that is the Soviet, was a decent man. A decent day, that's the conclusion, Doctor.

The river travels gently along the left side of the train. You never wade twice in the same primordial water, which never ages, and which is never the same. A fluid horizon, a fluid, therapeutic sleep.

The conductor taps him gingerly on the shoulder. The sleeper quickly grabs his bag and his coat.

And now he's off the train, addled, in the station, gazing at the wide and gentle river in front of him. The platform is deserted, mountains in the distance, the river a step away.

A cold, clear afternoon. The beginning of the world. The end of the world. In between them, a short armistice. The chronometer swallows the seconds of the calendar.

■

The day hasn't surrendered to the black waters, it isn't nighttime yet. Depleted, Peter moves from the old couch to the old armchair. He gets up, staggering on his long, old legs. One small step and a big step and another small one. To the vault of the bed.

Midnight. The rustling of the woods. Nocturnal waters surrounding the cabin. Murmurs, babblings. The numbed body, the mind besmirched. The body is our house, according to little Avicenna.

The day hadn't started in front of Barnes & Noble, where the TV producer Mr. Curtis had appeared, nor in the office of Dr. Koch, but in the cabin in the woods, in the all-forgiving vault of the bed.

You wake up a mole, a mollusk, a roach. Like yesterday morning, like the day before that. In no rush to free yourself of the night's tombstone.

You remember the chest pains of the previous night. The vise squeezes your forehead and the temples. Death? It isn't eternal peace, but a stubbornly recurring nightmare.

It was late, he could no longer call the doctor. The doctors are bored; to prove to them that it's a matter of life and death, you have to transmit a final whimper and die on the spot, and that's it. He swallowed two expired sedatives from the old Gomorrah and a fresh, perfect aspirin from the fresh, perfect Babylon, where he found himself now. You have to learn to get used to yourself, you vagrant. Night after night collected into a single night. Neglect, the dilation of membranes and a shapeless shell. Anxiety, numbness, sudden awakenings.

No, he hadn't died. Evidently, he was alive, thrown on the banks of the new morning by the alarm of the phone. He twists his pachyderm body from one side to the other, the bed whines; he rises, finally. In front of the mirror: an elephant! Not a mole or roach, but an elephant, unprepared for the day's little tumbling routines.

He lowers himself onto his heavy legs and sighs. A buffoon, in front of the mirror. The phone. The phone is ringing. The voice of little Dora, the delicate Spanish woman with the thick voice.

"The doctor arrived ten minutes ago. He received your message and is waiting for you. Dr. Koch is waiting for you. Today, at one."

"May I speak with Lu?"

Dora loses her patience, flustered.

"No, Lu isn't here. And I'm in a hurry, my sister is here to see me. Okay, we're waiting for you. One o'clock, today, Friday."

Soft legs, belly hanging, puffed like a sack.

He shouldn't have called Koch! He's in no mood for admonishments.

"You're in the strangers' country, where no one is a stranger. Unhappiness isn't the domicile of the chosen people, you should know! If you don't believe me, return to rotten Denmark like Hamlet and your obituary will be written in your native language!"

An arrogant little gnome, Monsieur Koch! Made to give lectures, not consultations.

The patient comes to the office of rhetoric for Lu. The mystery is no longer a mystery; the doctor's employee skips out every time. Ever since his stratagem was discovered, the pachyderm is no longer welcomed like an honored guest and admitted immediately into the office, as he had been previously. He must obediently wait his turn. So much the better! In a half an hour, who knows, a miracle might happen. What if Lu, hurrying to escape, accidentally forgets her purse? Maybe no sooner than she's left, she will reappear, carelessly, in front of the stalker.

The door opens. Koch makes a weary sign.

The patient follows him into the office. Flustered, he collapses into Avicenna's armchair. With an index finger, Koch sends him promptly to his own place.

"On the scale."

The scale is unfriendly. There will be admonishments, therapeutic offenses.

Koch seems to have lost interest in the spectacle, however. He takes a long look at the patient, from top to bottom, straightens his little, freckled finger toward the red needle of the scale, then toward the patient, then again toward the scale.

"An elephant! You're like an elephant. The scale doesn't lie. An elephant!"

Soon, the elephant finds himself outside on a bench, in a nearby park. He considers the passersby and their impatience before their weekly rest.

He leaves the park and looks at his watch. He gazes up at the sky.

The present! THE PRESENT, the pedestrian repeats the motto of his new life and enters Barnes & Noble, Broadway, corner of 66th Street.

"Do you, by any chance, have postcards of elephants?"

The young man behind the computer gives him a long and attentive look.

"I don't think so. I haven't seen any, I don't think."

"How is that possible? It's the country's political symbol. Are all the bookstores Democrats?"

The young man becomes more voluble.

"No, we don't have the donkey, either . . . I don't think we have postcards with elephants or donkeys. But you can look. Here, on the ground floor, to the left, there are albums, art prints, photographs. To the left, around the corner."

Peter rifles scrupulously through the posters, albums, piles of postcards and . . . finds more than he'd hoped for. A red sky, two elephants advancing, in the air, one toward the other, with immense burdens on their backs. Long, thin legs, from the sky to the ground. Dalí.

He leaves the bookstore with the print in hand, raises his gaze toward the sky; stupefied, he finds himself faced with an unknown man who stretches out a small, white hand.

James Curtis.

The day is over, Peter fills a glass full of water, and another. He doesn't turn on the light, the headlights from the parking lot nearby are enough. He throws himself into the armchair, moves to the couch, now fully awake. On the table, the pile of letters from a week, or two. Envelopes, ads, fliers, magazines, postcards. Junk mail. He pushes the heap to the edge of the table. The present becomes the past; yesterday morning, P.O. Box 1079, the taxi to the station, the river, the train, the crowd in Penn Station, the library, Koch's office where Lu was hiding, the consultation, the humiliation routine. The Dalí sky, the Dalí elephants. The producer Curtis. Lyova, the compassionate taxi driver from Babel's Odessa.

He gets up, he walks toward the coatrack; he finds in the pocket of his coat the business card with the golden name James Curtis, and he throws it onto the pile of letters. The proof of the day that was and wasn't.

The station, the train, the primordial waters, the small terminal station, another taxi. No longer Lyova Boltanski, but Red Hat Jerry. The throb in his left shoulder, the sickly hiss. Words barely get through. Nine dollars and fifty cents! If you have no money, be quiet until you reach the destination, the scatterbrained Peter Gaşpar had learned. You ask the driver to wait, you'll be back with the money in a minute. One minute, two, however long it takes to search the pockets of your pants and coats and shirts, where you forget your white money for your black days. In the end, you scrounge up fourteen dollars. The driver deserves twelve. Two dollars left. Two new dollars and two new dollars make four, four quarters make the whole.

The night follows, sleep, nocturnal turbulence. It comes again and again, the dawn, you wake up an elephant, unprepared for the day's little tumbling routines.

He'd learned recently from the papers that Oliver the circus elephant was having a harder and harder time memorizing his tricks. One evening he simply abandoned the arena, completely disoriented. Initially prepared to punish him, the trainer found himself behind the scenes of an even more powerful show; defeated and collapsing on his four giant legs, Oliver sighed and sighed heart-rending sighs. Tears poured down his ashen and wrinkled face. Peter gazed at him, troubled, in the mirror.

Another day, a new week under Dalí's cupola, Dalí the ringmaster.

He keeps reading books, magazines, letters. They accumulate, a year's worth, collecting since the day he plunged into the college in the woods, books, letters from students and professors and the administration, scholarly journals and political appeals and juvenile announcements. Tara's letter. He didn't forget where he'd put it, this he didn't forget. Any indictment should be preserved.

Dear Professor,

My mother called me with my midterm grades . . .

Why didn't you give me a "Fail," or at least an "Incomplete"??? I never handed in the final. Another professor treated me much better—he failed me! I respect him. It's the first time that someone proved himself honest with me, in terms I've established. That's a relief. Freedom. I was hoping for at least two shameful marks. So I can finally break down. You've deceived me.

The prologue described the tone of the rest.

I had even prepared my mother, warning her that I didn't have much to show for this semester. In response, she sent me lingerie. I wrote to my brother. He responded with a confession: he's gay. As in, what the hell do I know about depression?! He sent me a box of cookies and my stuffed rabbit from childhood.

Tell me honestly, do you ever fail anyone? Am I too vain to imagine this possibility?

"Careful, my dear vagabond," says President Larry, "these days the universities are run by the students, their parents, their money, and their lawyers. Professors are just part of the décor. You wake up, when you least expect it, in a mess you couldn't have imagined in that sweet penal colony that you escaped." And if Larry One says this, it must be true.

The extempore professor should inform the dean of any student-relation problems. That's what President Larry advises.

Dear Rosemarie,

As I've mentioned, Tara Nelson was one of the best students in my class that semester, but she never handed in the final. I gave her a good mark anyway. She'd done extremely well on previous assignments and her oral presentation was very strong. The same with class discussion; she frequently gave a perfect performance.

She has just sent me her final. It's very good. I am attaching her letter, as promised. Very unsettling! Just like the short telephone conversation I had with her yesterday, just like our short meeting last Tuesday, when she came to apologize for the letter. It is possible she is going through some kind of depression and may need help.

Tara didn't drop out of college, as she'd planned, nor did she go home for summer vacation. She found a job in the library archives. He ran into her one evening, walking alone along the campus alleys. Then, another time, having a coffee, in the library hall. Then, more regularly.

The yellow envelope appeared one morning in May. Here it was again, even more yellow, on the dawn of a March morning, after almost a year! In the mess that consisted of his papers and memories, the student's letter could have gotten lost. But it wasn't lost.

I am sending the final late. The product of an obligation, not of thinking. Does it stink, or does it merely have an odor? It's not a pedantic difference. A stink is repulsive, an odor merely unpleasant. Dirty lingerie stinks. Old food has an odor. Now that I really think about it, this paper is an inoffensive combination. A faint odor.

Five typed pages, in small font.

In his first year of teaching, Gaşpar failed six students in a class of fourteen. After another year, he learned generosity, tolerance, the humor of the multicultural. The marks varied among sufficient, good, very good, with a plus or minus here and there.

Here's the final, rambling, banal, redundant. The final itself might not be insipid, but I am furious. And it's clear with whom I'm furious. I was determined to obtain a beautiful bouquet of bad marks, a real cry for help. And then you come along and decided to be the Lord of Goodwill. A benevolent Hardnose. A kind man. "I'll give the poor girl a very good, no matter what. She has nice legs, she shows potential, and I have no idea, in fact, where I misplaced her final. In any case, good marks all around."

Freedom's spoiled brats! They ask for understanding, politeness, and sympathy, and you get a kick in the ass in return.

I'm in a downward spiral of wretchedness and you offer me sympathy! "Sweet," would be the right word. You're sweet, and I hate you for this.

I don't hate you, I detest you. I detest your sufficiency. You offer an undeserved mark, why? To command respect? Though you seem to be a distracted, absent dreamer, you have an unexpectedly profound relationship to yourself. You seem to be elsewhere, waiting, ready to intersect with the unexpected. Your adroitness and unhappiness seem precious to you. You flaunt your isolation, and that drives me crazy. The only conversation we could ever have would be on terms proposed by you. If those terms are violated, you become eloquent. In fact, the only thing I know about you is that you should shave more often.

What had remained with him from last year's epistle? *Nice legs.* Yes, those legs are the same. *You should shave more often.* Yes, this is still valid.

The only way to explain the mark you gave me, and the reaction it produced, is to call it ridiculous. Have you ever imagined something like this? Do you care?

What does the beauty from the American woods know about the refugee who doesn't shave regularly? And what does the wandering elephant know about the grief of the new generation in the New World?

My mother asked me to see a shrink. I slammed the phone in her ear; I cried, then I laughed. "How can you say you're afraid of air?" Of air! Air! Yes, of nothing, of nothingness. Next week when she calls me, she'll have forgotten what she said. I don't want pity, or empathy, or to be evaluated, as you did. Who do you think you are, to be nice to me? You passed me one morning on the way to the library. You mumbled who knows what. I mumbled something, too. I swore at you! Who gives you the right to be kind to me? I hope it rains on your entire vacation!

Gaşpar folds the letter back up and puts it in its yellow envelope, on top of the paper pile. He retreats. The all-forgiving bed. A long and gentle sleep. Saturday, even the Great Anonymous One rests.

■

P.O. Box 1079. You open it by turning the little disk on the little window, forming the code. If you forget or mess up the code, you can't open it. You take the little pink card out of your wallet, and you read the instructions. Did you forget or lose the card? The clerk behind the counter looks in her database, finds your name, you receive a new pink card, with instructions. Once, twice, three times. More than that would be too much.

In the end, Tara offered to manage Professor Gaşpar's mail. She was no longer his student, but they were seeing each other frequently. He'd entrusted her with the little card with the number and code, asked her to bring him his mail once a week, on Saturdays, after sorting it. Appeals from philanthropic institutions and commercial companies, invitations to conferences, shows, lectures, political demonstrations for a better world, the colloquium on terrorism, editorial catalogues, the new gym schedule, the list of student drivers, typists, gardeners, painters, IT instructors. The recipient is addressed by his first name, as among old friends. The lack of protocol reminds you that you are counted among the earthbound, and that they, just like you, receive messages from the terrestrial family.

He wasn't interested in the ads, and there was no one to send him personal letters. Tara would throw out the useless letters and keep the useful ones. It was the simple maintenance of junk. The final triage belonged to the addressee.

Saturday, at twilight, Tara knocks on the door. The door opens, Professor Gaşpar stands on the threshold and looks out at the snowy wood. He closes the door, turns on the radio. Mozart. Crystalline, like the winter.

Tara takes in the room with a single look, as she usually does, as if seeing it for the first time. A way of entering an event rather than a house. A couch, two armchairs. Bookshelves, folders. The calendar near the telephone. The curtain. The heap of old letters strewn on the table. Where is the imminent event hiding, waiting? The old yellow envelope is sleeping in the nightstand drawer.

Tara approaches the table, unloads the new pile on top of the old pile, throws her jacket on the couch.

Supple, pale, smiling. The youthful mane of her hair gathered into a tail hangs on her shoulder, over her sweater, which is as white as snow. Tight black pants, long legs, in boots. The red painted nail on the index finger points at the table full of papers.

"You didn't sort anything. Everything I did last week and two weeks ago and this week was for nothing. Better to just throw everything out. We'll tell Pegg at the post office to give your P.O. Box to someone else."

"You're right," smiled Peter Gaşpar. "Done; we'll decide together! It won't take long. If I keep putting it off, this garbage will suffocate me."

He lengthens himself out in the armchair. Props his legs up on the table, the way Americans do. Tara in the other armchair. Between them, the mail of the last two, three weeks.

Tara hands the professor an envelope. If it looks like garbage, he tears it and throws it on the ground, to the left. If it seems useful, he keeps it and throws it on the ground, to the right.

Through the window, the sleepy forest. On the radio, the crystalline child, Mozart. In the facing armchair, the young woman of the New World. The present's tenant doesn't quite feel up to the level of the surreal that is being offered him.

"A coffee?"

"Later. Let's finish this first. You threw away the card."

"What card?"

"The card with the text from the *New York Times*."

"Was it important?"

"You didn't even look at it, and you threw it out."

"It didn't interest me."

"I sorted this mail! And I kept that postcard."

"All right, let's see it. If I haven't torn it."

"You didn't tear it. I was watching you. You merely threw it away."

Peter bends down, rifles through the pile and recuperates the postcard.

"You're right, I didn't look carefully. And now that I'm looking, I'm not sure what I'm supposed to see. The image is too small. A hammer and sickle? I can see that. A letter to the editor. *I was amazed by the front page article of October 4, which talks about the State Hermitage Museum's intention to exhibit Impressionist art considered lost during World War II.* An old piece, from last October. We're in a different year."

"So much the more interesting. Read on to the end."

"Okay, I will read on. *In the mid 1970s, on a trip to Saint Petersburg, then Leningrad, I visited the Hermitage. I asked the guide if I could see the French Impressionist paintings recovered from Germany and brought to the USSR at the end of World War II.* Interesting? This seems interesting to you?"

"I thought you were going to read to the end."

"*Much to the delight of my mother* . . . eh, same old story. Russian mother, probably came here sixty years ago, when she was eight. *To my mother's delight, and to the delight of the other six Americans in our group, the guide brought us to a separate room of the Hermitage. We then entered an elevator that seemed unused, which took us to the floor above. There were several rooms full of celebrated works.* You want me to go on?"

"Yes, that's what I want, go on."

"*We were allowed to walk around and look at the paintings. I wonder how many other foreign tourists benefited from a similar privilege while visiting the Hermitage. Neither the guide, nor the museum's administration seemed surprised at our request.*

"So, they were lucky; they were privileged; the mother will tell her neighbors all about it when she gets home. Is that all? I see there's more. The end is in the interrogative. An admonishment addressed to the journalist. *What gave you the impression that this collection was a 'secret of the state'?* Should I look for the article to which this refers? Male or female? Did you find it already for me, the October 4 *New York Times?*

"I didn't look for it. The postcard has two sides. Text on both sides."

The professor turns it over.

"So, then, the frontispiece of *the New York Times, Wednesday, October 12.* A collage."

"Yes, a collage."

"The postcard is divided by a vertical line. On the right, the address. My address, *Professor,* and so on, *College,* and so on, et cetera. On the left, the text. A direct address. First name. As though between old acquaintances who've never even met. *My dear so and so. Dear Peter.* That's what the shops teach me. To dress elegantly, to buy cars, bathrobes and umbrellas, to frequent the gyms and the banks that offer loans and the magicians selling the castle I dreamed of in childhood. *Next time . . . Next time I kill you, I promise. The labyrinth made of a single straight line which is invisible and everlasting. Yours truly, D.* What's this?"

"I don't know."

"A joke."

"Maybe."

"Maybe something more?"

"I don't know. You need to show it to the dean."

"The dean? Nonsense like this must happen a million times a day. D? That's how it's signed. *D-Death?* Just like that, death?"

"Crimes are common in this country. We take jokes seriously. And you told me about a crime. It seemed like a farce, but it wasn't."

"That crime took place here, in America, but the cause for it was in a different place."

"A compatriot. Another professor."

"He actually was a professor. I'm just pretending."

"An unsolved crime, you were saying. The victim was the author of many books and a few doctorates. He entrusted you to write the review that scandalized your former country. A scandal followed; you both knew that it would. The professor was killed, and the reviewer, the impostor, as you say, was bombarded with the press's garbage."

"I don't see the connection. The assassination story was serious. Tied to the former secret police."

"So you've mentioned. The former secret police and the new secret police."

"It's more complicated than that."

"That's what you always say. More complicated. When you talk about the past and when you talk about the present. Complicated. Here, we're in the country of simplifications. For the masses' consumption, that's the rule."

Peter Gaşpar feels infantilized again, groping about in the unknown. A year ago, Tara was addressing him, a maladroit Martian and stranger to the lay of the land and the rhythms of the times, with ferocity and impudence. Now she was protecting him!

Peter Gaşpar is quiet. He doesn't look at his guest, he doesn't want her to see his hands, feet, hair, lips.

"You have to give the dean that postcard."

"The dean?"

"Yes, the sailor who conquered the oceans, became a doctor of psychology and is now the dean of a college. He trained the baseball team here, if you want to know. That's America for you! Mr. Carey, the dean of the college, not Rosemarie Black, the dean of students. So then, Carey, P.C. for short."

The professor listens attentively and is inattentively quiet.

"Or speak directly to Jennifer."

"Which Jennifer?"

"Jennifer Tang, the head of security. An elegant and civilized woman."

"How do you know?"

"I know a few things about a few things. Jennifer Tang is the widow of an extraordinary Vietnamese professor of Oriental cultures. He was wounded in the war the wonderful American forces lost. She cared for him to his death, like a nun. Then she got herself hired by the college and became the head of security. She's worth meeting with. Elegant, delicate. Made of steel. Blonde, besides."

"A blonde Vietnamese?"

"Dyed. Interesting, you'll see . . . So, Jennifer Tang, J.T."

"You know too much."

For a second, Professor Gaşpar seemed animated.

"I'm not done. She likes girls. It's known and it's tolerated. You've probably noticed that there's more tolerance now, for women and men with partners of the same sex. More than for others of us. In September, when classes start, there's always competition among the boys and girls for the new girls. The old girls usually win. You didn't know that."

"No, that's another thing I didn't know," the professor admits, modestly. "But I'm not going to go to the sailor, nor to the blonde Vietnamese. I don't want to look any more ridiculous than I already do. The role I've been sentenced to is enough for me."

"What role is that?"

"The refugee. The oddball. The weirdo. He connects, but he doesn't connect. Communicates, but doesn't communicate."

"Not true. I know someone with whom he communicates."

"But he doesn't shave regularly."

They both smile, but the mood doesn't slacken. Peter no longer stares at his knees. He watches Tara, who understands that he doesn't, in fact, see her.

"That's it, we're going to have a coffee. I've accomplished my mission; I sorted the mail, and I deserve a cup of coffee. If you want, I'll check once more, after I leave. If not, I won't. Now, coffee. Make some coffee."

Gaşpar gets up. On the way to the kitchen, he turns off the radio. Mozart is finished, and Wagner can be quiet. He could really go for a glass of wine. But he'd better not. "Be careful," President Larry had said, "and keep your office door open." The girls walk around with their tits hanging out. If you look too closely and you also happen to have glasses, they'll cry rape or God knows what. Keep the door open, or you'll get into trouble.

The cottage wasn't his office, though. The breasts of the student were covered by a sweater that went all the way up to her neck. Should he offer her a glass of wine? Better not. He'd bought Tara's favorite apple pie from the library cafeteria.

The professor appears with the tray, the student is flipping through a book. She doesn't help him, as she usually would; she waits to be served. She knows he's not too dexterous, but she doesn't get up to help him. She watches attentively how he arranges the plates and cuts the pie.

"I could really drink a glass of wine," she says.

Silence. The tenant of the present is silent.

"If you have any, I'd like to drink a glass of wine. You won't be arrested. I'm over twenty-one, I'm allowed. And it's a winter evening."

"In that case, vodka's better."

"No, no hard liquor. A glass of wine, if you have any."

"I do. Red wine."

"Perfect."

They resume the conversation. The Eastern European professor's assassin; the review published nearly two years ago; the famous compatriot's and the victim's memoirs.

Exotic subjects. Peter Gaşpar knows himself to be an exotic figure in the carnival of freedom.

■

Red sky. A burning bower. Two elephants on stilts approaching one another. Bodies in the sky, thin, infinite legs to the ground.

A fabulous dragonfly, with the body and aspect of an elephant.

A primordial stork-turned-elephant. Delicate, transparent, diaphanous extensions, they barely touch the ground. Astral, archaic insects out of the prehistoric wilderness. Elephant bodies on implausible, celestial baguettes. Giant, velveteen ears, imperial tusks, silt oozing from their trunks.

The backs of the pachyderms are covered with carpets, and on each carpet, a funereal stone. Between the stone and the carpet, space; the stones are floating in the air. The trunk of the female to the left is turning like a crank. The male lowers his trunk apathetically, gazes down and faraway: smoky hills, the landing pad, the guard's post, two scarecrows running with a flag and a torch.

The male and the female try, in vain, to get close to each other. The stilts move in place. The sky is striated with the arrows of their thin legs, which seem as though they might collapse under the weight of the bodies. The male on the right, the female on the left. The tombstones wobble; the eye painted on the carpet wobbles, about to fall into the abyss below, where the infernal alarm sounds.

Gaşpar jumps, awakened by the rattling windows. He's not in Lu's room; it's a different hotel, a different room, but the alarm has woken him up for good now.

The caravan of firetrucks in the Lunar City. At the fire station across the street, the sirens scream; the day's fire-breathing mouth opens. He lies numbly in his bed. The minute hand approaches eight o'clock. He lifts the receiver, slowly dialing the number of the all-knowing Gora. Gora picks up the phone, but Gaşpar changes his mind; he puts the phone back in its cradle.

The city of wanderers; skyscrapers scrape Dalí's sky. Below, the throng of that particular moment. The ogre stares ponderously out the window. The gangster of the garbage cans is as punctual as ever, carrying his great leaden luggage in his right hand. Military pants, yellow work boots, the tight tank top pulled over the bulging, battle-ready torso. In his clay head destiny has hollowed out large red eye sockets. Beardless, clay cheeks. Long, blond hairs covered in mucus extend from his nostrils. Cracked lips, crooked grin, toothless mouth, two yellowed walrus fangs, a stony neck, a long, flat, massive nose. His arms are short and pudgy, just like his body; the vigor of an assassin.

Watch him on the street corner, dragging his suitcase full of meteorites. At every step, he sags with the effort.

The first garbage basket. He rummages, he pulls out the bag, opens it, pulls out the opened can, throws it back, takes another bag, opens his luggage, bends over, stuffs the bag back in. He crosses to the opposite sidewalk; he bends over the basket. In his hand, another bag. He pulls out the remains of a loaf of bread, throws the bag, stuffs the bread in his pocket, waits for the light to turn green, crosses toward the opposite post, stops, bends over the basket, opens the luggage, closes the luggage. He sits on a bench in the small square. Nearby, the luggage filled with lead or mercury or cadavers. He slurps from the plastic cup gleaned from the last basket, sinks his mammoth fangs into the bread.

Head upturned, looking into the infinite. The nose sniffs out the danger; the nostrils' gelatin-covered antennae tremble. Mouth cracked open, exposing his prehistoric fangs. Passersby stop, then hurriedly move away.

Gaşpar can start his day. The void's gatekeeper has reconfirmed reality. He abandons the hotel; the library is nearby. You bookish hunter, you're looking for a needle in a haystack, some decoy in the fog of memory, a quotation, known to you at some point, lost in the jungle of another language; you memorized it in your own tongue; you recognize it, it seems, but you don't recognize it in the language into which you have migrated.

The mind rolls through the old refrains. Fragments unwinding, rewound. The threatening postcard! The quotation! The code of a different dictionary. The cadences of the past reject the language borrowed in this newer age. That was another time, inconvertible. *Next time I kill you* sounded different in the Gomorrah of juvenile jubilations. The look of the words themselves, their sound when read aloud; the hypnosis of the past won't migrate into the substitutions of exile. A pent-up memory; a frozen flower that won't open.

No, he couldn't place the quotation. The new words didn't bring back the old ones; yesterday's sounds wouldn't collaborate with to-day's, and the night that separated them in time was starless.

He'd fallen again in the trap of hunting for words. *Labyrinth? Invisible crime?* A new, impenetrable code.

The beggar who is no beggar rotates the empty, heavy luggage on the surface of the planet; he is here, a step away, bent over the garbage basket, then the next garbage basket and the next, until he throws himself into the last basket.

The square in front of the modest hotel. Gaşpar collapses, hu-miliated, on the bench. His eyes turned up toward the foreign sky. He doesn't have the courage to turn his gaze toward his neighbor; he sees only the military boots. Nearby, the guard of the grottos. Stubby, rough hands, legs of steel, the head of an ogre, bottomless eye sockets. Thin ropes running from his trunk, greasy hair. Sym-metrical tusks, yellow mouth.

Peter sits on the bench for a long time after the soldier of futility leaves, taking up his garbage route once again. His head back, gaze toward the sky and the elephants hauling the funereal obelisk.

■

Irresponsibility. A need for irresponsibility, that was how Peter Gaş-par defined his landing in the New World. The game of hide-and-seek with Death, whether at the wheel or by falling off a ladder.

The potential suicide doesn't seem frightened by death, except on the nights when the Nymphomaniac tortures him.

The large bell in the university chapel announces the lunch hour. The courtyard is blanketed with students and professors, hur-rying to fill their stomachs. Shouting, singing. All of a sudden, the square is deserted, quiet. The hungry crowd has disappeared. A white, clean toilet is waiting for them. Palade meditates, smil-ing, sitting on the toilet seat. A look of Nirvana across his face, wide, childish eyes, enchanted by bookish temptations. The reptile climbs, without a sound, along the wall that separates the neighbor-ing stalls; he climbs up to the top, stops, and from above, considers the squat body of the condemned, as he sits on the throne of waste, for one last moment. The killing shot rushes out from the mouth of the snake.

The assassin had stolen into the neighboring stall without a sound. One foot on the toilet seat, slowly, quietly, then the other foot; there, he's up. He could see over the next stall perfectly, the professor on the relaxation throne. A short, identifying look. The shiny revolver aims at the temple of the condemned; the bullet releases, without sound.

As he wakes up, Peter Gaşpar tries to remember the faceless mercenary, his hands, his neck, his shoulders. He can only see his black mouth, the phosphorescent flash. Poor Peter is sweating.

Lined up among other skeletons, Eva Kirschner. From in between her pale legs, the head of a baby with a mousy face. The prosecutor David Gaşpar extends his left arm to the sentinel with the Red Cross armband. With a razor, the nurse cuts the number out of the dried skin. Slowly, patiently, digit by digit. Small squares of bloodied skin thrown to the floor, one by one. One digit, then another digit. Five digits; the pseudonym of the dead who didn't die. The prosecutor is bilious, his eyes bloodshot, bulging out of their sockets, his head and hands trembling; the blood of the abattoir is draining from his arm.

After such a painstaking initiation, you wake up terrified. The Nymphomaniac has tested you again. Fear and insomnia don't just exhaust; they humiliate you. Peter relives, endlessly, the moment before the fall off the ladder. He lifts himself up on his elbows, covers his eyes; the film rolls on. The ambulance, the operating table, the rods that slowly penetrate the crushed legs, while the pain penetrates the kidneys and brain. Sedatives don't help. Mangled, sleepless nights; days dumbfounded by exhaustion.

He raises the receiver, slowly, slowly, dials Gora's number.

"Professor? I have a question."

Gora is silent, but he is there, listening, at the end of the world.

"You know that I was interested in deaf-mutes?"

Gora is silent, but he is there.

"Yes, I was interested in the deaf-mutes of deaf-mute socialism. I was one of them. Didn't you ever read the little story that gave me my fame and nickname in socialism? My hero, Mynheer, was a deaf-mute, like all of us."

Gora is silent, but his diaphanous breathing is audible.

"I don't know if I told you this, but I've been in a real crisis with insomnia."

"You didn't tell me. What happened?"

"Nothing happened; my beautiful cousin is fine, though I haven't seen her in a long time. You wanted to know that, I'm sure."

"No. I was asking about . . . "

"About me, you were asking about me; I'm enough of an idiot to believe it. Deranged by lack of sleep. Dreams, yes, dreams. No, drugs don't help. The doctor? Avicenna? Only if I can see Lu, and now is not the time for that; I'm in no shape for it. So then, the deaf-mutes, that's what we were talking about. Sometimes I sit all night long in front of the television, with the lights on. A few days ago, maybe yesterday, I don't even know, I saw a movie about deaf-mutes. Yes, a documentary. It was good, good, the way things are done here, professional, very professional. It's called, you won't believe it, *Sound and Fury*! You can't say that written madness isn't sellable. Bill Faulkner, of course. *Academy Award Nominee. Best Documentary Feature. Powerful. Insightful . . . emotionally wrenching*. That's how it's billed."

Gora is silent on the other end of the line.

"So, then, I've found my old friends, here. And here, I'm one of them. Deafened and silenced by everything I don't understand. Yes, there are plenty of things. Look, something happened recently, a threat, but never mind about that. So then, it's a family, three generations of deaf-mutes. Not all, but the majority. Now, of course, Technology, today's fairy godmother, offers remedies. The dilemma of Mr. and Mrs. S, both deaf, is whether they should take advantage of these advances for their daughter. Why so silent, Professor? You don't understand how that relates at all to me? It does. I've been dropped from the moon, onto another moon. Another world, another language, another deafness, another muteness. Another code.

I'm one of them, one of these deaf-mutes! But I don't understand *them*, either. Not even them. So, now you see why the insomnia?"

Gora is silent, but he's on the line; the connection is holding; he's listening attentively, to be sure; he's listening and taking notes.

"The child, Heather, is superb. Precocious, vivacious, excited by the saving implant. But what about her identity? What do you do about the great problem of Identity? How can you renounce the identity of the tribe, even if it's a tribe of deaf-mutes? How, how? The sect is very proud, of the way it lives, compared with the so-called normals. Maybe they're right. Solidarity, code, honesty, intimacy, everything you want! So then, Identity. With a capital *I*, with large, red letters. The magic key, sought by everyone, the one that opens any door, and all doors. I-den-ti-ty! That's that, liquidated, finished. Fig-ure it out. Un-load."

Peter no longer seemed interested whether Gora was listening or not. He'd given up on the pauses, he was merely chattering to himself.

"The child needs to choose between deaf parents and perfectly normal grandparents. They, on the other hand, can hardly wait to understand each other, at last, with the handicapped enchantress. Oh, I ought to slap myself; you can't say things like that. Normal, abnormal, it's not correct, it's not polite and it's not *politically correct*. Some time ago, there used to be a U.N. Day for the Handicapped. There was even a U.N. Year for the Handicapped, I remember. I was hoping that the United Nations would pull the handicapped East out of the socialist latrine. Now, we're proud of any identity at all, isn't that right, Professor? But what about me? I don't have the magic key; or, if I ever had it, I've lost it."

Gora's silence continued. He was probably smiling. He had no idea about the threatening letter; Gaşpar had given up on telling him.

"Yes, I have a dilemma on my hands. Every day I am faced with a dilemma. Now, I don't know if I should remain a deaf-mute, the way I was when I came here, or if I should throw myself, screaming, into the mouth of reality. I am going to call that child Heather; I absolutely have to call her. If she's got her hearing aid in, she'll answer, if not, I'll go on living just as happy as I am."

Gora was silent and still smiling, probably. The garrulous Gaşpar wasn't done.

"Professor, is there a country more formidable than this one? It has everything, everything. Even *I'm* here. Do you know anything comparable with the Lunar City? That's what I've wanted to ask you. You know everything, by the book; I'm sure you know the answer."

Gora was silent.

"No answer, I see. Should I help you? There is, Professor, another country that's just as formidable! Our quiet, faraway Homeland. A scholarly priest has managed to translate the Liturgy into sign language. A unique achievement in the Christian world! He followed the apostles' sacred mission, to speak to everyone's understanding. Now, barely now, there can be Mass for deaf-mutes. This is what's happening in our magic, superrealist little country on the edge of the world. They don't have the technological possibility to normalize the abnormal, but they have a spiritual one. And that's superior, isn't it? The sacred book is accompanied by photographs that explain every stage of the prayer in signs. The apostles of silence, that's what the new blessed ones are called. They even have a choir. They sing in signs. What do you think of that? Which is better, our country here, or that one, there? That's my dilemma. Should I go back?"

Gora was listening, silently. Probably smiling.

"Do you think I'm ranting? I'm talking about the Mavrodoiu Church in Piteşti. Do you still remember where Piteşti is? In the south of the Homeland, not in the Habsburgian Transylvanian north that was home to the Gaşpars, nor the Habsburgian north of Bukovina, which had the honor of bringing into the world the mathematician and philosopher Mihnea Palade and my cousin Augustin Gora. We're cousins, aren't we? Through alliance and semi-alliance and discrepancy. In Piteşti, then, in the south, where there were Roman legions brought from Palestine, Hebrews who impregnated the local women and propagated the race. Did you know that? Of course, you knew it."

Gora is silent.

"Anyway, that's my insomnia, my dilemma. Do I go back to the church of the deaf-mutes, or do I stay here, in the exile hospital? I hope you understand, so that you can help me decide. And there's something else. The new language of the deaf-mute church has facilitated two interpretations for some sacred texts. Parallel words, just as Palade had dreamed. What more can you ask for; what, what, tell me, Professor."

Gaşpar isn't waiting for an answer, he's merely breathing deeply.

"Do you vote? I need to know, it's important for my decision. You've been here for twenty years. Surely you've already voted a few times. Have you voted? With the elephant or the donkey? For whom does the bewildered citizen vote? Here voting is important, not like back in our homeland."

"Yes, it is. Too few vote."

"No one is interested in politics. The government is called the Administration. Wonderful! The building administration! And there are no identity cards, just drivers' licenses! Whom did you vote for?"

"I didn't vote. I've never voted in any election."

"Why?"

"When the electoral campaigns begin, you have the sensation that you've stumbled upon a children's playground. The voters cry, skipping, hugging each other, putting on masks, chanting. The candidates seem like robots, reciting slogans. It's a little frightening. No skepticism whatsoever."

"Democracy! All the rights in the world. The right to stupidity, as well, of course. It's important! Very important. No one shuns you, no one eliminates you, you're human. For-mi-da-ble!"

■

A long, narrow room with metallic walls and a floor made of silver metal. A long, metallic cage, without windows. In the back, at the far end of the office, a metallic table. Behind it, a rusted, metallic armchair. In front of the table, and on the sides, silver chairs.

At the table, the general. Tall, massive, white mustache and black hair. A brownish uniform; wide, golden epaulets with three large stars. Medals on his chest. The jacket and khaki shirt unbuttoned. Heat, as though from the inside of a kiln.

He presses the button on his desk; there's a ring; the metal door opens; two guards introduce Lu, each one holding her by an arm. They cross the distance from the door to the metallic desk with light, small steps. The detainee is deposited into the chair in front of the general; the soldiers come to attention, salute, do an about face; the metallic door closes without a sound behind them.

The general considers the detainee. Like a Russian princess. Short, fur overcoat, long, black knee boots. A peasant's kerchief, old and torn, covers her face.

Lu keeps her head down, holding herself in her short overcoat, shivering. Delicate green gloves protruding from the sleeves with the grayish cuffs. The gloved hands tremble; Lu clutches herself, clenching, in the fur that's too short.

The bell rings long and violently, like a siren, three times. The general is stiff in his chair; the detainee, stiff in her own.

The door doesn't open. The general stands up, waiting. He hurriedly buttons the front of his shirt and jacket.

At last, the metallic door opens gently to the side. A thin, little man in a silken, striped prisoner's uniform, striped cap over his shaved head, enters stealthily into the room. Heavy, thick, silk, elegant pajamas, with a skullcap, the beret of a wealthy retiree. On his feet, slippers made of felted fabric.

The general clicks his heels in a military salute, comes out from behind the armchair, moves respectfully to the side, making room for his superior.

The little man sits hastily in the general's armchair, and the general moves to the chair to the left of the detainee. The chief pulls a golden pen from the shirt pocket of his pajamas, extends it to the general, pushes a thick, black folder across the desk in the general's direction.

He smiles at the detainee, who doesn't raise her head.

"We know each other, don't we?"

She keeps her head down, her gaze on the metallic floor.

"I'd prefer it if you took off that stinking kerchief."

Lu slowly pulls the kerchief off her shaved head and lets it fall at the foot of the chair. She stares, resigned, at David Gaşpar, the cousin of her mother, comrade Serafim. Eva Kirschner's husband. Peter's father.

"I think you know what this is about."

Having gotten no answer, the prosecutor makes a quick sign to the general, who pulls a pack of Kent cigarettes and a golden lighter out of his breast pocket. He sets them on the desk. David Gaşpar pulls out a cigarette, the general lights it, David takes a deep drag, once, three times, with the thirst of someone who's been kept far away from such pleasures for a long time. The general pushes the ashtray from the edge of the desk toward the center, to the right of the chief.

"You come from a trustworthy family. Your parents were on our Party's side after, and maybe even before the war. In spite of their bourgeois origins and their wealth, comrades Serafim are people of confidence."

The general makes notes, conscientiously.

"They're not the ones in question. Nor their daughter. We're talking about the fugitive Augustin Gora. The son of former exploiters, owners of vast forests in Bukovina. Your husband."

Lu looks at him, unmoved, shivering in the too short fur.

The general unbuttons his jacket once again, as well as the buttons to the neck of his shirt.

"Have you divorced this man?"

"No."

A prompt, whispered answer.

"Hm, that surprises me. I don't think your parents were too happy with this marriage. Not that . . . no, I'm not referring to ethnicity. The Party doesn't discriminate among people; your family rid itself of the horrors of the ghettos and the arrogance of the chosen people, but I don't think they approved of the choice. And I doubt they're happy to have a son-in-law who ran away to the capitalists.

Lu looks at her relative, silently, trembling.

"Maybe Professor Gora thought that he'd received a passport on the merit of his intellect; maybe he hasn't understood that we gave him the passport. Not because he deserved it, but because that was what we wanted."

The prosecutor Gaşpar emphasized the word *we*, gazing at the general. The general was writing, concentrating on the paper.

"I hope you're not intending to follow him."

"No."

"Very good. This doesn't, however, excuse you from your duty to us. You've refused to answer the questions. You could be accused as an accomplice. Have you decided to answer?"

"No," whispered Lu, clutching her fur.

Cousin David had filled half the ashtray.

"While he was here, Augustin Gora participated in clandestine meetings. In those meetings, books by Nazis, Legionnaires, Trotskyists, Liberals, and Masons were discussed. Even books by Quakers. Decadent and religious literature was read. We know exactly who participated and when . . . "

Lu was silent; the general was filling his pen with ink.

"Is your eminent husband a mystic? Or is Mr. Gora a liberal propagandist?"

"He isn't," whispered Mrs. Gora.

"Yes, he is! He is all of those things. He read the Bible. He commented on the Scriptures. Even in high school. He would perorate in favor of Saint Peter. 'Peter's sect,' he would say. He debated *The Rights of Man*. He commented on Confucius. We have proof. Old and new. Not just from one, or a few of his former colleagues, but from many."

The prosecutor Gaşpar makes a short signal; the general rises, pours something from the carafe on the desk into the interrogator's glass; David sips the water of life, staring at the bareheaded detainee. Lu wets her burned lips with her tongue, clutching the short and expensive fur.

"And there's another thing . . . He wrote a letter for a student, a letter to American senators. Regarding an American scholarship. We didn't approve the passport. The student had dubious, idealist leanings. He talked too much, much too much. Conceited, arrogant, a know-it-all, he thought himself untouchable. We didn't give him a passport. And we're never going to. Your husband wrote the letter and gave him the addresses of the senators. And the address of a fugitive Legionnaire, who is now a celebrated professor of mystic studies. Moreover, Mr. Augustin Gora brought with him provocative, antisocialist, antihumanist documents, which were then played on Radio Şopîrliţa.* You know what I'm talking about."

"I don't know."

"Yes, you do. The capitalist gossip station, Radio Free Europe. You know it, Ludmila Serafim, you know it! Or is it Ludmila Gora? Or maybe Gaşpar? I've heard you like your men a little wet behind the ears."

The prosecutor slams his small fists on the metal table, once and again, and again, unable to hold back his anger.

"You know and you're going to admit it! You're going to admit it, Ludmila, I assure you."

He leans toward the ashtray, the cigarette is out, he takes it, he throws it, hysterically, onto the metal floor.

He gets up. The general follows, officiously, a step away. The felted boots of the superior are silent while the general's boots carry a deafening tread.

Lu takes her head in her hands, stiff, straight, in the metal chair, her shaved head, her narrow, pale face serried in between her green hands. She doesn't move. An effigy. Her face hollow, head shaved, her gloves covering her ears. Petrified.

*The word Şopîrliţa means "the gossiping lizard" [trans.].

Gora shakes a fist in the air, the pillow falls over the lamp on the nightstand; the lamp falls with a crash to the floor; the somnambulist twists, dizzily, wet with transpiration, awake.

"Green gloves," he murmurs. He sits, overwhelmed, he sits, worn out, on the edge of the bed, gazing down at the lustrous, wooden floor.

No, Lu had never worn green gloves!

He makes his way toward the bathroom, puts his head under the faucet. Wet, awake, he doesn't reach for the towel.

Peter Gaşpar isn't the only one having nightmares. The obituarist is also going through nocturnal trials.

Green gloves? Never . . . he pulls out the first-aid kit from under his bed, opens it, rummages around in it, pulls out Ludmila's old, black gloves, brought over from the Homeland of his youth.

■

Tara calls Peter Gaşpar on the phone, to remind him about the postcard. Wednesday afternoon, Peter has a meeting with the dean. The tall, blond sailor with curly hair and large, stained, freckled hands, smiles. Protectively, encouragingly. Gaşpar produces the card. He retells the story about his compatriot's assassination, about Professor Palade. Afterward, the biography of the mentor Dima, the author of an encyclopedic work. He summarizes the review that he wrote about the old man's memoirs, the scandal provoked by the revelation of the scholar's old political sympathies.

The sailor raises his blond eyebrows. He listens to the details of the scandal in the faraway country, the refugee's suspicions, the biography of the deceased scholar, the assassination of his apprentice, twisted, Balkan tales . . . as if they were sailor stories from the time when he was setting a course toward Indonesia and Dahomey. He's never reached the Black Sea (and that area's history certainly wasn't on the forefront of the planet's psyche), though it would have been worthwhile.

He doesn't have time for confusion. The decision is simple and prompt. Action! If one professor was assassinated without apparent motive, another could be assassinated for a minor motive. A mere review?! Just a review in a journal, and all this scandal on the other end of the world? It's a bad joke, naturally. The threat might also be just a bad joke. Still, we must be careful. So, then: action.

Friday morning, the Eastern European professor presents himself to Ms. Tang, the college's head of security. Small, amiable, elegant, precise, like a manager at a bank; laconic, determined, sparing in her gestures. Gaşpar can't take his eyes off her sleek, golden hair, her black eyebrows, her black and sharp gaze. Her dress suit is white, her shoes, small and white, with heels, small, dainty hands, short nails without polish. The professor sums up the twisted details of the twisted story, expressing his skepticism about the threatening letter. Ms. Tang has two clear dispositions: prudence and action.

"This is a death threat, Professor! A joke? Even if mortals are jokesters, death doesn't joke."

Maybe a Vietnamese proverb, co-opted by the American police? Gaşpar wondered.

"A death threat!" Jennifer was satisfied by the European's smile.

"We're all threatened with death," murmured Gaşpar.

Jennifer isn't in the mood to philosophize. She'd already alerted the local police. She requests permission for a visit the following morning.

"Where do you live on campus?"

"A cottage lost in the woods. Hard to see from the street."

The silence of Ms. Tang signals that the Eastern European hasn't answered the question clearly. So he describes the surroundings of the cottage.

"No one seems to know about it. Nonetheless, it's on the campus map."

Friday night. An agitated forest, neurotic animals, hysteric branches, whistles, rustling. The resident sleeps with interruptions.

At 11 in the morning, Jennifer Tang's car stops in front of the cottage. J.T. is wearing a red tracksuit and red sneakers and is accompanied by a tall man in police uniform. Slow with questions, even slower in the transcription of the answers. He introduces himself as Jim Smith, Trooper. J.S.T.? No, Trooper isn't a name, but a title. State police.

Questions, answers. The semester had started Wednesday, February 1. The first class, Monday afternoon, from 3:30 to 5:30. P.O. Box 1079 was full. He closed it; he wasn't in the mood for mail. Advertisements and information and letters asking for money didn't interest him. When he was younger, yes, he was always waiting for the miracle, the magic message. Here, the mail is a garbage can. He'd hired a student to sort it.

"The name?"

"Of the student? Yes, of course."

The policeman notes the information, makes a sign to Ms. Tang to note it as well. So then, he saw the mail only after a week? No, two weeks had gone by. The student had been busy; she'd brought the first batch only about the middle of the month. Then came another pile, and then another, and, then, the card appeared.

"Is it stamped, postmarked? Is there a date?"

No, you couldn't see the postmark. Just the stamp and the address. The address of the recipient was clear. Might the sender have ties to the college? The college's phone and address book wasn't accessible except to professors and administrators.

The police officer looks at the criminal exhibit.

"It could be a foreigner. You don't say 'next time I kill you,' but '*the* next time.' The next time I will kill you."

"That's important!" the invigorated J.T. intervenes. The professor's compatriots had been outraged by an article he wrote. Might the author of the letter be a compatriot?

The professor doesn't answer. Compatriot? Didn't Ms. Tang also become his compatriot?

"Do you have anything to add?"

"Two days ago, in the snow on the patio . . . there were footprints. Boots." Maybe some workman who'd come to check the plumbing or read a meter or something? Yesterday, there was sun, and the snow melted. The tracks weren't really visible any longer. Still, something. The steps go in a single direction. As if someone had just crossed the patio, inspected the cottage and didn't return to the patio. Someone inspected the area; that was sure. Now you could no longer see the tracks.

All three of them go out on the patio. Nothing special, says J. S. Trooper's look. He puts the evidence in a plastic bag, the bag in a leather folder. The object will remain with the police and the professor will get a copy. J.T. will send the claimant a front and back copy on Monday.

"Ah, yes. One other thing," the professor retorts. "I don't know, in fact, if . . . maybe this is stupid stupid, but . . . "

"Tell us everything," Mrs. Tang insists, under the bored gaze of the state trooper.

"Yes, let's hear it," adds J. S. Trooper.

Gaşpar pulls out a crumpled paper from his pocket and hands it to the policeman.

"I found it taped to my door. Maybe it's a stupid thing, I don't know. I can't tell anymore."

"*Lost cat needs help*," reads the Vietnamese over the shoulder of the policeman, who raises his eyebrows, taken aback.

A photograph, on a black background, of a striped cat. The cat sits, as if posing for the photographer, well behaved, has one blue eye and one white, blind eye. *Gattino is a 6-month-old, slender gray male tabby with distinctive spots and stripes . . . Gattino is a 6-month-old tomcat, skinny, ashy gray, with spots and stripes. He is blind in his left eye. If you find him, please call 658.2704. He might seem confused because he is feeble. He has one sick eye and chronic respiratory problems. But he has a home and we're beside ourselves that he's lost.*

Mrs. Tang and the police officer seem disoriented. The professor, however, provides some further information.

"There are also some lines written by hand. Under the typed lines, there are three handwritten lines."

They'd seen them, of course, but they didn't care. But now they had to care, there was no choice. *He's very short-haired & vulnerable. Please, please . . . if you see him call him by name, clearly and sweetly.*

If you have him in your home, please call us and we'll come get him immediately.

"Yes, yes," mutters the trooper and puts the paper in his pocket.

In the afternoon, Dean P.C. requests that the FBI be informed. They look for Officer Pereira, with whom Gaşpar had been in contact immediately after the appearance of his article on Dima, a year before, after the assassination of Professor Portland. The publication of the review coincided with the assassination, wasn't that right? They're waiting for a sign from Officer Pereira.

Saturday evening, Tara doesn't show. Instead, she calls to excuse herself; she's had an exhausting day; she has a migraine; even her workout has exhausted her. The professor retells the trials of the preceding days; the conversation lengthens. The subject animates her, she no longer seems tired.

Gaşpar goes to sleep late. Strong knocking on the door. Sleepily he weaves in between the bed and the nightstand. "Security," announces the voice of the woods.

On the front step, with a flashlight in the eyes of the suspect, the young police officer Garcia. It's a dream, that's it; Gaşpar is smiling, not daring to wake up.

"The rounds, you know. We were told that you've been having some problems. We're patrolling the grounds. We'll check in every three hours after midnight."

Every three hours? Could they check the grounds without knocking on the door? Gaşpar says he'll leave the light on. The police officer agrees.

Night, forest, gusts. Wind and cold. Barbed wire, patrols, dogs, phantoms in rags, gathered one in the other. Eva Kirschner. Peter is balled up above the child that he was once, above the body riddled with wounds. Frozen rags, skin and bones, the child of different time. The patrolling guards, security lights, livid bodies.

He awakes with the pillow rumpled and wet in his arms. He hears, somewhere, the grinding motor of a car; he doesn't want to go back to sleep, but he crashes into his pillow. Woods. Captives. Old, famished faces. Detainees. The frightened mob. The roll call. Patrol guards with dogs scrutinize the skeletons. The little boy easily became air, nothing to hold in your arms. The whimpering subsided, as well as the screaming of the sentinels. Heavy, leaden snow, not a single movement. A thick stillness; you can't breathe.

The nightmare doesn't belong to me, has nothing to do with me, it's my parents', Gaşpar decides in the morning.

Sunday he doesn't come out of his den. He tries to remember the text on the card. A word, a comma. He's not sure that he still has the phrase. He can't remember the newspaper article on the other side either.

A good sign, he'll sleep unhampered tonight.

■

Monday. The Security Office. J.T. sits in front of the computer, salutes with a nod, without shifting her gaze from the blue screen, extends her right arm toward a drawer, Gaşpar can see the large, thick, silver ring on the thin finger, she pulls out two sheets of paper, stapled to one another. The copy of the postcard, front and back.

"Don't let anyone see these."

Her gaze fixed on the screen. The small fingers caress the keys, and madam J.T. nods, *bye-bye*, see you soon.

After lunch, a walk around campus. The small cemetery on the hill. Gaşpar stops in front of every tombstone. Irish, Italians, Jews, a Portuguese, Germans, Dutch. The clan of the dead is disorganized, like nature itself. The pliant stone leaning slightly to the left is called Sabina. Nothing else. Sabina-Germany, and no other specification. The name of futility, like any name.

If the assassin is perfect, Professor Gaşpar will end up here, near Sabina, thankful for the brotherhood of exiles.

The library. Second floor, the magazine stand. Then, two hours of class. Calm and sarcastic, as in the glory days. In the evening at eight, the patrol car. Officer Garcia, fat, smiling. He will return in two hours. "Two hours? I thought we'd understood each other . . . "

"Yes, but Madame Tang thinks this is the right thing. At night we come every three hours, and we no longer knock on the door. Don't pull the blinds, and leave the light on."

The strangling of the invalid on channel 2. The debate about the rape on channel 4. The massacre in Rwanda on 9. Monsters on 11, vaudeville on 12, the jungle on 53, the basketball game on 22, shootings on 43. And back: 53, 2, 22. Alternative realities annul reality.

The *New York Times. Wednesday, October 12.* Postmark: *Old Glory.* The American flag. *For U.S. addresses only.* Stamp: New York. Yes, you can identify the stamp, the postal code, officer Jimmy Smith Trooper should have seen or actually saw the envelope's stamp in the meantime.

Typed text, the address written out by hand. Big letters: N looks like W, A doesn't have the unifying line, it's like a rooftop. The address is precise, even the name of the cabin, Boumer House, which no one knows. The college, the town, the state, the ZIP code. *Dear*—typed. The first name of the addressee written out by hand. Toni, Philip, Susan, Norman, Rosalind, Peter, whomever. The way you'd fill out a form. A trick, evidently, so that the threat won't seem individualized. *Dear* Peter . . .

Next time I kill you. Or *the next time? Kill you* or *I will kill you? Next time!* So then, a future date! Had there already been a failed attempt? *A previous try?* Signed: D. *Devil? Dummy? Destiny? Deity? Death?* Yes, *Death!* Ubiquitous whore.

A failed trick. No postcard was addressed to Larry or Madame Tang or the dean, only to an old and faithful target. Lady Death hadn't forgotten Mynheer. An encoded love note.

The fragment from the paper on the back was just another trick. To divert the amateurs, not the addressee.

The car, the brakes, the headlights. There are no dogs, no, the Van Nest patrol is replacing the Garcia patrol.

"Don't worry, we pass by here every hour."

"Every hour? I thought it was every two hours."

"Don't wait up for us; you should sleep."

"I wasn't waiting. I go to bed late, anyway. As late as I can. And I get up often, even without you."

"Routine check. You can go to sleep, the place is under surveillance."

Wednesday morning. A warm day, sun, scents of spring. The professor seems listless in the conversation with the two students who wait for him in his office. At two in the afternoon, he gets a call from the FBI Officer Patrick Murphy. He knows about Officer Pereira and about the scandal following the publication of the review; he's also heard about the card and the threat.

"Have you ever published anything on Rushdie?"

"Rushdie? The writer? The condemned? We're back to books again? Where does it end? The whole thing is absurd! I wanted to throw out the card, believe me."

"Please calm down and speak more slowly, I don't understand what you're saying."

Police Officer Patrick requests a meeting. Next Tuesday. Yes, at the office. Gray building, faculty offices, façade covered in ivy.

"There's no need for directions," Patrick cuts him off quickly. "I'll find the place. Tuesday, 1:30 P.M."

The grumpy Patrick was more interesting than the formal Pereira, with his gentle, stupid advice.

Gaşpar is tired of his solitary cottage. He calls a taxi, quickly packs up some things and papers, checks the faucets, the stove, draws the curtains. At the train station, he scrutinizes the passengers attentively, one by one.

The City on the Moon. The public library. Encyclopedias and dictionaries, the stories of the world looking for another world.

Monday morning, the return train, banal passengers. Night, disordered woods. Noises. Tormented birds, barbed wire, the routine of the sentinels.

Tuesday, at 1:30 P.M., without knocking on the door, a stout, solid man enters the office. Thick lips, small brow, the look of a bully. Hairy. His checkered coat barely reaches around his body. Dark gaze. A business card thrown on the table: Patrick Murphy, Special Agent. *Larry Number Eight*, yes, yes, Larry Eight.

"I spoke on the phone with Mario. He no longer works in this area. He told me the story of Professor Portland's assassination, about the scandal that followed. And your article, another scandal. How old was the professor?"

"Palade was young."

"Palade?"

"Same person. He changed his name here."

"Oh? No, not him. The Mentor. The celebrity."

"Cosmin Dima had died some years before. He was over eighty."

"Let's start with your review. The press piece. Fascism, nationalism, those kinds of things. Why did it provoke such a scandal?"

"A reminder of unpleasant things."

"New things?"

"No, they weren't new. The context was new. Post-Communism. New beginnings, new icons. The confusion of freedom. For the East, just as for the immigrants here."

"How famous was this Dima?"

"As famous as a man of letters can be famous. He wasn't an athlete or a movie star, or a sexy escort doing two weeks' time for drunk driving, whom the network is paying a million for an interview about her sadness in her jail cell. A million! Dima didn't get that much from all his books that appeared all over the world. No, no, Old Man Dima was something else."

"A nationalist?"

"In his youth. Maybe even afterward. In his country and mine he's a real cult figure. He's an icon, everyone used to say."

"Why did you write the article? Why now?"

"A new edition of his memoirs appeared. I hesitated, but I wrote it. I was asked to write the review. First I refused, but then I wrote it."

"Who approached you?"

"A journalist, a friend of the president of the college."

"I see. It was good for the college."

"Maybe. He argued that it would be good for me."

"Was it good?"

"Not really."

"Do you regret it?"

"No."

"My colleague Mario says you didn't receive any threats following the review."

"I did. In my former country, in the press there. I no longer live there. There were some here, too, a few, in the expat press."

"Was your wife threatened?"

"Wife? What wife?"

"Or, your partner . . . girlfriend."

"Partner? Oh, my *significant other*, as you say. My cousin Lu wasn't threatened."

"So then, threats in the press."

"Violent articles, insults, curses. There, far away. Here, just in the expat press."

"I understand that Professor Portland . . . rather, Palade, had received threats. Why? He wasn't writing about nationalism."

"He was. He had dissociated himself from the nationalists of his country. He published violently antinationalist texts."

"Did your review refer to him, too? He was a disciple of Dima's."

"I only wrote about Cosmin Dima's memoirs. I brought up his political affiliations of the thirties."

"Did he conceal or manipulate the facts? You said they weren't new pieces of information."

"Old information, new situation. The anti-Communist post-Communism. Or anti-Communism after Communism. It's easier to fight with a corpse . . . Dima didn't discuss his secret. Why should he confess in public? What matters is what you do, not who you were, isn't that right? Pragmatism!"

"Did he have followers? Other than Palade?"

"Probably."

"And were they scandalized by your review?"

"Probably. Not just them. General indignation."

"Mario told me that you avoid your former compatriots."

"I lived among them. There weren't only horrors; there, joys, too. But here, yes, I avoid them."

"Why did you contact Officer Pereira?"

"The college contacted him. After Palade's assassination. The president of the college was convinced that I might be in danger. Mr. Pereira didn't manage well in the whole Balkan mess. The motives for the assassination weren't very clear . . . Even now they're not clear."

The FBI envoy doesn't write anything down. He just scrutinizes the face of the interrogated.

"Why would the same group return after two years?"

"What group?"

"The group that threatened you then?"

"I don't know of any group that would have threatened me."

"Have you published anything else in the meantime?"

"No, nothing."

"Does the postcard seem to have been sent by an extremist group?"

"I don't know."

"A group of mystics, for example? I understand from Mario that the extremists from the thirties were mystics. Those with ties to Dima were mystics. Orthodox terrorism, no? Are there mystics here, too?

"I don't know. It's an odd text. It could be a ruse, to distract the investigation. We don't know who the sender was, we don't know anything. Certainly there must be extremist groups among the exiles, but I don't know anything about them."

"Is there anything particular to note about the handwriting of the message?"

"Only the name and address are handwritten. The rest, typed or printed by a computer."

"What do you think about the text?"

"I think it's a quotation. I don't know why. Just an impression."

"Something familiar in the text?"

"Labyrinth. The word *labyrinth*. One of Dima's obsessions. He wrote a lot about labyrinths. I spent a few days in the New York Public Library last week. I revisited his books. The obsession is there. The Greek labyrinth. Myth and ritual in the labyrinth. The world as a labyrinth. The city as labyrinth. The mystic spiral and the labyrinth of the cross. The Celtic labyrinth. The labyrinth of human viscera . . . "

Annoyed, the policeman stands up. Short, thickset, dumpy. Thick, black, wavy hair.

"We'll see each other in a week. Same time and place."

"Perfect," answered the professor, impatient himself to leave the room. Humiliated by his lapses of memory. He knew, and he didn't know the quotation. The past refused to render the bibliography accurately.

■

The moment has come to tell about the incident, to reveal the postcard to others, to get opinions, to solicit advice. Gora could replace an entire library, he might be able to offer the solution. Or to call Lu. If she learns about the threat, Lu will want to hear about the adventure, to listen attentively and with great concern.

Peter hesitates, with the receiver to his ear. He makes up his mind, dialing Gora's number.

"Yes, it is I, the Eastern Mynheer. Yes, you're right, we haven't spoken in a long time. But here we are, talking now. A lot, I assure you, we will talk as the condemned talks to his oracle. The impeccable oracle. The unvanquished. For the professor who has read and committed everything to memory, no question is too difficult. And so, then, I have to ask . . . "

He has the postcard in hand, the mysterious message in front of his face. He is ready, and then he changes his mind again. And that's how it goes, revulsion wins in the end.

"I'm asking you about the student uprising, which you witnessed. So that I can also understand the world into which I've landed. You've already told me about it, you're right. You told me everything immediately after Larry One hired me at the college. You described the atmosphere in the college; you were protective, concerned, as ever. An innocent produced by the library. I don't want to call you a mouse; a mouse isn't innocent, but you are a little angel, a milksop of words. Eh, tell me again about 'La Passionaria,' how they spoke from the balcony, the famous Dolores Ibárruri, Rosa Luxemburg, and Clara Zetkin, Ana Pauker and comrade Kollontai. And Señora Perón. Yes, I know, you never mentioned these names."

Naturally, there was silence. Hypervexed by Peter's ramblings, Gora yields, as usual.

"A student of mine. Quiet, civilized, I would even say shy. She used to come to class with her boyfriend. A handsome, athletic young man. One day this boy shows up in my office to tell me that the girl would like to speak to me. Babbling, he can't explain why she didn't come herself. Yes, there is a problem . . . Two years ago, after getting into the college, the girl went to a party for freshmen. She drank beer, she walked in the woods with a young man. And, and, and . . . what happened? Seemingly something and seemingly nothing. An embrace and then, then, no one knows, the girl doesn't remember exactly what happened. The only clear thing was that more than two years had passed.

"Yes, now I remember them. Then the girl came, troubled. It wasn't clear what happened two years ago, but it was clear what had triggered the flashback . . . Two years after the uneventful or half-eventful or a quarter-eventful or a fifth-eventful event, the aggressor passes by the new couple, on a clear, autumn afternoon. He smiles obliquely, as if with a certain understanding. The girl feels insulted; her partner persuades her to file a complaint. The student goes to the president of the college and explains what she can explain. The party, the beer, the woods, the embrace in the grass, the confusion in the dark. Larry One listens. It was around the time when you were charming Bedros Avakian's students, no? So, then, Larry one listened attentively to the narrative. Any accusation must be heard and resolved in a democracy. The presumed aggressor is punished:

he is not allowed to participate in rehearsals with the rock group The Blind Band for two months. He will also lose his privileged access to the gym and pool."

"The victim is unsatisfied, isn't that right?"

"The student feels that she's been strung along. The accused would reappear from time to time, at rehearsals and at the pool. He was from a wealthy family that donated to the college, that's what her partner maintained."

"You advised her to forget everything. You asked her if she has a good relationship with her parents. Yes? Then, take advantage of your summer break, enjoy yourself, protected, relaxed, that's what you told her. Don't make this twisted episode the center of your unhappiness; you're young, pretty, smart, your whole future ahead of you, not behind you. Is that what you told her, Saint Augustin? Like a retarded grandfather just out of the premodern cave, an Eastern European idiot. Misogynist, macho, without scruples."

"Yes, but nothing came of it. The students liked me; that was why the girl came to me in the first place. Avakian liked me, too."

"And the Uprising? It exploded the following spring. Slogans and posters everywhere, protesting the administration that encourages sexual harassment. The administration was under siege for three days. Speeches from the balcony of the besieged building. Demonstrations, reporters, negotiations, measures to be taken. And what happened to the erotic trio?"

"The female student received substantial compensation, transferred to a different college, and is now married. The boyfriend is now the president of an organization for the protection of immigrants' rights in the Midwest. The perpetrator who didn't perpetrate, or perpetrated a quarter of an act, graduated from the college, went to law school and now works on Wall Street."

"And Professor Augustin Gora? Did he refine his grandmotherly advice? What advice does he offer to a castaway? Should I be careful? What should I be careful of? Of female students, of gossip, of jokes, of demagogues and suspects and intriguers and envious people? Or our phantoms from far away?"

"Is there trouble? Did something happen to you?"

"No, nothing, but I'm preparing myself. I want to know how to prepare myself. The story of the three-day revolution is instructive, but banal. There's no mystery, not like Palade's case."

"Palade? What's come over you? It wasn't the students who killed him, that's for sure."

"Whoever acted knew the university perfectly well, the buildings, the schedule, the daily path of the condemned, his astrological and parapsychological and paranormal digressions. It's not the case with me. I'm an earthling. I trip over chairs, as well as weeds, but no stars. I'm inattentive, but he was too attentive. There's no connection, I hope, between us."

"No, there's no connection," says Professor Gora, without conviction, probably taking up his reading once again.

Peter Gaşpar could also have started up again with his nocturnal visions: the killer Charles Manson and the terrorist Timothy McVeigh and the cannibal Jeffrey Dahmer and other vanquishing experts, documentaries about deaf-mutes and cancer, about astronauts and populations in the jungle, American football, classical and box office film hits, chamber music, as well as jazz. After midnight, the games of distraction and pornography and karate videos or courses in exotic languages, everything an insomniac heart needs.

■

A long, vertical sign on a tall building. Dirty walls, dusty ornaments: the Hotel Esplanade. The corner of 48th Street and Eighth Avenue. Drug addicts, prostitutes, beggars, mystics, vagabonds of all races.

She stops, bewildered, looking for her companion. She sees him in the back of a sex shop. She moves toward the display with the sunglasses and plasters her palms on the glass.

A tap on her shoulder. "Here I am," Peter whispers into her velveteen ear. Lu gazes down at the pavement.

"Do you want me to go back to the place I escaped from? You're crazy with these sex shops! You can't restrain yourself."

Peter takes a step back.

"Crazy? This is mass culture! Therapy. The industry with the highest-grossing income. We can't ignore the well-being of the country. It's our country, isn't that right? They're our countrymen."

Lu is silent. She swallows, gloomily.

"It's my fault. I shouldn't have told you about my dream."

"What dream?"

"Last week, Friday. I was in a poetic state of mind. I was dreaming about a phallus. A child in the shape of a phallus. A tender form, it asked for protection, for tenderness. Like a child. And I was crying, emotional. It unsettles me even now."

Peter feels dizzy looking into her big, tearful eyes, which she was wiping, ashamed, with her trembling hands. Lu backs away, her gaze to the ground. Peter runs after her, waving, laughing. They disappear.

The street remains. The storefronts, the sex shops, the Chinese vegetable cart, the Turkish restaurant, the Mexican umbrella store, the bustle of the hookers, the pickpockets with the sombreros, the Pakistani druggist's shop.

A street, and another street. Clean, quiet, deserted. A solid building, stone and brick. An Anglican façade, gothic windows framed by wrought iron. Letters chiseled into the stone. The Young Men's Christian Association.

On the threshold, Peter. White, sweaty shirt. Sleeves rolled up, his gaze on the hunt. He surveys left-right, looks at his watch. He's waiting for someone, gives up, goes inside. Traffic, loud teenagers, suitcases and backpacks.

An immense black guard, an immense hand on the telephone. He watches the door and the elevator. The giant Peter in front of an even bigger giant, it's hard to win these caricature competitions.

They look at each other, without curiosity. One of them tall, fat, bald with a mustache, the other taller, fatter, black, thick, curly hair and black skin. A discharged hussar and a black American, ready to take out his saxophone.

"Mr. Joe?"

The man nods his big, heavy head.

"Madam Beatrice Artwein called yesterday, to . . . "

"Ah, Beatrice! Betty. That's what we call her. Yes, baby, the lady called. I have the key."

He smiles. Large, immaculate teeth. Large, black eyes burning with the delight of complicity.

"Yes, baby, I have the key ready. Two hours. That's it."

Peter doesn't return the smile, he's somber and distant.

"Perfect. I'll take the key and come back. I'll be back quickly."

The great Joe Louis bends toward the drawer, pulls out the key tied with a blue cord. He's no longer smiling, or looking at the client, he's become somber and distant.

Lu. Supple, tall, elegant. Red jacket. Her face is hollow, white, matte. Hair pulled back in a bun, her forehead free.

"A small, simple room. A bed. A shower, toilet, mirror. Without towels, but cheap," Beatrice had explained. "Without perfumes, creams, towels. You don't forget where you are, nor what you're there for. Promiscuity intensifies the promiscuous appetite. It defies conventions, sharpens pleasure."

Fourth floor. The hallway. Precise directions: 401–411 to the left, 412–419 to the right. 416. A bed, an armchair. A narrow bed. On the sheet, a brown stain in the left corner. Lu in the doorway. Mute, immobile. From one second to the next, she'll slam the door, abandon the room and her marriage.

Peter doesn't forget the risk, not even in his dreams: Lu wasn't made for squalor, it freezes her up.

In the middle of the room, prepared for shame and disaster, he records, attentively, the movements of the black plaits. Lu is no longer Lu . . . Slowly, she unbuttons the dress jacket, one button at a time. The red silk slips down. Nothing underneath. She holds her young breasts in her palms. She offers them to him! Smooth, bare shoulders, proud throat. She puts her long hands around her neck, like a coil. Velvety palms, thin fingers. She remains like that, exposed, looking at the narrow, dirty window. She pulls down the zipper of her jeans. She comes out of those blue pipes, naked.

Espadrilles. She looks at them with pity, first one, then the other, the left, right, she pulls out her foot slowly, the left, the right, she moves her legs away. Long toes, narrow foot of ivory. Her lips vibrate past the white stripe of her teeth. Lu isn't Lu! In her hand she holds a small, black, plastic object. She presses the button. A dull sound can be heard coming from the ceiling. Lu points her index finger to the low, gray ceiling, showing her partner the little television in the ceiling.

On the screen an angelic face and a body of an adolescent: Beatrice Artwein! Betty . . . at that very moment she's throwing off her golden bra, the golden leaf in between her thin, brown legs. Shaved head. Incipient breasts, prominent, electric nipples. Pink vulva warmed with the short fingers of a young girl. She's kneeling in front of the bald giant with the mustache, slowly unbuttoning the rigid jeans of the hussar, button by button.

Peter sweats uncomfortably, frightened by Lu, who waits for him naked on the bed, wetting her fever-burned lips with her tongue. On the screen, Betty ecstatically caresses the naked, hairy thighs of her colleague Gaşpar.

Peter stretches out on the bed, Lu imitates the movements of Madam Artwein! Simulacrum! Betty and Lu turn their backs to their partners, who bend over Betty, over Lu.

Lost gaze on the screen. Lu is in the bathroom, the shower can be heard. On the screen Betty, bent under the man, receives the penetration, quivering. The bodies accelerate the rhythm, hands searching for each other, as well as mouths, the professional and the client panting and gasping. From the threshold of the bathroom door, Lu listens to the moaning, smiling. Now she's wearing a red dress, short, very short. In her black bun there's a small white bridal tiara. White gloves, a pearl choker at her throat.

A click to the ceiling and the copulation disappears. Peter is on his feet. Black suit, giant, patent leather shoes. White bow tie, white kerchief in the breast pocket of the lustrous jacket.

The couple arm in arm in the courtyard of the socialist town hall of Sector 4 in the capital. In the far end of the yard, alone, Madam Eva Kirschner-Gaşpar is waiting, diminished, seemingly lower in stature, drawn into herself, gray haired, with a grease-stained, wrinkled and mottled apron over her golden dress. She lifts the hem and wipes her tearful eyes and dirty glasses with her apron. The festive couple passes by her, without seeing her. The entrance into the department of the city clerk's office. The official charged with the union descends the stairs solemnly to meet them.

It's Professor Augustin Gora! A little white beard, the gray goatee of a Slavic beadle. Nobility and the ridiculous in his timid manner, devoid of vigor.

The professor embraces the bride, kisses each cheek. He squeezes Mynheer's hand discreetly. He looks at him insistently, fascinated by the famous character, whose acquaintance he finally has the privilege to make.

Gora wears a green dress coat and a wide band, red, yellow, and blue, over his shoulder and across his breast. He makes a cavalier gesture to the bride, then to her partner, inviting them inside the building.

The mother-in-law suddenly intervenes, shaking with sobs. The professor smiles at the uninvited, invites the trio inside. The bride and the mother-in-law climb the three steps, the groom stands still and stiff like a statue.

The professor repeats the gesture, he tips forward again, like a mannequin, but the groom shows no sign of life. Dead, but upright. Stiff, with glassy, phosphorescent eyes.

Professor Gora smiles, bows toward the bride and hands her a large yellow envelope.

Peter sweats, pants, moans, twisting, throwing off the flaming blanket and sheets. He holds on to the edge of the bed with clenched hands, jumps to his feet, frightened and determined to talk to Gora.

Professor Gora isn't accessible. He sits for many hours in front of the computer, transcribing the agitated night from which he's just escaped.

■

It's not Saturday, it's Friday. Tara isn't bringing the mail, but reporting.

"I've become a suspect!"

"Who hasn't?"

"What do you mean?"

"The investigation doesn't exclude any hypothesis. Any suspicion. The easiest one: the reporter herself."

"I didn't report anything."

"You brought the postcard. The threat. You triggered the action. You could be complicit."

"That's what Ms. Tang thinks. I went to see her. I understand that you didn't like her either?"

"She was polite. As was Patrick Murphy, Special Agent FBI. Actually, I'm not supposed to tell you that I saw them."

"You can tell me; I'm complicit. I'm going to see Patrick again, too, says Ms. Tang. With me she wasn't polite. She asked me to transcribe the whole text from the postcard. In front of her. So she could compare the handwriting with those few words from the address on the card . . . All she had to do was get my file from the dean; she would have found handwriting samples there."

"She'll find and compare them, don't you worry. So you might be the author of the letter. Is that what she's suggesting?"

"She's not suggesting, she's investigating. Patrick is going to threaten me, I'm sure of it. 'Either you tell the truth, or I'll aggravate your situation.' Tang suspects me. 'How is it, then, that you take the professor's mail? It's addressed to him, not you.'"

"She's right."

"It wasn't my idea."

"Yes, it was."

"When I saw how overwhelmed you get by the mountains of mail! Plus, I'm paid to do it! You pay me! I told that blonde. I was sure that it would shatter the suspicion."

"The suspicion that you wrote the postcard?"

"No, that won't go away too quickly."

"Then, what?"

"That I sort the mail so I can come here."

"She said that?"

"It's a small college. If you try to hide, you just multiply the suspicions. My roommate sees me coming with the bag of letters for Professor Gaşpar. I sort the mail for the eccentric Peter Gaşpar."

"Eccentric, yes . . . And what else did Tang ask you?"

"If I tell you, will I be able to sleep better?"

"Has sleep become a problem?"

"Not yet. I'm not the one with a death threat hanging over me."

"We all have a death threat hanging over us."

"You've said that before. Are you having nightmares? Insomnia?"

"Maybe. I've lived my whole life in the city. I don't understand nature. I'm having a hard time adapting to nights in the woods."

"So you're alert. You're prowling. That's why you're not sleeping."

"Anxiety makes us childish. Only children are afraid of the dark. And the woods."

"Do you want me to sleep here? On the couch."

"Sleep here? No. Not in any event. It wouldn't help me. Nor would it dissolve Ms. Tang's suspicions. Why did the student provoke the professor's neuroses? So that he'd become dependent on her? To get into his bed and blackmail him?"

"If she entered his house and his bed, she must care about the professor. She'd have no reason to torment him."

"Maybe she's a monster. Dracula."

"A monster . . . it would bolster the attraction."

Tara continues to scrutinize him, like a policeman. Gaşpar does the same. Tara smiles; Gaşpar smiles, too.

"Don't be scared, there won't be sexual aggression. The monster won't attack the professor, and if the professor attacks me, I'll defend myself. Don't worry, I won't denounce you. I know you need the salary."

"No, you can't stay. Small college. People talk."

"I don't care."

"I do. As you said, I need the salary."

"You'd be less uneasy if there were someone here at night."

"No, I wouldn't. I'd be intimidated by another person. No, no. End of subject."

"Even if the first hypothesis is true?"

"What's the first hypothesis?"

"That I came up with the letter to make you need me, to make you dependent."

"Precisely. I need to be careful. Youth is irresistible."

"And if Patrick asks you to try? He offers you the plan of action: the neurotic who solicits the help of the student he took to bed. She'll also become vulnerable and will confess to everything in the end."

" 'She'll also become vulnerable?' What does Patrick know about her? We'll wait until Tuesday, after the meeting with the FBI. I'll tell you if I've changed my mind."

"Now may I sit down?"

The professor makes a motion toward the chairs, the couch. He hadn't noticed that they'd both been standing the whole time.

"Excuse me. I need to be at the office in fifteen minutes."

He looks at his watch. Yes, fifteen minutes.

"Okay. I'll come Saturday afternoon, as usual. Maybe, in the meantime, I'll find another message in the mail. Something more explicit."

Gaşpar looks at her, frowning.

"It wouldn't be bad. Not bad at all."

It sounded like a plea, or advice. He'd lost his humor. And it wasn't midnight, just three in the afternoon.

"Have you thought about that phrase? I learned it, I know it by heart. It's been in my head for a long time, I think. I've seen it before sometime, somewhere. I don't know where. I've gotten old. I don't remember."

"You remember enough, too much. If it's asleep in your memory, it will wake up. I know the phrase by heart, too. It doesn't evoke any memories, however. I'm uncultured, just like my entire generation. Conspiracies amuse me."

"We'll talk on Tuesday, after Patrick's interrogation. I'm in a hurry now."

Peter's in no hurry to get anywhere, the good-natured dialogue is putting him in a bad mood. He wants to go outside, to be alone. Tara retreats; the professor sets out apathetically toward campus. The wind is cold and wet. The library is warm and quiet. Books, magazines, newspapers from around the world. The sect of Saint Computer! At prayer, in front of the magic screen. Not even the Internet Generation, born from an electronic circuit instead of a woman's womb, can retain the quotation. But Tara never found the magic button. If only there were some kind of a hypnosis to trigger the phosphorescent needle of memory's magnet.

A fossil among the young servants to the God of Algorithms, that's what I am, the professor decided, abandoning the temple.

Alone in his den. On the nightstand, under the pile of socks and tank tops, the yellow envelope. Tara's old letter. Was that a different Tara, the one who was accusing professors of giving her too-high marks, while barely out of high school? A year ago, she'd confronted a professor who gave her a mark that was higher than what she'd expected. Now she was a gentle comrade. Was the past still part of the present?

In the envelope there was Tara Nelson's essay on the novel *Enemies: A Love Story*. It had arrived a few days after her impertinent letter and after the end of the semester.

Unhappiness revolves around an inability to interact with unfamiliar circumstances. Losing old habits feels like losing the self. The solution isn't to be found in the old habits, nor in a new identity, but in fantasy.

He'd read those pages on a July day, almost a year ago now. He'd discovered them, unexpectedly, in P.O. Box 1079.

Had Tara chosen the novel about the exiles to provoke him?

It isn't possible both to remain in the old identity and to integrate into the new one.

Was that true? We are imperfect impostors at home and away from home, on Earth and on the moon.

From the war experience forward, the hero is receptive only to his own thoughts. *The Christian woman who saved him and whom he is going to marry as a gesture of appreciation is an angelic Polish peasant woman, an illiterate saint, who, in the conversion to Judaism, becomes a sort of clown. The only escape from the real is the complicit relationship of mutual masochism, between the husband and the co-religionist, sexually voracious Masha.*

What's the connection to the threatening postcard? There's no connection. No connection at all! Just the fact that both preoccupied him now, simultaneously.

The escape from the real, like sexual liberation. Mental fantasy connection . . . the sex drive, the only labyrinth. Mental fantasy is their mutuality, physicality, sexual appetite, the only labyrinth that either of them can truly call his and her own.

Labyrinth?

A year ago, the word didn't seem suspect. Now it has definition, phosphorescence, wile. Peter stops, asks himself what the woods have in store for the night, whether the patrol will be more discreet. He wants to sleep. *The sex drive, the only labyrinth that either of them can truly call his and her own.*

In the novel, the true enemy is memory, the trauma imposed on identity. The terms of the biography become the morbid impulse. To incorporate past trauma into the new system doesn't require breaking down barriers, but rather to ignore its existence. To have a child, for example? Or to lose yourself in the labyrinth of sexuality?

Death. Lady Death! The Madame is gracing me with her imperial attention! *Sleep, everlasting sleep,* the somnolent Peter keeps repeating.

The red sky. The elephants on never-ending stilts. The insect-elephants, delicate cartilage. The astral giant from the prehistoric wilderness. Enormous, velvety mass, imperial tusks, indestructible ivory. Greenish silt draining from the trunk.

The female and male approaching, without ever getting close to one another. On the back of each, a carpet. On the carpet, the monument floating in air. On the trunk of the elephant on the left, an eye. On the female's, the ocular globe is in between her lips, which are as red as a cosmetics ad.

Below, the infinite. Gray hills, the landing pad, the watch post, two forms running, with a flag and a torch.

The sky is orange then pink then red again. The elephants. A sky striped with thin legs ready to buckle. The arrows of transparent bone, bearing the weight of the bodies and their burdens and the vault. The blood of dawn. The stones are slipping from the Indian rug, they hang in the air. The painted eye. The eye of Special Agent Patrick. On the rug covering the quadruped's spine, it says *Patrick*.

Sapped, Gașpar twists his body toward the nightstand, braces himself up in bed, props himself against the wall. The car brakes in front of his house. It's not nighttime, but another day. Dawn, thank God! He'd slept for many hours, hadn't heard the patrol until now.

The great volumes of the *Encyclopedia Britannica*. Thin pages, thin signs, the cryptograms of the past. The reader is pushed to the past that came before the past.

The Minotaur can't be killed, the Old Man argues in the chapter about the labyrinth. The Minotaur finds vengeance, transforming the modern labyrinth into a hell. The Minotaur, the Taurus constellation. The promise of rebirth, spring. Futile annotations.

The telephone; the taxi driver can't find the hermit's cabin. It's not the driver but Madame J.T. Peter has only just realized that the Vietnamese woman has an unnaturally low voice. The head of campus security wants to know whether the professor is going to spend the next few days on the grounds. Madame Tang alerts the dean about everything that goes on, who leaves campus, when, to return when, and in whose company.

No, Professor Gașpar won't be on campus for the next few days; in fact, he was just waiting for the taxi to take him to the station. J.T. advises him to close his curtains before leaving, to leave the front light on, as if he were home. And especially, to let the college know in the future when he plans to leave and for how long.

Deserted train station, no followers. An almost empty train car, no one but a hunched, pale old grandmother, sinking into a book, her spectacled grandson fidgeting nearby.

Did the mysterious postcard come from admirers of the Old Man, the alchemist? The encyclopedic scholar used to talk about the invisible fires of Hades, the underground world of the dead, the labyrinth of the cross, the bloodied thread of Ariadne, the knot as labyrinth. The labyrinth as initiation. The nomadic, exile, the underground. The serpentine maze made of a single line. The world captive in the modern tunnel, the tunnel of the subconscious? The Minotaur will devour the people from the tunnel! The Minotaur, in the invisible center of fatality, the scholar would say. *The labyrinth made of a single, straight line is invisible. A single straight line, which is invisible.*

Fatality hidden in profane numbers: temperature, speed, kilometers, cholesterol, blood pressure, glycemia? You don't need symbols to kill. Transcendent advertisements and trivial instincts, Maestro? Is that the secret of the proselytizers?

Mynheer raises his bored gaze to his notebook. In the window to the right, the river is keeping vigil. The winter fog. The majestic, imperturbable river. A single line. *Single, straight line, everlasting.*

He closes his eyes. He opens his eyes: the postcard. He reads the text on the back. A biomathematics professor at Cornell University is protesting against the State Department's harassment of the Mexican senator Castillo Martínez, blocked from entering the U.S., where he'd been invited for a public debate. Under this passage, the letter from the reader in Long Island about the State Hermitage Museum in Russia. The middle of the seventies, trip to Saint Petersburg, then Leningrad, the tour guide, the French Impressionist paintings brought back from Germany at the end of the war.

The postcard sits, aged, in Gaşpar's hand.

"What's that got to do with me? What connection do I have with this nonsense? I'm neither Russian nor German, nor a museum specialist nor a tourist. I'm not even an amateur painter. And I don't see the tie between the Hermitage, the State Department, and the labyrinth. Nor between the USSR, Ariadne, and the life of the Alchemist."

■

Saturday evening, Tara comes without bringing the mail. A bored gesture, a trifle; it doesn't merit attention.

On the table, two glasses and a bottle of red wine. The professor was prepared! Not just the bottle of wine and glasses, but even an apple pie. And a little delicate jar, and another delicate jar. A festive or ill-fated evening, or both?

He'd slept deeply and woke up revitalized. A clear mind, precise intentions: the Labyrinth! He will talk to Tara about the Labyrinth, he will show her his notes from the New York Public Library and the college library. "The Old Man, as we will call him, wrote a lot about the subject, including a chapter in the *Encyclopedia Britannica*."

Tara had also come prepared: white shirt, low cut, long black skirt, elegant, tall boots. Her hair up in a small, black bun. Black eyes and mascara, intense brows. The professor is freshly shaven.

"The conspirators force us to talk about the labyrinth! The Old Man, that's what we'll call Dima, wrote much on the subject. Minos, the king of Crete, was punished with sterility because he didn't sacrifice the bull he'd gotten as a gift from Poseidon, the god of the sea. The king's wife will conceive a son with the bull. The monster Minotaur. Half man, half beast. Shut into a labyrinth by Minos."

"Starts out well . . . what more could an American student on the threshold of her education wish for other than a lecture on mythology?"

"It's not a lecture. It's a preamble. For conversation. The American student might be of use. Through her acuity and freshness. She's neither uneducated, nor uncultivated, nor innocent."

"I've learned not to turn down compliments anymore."

"The labyrinth was designed by Daedalus, the king's architect. Every eight years Athens, the vassal fortress of Crete, would send as sacrifice seven maidens and seven young men to be devoured by the

Minotaur. One of them, Theseus, will kill the monster. He will come out of the labyrinth, with the aid of a ball of string, unwound behind him. The famous red thread, a gift from Ariadne. Theseus abandons her, however, in favor of Phaedra."

"Sex, then. The red thread is sex. In antiquity, too."

"Minos punishes Daedalus, the ineffective architect of the labyrinth. The labyrinth was imperfect! Daedalus is imprisoned in the labyrinth, together with his son, Icarus. The architect can't escape his own creation. Icarus, who is obsessed with flight, fabricates a couple of wings, making himself into an artificial bird. And he flies . . . ignoring the advice of his father not to fly too close to the sun. The wax in the wings melts. The flyer crashes into the sea. Then, the father Daedalus lands gently in Sicily."

"An animated movie."

"Let's drink the first glass. To the innocence of the audience."

The professor rises from the armchair, opens the bottle, pours the wine into the glasses, they clink, he sits back down into his seat.

Tara is docile and amused; the professor is in his new role.

"The Old Man wrote about such animated movies. Or the Alchemist. Should we call him that?"

"For the animated movies, the Alchemist is better."

"All right, I'll stay with the Old Man. The Old Man refers to modern interpretations, naturally. The urban reader. The solitaries of the city-labyrinth. The mythical Minotaur is the uninhibited part of man. The vital, prerational part."

"The beast. The beast of joy inside us."

"The modern city dweller wants to squelch this part of himself, says the passé-ist. Cosmin Dima is all for the inherent organic structure, he rejects modern artifice, the city labyrinth of modernity. Daedalus' artifices, and those that follow, hide the monster in the subconscious. A fatal mistake, the nostalgic says. The Old Man is skeptical of reason, disgusted by progress. The Old Man gets stuck on . . . "

"The Alchemist."

"For the Alchemist and for his friends, traditions, like pagan barbarism, are sources of energy and power. Civilization is forgetting. A lack of scope and center. The decline of the individual."

"Referring to us! The city dwellers! The solitaries from the city labyrinth. But what about those who live in the country, at the college hidden in the woods? Does that revitalize the beast?"

"I don't know what goes on in your dorms. Drugs, orgies? I wouldn't be shocked. Youth. The test of limits. I never participated. Regretfully."

"You can make it up. America offers you ways. You modify your look, body, mind, personality, anything. You can find the magic pill or the elixir invented only last week. You go to Arizona or Nevada or Antarctica under a different name. You're someone else. The New World encourages the new. Newness. A new start, we say."

"I was talking about the decline of the individual, not about impostures."

Gaşpar looks at his knees, but he's speaking clearly and audibly.

"It's not an imposture, but a new start."

"Substitution. A person who is a substitute for another person, that's how the dictionary defines impostor. I know what I'm talking about, I'm an exile."

"It's not a new beginning?"

"A lot of mimetics. The first step toward change is mimetic."

"So, then, you're with the Old Man."

"I don't believe in the idealization of the past. Or in any idealization."

"Skeptic."

"The only decency. The modern decline of the individual means the decline of the Nation, the retronauts say. The decline of the individual, the disaster of the Nation."

"Logical."

"Logical and true, if the past were a golden reference. But it can't be. It would defy human imperfection. Should we go back to the animated movies? The Minotaur can't be stopped, the Old Man and his apprentices maintain. The nostalgia of myth, the pastoral, idealization. The Minotaur avenges the modern labyrinth. The happy and prosperous hell of modernity, or the totalitarian, mytho-maniacal colony. Should we drink to the modern inferno? It's no worse than the infernos of the past."

"I prefer to drink for no reason. Just because I like the wine. The student is a hedonist."

"Not enough. I don't like the Minotaur. I prefer the labyrinth. As a game. As artifice. Antidote to boredom. We drink for Saturday night. Rest. Relaxation."

Gaşpar gets up. Big, massive. He is awake, as if no longer afraid to be awake.

"A sullen March evening. A sullen professor, a sullen lecture about a sullen labyrinth. The labyrinth as a game? It's a game for innocents. An innocent audience. A complicit audience, none-theless."

"Complicit? Yes, I am here. The student is present."

"It's the present."

"And the professor is also present."

"Maybe. He's not convinced. He should be convinced."

They clink glasses, in a good humor both of them. The game prepares for the crime or for the solving of the crime. The killing of the Minotaur or the key to its action.

"Under what sign were you born?"

"What do you mean? I don't know. I don't bother with that nonsense."

"Me, neither, but . . . Taurus means vitality. Spring. But I don't think . . . "

"But what . . . ?"

"My cousin Lu is obsessed with signs, zodiac, astrology, fortune-telling. Some things even seem true, naturally. The rule of proba-bility. I'm hopeless at this stuff. I am amused and then I forget."

"Horoscopes are another joke. Any game is good. You don't know how to play games, I suspect."

"I haven't for a while. Short amusement, that's all. When were you born?"

"You want to know how old I am?"

"You couldn't be young enough for an old man like me. It's the month that interests me, not the year."

"April."

"And the day?"

"You said just the month, that's all."

"There are two signs for every month."

"Okay, I'll take them both. Whatever they may be. Both of them."

"All right. A solar promise. Rebirth. The sun punished Icarus by melting his wings. Punished him for his arrogance in defying predetermination, for his faith in freedom, in options. For the ego's ambition. The modern self-made man. That's what you Americans say."

"Imposture! Mimetics."

"The first step to change. Some change, anyway."

"The wine isn't American, this time. The subject is Greek, the Old Man, Eastern European. The same as the host, an improvised professor, impostor. Targeted in the shadows by the phantom-killing ray."

A moment of exhaustion. Gaşpar doesn't know how to go on. He should probably consult Patrick, Larry Eight and the special agent, on how to manipulate the evening of the revelation. The stages, the pace, the surprises, the traps, the decisive moment when the coy and cunning fox will twist in the silk snare, unable to escape.

"Could you sleep here tonight?"

"Why? Do you have insomnia? Is it the rustling in the woods? Does the solitary city dweller feel the Minotaur close by? Bull, badger, owl. The night itself is a dark being. It seduces or kills. Do you have insomnia?"

"Last night I didn't sleep at all," the professor lies. That's why I'm delivering speeches. To stay awake."

"Take a sleeping pill. The wine is going to help, as well. You'll sleep after drinking Eastern European wine. Old habits help. They pacify."

The professor is waiting for an answer.

"I can't. I'm sorry, I can't."

"Why? Don't tell me you're afraid of the sexuality of the elderly. And you don't need to be afraid of yourself, either. As for me, I can fend for myself, if youth attacks. I'll get by. Don't worry, I wouldn't report you."

"You want me to sleep here? Here, on the couch?"

"Why not? I'd feel better."

"No, absolutely not. My roommate is waiting for me. It's a small college, everything gets out."

"I don't care."

"I do. And you need your salary."

"We'll tell Patrick that we spent all night talking about the labyrinth. It took all night. We drank wine, you were tired, you stayed. We'll see how he takes on the new cards, what hypotheses he offers."

"We could tell him that, even if it's not true. I like the game, I told you. The game, as a labyrinth."

"Games with Dracula?"

"The professor is an eccentric, not a monster."

Tara continues to prod him, like a policeman. Professor Gaşpar does the same. She smiles, he smiles.

"The game, as a labyrinth. That's what Gilbert says."

"Gilbert, which Gilbert?"

"Anteos. You don't know Gilbert Anteos?"

"The guy with the shaved head?"

"Yes, professor of Greek, Latin, and ancient literature."

"You're in his class?"

"Yes, I took Greek Mythology and Modern Life. An eccentric type."

"Like me?"

"He took refuge in America from the colonial dictatorship in Greece. He's an exile, too. A nomad."

"Why didn't you tell me?"

"About Anteos? You never asked what classes I'm taking."

"You just let me go on and on, like a dilettante, about the Minotaur and Ariadne and Daedalus."

"I don't look down on dilettantes. America is full of dilettantes. They respect all hobbies. Among dilettantes, you discover clairvoyants and unexpected suggestions."

"So, then, the expert with the shaved head talked to you about the labyrinth. Did he also quote Dima?"

"I don't remember. Otherwise, yes, all the references, the entire inventory. The invisible fire transforms the bodies arrived in Hades in the underground dwelling . . . the labyrinthine dwelling of the dead. The transition from the spiral to the cross. Christ, like Theseus, descending into the Inferno. *Descensus ad infernos.* The red thread of Ariadne, the bloodied memory."

The professor is silent, gazing at his postal woman who didn't bring the mail.

"I should check my notes. I didn't retain that name, Dima. When you were talking about these Balkanic, sinister things, I didn't make the connection. But Anteos, yes, Gilbert talked about the labyrinth and the rest. I took notes, I'm sure. What I didn't write, I remember."

"Meaning?"

"Gilbert told me, at some point, about the eccentricities of the refugee Peter Gaşpar."

"Aha, you mean Dracula's eccentricities."

"Not quite. Maybe Gilbert didn't have all the information. He was talking about childish, endearing eccentricities."

"For example?"

"You eat every day in the faculty lounge, I understand."

"Where else?"

"Greeted with happiness. There are amicable signs from all the tables, they call you over. They want you among them."

"The advantage of the exotic stranger. He rouses curiosity. They want to hear stories from the Stone Age."

"Especially when the stranger is generous. He tells stories, but he also brings gifts."

Gaşpar doesn't ask any more questions. He understands what she's talking about.

"You bring them all kinds of wonderful things. The Belgian chocolate and Swiss chocolate impressed everyone."

"That's what I was after. The stranger is curious, too, wants to understand the robots of the postmodern millennium. I brought first-class chocolate. To see how diets and discipline and Protestant austerity get swept under the rug."

"And did it get swept under the rug?"

"Yes. Truffles are magic. Demonic. I'm a fat foodie, as you can see. I wanted to see how the fitness fanatics would react. I watched deliriously to see the first truffle in the mouths of the ascetics. Just one, that's all. After that, the drug takes its effect. Ir-re-sis-ti-ble. You want another and another, as many as you can, to fill you with happiness, until you choke."

"Yes, Gilbert told me. After a few sessions of that kind of intoxication, you switched the drug."

"I brought jars of pickles. Pickled in salt, not vinegar, as they're done here. Amazing stuff. The wonder of the wild East."

"And then, other wonders."

"Roasted peppers. Eggplant salad. Divine."

"I know. Gilbert hadn't forgotten any of the temptations. He's Greek. You floored him. Same with the postmodern natives. Robots, as you call them. Where did you find these things? How did you haul them here?"

"I found the chocolate at the Chocolatier. In the Lunar City. I ordered, they sent. It awoke my national ambitions. In Queens I found all the charms of the East. Serbian, Russian, Greek, Hungarian, Romanian. Stuffed grape leaves, stuffed cabbage, pickled herring, roe salad, stuffed chicken, lamb meatloaf, brains, kidneys, fries, feta cheese, *burduf* sheep cheese, eggplant salad, black pudding, Romanian and Serbian meatball sausages, preserves of all kinds. I couldn't take everything. A jar at a time. Just to try. A taste of the East. The tongue that tastes and the tongue that speaks. The essential. The matrix, as they say."

"You took care of everyone but me."

"That's not true. I took care of you, am taking care of you. I didn't want to replace the American pie with a Carpathian pie; the comparison would be humiliating for a superpower. Apple pie, with cheese, doughnuts with sour cream, "poale-n brau" Danishes, pudding with raspberries, dumplings with prune jam or blueberries or cheese or rose preserves, crepes with ricotta, cinnamon buns, honey buns, Moldovan sweet bread, cheese bread, this is the gastronomy of my friends from the former Eastern Empire, from Bukovina, not mine, since I'm on the former Habsburgic Empire's border! But today, however, next to the Yankee pie, we have a miracle. Mir-a-cle! The gift of the gods. Sour cherry preserves. A singular delicacy. From Bukovina, where a friend of mine was born. He was a mathematician, murdered by someone in a bathroom stall. My cousin's husband is also from Bukovina. In fact, he's my cousin, too, isn't he? Small, sour-sweet, black and wily, inestimable cherries. The recipe of the gods. With no equal. Unearthly. Ce-les-tial!"

Peter shows Tara the small, black jar next to the small, yellow jar.

"Sour cherries from Bukovina. You should learn geography."

"I will learn. I bet this is an aphrodisiac."

"Naturally. I hope you won't turn it down."

"I won't turn it down. I don't think Gilbert would turn it down, either."

Gilbert?! A venomous fly stings Professor Gaşpar's viscera. It didn't matter that he'd slept well and prepared himself for the Saturday night meeting. It didn't matter one bit; he was losing the game.

"The thread that gets tangled. The knot, as labyrinth. Initiation," continued Tara, putting down her glass, then the slice of pie, then the spoon with traces of the black and yellow miracle. "The serpentine maze leads to the center. Is the center the female sex? The arrow aims for the center, the sperm aims for the ovum. *Regressus ad uterum.* Is it the same as *descensus ad infernos?*"

The glass frozen at Gaşpar's lips. He slurps it to the bottom. He puts the empty glass on the table. He's regained his composure, ready to confront all banalities and surprises.

"So then, you want me to sleep here, on the couch? To make you feel better, less alone. So that I can be here when you get panicked and need a nurse. That wouldn't intimidate you?"

"I've gotten used to the idea already."

"You're not afraid of becoming dependent."

"I'll be careful, that won't happen."

"I'm sorry, I can't. Let's change the subject."

"Very well. But we should still tell Patrick, no? We'll tell him what we want?"

"It isn't what I want. Not anymore."

"Something has intervened."

"Something has."

"But you accept the game, the substitution."

"The imposture, you mean? There's no point. It will complicate things. We won't be able to sustain the lie through other interfacing lies. Patrick is no joke. Nor is Jennifer Tang. Here, the authorities are no joke, I don't know if you're aware of this."

"Nor anywhere else."

"I'd like more wine. Aren't you afraid of losing your lucidity?"

"Or of you losing yours."

"The student isn't sure if the professor is speaking the truth."

"I'm embarrassed, I don't have another bottle."

"It is possible that this is also a lie."

"It isn't. I don't have another bottle of the same wine, I mean to say. I didn't think it would be necessary. I wasn't even sure it would be good. I have American wine."

"California wine is excellent. Better than what we drank. No offense."

"None taken. I wanted an exotic atmosphere, with wine from exotic places. But it's not a good idea to mix the past with the present."

"And between them, we eat pie."

"American pie."

"Yes, American. We are in America. American student, American professor."

"Okay. Until the touch of invisible and perpetual death, the game continues."

The evening extends past midnight. Tara proves herself to have quite a high tolerance to drink and to the dialogue's traps.

■

"Professor, forgive a poor, ignorant wanderer. I need some guidance. I'm about to have a new meeting with the free world's police department. Larry Eight. Mr. Murphy."

Gora was silent, used to Peter's casual entrances.

"Police Officer Murphy will again subject me to a long interrogation about Dima and Palade and the elite of our little elite homeland."

"I've told you everything I know."

"Palade remembered a certain Marga Stern, information received from Saint Augustin Gora. A lover from Dima's youth, with whom he maintained an unclear relationship even after he was married, after her own marriage and divorce. I understand she was deported to Transnistria. I don't know if she survived or not, the important thing for me is Dima's indifference in relation to Marga Stern and other coreligionists. The real danger was imminent around that time. He didn't look into her fate, didn't send a single word of encouragement. Palade wasn't sure about the information from the professor. He suspected that it might be a fabulous fabrication."

"There was a rumor that Marga died in Transnistria, but it isn't true. She survived, God knows how, and returned to the village where she'd tried to hide during the war, and there, two weeks later, she killed herself. There's a short note about her in Dima's *Green Notebook*, at the end of the war: *Poor Marga, how much she must have suffered.* That was all. A late tribute to youth, maybe a conjectural obligation."

"Ah, so you know more about her."

"I learned about it when I spent all that time in the attic room, where all the talk was about Dima. I researched it, looked into references and discovered the story of Marga Stern."

"Would that interest Police Officer Murphy?"

"During the time of anti-Semitic laws, then later when the deportations started, Dima never once looked into Marga's situation," Gora continued, as if he hadn't even heard the question. "He could have, even though he was far away and overwhelmed with his own problems. There would have been means of communication."

"Did he have other friends from her community?"

"I don't know, I don't think so. I only know about Marga. Immediately after Dima got married, she did, too, but she divorced quickly, after a few months."

"Was she beautiful? Like Madam Gora? Like Ludmila Serafim, married to the eminent professor Gora?"

"It was said that she had no capacity for generalization and that she was proud of this. Never pathetic, scared of abstractions, concentrated on facts, objects, sensations. Good sense, moderation."

"It's as if you knew her directly."

"Dima would call on her, alert with desire, then would retire from her, then call her again. A delicate, discreet, loyal partner. Biologically calm."

"Biologically calm, is that what you said?"

"Yes, that's what people who knew her said. She loved Dima. Marga Stern seemed to me a very memorable character. Absolute respect for the real."

"Indeed, but maybe it's a bit much for Larry Eight. Police Officer Murphy wouldn't understand Marga's chaste intelligence, nor Dima's indifference, he'd call those things pragmatism, the only thing he understands. He has the head of an army officer and a notebook in which he doesn't write anything."

"I'm sure he recorded you on tape."

"I didn't see any recording devices."

"You don't need to see them. Maybe he doesn't even have any, but has a perfect memory."

"It's not enough. He would have to provide a faithful report at the trial. Otherwise, it has no value in the face of justice."

"You haven't gotten to justice yet, you have a ways to go yet. It's possible that . . ."

Peter, however, had hung up the phone.

■

"Officer Pereira confirms that two years ago you refused to write a certain article. Did then someone force you to write it?"

"I wrote it of my own free will. After much hesitation. And with little pleasure."

"Did the president of the college convince you to do it?"

"I asked him for advice. He advised me to write it."

"How long did it take?"

"Six months."

"And the hesitation?"

"I don't remember. Two, three months. I was doing research during that time. The bibliography wasn't accessible. Some things are known; other things remain obscure. Or inaccessible. In secret archives."

"Communist archives?"

"Probably. Not only. Maybe C.I.A."

"C.I.A. documents?"

The eyes of the thickset Patrick flicker. He pulls the notebook in which he writes nothing closer.

"The entrance visa to the U.S., for example. As a member or sympathizer of an extremist political organization, the Old Man should have had a lot of difficulty obtaining a visa. His old political articles had appeared in a time when there were still democratic options. The C.I.A. is more lenient with the Germans who became Nazis after Hitler prohibited political parties than those who did so when there were still other options in Germany. This should hold true for all countries, don't you think? Additionally, the Old Man had been a diplomat during the war. On the side of the Axis Powers. The C.I.A. knew all of these things. But he didn't have any problems. Or maybe . . ."

"Maybe what?"

"The anti-Communists were useful during the Cold War. The past can be forgotten, if necessary."

"A pact with the devil, then?"

"Not with the devil. With the C.I.A."

"You hesitated to write the review because of the C.I.A.?"

"No. I don't even know if the C.I.A. hypothesis is valid. I hesitated because I don't like public scandals. I'm tired of the just cause. Communism was a just cause. For my father, it was. And not only for him."

"Shutting people up, confiscating the property they earned through hard work, you call that a just cause?"

"Not those *things*, necessarily, no. But opposing fascism, for example. To maintain the illusion of a more just future. The luminous, humanist future, that's what the slogans promised."

"So, then, what was the accusation against the Old Man? A valuable man allied with killers?"

"This, too. During a time when, let's be honest, all of Europe had gone insane. But after the war? Amnesia. Immoral amnesia . . . amoral. He didn't seem to care at all about his complicit involvement in the tragedy. He'd arrived, after all, in a pragmatic country, hadn't he? What mattered was what he did, not what he'd once thought. America encourages change."

"And had he changed?"

"I don't know. Every man changes now and then. I don't think he'd changed his mind about democracy, if that's what you want to know."

"What did he think about democracy?"

"Corrupt, vulgar. Infantile. Demagogic. Chaotic. Stupid. Decadent. Hypocritical."

The police officer doesn't seem at all discouraged by the avalanche of adjectives.

"Did he promote these ideas?"

"At one time. Now, it would have been idiotic. He discussed them, maybe, with his old comrades. He kept in touch with them.

Nostalgia for his youth, perhaps, when he believed himself to be part of the marching rank and file? Now he was doing his duty at the university, he was writing books and becoming famous. Would it have helped him to undermine himself with confessions? Self-indictment? Here, in your country, I mean, in our country, you can refuse to accuse yourself. Would it have made the world a better place? Would it have improved the future? No one was asking him to proclaim his own mistakes and guilt."

"Then why did you write the review?"

"I was asked to write it. Not to unmask Dima, who was dead. It was just the review of a book, in a weekly journal, not even a daily paper. The book had been published with the author's approval. He had produced all kinds of memoirs, diaries, he liked looking in the mirror. A mirror ruined by flies and fogged up by the breath of the author. I wrote an honest review. No more, no less."

"Without a moral subtext?"

"A review in a journal with modest circulation."

A long silence followed . . . "Angels don't write books," the Eastern European had whispered. He didn't know if it was part of his answer or if there was any connection at all. The inaudible thoughts of a mortal . . . Police Officer Patrick had heard, however. He stared, intrigued, at Gaşpar's face and was silent.

"Angels don't write books . . . " Was that some sort of bitter and light conclusion about Dima, or about all the scribes delirious with the vanity and infantilism of uniqueness? Hard to say what Peter's muttering had meant or if it had meant anything at all. The silence between the interrogator and the interrogated had grown.

"Mr. Murphy, I am ready to confess."

Mr. Murphy was listening, imperturbable. The decisive moment had come, the interrogation was proving very efficient, because of the sleuth-hound, the guilty party was ready to confess to the villainous operation. Mister Murphy put his hands on the table, near Mister Gaşpar's large hands, and bent amicably over the table, to be closer to the miserable wretch.

"I realize, talking to you, that I'm the product of my country.

This I want to say. I circle around certain ambiguities, I cultivate them, through all kinds of copouts that are nothing but copouts. I avoid the essential. I thought I'd healed myself. I haven't. Over there, there's a difference between the sins of a beggar and a celebrity. A big difference. They are treated differently, very differently."

"That's true everywhere."

"Probably, but I feel infected. There, the question that takes priority is who are you, not what have you done. I'm not immune, I've realized, specifically in the case of Dima. It's probably that it intrigues me, contradictions appeal to me, as well as ambiguities, secrets, subterfuges, subtleties, everything that is more than the essential. That's it. That's my confession, so that you know whom you're dealing with. An infected man. Maybe, not totally. No, not totally."

Mister Murphy gazed at Mister Gaşpar and for the first time smiled. Mister Gaşpar gazed at the large hands of the interrogator nearby on the table, smiling himself.

"I only want to understand. Your fellow countryman dreamed of a better world?"

"All preachers say that. He thought that we lived in a desecrated world. That's nothing new, nor is it altogether wrong."

"De . . . what? De-se-cra-ted?"

"A world where there's nothing sacred. Desecrated. But the sacred is hiding in the profane. That's what he would say. So then, it's hiding . . . around us, inside us. Whoever is hiding can't show himself in the light of day. He's not allowed, he's in danger, expelled from the light. The sacred is expelled, but hidden, persistent."

"Why is it hidden? The world is full of churches. And synagogues and mosques. And Buddhist temples. I go to church. I'm a believer."

"I'm not. I hear that in Los Angeles there are 250 sects. Two hundred and fifty gods? Maybe that's better than a single god and a religious tyranny. I don't know exactly what Dima was trying to propose. Ideas aren't dangerous until they become reality. I don't think a sanctified world is exactly sacred. I would be afraid of a world like that."

"The founding fathers of America were people of faith. They read the Bible."

"But they defined the individual as a citizen."

"Religion helps man."

"Maybe. But the state? Iran isn't the only example."

"The fact that you were asked to write the review doesn't mean you had to do it. Was there some kind of revenge?"

"Revenge? Toward whom, and why? I never even knew Dima."

"It's not about Dima. People like Dima. Your family has suffered."

"My family? Yes, they've suffered, but I was born after the war. My parents wanted to forget those horrors. And besides, they were deported by the Hungarian administration. Dima isn't Hungarian."

"It's not about Dima, but about people like him."

Peter is quiet, frowning. His family? So then they know everything about Dima and Palade and about him. Now the police officer will ask for details about the watchmaker who became a Communist prosecutor and the wife he met at the door of the crematorium. He shouldn't have written the review! He'd foreseen the suspicions. All of his circumspection, allowances, ambiguity, in vain. Just listen to that! Revenge, resentment, rancor.

"No, it had nothing to do with revenge. The review was gentle, the American papers say. They say I was paying homage to Dima. Is that true, I wonder? I'm not immune to the culture that formed me, to its sophistication and affectations. Provincial elitism from the other end of the world. Anyway, Communism cured me of the need to unmask sinners."

"You said it was nothing new. Then it wasn't unmasking."

"Well, yes . . . I was formed by a culture of ambiguities and copouts. America is reeducating me."

"Through that female student?"

"Maybe. I hadn't thought of that. I should have."

Yes, he should have. Murphy's suggestion was welcome.

"Students have something to teach me, too, yes. Tara, as well, probably. I am curious; I want to understand the place where I've arrived. And you want to understand the place I left behind."

"In the review, you mention that he was fascinated by tyrants. Did Dima admire tyrants? Why? Didn't he also live in a tyranny?"

"The military dictatorship was established only after his political engagement. Military, but Balkanic. Not German or Chinese. The advantages of corruption."

The police officer opens his eyes wide at the praise of corruption, but he doesn't comment.

"He was to know a Western dictatorship, as well. During the war he was working at an embassy, in a Western, authoritarian state. The "national, unitary, sacred state," as he used to call it, didn't bother him. God's involvement in the administration of society, sacrifice, and decency and Christian redemption, the reintegration of man into the cosmic rhythm, the organic family, all in opposition to degenerate individualism. I read those things here and there, superficially, as I tend to do."

The theories seemed to be tiring Peter out, as well as Patrick. Gaşpar sighed heavily at the final thought, as though after too long a toil.

"Was the president of the college hoping to help you gain prestige? He hired you in spite of a lot of opposition."

"I don't know that there was so much opposition. Larry—excuse me, President Avakian—was convinced that the review should be written. A just cause, he said. I have to cure myself of my Eastern European equivocation, he said. He'd been a student at the university where the Old Man became a great American professor. The coincidence irritated him."

"Why did you refuse to be presented as a dissident?"

"I was never imprisoned. I didn't even demonstrate."

"You asked to have removed from the college's guidebook the part in your bio where you're described as a Holocaust survivor."

"I was born after all that; I'm not a survivor. In my family, the use of that word was forbidden."

"Why?"

"Humility. A friend of my father's who came back from Auschwitz asked a doctor to remove from his arm the piece of skin that had his prisoner number. It was the first thing he did when he came back! He never again mentioned those years."

"You made anti-Semitic comments at Club 84, at the first job you held in America."

"The owners were wealthy Jews. I protested to their arrogance, not their Jewishness. The arrogance of wealth. They were throwing away massive quantities of food. I came from a country that was starving. I would have protested to a Chinese club, as well."

"But in the end, why did you really write the article? That review."

Peter is quiet. Not to find the appropriate response, but in order to look the interrogator directly in the eyes.

"I had a long conversation with Professor Palade before he was assassinated. Neither of us suspected what was about to happen. I went specifically to see him, to talk to him. He was an expert on the subject."

"Did you know him? Were you friends?"

"A mutual friend made the acquaintance. Palade felt he was in danger, but I didn't give it too much attention. I was obsessed with my review. I wanted information, advice."

"And did he advise you?"

"The Old Man had been his mentor. He'd helped him come to America. He adored him. He knew all of his work and his life. He was the one who asked me to write the article."

"Why?"

"After the Old Man's death, a lot of old secrets were uncovered. Palade found himself implicated, without wanting to be. He began writing against nationalism in the exile journals. Violent. Incendiary. He'd discovered motes on the sun. His sun. He was suffering.

The pieces he wrote were an announcement, perhaps, of a re-evaluation of the Maestro. I'm not sure. In any event, they cost him his life."

"Was he afraid?"

"I don't know. He was an odd fellow. Obsessed by mental constructs. Presentiments, parapsychology, esoteric codes. I wasn't . . . I'm no good at these things. I'm blocked. I didn't pay attention. Afraid, yes, I think he was afraid."

"Was the meeting useful?"

"It was decisive."

"Did he tell you things you didn't know?"

" 'Your text will resurrect the Old Man,' he said. 'Even if as the result of a thrashing, he will live again. His postmortem prestige couldn't be damaged any more than he damaged it himself when he was living,' Palade said; 'the reaction to the text will reveal the paltriness of his admirers, that's all. The posthumous paltriness. The paltriness of sanctification.' That public lynching was reserved for me, but Palade didn't talk about this."

Patrick was silent, waiting for the revelation, the true revelation, as opposed to trivial diversions.

"A minor, but real detail shocked me. It's verifiable. The Maestro's doctor."

Patrick waits for the great moment.

"The drop that tips the glass. The small, but decisive drop."

Patrick isn't taking notes. The notebook and pen wait, humbly, at the corner of the table.

"The Old Man had hired a driver. Specifically for visits to his doctor. Frequent visits. He could have taken a taxi, but he wanted his own chauffeur, a man he could trust. He didn't drive, of course."

"Of course?"

"Palade didn't drive, either. Neither do I, for that matter."

"You don't drive? And how do you get by? The campus is completely isolated, you can't get to the city except by driving. Does that student, Tara Nelson, drive you?"

"Sometimes. Rarely."

"So then, the scholar had a driver. He brought him to the doctor."

"Hired just for these trips."

"Having a driver is nothing out of the ordinary. And we all have doctors."

"A special doctor. A comrade from youth. Immigrated to America after the war. Old himself, now."

"Renowned?"

"Somewhat. Dima could have found someone better. He lacked neither money nor fame, he could have the best doctor at his disposal, but he chose his old friend with connections to Fascist circles, in America and South America. That doctor published a book. I own it. Propaganda. Terrorism. In the name of anti-Communism."

"What's it called?"

Gaşpar dictates and Patrick transcribes the title, year, publisher.

"What kind of Fascist circles?"

"The World Anti-Communist League. The founder, Otto von Bolschwing, was convicted as a member of the SS. He collaborated after the war with the American Army's Corps of Counterintelligence."

"A just cause."

"Maybe. American counterintelligence offered protection to people like the doctor or the former SS commander Bolschwing, who immigrated to the U.S. in 1961. Bolschwing lived here over twenty years, until his death. The doctor, Dima's comrade, was just presenting the same old Nazi and Fascist slogans, repackaged in a new language. The wrapping of the present . . . and the League . . . "

"I don't see what you oppose in an anti-Communist organization."

"Its members. A former dictator of Guatemala. He was an official in Mussolini's government. Eight former Republican members of American Congress."

"American congressmen represent a free country."

"Naturally, but they stand behind a former SS commander from Holland. A distinguished Englishwoman, a baroness who stood militantly for European freedom, and a former minister in the Nazi government of Croatia. A former adjunct to the American Secret Service and a former Belgian general and a former founder of the Japanese Liberal Party and a former member of the Egyptian parliament, known for his ties to former Nazis."

"A lot of formers."

"Yes. And a member of the former Argentine junta. A member of the Saudi Arabian royal family. The leader of the Spanish anti-Marxist group. Two Yale professors. A varied team. Not without Nazis and Fascists."

"The anti-Fascists were Communists."

"There were some non-Communist anti-Fascists, as well. The Old Man Dima could have chosen a different doctor. The past should have made him circumspect. He visited his former comrade often. Was he complying with some kind of arrangement with the C.I.A.? The possibility is worth looking into."

Patrick doesn't seem at all interested in the suggestion, doesn't take note.

"So then, Old Man Dima, as you call him, wasn't just a great professor in a pragmatic world. He doesn't seem very pragmatic . . . but his apprentice? Mr. Portland."

"Palade."

"Okay, Palade. A scholar who was just as important, you say, a mathematician, parapsychologist, philosopher. And antinationalist. Why was he assassinated? By whom? By people involved with Dima and the doctor?"

"I don't know. There was talk about cooperation between the secret police from the old country and American nationalist exiles. There's no proof of anything. And there will never be, I'm sure."

"Does the threat letter you received come from the same source?"

"I don't know."

"You were insisting that it might be a joke."

"That was what I'd thought. Gradually, I entered the psychology of the stalked. The president, dean, and head of campus security convinced me."

"Or the student who sorts your mail?"

"She, as well. She agreed with them. I am worried about the letter, I will admit."

"Do you regret publishing the review?"

"I had reservations, as I told you. I published the text, and the reservations remained. It doesn't mean I regret it. No, I don't regret it. The facts I exposed were absolutely accurate. Then I had dreams about the Old Man. Several times. In front of his burning library. The flames were engulfing me, as well. Burning, without escape, on the pyre. I also dreamed about his apprentice, Palade. Conversations with a cadaver. A skeleton, a dead man."

Patrick doesn't seem interested in such digressions, continuing to suspect the Eastern European refugee.

"Do you trust Tara Nelson?"

Professor Gaşpar doesn't respond immediately.

"Yes, I trust her. You've also suggested that she's useful to my American reeducation. That's not a negligible advantage."

"Has she ever written you any letters?"

"What does that have to do with anything?"

"We would compare the handwriting style. Which can be faked, of course."

"She's never written me any letters."

"Other students? Do you receive letters from students? Or anyone else?"

"Not really. And I don't hold on to them."

The interrogator appears to be finished with the interrogation. He closes his notebook and sinks into his chair, massive and relaxed. He needs a break, he gives the suspect a long, calm look. He puts his large hands on the notebook on the table.

"I'd like to understand a little better."

Finished, but not finished.

"To understand where Palade and Dima intersect and then come apart. And how you relate to them."

The policeman and the suspect look into each other's eyes. Gaşpar hesitates to answer, has too much to say, too much to explain.

"Dima's political choices probably correspond to his philosophy.

He seemed to prefer polytheism over the limitations of monotheism. He found the universal in nature and vegetation. Interested in myth, without being a mystic, he opted for an organic world, a return to nature, to the cosmic. An agrarian vision? It's more complicated than that. Antimodern, probably. Palade was intoxicated by the mysteries, and he paid close attention to the theories of information and cognitive studies. He sees exile as an essential cosmic condition. Obsessed with parallel and permeable worlds, quantum physics and infinite universes. His death wasn't natural like Dima's, but abrupt and enigmatic. Horrible."

"And you studied all of these theories before writing the review? Or did you discuss them with Palade?"

"With him, as well, but mostly with another mutual friend of ours. An erudite scholar. He explained everything I didn't know and gave me a list of books that I don't at all feel like reading."

Patrick wasn't interested in erudite scholars.

"I understand," the policeman announces in closing, slapping the notebook on the table with both hands. We will talk again Friday morning."

The interval is shortened! Neither the interrogator nor the interrogated comments on the change.

After two hours, in the library café, Tara Nelson informs Peter Gaşpar about her meeting with Patrick.

"Did he ask about the student-professor relationship?"

"Yes, he didn't forget."

"And what did you tell him?"

"That we're friends. I help you, sometimes. Not just with the mail. On Saturday I slept on the couch in the hallway. So that you wouldn't be alone. The woods scare you at night."

"I asked you, that is, to sleep at my place? Is that what you told him?"

"Yes. Isn't it the truth? Didn't you ask me?"

"I made that mistake. You refused. Did you tell him you refused?"

"No."

"You told him that you watched over my sleep?"

"Yes. I told him that I don't ever make gestures of charity, but since receiving the letter you've been having insomnia. I think it's good to have someone in the house."

"A lie."

"That's not a lie. The lie is that I slept in Professor Gaşpar's house. But you proposed playing games."

"And you said it wasn't worth it, it would mean going from lie to lie, we won't be able to pull it off."

"I changed my mind. It seems interesting."

"Interesting? Patrick asked me as well if you do anything for me other than sort my mail. No. I answered no, nothing. He didn't correct me. He didn't point out that you said the contrary. So, he knows we're lying. Or, at least, one of us. Or both. I lied, too . . . that you never wrote me a letter. The dean of students knows about Tara Nelson's impertinent letter. I hope Patrick won't come across that detail; he already seems bored with all of this nonsense."

He wasn't convinced that Tara had actually played the game with the cop, as she said. What if she was actually playing with him, rather than with the police officer?

Before saying goodbye, Tara hands him another envelope.

"Another message? Another death threat? With the date and the place where the assassin and victim should meet?"

"No. I brought you a little book, to amuse you."

Gaşpar thanks her, he's irritated, he doesn't open the envelope. Once home, he pulls the small volume out of the envelope.

Ambrose Bierce, *The Devil's Dictionary—Unabridged*, Dover Editions, Inc., New York.

A note at the beginning of the volume, "A sardonic partial lexicon of the English language. Ambrose Bierce (1842–ca. 1914), a Civil War Veteran . . . recognized as one of the most influential American journalists of the end of the 19th century and a notable writer of short fiction and light verse. Two years after the publication of this volume, Bierce ventured down to revolution-riddled Mexico and was never heard from again."

A marker in the book. Page 42. Geology, Ghost, Ghoul. Yes, *Ghost. The outward and visible sign of an inward fear.* The definition is worth re-reading. The outward and visible sign of an inward fear . . .

■

Even during the cold nights, when it's pleasant to remain in bed, Augustin Gora would wake up early. Since he'd changed the country and language in which he lived, he slept only with the help of sleeping pills. Short sleep. He would wake up without any difficulty, would start working so as not to feel his exhaustion. He'd often find himself in front of his computer. He would look at the calendar: Thursday. He would turn the armchair to the left and look at the receiver. Turn the armchair to the right, bend over the desk, pull out the bottom drawer, place the folder titled RA 0298 on the desk. The phone would ring. He would look at it, without pleasure.

"Saint Augustin? Are you in your lair?"

"What lair?"

"Between book covers."

Gora was silent, annoyed by the glibness of the intruder.

"Yes, between."

"I'm looking for a bibliographical reference. You're the authority, you know everything."

Gora looked at the folder, smiling. The summary of his conversation with Bedros Avakian about Peter's hiring.

"A quotation. I can't place it. I know that it's a quotation. I've seen it somewhere. I know it, but I don't know it. It's not in the language of my birth, but the language of my death. I'm counting on your speedy reaction."

Gora listens and moves on to the second file in the folder.

"I know I saw this phrase somewhere. A long time ago, when we were young and bookish. In your English, I don't have the key."

Gora was silent, looking at the Avakian page.

"The author could, in fact, be Lady D. Madam Death. The whore with the scythe."

"I see you know who the author is."

"But I don't know the pen name. I repeat the quotation daily to myself. Five, ten times a day. When I am awake and when I sleep. When I walk, and when I remember, while on the toilet, that I was young at some point. Then, I reread the black paper. The devil, the whore's lover, sent it to me. *Next time*, says her Ladyship. *Next time, I kill. I promise* . . . that's what the goblin of the night says. Should I believe her? You never know when she's joking and what the joke is concealing. *Next time, I kill you*, gurgles the filthy monster."

Gaşpar stopped, then took up the entire text with a sigh.

"A quotation, no?"

"Maybe. I think so."

"Madam Bordello reads literature! I was sure of it. A snob."

What follows is a tangled story with digressions and parentheses: a few weeks back, Peter received a strange death threat. A joke. The authorities took it seriously. They ordered him to do the same.

"The review about Dima . . . you remember. Then, I was under protection, without the protection of the FBI. These people make you give up your soul with all the questioning. After they are sure that you're no criminal, they give you senile advice. Now, another investigator. You know what Larry Eight told me? *Don't relax.* But that's my nature, sir. That's who I am, Mr. Murphy, I'm whistling all day long, but I can't relax . . . "

Had he stopped or not? It wasn't clear.

"I'm bothering you at this early hour in the morning because I'm under a lot of pressure. I can't die illiterate. I have to find out what books the two lovers Mister Devil and Lady Death read at night before going to bed. *Next time I kill. Next time I promise you. Next time, a single line. Labyrinth. Invisible labyrinth.* Eh, what do you say to that?"

"I'm thinking," Gora whispers. He'd moved the folder to the edge of the table. The Computer knows the answer, and Gora also knows the answer, and is dumbfounded.

"Assumptions. I am weighing things out, and thinking. It's by . . . so and so or so and so."

He was smiling. How could you not think of the apprenticeship of exile: from the old typewriter, heavy and rusted, presented annually to the socialist militia for approval, to the American electric typewriter, then to the fax machine, the pages transmitted instantly to the other world, then the computer that often gives birth to another computer. Cosmic schism, the planetary uproar of banality. You are the same Gora who is no longer the same.

He pushed down on the piano keys, humming the magic phrase, the computer hesitated, then the confirmation appeared on the blue screen. He'd wanted to check if the robot knew as much as a professor educated in the old school. It did, look at that, it did.

Saint Augustin, the wizard, knows all the books in the world like the back of his hand, all the books that now a poor kindergarten computer also knows.

"The Old Man? Old Man Dima? Is he writing to us from the other world?" Peter Gaşpar asks excitedly. "These were all his concerns . . . magic, the labyrinth, mysticism, the fantastic. It's he, isn't it? He wants me to meet him, he loves me, he wants to save me from our sinful world, isn't that right?"

"That's possible. I'm leaning toward somebody else. *I've known what the Greeks didn't know: uncertainty.* Do you know the quotation?"

Silence. Gaşpar, the basketball player, doesn't know this quotation. He has no idea about the suspects in the attic; around that time he was still playing hockey and *turca** and basketball.

"I've known what the Greeks didn't know: incertitude," repeated Saint Augustin. A phrase once heard in the socialist attic.

Silence. The deathly silence of the grave and the illiterate.

"I'm leaning toward the blind guy. The Great Blind Man," whispered Gora, more to himself, convinced that Peter wouldn't know what he was talking about. Peter had no idea about the attic of the past. He allowed the intruder and himself a breathing pause, to allay

*A Romanian children's playground game, the point of which is to toss a short stick with the use of a longer stick [trans.].

his agitation and his memories. The attic! It was just too much . . . Peter had no idea about the attic of suspects.

"Hello, hello!" the happy intruder exploded. "Perfect! That's right, I knew you'd have the answer. Bull's-eye, perfect. Li-qui-da-ted."

That precious, cunning Augustin offered the magic key, Peter Gaşpar was surely mumbling to himself. Just like that, the sonorities of youth in Gomorrah reclaimed! The language of so long ago! The juvenile cadences! Jubilation. Memory reborn, triumphant, all of a sudden!

Gora knew that bewilderment, its whirlpools. He knew the tears of joy of the reader in the corner of the library who, book in hand, suddenly untangled the riddle. Transformed all at once from a deaf-mute toad into the prince of youth without aging and life without death.* A god, in the magic of his language! Now, he could defy the anonymous crowd in which he was lost: no passerby could understand those words or understand the murderous quotation, hidden in the language unknown to anyone outside of himself, the crowned wanderer, the king of the world, at least for one second.

Professor Gora was left with the receiver in his hand. He waited for the gasps and fainting spells of the phantom. Nothing.

Folder RA 0298, on which the word MYNHEER was written, sat still near the white gloves, pushed to the edge of the table.

He listened for the noises of the house. Nothing. He retrieved the yellow folder. Stalled for a second, reopened it.

He instantly identified the passage discussed so often in the attic in Bucharest, a passage to which he referred regularly, then read Palade's and Dima's comments. Now, he confronted the variations of that conjuncture, while the buffoon ran to the library, exalted, to settle the question of the code.

After two hours, Peter's voice:

"Purim! Purim! That's the key. Perfect! I have the key. Fin-ished!"

Gora taps on his computer, the word doesn't appear.

---

*Folk tale by the Romanian writer Petre Ispirescu [trans.].

"You don't know what Purim is? You never learned? Even in the family of my Communist in-laws people knew what Purim was. I knew Lu's grandparents. They went to synagogue on holidays. You knew them, too."

"It's been decades."

"So you haven't understood the millennial madness, either . . . Although, you stand by her captives, I know. No small thing, for someone born in our parts. And then abandoned by a wife who wasn't exactly Christian. The poor woman was unsure if you had chosen her for a symbolic reason. She told me you were reluctant to write to your friend from childhood, Izy Koch, about the marriage. You were afraid he'd think you chose the otherness of her community, the otherness of her tribe, her ethnic identity, rather than the woman."

A venomous comment, entirely unnecessary. Not at all necessary. Gora was boiling.

The voice stopped, Gaşpar probably wanted to excuse himself, to correct himself through a sporting remark.

"There aren't many reasons for us to be loved. Any irritation is enough, to stand as proof of our many defects. One of our many defects. Even one defect, just one, and it's over with us . . . li-qui-da-ted. Fin-ished!"

He pants, just like Gora, and can't regain his composure, just like Gora. He'd never before spoken with so much passion and bitterness. A long silence would follow. Gora gathers his strength, bracing himself for another avalanche.

"Purim is the holiday with masks. The people of the book don't have joyful rituals. This one is fun, childlike. Haman, the guide of the king of Persia, an anti-Semitic Iago, plots the massacre of the sinners. Esther, the king's concubine, saves her people. Maybe she was the favorite from the harem. And so the wandering people pardon the sinner and celebrate their salvation. They wear masks, enjoy themselves, eat triangular sweets named Hamantaschen, which means, "Haman's pockets," or "the monster's hat," as some others call them. They feast every year, for the whore who saved them.

Victory over the world's Hamans. And there are many Hamans, the chosen people feel."

Peter repeats, with pleasure and venom, "the chosen people." The bitterness hadn't disappeared, but the voice was growing thinner.

"Many wise people say that the Holocaust canceled the contract of the All Powerful with his chosen people. So, then, the Bible is no longer valid. Miracles, covenants devalued, expired. With one exception! The legend of Esther, where God is missing from the scene. A hellish tale, whose moral is that the mission of the exiles is to save themselves. Themselves! That's all. Purim, the celebration of the masks, reminds us of that summons."

Gora the all-knowing doesn't know this story, doesn't see the connection to the threat letter. His fingers run frenetically over the keys of the moment. Bent once again over the folder, he is ready to listen, to learn, to remedy the lacuna and document what he's learned.

"Look, I bought *Ficciones* and *Labyrinths* from the bookstore, as you advised me to do, both editions. I found the text of the Great Blind Man. The first crime. The first letter of the sacred name was pronounced. The second crime. The second letter was pronounced. That's what the great Argentine writes. A third crime follows. The third of February. The time for carnival. The festival of masks."

"Does it say that there? The festival of masks?"

"It says that in both volumes . . . Carnival appears in both translations. Carnival in Argentina is in February. The message Tara brought me came at the beginning of the semester. Beginning of February. I discovered it late because I don't get my mail in time. It had arrived at the beginning of February. So then, Carnival is the festival of masks. For the chosen, exiled people, the perpetually threatened, this is Purim. Purim in the lunar calendar . . . you know what the lunar calendar is."

Gora knows, naturally, what the lunar calendar is. He knows at least this much, but the all-knowing Gora is silent.

"So then, in the calendar of the ancients, the calendar that follows the moon, not the sun, Purim should come shortly. The date of the crime. Purim is soon. Soon. So then, the countdown. That's what the quotation is announcing. As you know, the three victims from the story are all members of the chosen people."

A poisoned silence. Gora opens the folder.

"Have you notified the police?"

"I first called the distinguished Professor Augustin Gora, who was known, in my family, as Gusti. An all-knowing expert. To find out where the quotation came from. I haven't been able to figure it out until now, though I thought I was smart, capable of untangling the riddle on my own. Somnambulant, lost, all the nocturnal wild beasts in my head, but I considered myself smart nonetheless. The professor saved me. He offered the solution, just as I'd anticipated. Saint Augustin knows everything. I found the source of the quotation. *Labyrinths* and *Ficciones*. I have both volumes. I read, reread, confronted. I hit on the Carnival. The festival of masks. Purim. Should I notify the police about Purim?"

"Yes, you should, yes, notify them now, right now, immediately! Do you have a contact number, in case of emergencies?"

"Yes, of course I do. Little Patrick must be used to being snagged from his wife's side or from the side of whomever or children or television. However, I'm not going to perform this kindliness. He's going to come see me tomorrow, in any case. Routine meeting. Tomorrow I will tell Larry Eight. He'll gape, eyes and mouth, like a crocodile. Convinced I'm pulling his leg."

"You say what you discovered."

"What did I discover? A course in fantastic literature? An Argentine author of fantastic literature? Should we go to Argentina, Patrick and I, on the tracks of Lonrot and Scharlach, Borges' characters? Or should we go on a pilgrimage to Palade's grave? Or, better yet, to Cosmin Dima's grave? We wait, hidden, in the cemetery, to see who comes to bow at the sacred gravesite and who brings flowers and petitions? Dima's zealots, Palade's assassins, my stalkers? What should poor Patrick do? Should he learn about the archaic calendar, the lunar holidays, the Purim rituals? Or about the tricks of Communist and post-Communist espionage? Or should we go to the little Paris of the Balkans, as Bucharest was called during the interbellum, grab a beer with the old and new informants who decided to murder Mihnea Palade while he meditated on the toilet throne? What should Mr. Murphy do? He will become increasingly suspicious of the Eastern European professor, that's what he will do! Professor Peter Gaşpar, hyperbored of the America of all possibilities, where he regrets he did not come twenty years earlier, in the example of the wise Professor Gora, the husband of his cousin Ludmila Serafim, *the significant other*. That's some hypothesis, no? Here when they find a body, the first suspects are the poor people who mourn the dead. You start the investigation with them. Those who reported the crime. What should Patrick do? What would we do in his place? 'Scrutinize the surroundings for anything unusual,' the FBI officer advised me. I can't. I am absentminded and neglectful. Is it 'happy anxiety' or 'anxious happiness?' "

"Careful with the warning," repeats Professor Gora, irritated. "Don't forget that Lonrot dies because he's too rational. He allows himself to be fascinated by a rational scheme, but the perfect reader eliminates logic and good sense and sufficiency and skepticism. He gives himself entirely to the will of the text, he lives it. There are warnings and there are warnings, you have to be vigilant."

"Warning? They can kill me without warnings. To subdue me? Anyway, I'm subdued now. I'm not going to reenter the nebulas of the Homeland. I did it for Palade. He'd asked me. That's it! I left the place, definitively. Ciao!"

"Palade was warned, then killed."

"Because he wasn't obedient. They repeated the warnings, and he still wasn't subdued. He enraged them. And then, he was a renegade. Renegades are punished."

"What do you mean 'a renegade'?"

"Dima's disciple had become antinationalist, offending the sacred symbols. Paired up with a young, pagan witch, in love with America, where he changed his name, ready to change his religion. I'm the old nuisance. Fin-ished. Basta. One more blunder shouldn't matter. The review was my only work. Li-qui-da-ted. A trifle."

"There's also the famous and well-known text *Mynheer* and your unknown masterpiece. That was the gossip."

"Maybe the gossipers wrote it."

"You received a threat, don't forget. A condemnation."

"To temper me. I'm tempered. Mute, the black swan. Deaf like the Buddha's statue, mute like Moses' sculpture. Deaf-mute like my deaf-mute brothers of anywhere and anytime. I don't care about imbeciles allied with other imbeciles. They will forget about me, they'll find some other targets. The threat is the joke of a semi-literate failure."

"Failures can be very dangerous. Hitler was a failure."

"Condemned to death? We are all condemned to death. Death, invisible authority? Invincible? A half-wit with cultural pretentions. The author of the letter wants to appear as something he's not."

When Gora heard his voice again after two weeks, something had changed.

"The woods. It invades at night. The patrols, the dogs, skeletons, barbed wire. My guilt, or the guilt of others, I don't know. I sleep very little. I wake up sweating, terminated. At the door, at the window, the dogs of night, the patrols. Lucky that my mother can't see me. I crash into sleep, into nightmare, I wake up exhausted."

Had he notified the police? He'd notified the college's administration. A student had advised him.

"A student? How?"

A female student with whom he'd had some kind of conflict at some point.

"Beautiful?"

"It's not Lu, don't worry . . . she's no double for Lu. I am talking to someone, that's what's important. W.A.S.P. *White Anglo-Saxon*

Protestant, that's as much as I learned. She doesn't have our neuroses. She has others."

The student had persuaded him to notify the campus administration.

"It was worse."

"How could it be worse? Why would it be worse?"

"The patrols. The night patrols. Every two hours. No . . . "

Saint Augustin babbled something. Who knows what, but he was writing madly.

"I'd forgotten to tell you something, Maestro. I talked to Palade. His brother, I mean. Lucian, Luci. Luci Palade, who's still back in the old country. He told me that the attacks against the foreigner that I am continue in all the papers. Only the cliché has changed, they don't call me a foreigner, a traitor, but a failure. I never wrote anything, I have no talent, how do I dare speak out? They're right. The universal vote gets suspended if you have no talent. You have no talent, you have no vote, no voice in the country of the talented. The idiots forgot the national proverb, 'the mouth of the fool speaks the truth.' Isn't that right, they forgot?"

"They consider you an enemy. Failures are dangerous, as I was saying, and vengeful, be careful that you don't . . . "

Saint Augustin didn't get to keep prattling on. Peter had disappeared, his voice had disappeared, the phantom had moved his tricks into the void.

■

The phantom, however, still sends riddles, suggestions, traps.

Left alone, Saint Augustin recapitulates. Could the basketball-star-turned-reader actually never have heard of the Borges story? Hard to believe. Lu might have told him stories about the attic of suspects where the suspect fable was read. She might also have reminded him about the evening when Palade debated Borges' parallel worlds. Or even if Lu, discreet and dignified as she always was, avoided the past, Gașpar would have found out about the story from

Palade. Inevitably. They had talked so much about Dima, and Borges should have been an unavoidable reference; Dima and Palade had published exegeses about the blind man from Buenos Aires.

When he was speaking about the nights with Palade, however, Gaşpar had never mentioned Borges! Not a single allusion, not a whisper, nothing! He doesn't even appear in the review about Dima's memoirs. Was he already preparing the game with the masks and quotations back then? Animated for a short time by the Dima dilemma and Palade's strangeness, was he already putting into motion future amusement? A death threat! Let's be serious, criminals don't need quotations from esoteric books.

Angels don't write books. And what exactly is that, wise guy? They don't write books, so then, neither do they write death threats borrowed from books. Gora had found the aphorism in the draft of the meeting between Patrick and Peter and was once again amazed by the buffoon's conclusions.

And from where to where . . . a basketball star raised in the house of the Communist David Gaşpar and in the Communist schools of the Red era, and now so many sophisticated Talmudic speculations about a postcard with excerpts from the *New York Times*?

Professor Gora wasn't convinced that Peter hadn't just gotten bored of the New World and tried to regenerate his own irresponsibility. He'd announced from the start that he'd moved his game with death to foreign soil, and now he was staging his nocturne of threat.

He'd wasted time with this ridiculous farce, he had half a mind to call the police himself, to inform them that a good friend, a recent refugee from the East, has found his life in danger here, in the Country of All Liberties.

An obligatory paragraph in the obituary on which he was working at that very moment.

■

Life after death is nothing but a poor obituary, Gora says. Futility after futility has its scribes, professionals, intermediaries, clients, giant archives, and giant advertising agencies. Every story with a beginning and end is an obituary.

Because of the short time between the notification of a death and the next publication deadline, many press agencies have obituaries ready for the right moment.

The last validation of passing from the world can't be brief and formal. The truth consists of fantasy and of potentialities, reality isn't confined to facts, but also to hypotheses and enigmas, unfulfilled chances, expired within the unique that has itself expired.

He'd consulted editing guides for obituaries, from the *Know How* series, which gives instruction about gardening, marriage, electrical installation, diabetic diets, sexual appetites, and winter sports, as well as the inevitable funeral end. The last great event: copulation with the Nymphomaniac.

An obituary can be basic, with publically known facts about the life of the deceased, but also a very personal look at life, with details that probe the uniqueness of the loved, or of the detested, as the case may be. The obituary has evolved from a summary note of farewell to a multilayered and durable memorial. It can by a dynamic and illustrated biographical history. One can consult the National Archive of Obituaries. Millions and millions of examples can be found in The Daily Book of Obituaries, *military and athletic anthologies, obituaries of heroes and impostors, refugees and adventurers, exiles, animators, courtesans, panderers, politicians, bankers, clowns and nuns and magicians and madmen. Modest and villainous and eccentric lives.*

The obituary isn't just a simple farewell note but the memorial addressed to posterity. The history of a life with everything that life contains and didn't get a chance to contain. Unfulfillment can't be ignored, what you wanted but didn't get a chance to do or to be, the failures that never got second chances. Something apart from a recapitulation of the calendar, apart from the daily chaos.

He'd listened many times to the famous band *Obituary*, which had launched the death metal genre in Florida at the end of the eighties, he'd bought the album *Cause of Death*, made notes on the subsequent records, *The End Complete, World Demise, Set in Stone,* and *Buried Alive.*

"Do you know what Peter told me when I asked him about Eva?"

Lu had stopped, they were on the sidewalk in front of Gara de Nord, the central station in Bucharest, after dropping the high schooler Peter Gaşpar at the train heading to the north of the country.

"Eva is obsessed with him, not with her husband. The son isn't too pleased, but he doesn't protest, doesn't pay attention, he only thinks about basketball. Eva told me about his visit to the cemetery in Săpînţa, the merry cemetery."

Gora had no idea that such a cemetery even existed.

"The Merry Cemetery in Săpînţa, near Maramureş. The tombstones have colored, comical stories drawn onto them. Death isn't comical, Eva said. I asked Peter about his mother. He said that David forbade any mention of the theme of death after Eva said at some point that from the concentration camp they came not home but to a cemetery."

In recent years, a new journalistic genre has developed: the obituary as entertainment.

What is anything, if not *entertainment?*

Publicity, attraction, distraction. The merchandise has to be attractive: the book and the carrots and the shoes. Otherwise no one buys it and it rots and disappears. I buy, therefore, I exist, I sell myself to buy. If I don't sell, I have no value. The obituary is evidence that I existed! If it's not interesting, then I didn't exist. I don't exist because I didn't exist.

It's a new industry, a cavalcade of performers and healers, bachelors, spies, acrobats, sports stars, movie stars, jazz stars, eccentrics and killers and bureaucrats. Anecdotal, discursive products of a cynical frankness, touching and, of course, amusing.

De mortuis nil nisi bene doesn't apply anymore.

Amusement, the lack of prejudices and restrictions, infantilization. What's wrong with that, Professor? What's wrong with it, the professor was asking himself.

Gora was smiling, tired, dreaming, fondling the blue gloves, on top of the folder, which he hesitated to open.

Thin, loose pants made of green satin. A sleeveless, transparent shirt. Sandals with a single strap, on a bare foot. Lu, pale Andalusian. Intense gaze, intense expectation. She's thrown off her sandals, pants, small underwear, no bigger than a rusted leaf. Full breasts, hot belly, long arms and long legs, electrified. The supreme moment, supreme youth. Open the bottle, pour into the glasses. The clinking of old crystal. On the table, raspberries, cherries, wine. She is here and faraway, in the green of the great trees.

Dressed in a light, linen blouse of red, yellow, and white, she was meticulously cleaning the vegetables. Then she washed the fish and the fruit. She was wearing thin rubber gloves, like a surgeon. White, yellow, red. She cut the vegetables scrupulously, piece by piece. She was celebrating the silken morning, the alert ecstasy of the human fully alive. She breathed in the physical and metaphysical day, she loved concrete things and the sacredness they contained. Concentration and sensuality.

Old aphrodisiacs. Gora was watching the wood and glancing, now and then, at the screen that delivered the disasters of the day. After a while, he let himself fall back into the chair, covered his eyes with his palms, eager for relaxation.

The thin, loose pants, the linen transparent blouse. The sandals, the bare foot. You wake up, stupefied by wrinkled, old skin. The dried body, skin like parchment, white hair, like snow and like the pall of the dead. Long, quick tongue, long, livid, dried hands, long, dried legs: a skeleton with a lugubrious sound, swept away at the first touch: a heap of dust.

She threw off her sandals, her pants, her small, thin underwear, no bigger than a rusted leaf. Dried breasts, the skin of her belly purplish, old thighs, the burnt lips of her sex under the puff of white, curly hair. She takes your palm in her narrow, long, wrinkled palm. She folds it into a fist, which she pushes into her center, moaning. Her eyelashes tremble, just like her voice. A short cry, like an owl.

He opens the green bottle and pours into the glass. The clink of the past. The raspberries, the cherries, the wine. She places the cherry on the lips of the dying man. She pushes it delicately into his mouth. Deeper and deeper. Bitter, old fingers.

"What was your youth like," she asks. "You started late, didn't you?"

For a moment, she remains lost in the green of the great trees. A burned look in her eyes.

"Oh, yes, me, too. Late, much too late. I regret it, yes." The lips lick, the teeth bite, the tongue caresses. The dying man pulled inside, into the deep, his gaze hungry, his body thin, senile, an exhausted moan, a scream. Hunger and satiety, copulation with death.

Old phantasms. From time to time, he raises his gaze toward the small blue screen: the chess player wipes his brow and bald head with his wide and hairy hand. There's no visible adversary, just the board with green and red pieces. The red team and the green team. The king, the queen, the knights, the bishops, rooks, and pawns.

The bald hussar with the black moustache holds the red pieces. He touches the crown of the queen with his index finger, stops thoughtfully, gazing amazed at the battlefield. The kingdoms are no longer black and white, but colored, as the hypercolor era demands. He raises his hand, brings it to his brow, scratches his baldness, tousles his eyebrows, first one, then the other. The right hand holds a brightly labeled Coca-Cola can. Peter brightens, as if responding by a divine sign.

Gora smiles, also awake. The astringent liquor pours into the tall and narrow glass. Frothy, cold, fresh, an elixir. Salvation.

He sips once more. Drink your salvation! Salvation. It preserves memory, fortifies the present, defies the future, age and the obituary.

On the table, the folder. At the edge of the table, the gloves from the past.

■

Pale, unshaven, sleepless, Professor Peter Gaşpar—the stalked, in fact, the plaintiff—seems ready to accept the role of the guilty party.

His gaze, his tone, the questions with which he opens the newest meeting all confirm the change. The discussion is unfolding differently from the preceding ones. Peter looks tired and slow, defeated by the guilt that he seems ready to admit, resentfully and out of sheer weariness. But after a few minutes, the scene changes: he puts his large hands on the table, next to the large hands of the policeman. He raises his hands. The index of the right hand points to the two volumes on the table.

He announces in a low voice, "I found the quotation and the author."

On the table, a book with a hash-marked, colorful cover. Typed in three steps, with golden letters: FIC-CIO-NES. Next to it, another book. A shiny, black-and-white cover. LABYRINTHS, *Selected Stories & Other Writings by Jorge Luis Borges.*

Patrick writes. He doesn't raise his eyes, bent over the spiral notebook. He pulls it out of the large, old bag made of cankered leather only for unusual circumstances. This time, he is writing. He measures up the suspect disguised as plaintiff, then begins, surprisingly, to write.

He transcribes the name of the publishing house, the year, while holding the book in his left hand. He takes a sheet of paper off the table. He tears it in half and puts one half in each book as a bookmark to the right of the text *Death and the Compass.* Page 129 in the first book, page 76 in the second.

"Argentine, you say?"

"Yes, a great Argentine writer. Born in 1899 in Buenos Aires. Into a family of Spanish, British, and vaguely Judeo-Portuguese origin."

"Dead, then."

"He postponed his death in the hope that he'd receive the Nobel Prize. He was stretching the compass as far as possible, but death found him, finally, at eighty-seven years old. Old and blind."

"Did he receive the prize?"

"No. Those awards are a lottery. The Great Prize so much the more so. He had the chance, but there appeared attacks in the press that he was a Fascist."

"Was he?"

"Nonsense, he couldn't have been a Fascist."

"But the Old Man alchemist might have been?"

"You can't compare the two. Even though Dima was fascinated by Borges. Just like Palade. Maybe the fanatic who is honoring me with the threat letter, too. Neither Borges nor Palade were Fascists. The case of Dima is more complicated, as I explain in the review. Anyway, he wasn't a standard Fascist."

"Meaning?"

Peter doesn't answer, and Patrick stops writing. He gives the suspect a hostile look, the same as when he'd first appeared, very bristly and determined. The tangled cultural traps increase suspicion. Wearisome digressions, that's what could be read in Patrick's gaze. He rifles through the pages, retains a line from here and there, soured by the opacity of the sentences.

"A police story?"

"We could consider it a police story. The hero is a detective. The heroine is Death. A logician who works with a compass and a square."

Annoyed, Patrick seems ready to draw his gun, to escape the pretender's oblique language.

"Lonrot. Scharlach. What are these names?"

"I don't know. Nordic names. Names from a story."

"And the quotation? Where's the quotation?"

"Here, page 141, *'The next time I kill you,' said Scharlach, 'I promise you the labyrinth made of a single straight line which is invisible and everlasting.' He stepped back a few paces. Then, very carefully, he fired.* In the other volume, on page 87, *'The next time I kill you,' replied Scharlach, 'I promise you the labyrinth, consisting of a single line which is invisible and increasing.' He moved back a few steps. Then, very carefully, he fired.* My assassin used the first book. Published in New York, by Grove Press. Only he cut the article in front of the subject. *Next time,* instead of *the next time.* Your colleague Trooper was right."

"Trooper? Which Trooper?"

"Mr. Jim Smith, from the state police. From the state troopers. He was saying that it should say THE *next time*, so then the sender could be foreign. He sent the postcard to the investigations lab in Washington. For print analysis. Are there any results yet?"

"I don't think so. It takes time. The lab is very busy."

"Naturally. In the land of freedom, crime is a form of freedom. It doesn't matter if my assassin uses proper grammar."

"Your assassin?"

"The one who calls himself my assassin. The foreigner."

"The foreigner?"

"That's what Jim Smith said. It should have been THE *next time* and I WILL *kill you*."

Patrick is smiling. The state police officer doesn't inspire any more trust than the professor he's investigating.

"There are Americans of generations and generations who don't write correctly."

He looks at the foreigner in front of him once again, intensely.

"May I take these books? In fact, just the first, the one from Grove Press."

"Of course."

"Okay, I will read the story. I don't think I'll find anything, outside of that quotation. Is there anything else in the text that we should pay attention to?"

"The festival of masks."

"And what's that, now?"

"On the first page Doctor Marcel Yarmolinski is mentioned. A delegate to the International Talmudic Congress, from Podolsk. Podolsk is a place in Eastern Europe. The Talmud is . . . I think you probably know what it is."

Police officer Patrick Murphy is silent. His black gaze is increasingly blacker. Larry Eight knows, doesn't know, hard to guess.

"Yarmolinski endured three years of war in the Carpathian mountains. The mountains in my country, Old Man Dima's country and Palade-Portland's country. The story says that the third crime takes place in February, the month of the Argentine carnival. The letter arrived at the college in February. A month has gone by, maybe more. And now the Judaic Carnival is approaching."

"The Judaic Carnival?"

"Yes. It is, in a way, a Jewish story. The three victims are Jewish. The author was obsessed with the old Judaic texts and the Kabbalah. And with . . . "

Gaşpar searches through his left pocket, then the right, out of which he finally pulls a crumpled page from a notebook. He uncrumples it.

"*Sefer Yetzirah*, the Book of Creation, written in Syria or Palestine in the sixth century and . . . and the Tetrarch of Galilee . . . who never even existed."

Patrick scratches his head, Peter returns to the dialogue.

"Purim is a festive celebration, with masks. For children. In Borges' story, the carnival forecasts the crime."

The stupor proves beneficial, the policeman is struck by an idea.

"This writer, what's his name . . . "

"Borges. Jorge Luis Borges."

"Is he in the curriculum?"

"No. Maybe in the graduate studies, at a big university. But some students here would have heard of him, I'm sure."

"Have you ever mentioned his name in your class?"

"No, never. I don't think so. I'd have had no reason to."

Patrick picks up the phone.

"Tang? Find out if anyone's taught a course about the Argentine writer Jorge Luis Borges in the last three years."

This time he pronounced the guilty party's name perfectly.

"Yes, the name of the professor who taught the course and the list of students who took it."

Patrick puts down the receiver, standing up now. He doesn't extend his hand, just merely announces, gruffly, "I'll call you. I will call. If something comes up, tell Jennifer."

The grenade in the body. The hidden tumor, the knot of toxins. Death in a can, ready to explode. Postponement, postponement, hummed the obese body. The caricature in the mirror in front of the bed asks for compassion: belly swollen with rot, the shaved marble of his head, his thick, livid lips, his gelatinous eyelids.

"The effort isn't worth it, dear Almighty One," the condemned whispers. "It would be a ridiculous victory, Dulcissima, postpone the execution."

After half an hour, fat Peter Gaşpar stops asking for postponement and tries asking for refuge. The wind swells under the stiff branches of the trees, the darkness advances fluidly around him and in the surrounding wood. This is the nocturnal tribunal from which he asks allowances. He hears the purling, the furtive whimpering of the night. He wanders around the shack, he's in no mood to reenter the cage. He's enraged less by the threat itself, and more by the people behind it. He doesn't like martyrs, or heroes, and he detests the role of victim. He prefers a banal death, without drama. Illness, suicide. The appearance of normality or of an accident. He carries his flesh with difficulty. His body has dilated in exile. Perplexity and insomnia and ravenous eating.

The night will bring the acoustics of the hunt again. Skeletal shadows covering their ears to drown out the sound of the dogs, covering their eyes to block out the blaze of the sentinels. Shivering from cold and fear, Eva Kirschner is there, head shorn, in a striped uniform that hangs loosely on her skeletal body.

The message of the blind man from Buenos Aires had incited the pack of neuroses.

Peter ambles in a circle around the cabin. He ignores the forest and the cabin, both bewildered with anticipation. He tries to regulate his breathing. He breathes in deeply, holds the air in, one, two, five, more, exhales slowly, very slowly, a small, even dose of air, just like his inhalation. One, four, slowly, as slowly as possible.

In front of the door, Death. A smiling woman with whitened blond hair and the large teeth of a wild beast. A black dress that reaches to the ground. In her hand, a piece of paper. The death sentence. The Decree.

"Do you . . . live here?"

Peter looks at her, dazed, slow to answer. No, the assassin has no weapon, just the Decree.

"Please excuse me . . . I'm sorry, this is the notice, the witch stammers. Excuse me . . . I came by before. But you weren't home."

Peter gazes at her mutely, happy that he hadn't been home.

"I came by, but you weren't here, I left a note. Gattino. It's about Gattino. He's blind, poor guy."

Yes, the condemned had received the message, a month before. The Argentinian Blind Man, the morbid note.

"He's only six months old. He's gray, and blind in one eye. With a respiratory infection. Have you seen him? Have you seen him around by any chance? He has short fur. He's shy, very shy. He needs to be called by name, quietly, sweetly. Gatti-Gatti-Gattino, pss, pss, Gat-ti."

She extends a photo of the cat with the white, dead eye. The Old Woman smiles sweetly, with the large teeth of a wild beast.

"Yes, ma'am, I found your sign posted to my door. I haven't seen the orphan. I mean, the wanderer. I promise, of course, yes, I know the number. Both numbers. Yours, Helene, and your brother's, Steve. Yes, yes, I have them. I will call, I will call you immediately."

The sky is darkening. Muted décor. The disoriented wanderer is also muted, and alive. He forgets about suicide and melancholy. Troubled by the fate of Gattino. Italian name, from Buenos Aires.

He gazes up to the illegible sky, then to the ground in front of the steps, a carpet of leaves and insects. He inhales deeply and exhales slowly, in small doses.

The headlights catch him in between two bands of light, the car stops in front of the shack. Jennifer! The elegant head of security, in an Armani trench coat and a Dior scarf, the color of the wind. She gets out of the car, alert and smiling.

"Taking a walk? It's good for the sleep, it's good. May I come in?"

The elegant Vietnamese woman ignores the disarray inside.

"I brought a list of the students. There was, in fact, a course on Borges! Two years ago. A professor from Spain. I brought the list of her students. We're going to compare the handwriting of each of them with the cursive on the postcard. The question is whether any of these was also your student at some point."

The professor looks down the list.

"No, I don't think so. None of these names look familiar. I will check. Tomorrow, at the registrar's office."

J.T. leaves the list on the table. Tara is not on the list. He doesn't remember any of the names in front of him. Did Palade's assassins infiltrate the killer among his students? There would have been no need, the killer could easily enter the campus, find the hermit's cabin, watch for his return, appear smiling out of the bushes and calmly unload four bullets, four for the four crimes outlined by the compass of Buenos Aires. Or the killer could repeat the Palade scene: after two hours of class, Professor Gaşpar hurries stiffly to the bathroom, his bladder demanding its rights. The stranger enters the next cabin. For some years now, the professor has risked soiling his trousers in the bathroom. Standing in front of the toilet, he moans quietly from the sting.

Climbed up on the seat in the next stall, the Messenger of Death targets the victim's temple. It's simpler than it was with poor Palade: he's aiming at a standing victim, instead of sitting. It would be simple in the cabin, as well. It's simple enough to duplicate the key. The nomad's insomnias and nightmares would only help the killer. At two in the morning, Gaşpar is in the middle of a neurotic episode, at three, at dawn, he's riding an elephant, out of whose trunk flow heavy streams of tears. From the sky to the earth. The cinephile watches on the screen to see the aggressor approaching, twirling the shiny toy in his fingers, turning it toward the condemned. A murderous trajectory, the invisible labyrinth, eternity.

Peter smiles. He'd dozed off smiling. The paper J.T. left behind was trembling on his ample chest. He inhales deeply, snoring slightly, like a fat and tired baby chick.

On his chest the list of students who took the Borges course. A white, thin shield.

■

"We have a suspect. We compared the handwriting from the postcard with that of the students in the Borges course. There's a suspect."

"The text was typed."

"But the name of the sender is handwritten. As well as the address."

"Well, then?"

"The suspect is from California. Appears to be Polish, is here on scholarship, studies political science and is the editor in chief of the *Journal of Political Studies*, which the college publishes. Very intelligent, very social, and with a very cultivated mind."

"Very, very, very. What's his name?"

J.T. pronounces the name from the sheet on her desk, syllable by syllable.

"E-rast. Erast. Lo-jew-ski. Erast Lojewski. Lojewski. Polish parents, most likely. He graduates this year."

J.T. was satisfied; she'd worked quickly, and her makeup did her justice.

"Did you take him in for questioning?"

"We can't. We sent the writing samples to the lab in Washington. If we get a positive match, we'll ask the prosecutor for permission to question him."

Gaşpar smiles, moved. The byzantine socialism that he was used to hadn't prepared him for such scruples. The barbarian, I'm out of the cage. Captives and captors considered me a liberal buffoon, freethinker, good to let loose in the jungle of freedom. Yet I was a slave, just like everyone else. I had the mentality of a slave. More detached, maybe, longing for some kind of evasion. A barbarian, still. A real barbarian.

"Are you watching him?"

"We're not allowed to. Not until we get the results from the lab. Would you feel more secure if he were under surveillance?"

"I don't know ... yes. I would. I didn't sleep at home two nights ago."

"Where did you sleep?"

"At a motel. On the main highway, not far from the college. I called a cab, I asked for the nearest motel, and the driver took me there. In the morning he brought me back."

"Motels aren't the safest of places."

"I know. I've seen many American movies."

"You should have called me. We would have figured something out."

"I survived. I'm here. Honored both by the stalkers and the protectors. Excitement! I don't have time to get bored."

That same afternoon, J.T.—in a new, afternoon outfit—informs him that he wasn't the only target. Two other professors had received the same threat! No, she couldn't reveal their names. The information had surfaced during a discussion in the professors' lounge; security had come by it accidentally.

One of the letters was written entirely by hand! The handwriting was identical to the other, and similar to Erast Lojewski's writing. On the back the image of the Hermitage was replaced with a photograph from the *New York Times*, one image of Arafat and one of Pinochet.

The two American professors hadn't notified the administration. The postcard had seemed a joke and didn't warrant serious consideration. Was the Eastern European obsessed with specters and horrors? Is that what the Vietnamese American was suggesting? Hadn't Professor Gaşpar tried to convince Larry One and the Sailor Dean and the taciturn Vietnamese J.T. that the threat was a farce?

The calming news did little to calm him. If there were more of the same letters, it means that he's not the only target. The sender isn't necessarily a compatriot, Dima's admirer or Palade's assassin. But it might be a simple diversion to calm the potential victim and misguide the police.

"Professor Gaşpar? I'm Gilbert. Professor Anteos Gilbert. Latin and Greek, ancient history. I hear that you've received a threatening letter."

Aha, Tara's professor! Tara's letter? Yes, her letter, too, had been threatening at one point, in its own way.

Gaşpar understands just in time that another letter is in question.

"I also received one," the Greek continues, patiently.

"I hadn't known."

"You'd have had no way of knowing. These robots at the police department don't communicate among themselves. Three hierarchies. Federal, state, and local. The local police don't inform the FBI, and those guys don't care one bit about the state and local cops. It's every man for himself. I went to the New York State police. On the very night that I got the letter in the mail. Valia, my wife, had panicked. She insisted that we go immediately to the police to show them the letter. Valia is Russian . . . "

"I didn't know. And I don't see . . . "

There were a lot of things that Professor Gaşpar didn't know, a lot of things he didn't see around him, blinded by invisible charades.

"There is a connection. Kosovo, the Serbs, Chechnya. You understand."

The listener does understand, but he's in no hurry; he waits.

"Valia was afraid that it was an Islamic extremist threat. Because of the Russian repression in Chechnya or the support that the Russians gave the Serbs in Yugoslavia."

The Eastern European is no stranger to the complications of the region. He breathes heavily. The excess of news means more boredom. A dearth of events has the same effect.

"What happened? What happened at the police?"

"I spoke with a man named Martin. I told him the story, showed him the card. He questioned me for a few hours. He made me make a statement. I made it. I left the place in the middle of the night."

"Did you locate the quotation? Did you tell him who the author was?"

"What quotation? That absurd proposition? A labyrinth! A labyrinth out of a single line. Invisible, eternal? One fell swoop! Next time I kill you with one fell swoop . . . No, I've no idea if it's a quotation. I don't know, and I don't think it matters. That's not what interests the police. I told them who wrote the card."

"Who? You know? How do you know?"

"A student. A student in my seminar. I recognized the handwriting."

"Tara? Tara Nelson?"

"Tara Nelson? No, not a chance. An international student."

"Where from?"

"Sarajevo. She came here on a fellowship. Deste, that's her name. D., signed on the card. Deste."

"Sarajevo? You recognized the handwriting? How? Just a few words written by hand . . . it would be hard to say."

"She used to write me notes before class. Asking for bibliographies, advice. I seemed to remember the writing, but I wasn't sure. And I didn't want to find out. I left my statement with the police, for them to beat their heads with it. The meeting had been decisive."

"What meeting?"

"In the library. After about a week, I ran into Deste at the library. She was at the computer. I went closer. I asked her what she was doing. She showed me. She was typing a text. I froze. It was the text I knew too well. I told her that I received her letter. 'Yes, you got it?' She asked me. Good, I'm glad. She was laughing. She has an irresistible laugh."

"Did she explain? Did you understand? What follows?"

"I asked her if I was the only addressee. Not at all. Forty. Forty letters! She'd sent them to all corners of the country! I told her that such things were lawfully reprehensible. She seemed amazed. Amazed, amused. Candid. The girl is enchanting. Innocent, but ironic. Full of charm."

Professor Gaşpar learned more than he'd expected to learn; there was nothing else to ask.

"I wanted to know how she'd chosen her addressees. Interesting people! That was the criteria. That's what she said, candidly."

"She doesn't know me. She's never met me."

"She'd probably found some things about you. Your biography published in the college handbook, or she heard something from other students. Only four addressees from the college. That's all. We're among few, you must admit . . . Who knows to whom and where she sent letters. I told her I have to inform the police. 'The police? Why the police?' I explained to her that there's no knowing what kind of effects such a game could have. She was stupefied. This was, in fact, her intention. The unknown! I tell you, she's enchanting."

"What was? What was her intention?"

"An exhibit! An art project, a conceptual installation. *Installation*. That's what it's called now. Something about the Byzantine Empire. I didn't really understand, and I didn't care to. That night I called the police."

"So you denounced the innocent . . . "

"To the contrary. I withdrew my statement."

"Withdrew? But didn't you say that in the end you gave the name of the person who . . . "

"In the end, but not then. Then, I withdrew the statement."

"Why? The student represents the Byzantine Empire. Exactly what Valia, your wife, suspected . . . "

"Nonsense. Deste is not a nationalist. Nor a terrorist. She's got nothing against the Russian. Dr. Gaşpar, you yourself know what it's like to be an old man, bald and fat, in front of a young enchantress. You know?"

Dr. Gaşpar knows, and keeps silent.

"We haven't even met yet, and look, I've started to babble . . . I'm asking ridiculous questions. Forgive me! If we're on the topic anyway about this letter and Deste, then . . . Anyway, I withdrew the statement. There was no point in putting her through stupid questioning."

"An old man in front of the young woman?" Professor Peter Gaşpar asked himself suddenly and out loud. "Frustration? That's it, isn't it? From timidity to frustration, to revenge, a quarter of a step . . .

You changed your mind, and then you changed your mind again. In the end, you did denounce her, isn't that right?"

The Greek Gilbert Anteos had come across a Balkan neighbor, was in the mood for gossip, all of which meant that the story had ended well. *Happy endings, Hollywood; everything can be fixed.* Peter had no reason to be impatient; he'd been given a happy ending as only someone as ridiculous as he deserved. The elephant guffaws, humiliated.

"A month passed, Professor. A month! The FBI doesn't connect with the Trooper, and these guys don't connect with the other guys. For a month, neither knew about the other's existence! I withdraw the statement, and Officer Martin calls me. He asks for the name of the person who sent the postcard. Why should I give you the name, I said. I withdrew the claim, the case is closed. It was a joke, I tell you, a stupid joke, I withdrew the grievance. Police Officer Martin gets angry. 'You're not the only one involved!' he screams. 'There are others, awful things could happen. Either you give me the name or I'll arrest you.' Arrest me! We're not in North Korea or Iraq, not in the *Axes of Evil*. Neither in Sarajevo, nor Saudi Arabia. But I yielded."

"You gave her name?"

"No, I didn't give her name. I refused. Again and again, I refused. Valia was desperate. You know how immigrants are, fearful of the police. I kept on refusing. In the end, however, I promised to send the person to the police station. He took my word and left me alone. I had to convince Deste to turn herself in."

"The old man in front of the young woman," mumbled Peter. Enchanting, irresistible. The old, fat man in front of enchanting youth. "Irresistible youth, isn't that right?" Gaşpar asked himself, into the receiver.

"I explained to Deste that the story had taken on new proportions. There was no time to postpone. She must go to the police, explain everything, prove her innocence. She was questioned for eight hours. But this wasn't why I called you."

Ah, the bomb hadn't exploded yet. The banter was just preparation for the shock. Gaşpar pulls in his knees, ready to take on a new hit.

"I'm calling you on Deste's behalf. She wants to apologize. But she doesn't dare. She asked me to bring you up to date with the events."

"Of course, yes, of course," stammers Peter, short of breath. "When was the whole thing settled? When did she go to the police?"

"About ten days ago. In the end, they contacted the college. Not the FBI, but the college. The college had had no idea. I don't like Ms. Tang. She's got her nose in every pot, and so I didn't tell her anything. Other consequences. With the dean, the president. The poor girl finally understood that, in the land of jokes, there's no joking allowed. She wrote you at the hotel where you live. The president asked her to write to you, to apologize. She wrote you. You didn't receive anything, it would seem."

No, Professor Peter Gaşpar hadn't received anything but the labyrinthine threat of an eternal and invisible strike. Ten days? Poor little Deste . . . she's been putting up with consequences for ten days? What was happening with Gaşpar the elephant during this time? He remembered only the nights. Intense nights. An exile can't hope for more than ephemeral intensity. The days and nights had been intense, and, as it turned out in the end, also ephemeral. He couldn't remember a lot, and didn't even want to remember when and how he'd spoken with Jennifer Tang and Larry One and Larry Eight and Tara and the Sailor Dean and so and so; he wanted to forget everything quickly, to sweep it away, as if it had never been.

After half an hour, the old man who wasn't quite that old, just fat and bald, speaks on the phone with the enchanting assassin. This he would remember, for sure. He's determined not to forget anything about this, to speak to his erudite friend Gora about the burlesque *Commedia dell'Arte*; Saint Augustin will quickly find the bookish cross-references, enchanted by the farce's finale.

An irresistible voice. A child with an irresistible voice. The specialist on the ancient world was right. The assassin wants to invite Professor Gaşpar to *dinner*, to talk to him. More specifically, to cook for him a special meal. Balkan cuisine. Does Professor Gaşpar have a kitchen? Yes, the kitchen could be set up. Perfect. She'll take care of everything. He should just tell her when she should arrive with the ingredients. She'd prefer not to disturb him. That is, to cook while the professor isn't home.

"Yes, of course, that can be arranged, why not . . . " mumbles Gaşpar.

"There's something else, something important," adds the child. Is the professor on a diet? It wasn't that . . . she doesn't want to . . . you understand, don't you? Yes, the elephant understands and sweats, reeling from the most recent blow. How should the old, fat, bald man speak to an enchanting young woman about diet? How? He must admit the truth: it hurts him here, and there, every morning and sometimes in the middle of a seminar, gastritis, colitis, ulcer, hemorrhoids, kidney stones . . . are these subjects to discuss with the young woman from war-torn Sarajevo?

Deste waits; her enchanting voice allows itself an enchanting pause. All that can be heard is the sound of her breathing. Her breathing is diaphanous, like a summer's night.

"What did you say? What was that?"

"I didn't say anything, no, nothing," the elephant burst out. "Nothing."

"So then, nothing. No diet. Perfect!" decides the homemaker, victorious. "See you soon!" Professor Gaşpar hears the flutter of the girl mirage.

That very afternoon, he finds an envelope blue as the sky under the cabin door, bearing the name and delicate handwriting of the Sarajevo Siren. Within, some typewritten sheets.

Dear President Avakian,

Following our meeting in your office with the Dean and Ms. Tang, I sent Professor Gaşpar another letter. I reformulated the first letter, with an addendum. It seems strange that Professor Gaşpar has not received any of my previous letters. I will send this one with Express Mail. As I've told you, it wasn't my intention to provoke misunderstanding and trouble. I thank you for your help in calming the tensions.

Yours,
Deste Onal

Another letter, this one on blue paper.

Dear Professor Gaşpar,

This is the third letter I am writing regarding my tortured art project, The Lottery of Babylon. *I regret the unease that I've caused. The first letter, sent to the campus address, contained nothing but apologies. During the conversation with President Avakian and Ms. Jennifer Tang, I understood that you never received that letter. A second letter was addressed to the hotel where you live with your wife. President Avakian told me that this letter also didn't make its way to you. Annexed, I expedite the copy of the letters, as well as the proposed project.*

With deep respect,
Deste Onal

And stapled to this letter, the previous letter. The paper was white, like the soul of virgins.

Dear Professor Gaşpar,

In the framework of the artistic installation entitled The Lottery of Babylon, *I sent you, as well as other intellectuals, journalists, artists, writers, professors, and politicians, a postcard written by me containing a quotation from the short story "Death and the Compass," by J. L. Borges, "Next time I kill you, I promise you the labyrinth made of a single straight line which is invisible and everlasting." I found out that the letter made some of the addressees very uneasy. I neglected to consider such a possibility. It wasn't my intention to threaten or frighten anyone. Please accept my apologies for the trouble I have caused.*

With all of my respect,
Deste Onal

To the two pages, the white and the blue, another four typed pages were attached with a paper clip as red as the fires of hell. Thick, yellow paper.

I'm a Bosnian citizen, with Balkan, Lebanese, Jordanian, Egyptian, and Syrian roots. My olive skin and green eyes make me look downright Ottoman, which is what I consider myself, in fact. My generation asks itself why Ataturk—Mustafa Kemal (without being Jewish, as some claim) abandoned his home in Thessaloniki. I ask myself why my grandfather, my aunts and uncles, had to leave their entire histories behind in Srebrenica. If the Berlin Wall could fall, why wouldn't other walls fall? And even if they were to fall, I doubt that hatred would disappear. Hatred always conquers new captives. Even though they drank the same bitter, black coffee and ate the same mutton over centuries, and suffered together the brutality of modernity, Serbs and Greeks and Turks, Kurds, Armenians, Azerbaijani, Shiites and Sunnis, who eat the same salted cheese, inject into their children's blood the traditional hatred. The dignity of hatred! The time has come at least for us Ottomans to define our failures. The installation The Lottery of Babylon *will illustrate this conviction. I use texts from Jorge Luis Borges, his obsession with maps and labyrinths. A labyrinth of compartments and maps, held together and still independent. The red wall of the first room represents Glory, Heroism, Hatred. The bottles of booze and slivovitz and the cups with the half-moon belong to the nations assaulted by modernism.*

The telephone. Startled, Gaşpar drops the papers. He grabs the receiver, drops the receiver, picks it up again.

"Did you hear? Surely, you've heard. Miss Deste! Polyglot and cosmopolitan. She didn't make a peep. Not a whisper. Nothing. Nothing. I had no idea about her great artistic conspiracy."

"You know Deste? Deste Onal."

"Know her? She's my roommate! She's the reason I didn't want to stay nights, so that she wouldn't get suspicious. She blocked me from soothing the insomnia of the exiled Peter Gaşpar. Exile, the exiled . . . I hear this story all the time. Displacement, dispossession, death. What about rebirth, and freedom? You run from one place because it isn't good for you, isn't that right? So then, what's all the nostalgia about? Explain it to me. I'm a dutiful American. I want to understand. Miss Deste! She was scheming, without anyone's taking notice, the great aesthetic-political experiment of the century! She kept asking me who were the most interesting, most bizarre professors? People with a code. I'm quoting her, a code! That's what she said. With a code, listen to that! Peter Gaşpar, Gilbert Anteos. Mr. Avakian? Did she also send President Bedros Avakian a threat? Maybe there's something going on between them? She's capable of it. Now I think she's capable of anything! Pent up and craving admiration and dubious connections."

Peter didn't get a chance to interrupt the avalanche, bent over to pick the papers off the floor. The receiver at his ear, not to miss a single word from the indictment.

"Without even a word! A vowel, a comma. Nothing! The Ottoman Empire! Secrets, plots, traps. Perfidy, dear Professor Gaşpar, that's what it is. Elegant, collegiate, brilliant, seductive, yes, yes, a joy, that's our sweet Deste. The Oriental witch from the Oriental forest, in the next bed over. Right next to me! The American who believes in what she can see, not in the invisible labyrinth."

"Did you find any letters from Deste among my mail last week?"

"Letter? I don't know. A pile accumulated, I didn't have time to sort it. I'll do it, I promise. The letter from the conspirator? Let's see what she has to say."

"She called me on the phone."

"On the phone? What nerve! After everything she did?"

"She said she didn't realize. She didn't expect the proportions it would take . . . "

"She expected it, you can be sure! Not only expected it, she was provoking it. To see what would come of the provocation. The Unknown! To become visible, to break out on the scene. She's waiting for her big break. She's waiting for it even now."

"She wants to explain, to apologize. She proposed a meeting."

"A meeting? What kind of meeting? After what she did? After everything she did to you?"

"Precisely. She wants to explain."

"She should explain it to the police! Or to the judge, in court. I hope you didn't accept."

"I accepted."

Silence. Not a sound. Tara had probably thrown the phone, out of outrage. No, she hadn't thrown it.

"How could you do that? How? After all you've suffered . . . did she hypnotize you? What did she do? Tell me, tell me. I'm curious. The Balkan enchantress has spells that are different from the little American girls. This, yes, I understand. Believe me, I understand. I don't understand, however, how a man who's just gone through the Balkan storm can concede so easily. He falls just like that, at the first breeze, the first lure? The first one! Or were there other conversations? Other phone calls?"

"No, there weren't."

The old, Balkan man takes advantage of the fact of not having been as yet confronted with the young woman's presence, only her voice. He'd yielded, the geezer, at the first breeze of elixir, it was true, the elixir of youth without aging and life without death. Basta, liquidated, my girl, finished. No, no, he won't yield any more. That's a solemn promise. He'll resist, the way he resisted the American young woman for so long. He'll resist the Balkan as well, that's all. Done, finished, he'll resist. He promises that he will. Basta.

"You're right. I made a mistake. Besides, she sent me a written explanation. I don't know what else she'd have to add."

Tara doesn't seem impressed with the professor's regrets. She's silent.

"Yes, I should recant. I should call her, find a pretext for a permanent postponement."

"You don't need a pretext. You don't need any more pretexts and labyrinths."

"You're right," yammers the elephant.

They plan to meet that evening. No, not in the cabin. Professor Gaşpar prefers, this time, the library's cafeteria. Tara's not surprised. She accepts. Fair play American! Peter drops the receiver in the cradle, exhausted. He stretches out on the couch, with his eyes closed. Boredom, dear Jennifer Tang, the boredom of new information is even more oppressive than the void. He shouldn't have accepted the meeting with the Mata Hari. And once he'd accepted, like an old, easily swayed dotard, to eat the poison that the Sarajevo spy would prepare for him, he shouldn't have read the project. The Babylonic pages were boring. A cold shower, after which a bath of narcotics. Not cold, just lukewarm, banal, to allay his illusions. The antidote to the attraction is here, on paper. He just has to reach out his hand.

The second room is called the Library of Babel. The hexagonal space, Borges' logic about the universe and mathematical order. Shelves, monitors, video, scenes from Citizen Kane, Grand Illusion, Ivan's Childhood, Modern Times, Battleship Potemkin, Roma: Open City, The Seventh Seal, L'Avventura, Zorba the Greek. *Scenes rolling on two monitors. A labyrinth of the images of history and our confusion.*

Boredom, numbness, from top to bottom and from the bottom to the top and laterally. He ought to do something, call the ambulance, run to Borges' grave, call Gora. Yes, he should offer the enigma's answer to the professor. Saint Augustin deserved at least this much. Or better yet, he should call the former Mrs. Gora, to ask her if the letter from the young Bosnian woman has arrived at the miserable Hotel Esplanade. Or did no such letter even exist? A candid, voracious, and enchanting spider, my adorable Deste! En-chan-ting, pure and simple, yes, and candid and vo-ra-cious. Oho, he likes that word, he repeats it, syllabically: vo-ra-cious. Suddenly, a terrible, sickly longing for Lu. Family, his only family . . . He sees her, as if through a fog, in the divine moments of long ago. He closes, opens his eyes, waves the impossible away with his hand. Should he rather raise his eyes toward the burning sky, to watch his likenesses advancing in vain on their thin, infinite, in-fi-nite, stilts, the female toward the male, the male toward the female, without ever getting any closer? Delicate and transparent articulations. Long, diaphanous. Giant, velvety ears, vel-ve-ty. Prehistoric tusks. The funereal burden on their backs, the silt of tears pouring from the flaccid trunk. The female's trunk turns, the twisted neck of a swan. The male apathetically lowers his trunk toward the ground below.

The third room is dedicated to the Book of Sands. In the middle, a large volume with canvas leaves, reproducing military documents, maps, statistics, weapons, clippings from old newspapers, diagrams, portraits, obituaries from right after World War I. The projectors in the ceiling often send different images to the pages of the book. No visitor sees the same page. I'm illustrating the individual's perception and the collective perception of History.

Oof! He feels the need for some amusement. The urgency of some amusement. A voice. He needs a real woman's voice. Lu's inaccessible voice, which he hasn't heard in ages.

In a few hours, Tara will appear, his young American comrade, but now, right now, he needs to hear Lu in the receiver. Maybe not, maybe even Lu wouldn't save him. "I need irresponsibility," the elephant says, finally.

An irresistible voice, Gilbert said, about Deste. The stiff phrases on the page don't, however, make the best pleas for the mysterious dinner.

The last compartment, an obscure place. Death and the Compass—*a favorite text from Borges. Detective Lonrot tries to untangle the labyrinth of crimes that will bring him to his death. The projectors cast images of enigmatic codes onto the walls, maps, obituaries, decorations, weapons, war craft, planes. Chasms and idyllic valleys, ski and vacation resorts. The modern labyrinth, one metropolis after another with hundreds of Babel Towers touching the sky. A large, phosphorescent banner from one end of the room to the other:* NEXT TIME I KILL YOU, I PROMISE YOU THE LABYRINTH MADE OF THE SINGLE STRAIGHT LINE WHICH IS INVISIBLE AND EVERLASTING. *On the floor, 40 envelopes to various addressees and, eventually, their responses. Sudanese, Americans, Russians, Latvians, Greeks, Nigerians, Armenians, Jews, Chinese, Bosnians, Argentines, Rwandans, Australians, Italians, Cambodians. Short biographies of each. An enormous blue ribbon crosses the space. Large, white letters: Exiles of the world, unite!*

The papers tremble in the trembling hand. Weary, he lets them fall to the floor. He dials Gora's number. A long ring, once, three times. He puts down the receiver. He raises it again, dials the number again. A long ring, once, three times, four times.

Recorded on the tape, Gora's voice invites the caller to leave his name and number where he can be reached.

"Important news, your Holiness. The whore with the scythe mocked me. She rejected me, the Nymphomaniac. She made a fool of me. She refused me, humiliated me. She made a laughing stock out of me, Saint Augustin. She's leaving me to wander, she's in no mood for me. She insulted me, rejected me, as you'd reject a sickly runt."

Click, the receiver. In the mirror, Oliver the Elephant, the tightrope walker, tosses and turns, powerless and overcome.

Peter collects the papers from the ground, lays them on his chest. His certificate of immunity. Exhausted, he closes his eyes.

■

The meeting with Deste took place in three stages, during his afternoon nap.

The gong rings: the agreed upon hour. Peter knocks lightly on the golden door. He doesn't wait for it to open. He turns the charmed key in the charmed lock. Courageously, he enters the room. Brief courage. Only a moment's worth. He stiffens on the threshold.

The conspirator had swept the floor of the cloister cell and washed the dishes in the sink. She'd rearranged the books on the shelf, the carpet on the floor, the cover on the bed. The windows were no longer dusty, the giant shoes and boots and slippers were aligned, obediently, all in a row in front of the coat rack. The clothes put neatly in their place, as if in a dream. On the table, clean plates and glasses, napkins as yellow as lemons, an immaculate tablecloth. Fairy tale. Red wine, black bread.

Destiny had thrown the die. No, Death hadn't abandoned him. She was, evidently, positioned on the ramp, cloaking herself conscientiously, in order to maintain the game and the tricks. She'd improved the décor, prepared the range and the oven for the fatal supper. Picturesque, tasty morsels, a Byzantine dinner party. Perfect décor, perfect Deste, perfect Death.

Peter takes off his windbreaker, hesitates, turns his back on hell for a moment to hang his windbreaker on the coat rack, keeps his back to the table and the peril.

"I'm going to wash my hands, I'll be back in a moment."

Immaculate bathtub, towels folded on the stool. The yellow glass with the brushes and toothpaste. The red robe on the hook. The cabinet behind the mirror. Neatly aligned, razors, deodorants, the green aftershave bottle.

The mirror above the sink shines, hostile. Deep, blue rings under his eyes.

Nearby, he feels the presence of a woman's body, the hysteria of desire, he twists in his sleep, tortured by the aged Nymphomaniac in the guise of a virgin.

He writhes. Lubricous, a lubricous old man in his sleep.

"Done, I'm ready!"

Professor Peter Gaşpar in the frame of the door.

The salad bowl, the basket full of sliced black bread. Individual clean pieces of cutlery and glasses. The carafe full of water and the small, empty carafe. The yellow paper napkins.

"No, I didn't bring candles," the student explained.

She unties the short, white apron over the short, black skirt, pulled up over her knees. Round, pale knees. Three-quarter black socks. She's no Ottoman missionary, but more of a Parisian lady's maid serving Donatien Alphonse François, Marquis de Sade. Blackness, just like at the cinema, interrupting the scene. Interrupted, yes, Peter is sleeping and isn't sleeping, yes, he's asleep, then again, sapped, asleep and unharmed, back in the scene.

"I made eggplant salad. Couldn't go wrong with that one."

"The salad of nostalgia."

"I asked an American friend to take me to the organic grocer. The cooking and peeling of the eggplants weren't easy. An operation at a low flame. And where was I to find a mallet? The little, wooden yataghan, absolutely of wood, otherwise the taste is altered. I tasted it over and over, a hundred times. We make our salad with garlic, you with onion. I diced the onion, mincing, mincing."

"Let's have a drink. Where I come from, we start with hard liquor. Țuică, plum brandy."

"I know, it's like șliboviţa, but more subtle. Even though, where I come from . . . "

"Yes, yes . . . religion . . . "

"The family I grew up in wasn't very religious. Bosnia went through a socialist secularization. Then de-Titoization, desecularization. But not in our house."

"I understand, we'll have wine, then."

"I prepared a carafe! A small one, for wine. That's how I like it," the assassin chirped.

"You prepared everything perfectly, like a crime."

Interruption, snoring, pitch blackness, whimper, Peter motions with his large hands like shovels, swimming to escape.

"I forgot to give you money for the groceries."

"I made the invitation. I have money from my husband."

"Ah, he's here, in America."

"He left. Austria. He has a café in Linz. He orders flowers over the phone and sends money. The beast! Just like all the rest from where I come. But I prefer those kinds of men. I can't stand a Mr. Know-How. Mirko is complicated, insufferable. Serbian. The Bosnian conflict destroyed him."

The story from Scheherazade's thousand and one nights. The victim's large body unwinds. An old, bloated child, in his cradle once again.

Scheherazade looks straight into the eyes of the victim. Peter cowers . . . the small pale fingers massage his temples.

"My American ennui has embittered me, provoked me. The exhibit, the demented letters, I wanted to see what would happen, to detonate the void, the discipline, the naïveté of the Yankees."

Peter looks down at his shoes, prehistoric fossils sheltering old ghosts.

Hearing annihilates sight, the old man doesn't raise his gaze, and he avoids the green ray. He tries, finally, to raise it. His leaden lids heavy, impossible to budge them. The student has the head of a boy, hair cut short in a French bob, thin Tibetan brows, hemlock green eyes, a delicate neck, a silk eyelet T-shirt, the skirt too short. A nymphet.

He gets up, he doesn't get up, the chaos is starting. That's how the chaos of youth used to start so long ago.

Unhurried, he raises the burden of his body. He feels the green arrow in his chest cavity, in his brain, in his kidneys, which are crushed by the belt that digs into his skin.

A last effort, the movement flips him out of bed and onto the floor. Shaken, awake, happy, a miracle!

■

Didactic guidelines. Smiles to the left and right. A polite greeting and a polite smile, left to right and all around. The door of the office wide open for any visit. Lower the gaze, so you don't see cleavage, bare breasts, bare legs hanging casually on the back of the chair to the left of the table. Embracing couples in the alleys of the campus. The nocturnal moans of orgies. The screen. TV commercials. Fresh vegetables and toothpaste. Water skis. A nude young woman, smiling at the amateurs. Avalanches of libertine, apocalyptic images, defying the rhetoric of the moralists. Bare breasts must be ignored, the same with the nymphs' belly buttons pierced with colored rings, Gauguin's nymphs, bare feet shuffling through wet grass, knees springing out rhythmically on the bicycle, the mane of blue, green, and orange hair.

The carnival of final copulation before life's end. The teachings of the Lord and proletarian ethics and political correctness. The indecent, public announcement of the moralist public debate.

It's the end of the world, my dear old vagrant! Nero's Rome, the Athens of the end. Prudence rules without the rule of capitalist pragmatism, the contrasts of freedom in the free world.

Instincts don't die, however. Brutal and living impulses persist. Professor Gaşpar sees himself as a blind and naked recluse along the college alleyways! The male instrument shudders in the fog. An empty weapon in plain sight. A maniac escaped from the exile of the hypocrites, liberated at last from the therapy of convention. Irresponsible, just as he'd wished. The eyes of a hungry wolf, hands trembling impatiently around his prey.

Afternoon, at the library café, the professor no longer has the eyes of a wolf, and his hands don't shake. He watches Tara calmly, smiling, waiting for the questions and advice.

"Did you call off the Oriental soiree? Did you have the courage to refuse hypnosis?"

The guilty party gives no response, just smiles indulgently.

"If you haven't done it already, it will be very difficult to back out. The conciliatory supper is fatal! She's going to anesthetize you. My delicate roommate knows what she wants and will persevere. She'll entrance you and then will deposit you, her trophy, into her biography, under the chapter "In Case of Need." You don't know what a plotter she is, you don't know her at all."

"Why are we here? Last night we decided to meet in the city at a restaurant."

"I have no appetite when I'm confused. I want us to clarify things. To know if you called off the interview."

"Don't worry. Nothing disastrous will happen."

"You already saw her, or you're planning on seeing her? When?"

"I'll cancel the date. I shouldn't have accepted. She took me by surprise, and I was curious. Curious and childish."

"You've said this before. Meaning you haven't canceled the fairy tale soiree."

"I don't understand why you hate her. She poisoned a few months of mine, not yours. I'm entitled to refuse her offer."

"Entitled, yes, but you're curious. You want to see the phantom who sent perfumed letters from the other world up close. I have no reason to be curious. I know the conniver."

"You thought you knew her. Then your image of her was up-turned and proven false. Once again, you think you know her, but maybe she's someone else. Let's get dinner. You have your car, I assume."

"Yes, let's go. After dessert we'll escape. To the wilds of Nevada. I hope that appeals."

"Impressive and frightening."

"American girls are all about fair play. They announce their intentions, not like the slaves of the Orient, who surrender only to dominate."

"American girls are more dangerous. Insufferable, in fact. They always feel entitled, vindictive. No misgivings, no melancholy. No flirting. Flirting is ambiguity, isn't it? Unacceptable, incorrect?! Politically, morally, and religiously incorrect. The American suffragettes have very just and personal criteria, and they respond promptly when ignored or offended, or when they think they are ignored or offended."

"Oho . . . now that's going too far. I invited you to run away to Nevada where we can live like savages for a few months. The adventure compensates for the flaws. A regimen of freedom and primitivism. We'll retreat to my little provincial hometown. Full of convention and good sense. I'll introduce you to my aunt. My mother's unwed sister. You'll like her. She contradicts the cliché. She has both misgivings and melancholy. Just like I do, besides . . . but also a sense of fair play. Clarity, humor, vitality. Wisdom. And she's attractive. America is offering you an American partner."

"So then, we're going out to eat."

"We're going, but first we'll go to the bear's den. So that I can get the scent of the betrayal. I parked the car in front of Professor Gaşpar's cabin. Let's go to the bear cave first. Just for a second, no need to stay longer. I can sniff out foreign tracks very quickly."

The red car in front of the cabin. Gaşpar opens the door to the den, wide open.

"You want to come in? Come in and pick up the scent."

Tara hesitates. Smiles and hesitates. Concentrating. You can tell by the furrow in her brow, above her nose. When thoughtfulness becomes worry, that furrow becomes visible.

The professor on the threshold, in front of the wide open door. He makes the grand gesture of a hotelier.

"No, I'm not coming in. I'm not with the police. I'm not even Professor Gaşpar's student any longer. Nor the mailman. I have no entitlement, to use Sir Gaşpar's term."

The restaurant is empty, Tara is direct and full of fair play, even if not always sincere, while Peter is no Pieter, Gaşpar is no Mynheer Peeperkorn, doesn't have the ease, the Dutchman's irresponsible grace, nor the vitality to sweep away his blunders. The interbellum character multiplied himself, all around, not just in the pages of long ago, in the picturesque variations of the present: a man married for the fifth time, to a woman younger than his daughter from marriage number two, husband renewed by Viagra—the new Peeperkorn.

The quiet Italian restaurant, lit discreetly by a single candle on each table, promises a good premise for the Nevada experiment. First glass of wine. Silence, the tick-tock of thoughts, hesitations flickering in the gaze. The professor extends his hand, the student doesn't withdraw it, nor does she yell or seem appalled at the touch. No talk of morality or Protestant Puritanism.

The professor squeezes the student's fingers and leans toward the playful curls. He allows himself to be won over too quickly instead of becoming, through purely his presence, the possessor of the prey. Tara appears grateful for what Peter had changed in her over the course of the last few months. Natural, alive, more present and stronger than the clichés that overwhelm the vocabulary and imagination of so many of her generation, she'd learned to protect her companion with the naturalness of a comrade. A comrade who was deepening their intimacy that evening.

Tara's car remained parked in front of Professor Gaşpar's cabin over the following weeks. Gossip was kindling and intensifying, but President Larry One impeded the indictment. He frowns wearily when Jennifer Tang informs him laconically and dutifully during the pause of a routine check-in that Professor Gaşpar was seen walking aimlessly and negligently around campus, his pant legs dragging on the ground, his fly down, restive and bored, and a car parked outside his house, precisely the car of the suspect tied to the letters.

At the end of year celebrations, Tara receives her graduation diploma, Deste announces that she's transferring to another university for her last year of study. Gaşpar disappears from campus not long after that.

No one knows whether it's merely a temporary leave, for the duration of the summer, or if he's disappeared *forever*.

■

A temporary absence or gone *forever*? No one can answer, not Gora's obituaries, which compete with destiny, nor the disloyal narrator, as Palade used to call me. The narrator who manipulates reality.

During those dizzying days, Gora called me. We'd known each other for a long time, through Mihnea Palade, the Bukovina native who'd finished high school a few years after me, in our little town of trees and idylls. He was the one who introduced me to the suspects' attic.

Palade had stopped me in the center of the capital, in front of the Italian church. We hadn't seen each other since his arrival at the university. On a long walk around the beautiful Ioanid Park, not far from where he'd found me, I shared with him my elation over the anonymity of a large city, and he told me all about his new circle of friends with whom he debated literature and religion and philosophy and art. He seemed vitalized and enthusiastic, happy that the same temptations appealed even to a polytechnic man such as I was. He was studying mathematics himself, not quite born with Leopardi's milk bottle in his mouth, either. And he sought to forge a sort of cultural solidarity between us, not just a geographic one. He gave me the address of the attic, adding maliciously, "It's not like drinking with women. It's much, much worse."

A few boys, a couple of girls. The excessively esoteric discussions, and the juvenile assurance by which those discussions were amplified, bored me, and the open anti-Communism seemed suspect. Blowhard interventions, like some spoken essays, irritated me. I don't have any special recollection of that night, except for my obsession with Lu.

Neither Gora nor Palade forgot the bizarre state of embarrassment and skepticism of the bibliophile that I was. Gora had participated—with increasing fervor, as I was to find out—in the heated controversies, which he himself directed gradually away from politics and toward literature. That was where Mihnea Palade expounded on Borges' *Death and the Compass* and Kafka's *The Trial* or Orwell's allegory, Dima's books and life. That was where he reencountered Lu, whom he'd known from some Saturday night parties with other young people captivated by music and dance. I still haven't forgotten his first descriptions of her.

"She's beautiful, but there are times when she isn't. When she can't avoid or hide her timidity, her spark leaves her. She's used to glowing, she's unstable, fighting with her instability. Other times . . .

other times she's happy, sociable, her thoughts elsewhere and no-where. Liberated by absence, then drawn in deeper into herself. I felt her emotion, and her emotiveness. Just when she seems to be made of steel, perfect, in control of herself. In a familiar context, however, she's irresistible. Sovereign and self-sufficient? Not at all, not at all! Fragile, with an unwieldy discipline for appearances. Emotion, then. An extraordinary sexual premise, no?"

Even later, Palade never hid his envy in relation to Gora, tied not only to the mysterious Lu, but also, once he arrived in America, to Dima. Even though he'd given the entitlement of his will to Palade, it seemed that Dima secretly preferred Gora. His wife in exile, Merrie, a distinguished Englishwoman, elegant and credulous and fashionable, also seemed to trust Gora more. After the Old Man's death she allowed him to consult the secret *Green Notebook*, written during the war years. Gora promised not to tell anyone about it and never to write anything about the secret text. He never mentioned the *Green Notebook*, not in his meetings with Palade, nor in the bibliography he suggested to Gaşpar for the review.

I was bewildered by Gaşpar's sudden disappearance, but also by the fact that after Gora related to me the sensational and troubling news, he moved on immediately to the subject of Dima, with no apparent segue. As if there had existed some connection between the two subjects that he wasn't mentioning.

"Dima had access to all the information about the war, he knew the horrors committed by the Germans in the East, but . . . not a word in all his notes, no concern for the fate of Marga Stern, his lover in his youth. He'd shared her for some time, it seemed, with his pre-decessor, he'd become jealous, forced her to choose, and she'd preferred him. Then to read that he was horrified merely by Sta-lingrad! What about what would happen to Marga, and not *just* to Marga, if the Germans had won? Not a word about that in his diary."

Was Dima's admirer disassociating himself from the Maestro because of Peter Gaşpar's disappearance!? Because of the review that he himself should have written instead of guiding the neophyte

Gaşpar according to his own designs? Was the Old Man worried for his people?! Wasn't Marga Stern a citizen of his country? Wasn't she a member of Dima's people?

Gora didn't suspect that I knew everything about Marga Stern the whole time that he was informing me about it; his pathos was amusing to me.

"It's not a matter of a single person, but of all the people of which the world simply disposes. With indifference, no?"

Gora appeared ransacked by memories and resentments, fueled by Gaşpar's disappearance.

"People of which other people disposed, pure and simple. Ideas are ideas, abstractions, games of the mind. The real test of ideas is people, how people relate to people."

For a loner such as Gora, this affirmation signaled serious trouble. I telephoned him after that, he called me, too, we kept debating Gaşpar's disappearance.

I was convinced that I was a mere replacement. He couldn't talk to Lu about the disappearance or perhaps he'd tried and wouldn't allow himself to try again, and he needed someone else from his former country. He would have preferred Palade, he didn't know about my last meetings with Palade.

■

When he decided to return to his native country for a week to see his family and to introduce his fiancée, after two decades of being away, Palade called wanting to meet with me. I'd been here for only two years at that time, and I was dazed by the lessons of the unknown.

I'd written him that I'd arrived in the New World, he answered, we spoke on the phone several times, he put me in touch with Gora, and then the dialogue ended.

We met in Central Park, not far from the children's playground, in front of the characters from *Alice in Wonderland*. He'd come to New York specifically, he alleged, for that unexpected rendezvous.

His oddities and extravagances were multiplying, I'd discovered, but I made no sign of surprise or protest.

It was spring, a superb day, neither hot, nor cold, nor rainy. We saw each other, smiled at each other, embraced. Palade seemed hurried, he went right to the point.

"I'm going home to our humorous little homeland. Maybe to die there."

I wasn't expecting such a direct approach, I was determined to intervene as little as possible.

"You might ask why I chose precisely you. Very few know that we're from the same town. We haven't seen each other in a long time. Since that memorable evening when I tried to introduce you to the literary youth of the moment. You retreated. The group seemed suspect to you."

I hadn't remembered being quite so expressive. He was, however, exactly right about the motive for my disappearance from the enchanting attic. The wisdom of cowardice. I avoided risky situations, which, in any case, were many.

"Unfortunately, you were right. The Secret Service files that remain and that weren't forged show that you were right. Yet another reason for this meeting."

He watched me, frowning, and lit a cigarette.

"Maybe you've heard that I occupy myself with esoteric adventures. I read the coded signs of destiny. The signs around me, as obscure as they are, signal danger . . . *They* can liquidate me here, too, naturally, but also there."

I waited for him to clarify. He didn't.

"In our past, everything was about compromise and complicity. The very fact of breathing that air . . . all compromise and complicity. Why did they give me a passport? Usually, it was a bargaining process. You gave them something, they gave you something. There were all kinds of schemes, as well. A Byzantine country, life under the table as opposed to on the table. Relations, interests, the chain of weaknesses. Don't ask me any more about it."

I had no intention of asking anyone anything, except myself.

"Language wasn't my essential loss. I left that place a young man, I wrote here from the very beginning. I've published books, I have more in a drawer . . . It's a great danger always to be asked for manuscripts and to have everything you write be accepted. Dima, for example . . . published too much. Apropos, the sentinels were, of course, interested in my relation to him. They wanted to organize his festive return to the Homeland. They didn't care about his anti-Communist past. The masquerade would have legitimized their regime. As a young man, Dima imagined himself as a reformer, only the reform was reactionary."

He'd stopped, to think, or to remember.

"Have you heard about Heal, the physician? And his group? They walk on burning embers without feeling anything. We were also walking on burning embers in that attic, weren't we? However, we were afraid, suspicious, sensing the duplicity. In California they do research about the technical modification of consciousness. What do you think about this country? It would be more worthwhile to talk just about the New World, the old one has gotten old for good; it was always old. There, in the old attic of the old country, I started the cult of Dima. But neither of us knew about Marga Stern. I think that Gora invented her. Potentialities become realities in his obituaries. I agree that life isn't made solely from the real and visible. But potentialities are codified. Gora is under the trance of books . . . though he also has some revealing insights."

A long, long silence. Endless. Palade had grown silent and was no longer looking at me. I had disappeared for him.

"Indifference is human, isn't it?"

He didn't hear me.

"Estrangement, human, as well. Human. Isn't that right, Mihnea? We're human."

"Yes, yes . . . the Nazi horrors in the East weren't Dima's priorities. He wasn't vilifying the people of Marga Stern's religion. They just weren't his priorities, that's all."

He lit his cigarette and was seeing me again.

"Soon the last survivors will disappear. Do we forget or do we retain the symbol without which we won't understand ourselves?"

He shook the ash and angrily tossed the unfinished cigarette.

"Yes, indifference, estrangement. Self-obsession. Still, he was generous, eager to help, sensitive. He was like that in the past, too, when he was propagating nightmares wrapped in green foil, with saints' faces. I believe in parallel worlds. Multiple worlds. Then, also duplicity. Not always a negative thing. Man isn't an unequivocal being. He has fissures and secrets. Obscure potentialities. You think I'm an obnoxious sophist, don't you?"

He'd lit another cigarette in the meantime, he'd remembered to offer me one, too; I was happy that I'd quit smoking. He watched me with excessive attention.

"You, sir, ought to understand Dima's ambiguities. People always expected you to be perfect, and you couldn't be. Angels don't write books."

Only after many years I was to discover that Gaşpar had used that aphorism, which evidently wasn't originally his own.

I didn't like to be addressed formally, but, like Mihnea, I was also drawn by contradictions and fissures and secrets and unexpected potentialities, only for me, people seemed more important than ideas. "*People are more important*, Mihnea," that was what I wanted to tell Mihnea Palade. I didn't get the chance.

"Imagine that, they didn't allow me to see the archives! Me! I was his loyal admirer and apprentice. They didn't let me see the archives from the moment that I began to ask questions. I advised him to stop seeing that old, fanatic doctor. The correspondent for the Iron Guard in the United States! Absolutely ridiculous! I assume you've heard of the doctor in question."

My silence was a sign of consent. Palade wasn't looking for consent, however, he merely wanted to spill his poisons. I'd become posterity's witness.

"I hear that Gora saw the secret archive. I doubt that he saw it."

He was jealous. He'd adored Dima, he didn't expect someone else to be favored.

A good moment to attack. I asked him whether Gora could have been an informant. It was a way of asking him, indirectly, about himself.

"Could he have been? Anyone could have been. Not because he was predestined, but because destiny was enslaved to the Supreme Institution. The Devil had become a little intermediary, a bully and a bureaucrat, and man has unimaginable capacities. Integrity and duplicity, just as surprising. Think of the adulterer . . . parallel lives. Sometimes, for years, decades. Pent-up mysteries in the fragmented depths. Parallel worlds. Computers are going to perfect these opportunities, all the way to an absolute bewilderment. You've heard, I'm sure."

I'd heard a little bit, but not much; I was prepared to hear anything and commit it to memory.

"You put on some special gloves and the computer program suddenly gives you access to the world into which you've entered. You operate in a different world. Through the gloves, the hands take hold of the objects of other worlds, they touch and handle and modify them."

He digressed. Was it an allusion to Gora? It wasn't clear.

"Ah, yes, but you asked about Gora. I was his student, we were close. He left before me, as you know. They say through the interventions of his wife's relations. I don't think so. It would have been too much if they'd wished to separate her from him. In any case, the suspicion remains. Just as in my case. The great victory by the system. Generalized suspicion has a longer life than the system itself. An unflinching, motionless posterity."

He looked me straight in the eyes once again. Not to dispel suspicions, but seemingly, to fuel them.

"Gora is a civilized man, through and through. With all of the hypocrisy and lacquer that civilization implies, naturally. I wonder, is the obsession with Lu credible? There are plenty of erotic services available, with superb and costly young women fit for a solitary aristocrat. An aristocrat, yes, not by birth, but by erudition. Gora's nights? Secretive nights, you can be sure. Books need the company of women. Women, not just one woman. Lu isn't just one woman, but many. What I know is that Gora left legally, with the approval of the authorities. He tried to bring Lu. Did he need the Institution's help? I don't know. Dima tried to help him. Gora was bitterly opposed to any visit by Dima to his Communist Homeland. No, no, no, not at any price, Gora would yell, red with indignation. Dima wasn't as intransigent. Old as he was, he'd lost hope in the death of Communism. He was homesick for the places of long ago, he thought a visit would also serve his international prestige. The Institution's propagandist alibis succeeded in convincing the Occident that our adored dictator, the Genius of the Carpathians, was building a special socialist democracy. A special democracy, within a special socialism. We were becoming, one would say, a special species."

I'd heard of Dima's intention to negotiate a compromise for a celebratory visit in his, that is, our country, and Gora's opposition was proof of his integrity. None of this was news.

"Have you heard of the former Polish dictator of Free Europe? Great assets in the anti-Communist crusade. Have you heard about the latest discovery?"

I was all eyes and ears.

"A very cultivated man, of a great presence. The author of a very appreciated monograph about Joseph Conrad. The best, some say. The Polish Communist government, exasperated by the programs on Radio Free Europe, condemns the anti-Communist director to death. Condemned to death, in contumacy! But what do the archives of the Polish Secret Service show today, however? That the distinguished intellectual and anti-Communist had been an informant! Nicely worked over, don't you think? How was it that they didn't assassinate him? Some they killed because they refused, and others after they did their work."

Palade was mixing up the chronology, in fact: the suspect had first been an informant for the Polish Secret Service, then refused to continue, then escaped and worked for the enemy.

"You were right to steer clear of the attic of suspects. Who was and who wasn't an informant? Me, Gora? You? Weren't you questioned? Weren't you visited by agents? Who knows what they wrote or modified in their reports. Even now they modify them, I'm sure . . . Those who might have forced us to become informants are in their mansions. The scribes who praised the Party and the genial Comrade Number One, who beat their breasts, in pubs or in safer places, with one, two, five Secret Service generals . . . they don't have files saying they were informants. Or they had them but they've disappeared. Eh, what do you say? A good, Byzantine tradition found an alliance with a good, Communist tradition. Or a policing tradition. Or both."

He was smiling, Mr. Palade, satisfied with the discourse. He'd come to divert my doubts, not to sweep them away. I had to ask the question that I kept postponing.

"But what about Lu? What do you think about her?"

He was increasingly hurried, he responded immediately.

"She was in the attic, as well."

"Well, they weren't *all* informants . . . "

"Not at all! It would have become a theatrical cast. No, no. I wanted to say only that we saw each other there. That was where Gora met her, and he hasn't left her even to this day. It isn't just some sort of bookish delirium, as one would think, nor the claustrophobia or agoraphobia of those lost in books. That would be understandable, we're not far from that disease ourselves. But with him it's something else. Lu isn't a woman, but rather many women. Not a negligible opportunity! I know her from the evenings in the attic, but also from the nights of dancing in the more fashionable circles. A beauty. She would appear in groups and dance to rock music and do the twist and the shake and the hula-hoop. Serene, happy, pleasant. With certain abrupt reactions, as if from a shock. I recall one evening in particular. After midnight, after hours of dancing and flirting, the atmosphere had become propitious for the act that might follow. Some couples retreated to rooms, many of them, children of state officials. Sometimes there were even homes of former noble families that had somehow succeeded in holding on to their properties, through God knew what arrangements. Dance and love. Couples would swing partners, some orgies would commence. Lu took notice of the movement. She became instantly pale. She grabbed her purse and bolted. I called her the following morning, worried. She told me that she walked by herself for an hour, in the middle of the night, from the neighborhood by the lakes all the way to the Arc de Triomphe. It was only then that a taxi appeared. She had no money on her, so she offered the driver her bracelet. That was how she got home, finally, around dawn."

I understood that I wasn't to expect clearer responses from the inhabitant of parallel worlds.

Palade wasn't assassinated in his Homeland, from where he returned more troubled than when he'd left. He informed me that he had a few hours free at Kennedy Airport, where he was changing planes on his way toward Middle America.

A murky day, torrential downpours and storms before the unexpected arrival of Mynheer Peter Gaşpar and his cousin in America.

The flights had long delays, some were canceled entirely. I waited many hours at the airport.

"It was a good trip. That is to say, bad, but beneficial. It woke me up, as if there were further need for that. That revolution, if we can call it that, was postmodern. That is, it is postmodern. It continuously produces its own parody. The impostures, the codifications, the relativities, the uncertainties. A postmodern revolution in a superrealist country, what do you say?"

I wasn't saying anything. A superrealist country in a postmodern revolution described by a researcher of the esoteric and the paranormal deserves attention.

"They're proud of the revolution, they invoke thousands of martyrs, but they've told me of massive infiltrations of terrorists, KGB conspiracies, as well as the involvement of the Occident and the Orient, the South and the North. They're talking about a transition, but more toward the year 1938 as opposed to toward the year 2000, modeled after Dima's thinking. We've passed through the moments of daze and fury . . . They were looking at Ayesha, my dear Indian, as if she'd just walked out of a cave."

I was trying to guess what, nevertheless, had been the benefit of the visit. Palade didn't wait for the question.

"It made me happy to see certain friends. I returned to my youth, the places we both loved. And the attic of the great polemic debates. Their dreams and ambiguities."

The word *ambiguities* was promising, I was hoping some confession was to follow. It didn't.

"And then, I received signs. Signals. Calls. I didn't decipher all of them. My brother . . . you know, my twin brother. Twins with the same cosmic premise. Well, he began to dream odd things, while I was there."

I was afraid, I had been afraid in the previous meeting, as well, of such immersions in the world of magic and the phantasmagoric.

"Fiction is a part of reality, as you well know, as you yourself manipulate reality. *An unreliable narrator,* as they say here. Gora does the same thing, but he pretends it isn't fiction. Fiction is created by and received from the real, from people, but also from the imaginary. Dream and imagination and presentiment, these things are human. Even science can't advance in any other way. To discover something, you must be able first to imagine a new possibility."

I raised the cup of coffee to my lips, I sipped, without looking at Palade. The sickly pallor of his face had struck me when he first came out of the gate, and would preoccupy me long afterward. He understood that I wasn't interested in complicated theories, but in the experience of his journey.

"You believe, then, in these signs . . . "

"I know, I look for adventure, even in or through objects. Ads lure me, their lies, their successful bankruptcy. Their cipher! If I go out to buy an ice cream, I return with a load of other useless things. Just because I saw them along the way. Or, at least, with eight ice creams of different flavors and colors. Just as if I were forcing an encounter with the unforeseen, the unseen. I disturb the sleep of things. Just now, when I was home, my mother asked me one day to look for some knitting needles in the city. Thick gauge needles, for a woolen vest she was knitting. I was lured by the encounter with the knitting needles. It had been two hundred years since I'd made such a banal and fantastic trip, to buy knitting needles for my old mother. On my way back, on the corner of the street, a gypsy. Young, enticing. She was begging for money. She stopped me, I looked at her, I gave her money, more than she'd dreamed, she looked at me with flames in her eyes. 'Want me to read your palm?' I stretched out my palm, I looked at her again and again, at length, disbelieving, she hesitated to speak, she seemed horrified. You're born in the same month as me, she mumbled. Not the year, just the day and the month. And she told me the day and the month."

"And when is your birthday?" I asked, to break the tension.

"The beginning of January," Palade hurried to return to the story. "'Capricorn. I see blood. Blood on your temple,' the witch said. 'You're on a kingly throne, and blood is pouring from your temple. A bad omen. Guard yourself from enemies, young man. From enclosed spaces, from strangers,' said the oracle."

"So, then, you believe in these signs, you read the ads."

"The life of the mind has its own dangers. Not just the apparent truth, but also the hidden, dangerous one. Coincidences, errors make up a codified game."

"And whom else did you meet from the attic?"

"Ah, you're thinking of Lu, you seemed to be interested in Madam Gora . . . you asked me last time, too, what I think of her. I ran into her. At the theater, *The Master and Margarita*, actually. A mystical play, isn't it? Or magical? I remembered the play from when we were there. Imagine that, it was still being produced. Lu, yes, with a younger cousin, or that was how she presented him. A tall, bald, solid man with a moustache, very quiet, but ready, it seemed, to let himself go at any moment. Lu intimidated him, and I intimidated him. I asked her to a coffee. She even came. We talked a while. About Gora, as well. Even about Gora."

The word *even* kept repeating itself: she *even* came, *even* about Gora—the unusual was Mihnea Palade's routine.

"She said she was cured. Short hair, very short, like a boy. A shock. A slender face, vibrating movements, the vibrations of her fragility, deepened eyes, same hands as ever, superb hands. She seemed taller, lighter. Illness is a mystery, it has its own magic, it brings you closer to the unknown and the mystical. Especially such a grave illness . . . you're in transit. In between. Closer to death, you feel more intensely the mystery of life. Illness intensifies sensuality. Out of words and gestures I was guessing at the unperceivable, reprimanded by decency and fear, fear of the self, not just of others. Lu is more than a single woman, as I've said. That was how I first saw her long ago, and how I still see her now. It's just that now, after her illness, she seems more accessible, open, freer, more thirsty . . . "

I was listening to him, I wasn't listening, I craved more details, that was for certain, but I changed the subject, to escape my own self.

"Do you think that former Secret Service agents have special reasons to follow you here, as well?"

He didn't answer right away, as I would have expected. It seemed that he needed time to decide how and what to say.

"I don't know what they have in their files, I wouldn't rule out any hypotheses, I am a man of hypotheses, I believe in secrets and secret needs. A double or multiple life. The imposture is only another embodiment, apart from the known, accepted one. See even here, in the United States of freedom and taboo, a politician slips into the whirlpool of a short erotic adventure now and then. An enormous scandal erupts, and the politician is ruined. In France he'd be admired. The old adulterer has been proof since the beginning that man lies in everything. Doesn't he care about the poor, about religion, about his children, about America's future? Of course he does!"

He was quiet for a moment and took a long look at me.

"No, I wasn't an informant, if that's what you want to know. That isn't why the agents of yesterday and today would be following me.

I don't know the reasons why they would. And maybe it's better that way."

He was saying that this would be our last conversation, so then, it was a confession.

"I was living in blasphemous, admired America, chaos obsessed with order and freedom, pragmatic and religious, corrupt and idealistic, hundreds of sects, thousands of armed racists, illiterates of all degrees, corruption and lunacy and spectacle. And grandeur! Imperfect, fortunately. Only a dictatorship is perfect."

"What did she say about Gora? What did Lu say about Gora? Did she agree to talk about him? Why didn't she follow him here?"

Palade searched my face, disappointed. He was smiling, with sly complicity, as if the questions had been a failed copout from the unmentioned question.

"It's quite possible that Lu is abandoning, barely now, the place she never wanted to abandon. I asked her about Gora. Why hadn't she followed him? 'I don't know. I don't want to know yet,' was what she said. 'We're all irreplaceable and our ages are irreplaceable, we can't be replaced even by our own selves, in another age and in changed surroundings,' she said. 'I don't know and I don't want to know, I shouldn't know.' What's certain is that she's become less retractile and equivocal. Okay, we'll end here, I'm in a hurry, I'm preparing three different books, I have publishing contracts to look at, a lot of work, until next May. The month of May is inscribed in my brother's dream."

"What are you trying to say?"

"A session with the Political Bureau. The former Political Bureau. Lilliputian marionettes made of straw and cotton and velvet. Just like in the puppet theater. The obese chef, the gardener with his rake, the stenographer with his small glasses. Generals, youths in the green shirts of the Legion, workers with caps and red bands, activists. A large banner across the entire wall. *Nationalism, Communism's last refuge.* In our day there were others: *Workers, the Party's golden foundation,* or, *Man, the most precious capital.* They were discussing my case, the date of my execution, waiting for a sign, some indication. The Genius of the Carpathians seemed be-fuddled, turning toward one of the capped guides. This is what my brother Lucian told me. The dream."

Palade wrapped his scarf around his neck. He was in a navy blue suit, as always, with a white shirt, open at the neck, red scarf made of soft wool.

"The marionette responded hoarsely, like a ventriloquist's doll. 'The holiday of the Orthodox saints.' The Genius smiled, he liked the crudity of the guide, he nodded his head and waved his hand in approval. The marionettes took out their notepads and noted the date, the holiday in May. This year I got off, nothing happened. Unfortunately, I don't have that gypsy here to untangle the mystery."

He tightened his scarf again around his neck, though it was warm and humid. His thick, woolen scarf around his neck like a kind of useless armor.

It was our last meeting.

Some time has gone by since then. Peter Gaşpar might also have met with Palade again in the parallel worlds of the transmigrations, and he will communicate to us if the enigma of his disappearance is the same as Mihnea Palade's.

■

Gaşpar's telephone message seems like a challenge. Had he guessed the whole time that he was the hero of the obituary on Gora's desk? The message was promptly transcribed into Folder RA 0298. The funereal diversion requires professionalism! Gora had specialized, he'd learned to maintain the good disposition of those still living; the farce named biography became the obituary farce. He would select a fragment, then another, for those left on this side of the River Styx.

She mocked me, the whore! She made a laughing stock out of me. The Nymphomaniac . . . she's in no mood for me. Transcribed from the tape, the words rest obediently in the *Mynheer Folder.* Gora had listened to the message dozens of times, he knows it by heart. With the transcription in front of him, he listens for the inflections in the voice, comparing the phonetics and the written page, looking for new meanings. He ignores the transmigration of the soul, in which Mihnea Palade believed.

Was Peter Gaşpar going to take advantage of the postponement by continuing to play with the Nymphomaniac, as he'd promised when he first arrived in the New World? Or would he put an end to the game, embittered, proving that he decides the epilogue after all?

Suicide doesn't seem likely.

The grump left a grumpy message and disappeared. Not a word afterward. Did this message preclude the kind of assault with which Mihnea Palade was honored? The telephone in the Eastern European professor's shack rang and rang, while the college's secretary maintained that the professor had solicited a leave of absence, an unpaid vacation. Was there a forwarding address? No answer to that question, the bureaucrats aren't allowed to violate the professor's privacy.

Had he taken off, in the end, with Deste? Or did he go with Tara to Nevada's Nirvana, to discover the true America, the wilderness of freedom? Which Tara? The one who examined the relationship between underwear and moldy pasta, the difference between an odor and a stink, or the mailwoman who delivered threat letters? An easygoing, cordial, wise partner, no relation to the neurotic who yearned for bad marks?

Disappeared in America's labyrinth, Peter doesn't answer. Did he encounter the Blind Man from Buenos Aires at the Grand Canyon?

Gora considers himself an untrustworthy columnist. Revitalized by the alternative, he passes his hand over the folder, looking at the corner of the table, where the red gloves rest.

Part III

Before disappearing, Peter had a last meeting, with Lyova Boltanski.

Penn Station! He emerges from the crowd, his gaze up to the sky. The present! The pres-ent, the traveler was mumbling. The motto and prayer of his new life: THE PRESENT!

The yellow cab brakes at the curb's edge. Lyova was waiting for him, just as they'd agreed.

"Thank you, you're a man of your word. The Soviet is a man of his word."

"The American is, too, if he's paid well enough. You paid me well. Too well."

"Well, what do you think . . . I owed you. *Noblesse oblige*, say the French. What do the Ukrainians say?"

"Why the Ukrainians?"

"Well, aren't you from Odessa?"

"I'm a Soviet. I told you but you didn't understand. *Ein Man ein Wort*, this I know from my family. It's not French, but I think it's the same."

"Almost the same."

"Okay. Where are we going?"

"I don't know the exact address, but I know where it is."

"New York isn't a village, we need an address."

"Do you know how to get to Lenox Hospital? A major hospital. Near the hospital, there's a doctor's office."

"Again to the doctor? The girlfriend moved to Lenox? The girlfriend or the partner or the wife who doesn't want to see you and who disappears before you appear."

"No, she didn't move. It's not for her I'm going."

"Are you ill? Or is it a psychiatrist? I asked you last time, and you didn't answer. A psychiatrist?"

"I answered last time and I am answering now. No, he's not a psychiatrist. Dr. Koch is an internist, an unfashionable profession in America."

"That's right. Specialized doctors. For the left hand and for the right hand, for knees and tendons and for headaches or baldness aches. Ten digits in the hands and feet? A specialist for each one. Twenty specialists! And a specialist for each nail of each finger. Another twenty! Dentists who do only fillings and others who pull teeth, others who take care of gums, other who implant new, more durable fangs. The Ford method, the division of labor. Maximum output. Charlie Chaplin's film. I saw it dozens of times in the Soviet Union."

"*Modern Times*, that's what it was called, wasn't it? Efficient and ferocious capitalism. So, you saw movies in your socialist country. What about books? Did you read books?"

"I read. Whatever I could get my hands on."

"Whatever you could get your hands on? We all fell into that trap of books."

"Why trap?"

"Oh, I'm just saying . . . it was a den where you could be alone, we had nothing else, just books."

"Doctor Koch . . . Koch you said?"

"That's his name."

"So then, it's the lungs. Bacillus Koch, that's all I remember from school. Something wrong with your lungs?"

"Not a goddamn thing. I don't call him Koch, I call him Avicenna. You know who Avicenna was."

"I know, and if I don't know I still don't care. So then, you're ill in general, not in the lungs. The nail of your little toe on your left foot?"

"I'm not going for a consultation. I am bringing him a present. This tube."

"Aha, you don't have that heavy briefcase, now you have a tube. So then, you're not going to the library, or to the library café, and you're not going to lose your wallet."

"No I'm not going to lose it. And I have money, don't worry."

Peter holds a long tube made of blue cardboard, with a lid, under his arm.

"I'm bringing a message."

"That big? About the girlfriend who works with him? You're begging him to help you with your unrequited love, to prescribe an elixir? Tubes for unwanted maps or diplomas, like this one, could also be used for a papyrus with the magic formula for love."

"I am bringing him a gift. A rare engraving. I bought it for him."

"Ah, a gift. Of gratitude. Conventions from the old world. *Noblesse* . . . how did you say?"

"*Noblesse oblige.*"

"Yes, yes, *oblige.* Something other than *Ein Man ein Wort.* Now I understand. Something else altogether."

"Not altogether."

"Gratitude for treatment."

"Not only."

"You were saying it was a message. The message is separate?"

"Separate. But the gift is also a message. The letter is another message."

"Aha, about your friend."

"About a friend. A mutual friend."

"Aha. Something pleasant or unpleasant?"

"Unpleasant."

"One warm, one cold. The gift as a thanks, the message as poison."

"Something like that."

To the right of the hospital, traffic, cars, taxis, ambulances.

"We're here, I think we're here. Now where are we going?"

"Ahead, just a little farther. We'll pass the intersection, the first building after the intersection is Koch's office. Avicenna."

Lyova stops in front of the clinic. Peter has his money ready, he counts it, he doesn't want to give too much, it would offend the Soviet.

"Thank you, Lyova. You're a man of your word."

"I am. Whenever you need me. You have my phone number."

"Yes, I have it. I took it down, I won't lose it."

Abruptly, he changes his mind.

"In fact, wait for me. I'll be right back and we'll go."

"Where, to Eastern Europe?"

"No, to Penn Station. The train leaves in an hour."

"The big city tires you out, you come and you run."

"It enchants me. There isn't another like it in the whole world. The City on the Moon. But I'm in a hurry. A big hurry."

Peter enters the little waiting room, full of patients, doesn't look around, two steps to the window where little Spanish Dora sits in vigil. He hands her the tube, shows her the white ticket on the blue tube, where it says "Dr. Koch-Avicenna." He turns on his heels.

Lyova is at his post, the train is at its post, America functions perfectly, Peter disappears.

Gora also has Boltanski's number. "Use it whenever you need, it will remind you of our youth!" Peter would say. He'd never used it and he had no idea that, right before disappearing, Peter had traveled in Lyova's yellow cab.

Naturally, Koch-Avicenna could have provided information about Peter Gaşpar's farewell visit, but the information was neither pleasant nor urgent. Doctor Koch was waiting for the right moment.

■

She mocked me, the whore! The Nymphomaniac . . . she's in no mood for me.

But maybe she was in the mood and hadn't concluded the game. The postponement only proved that the adventure hadn't reached any kind of conclusion.

The time is 7:30 in the morning. Gora is awake, ready for the adventure. The adventure of looking for the disappeared.

The Magic Mountain is nearby in its known place, on the hospitable shelf, all you had to do was extend an arm, but Mynheer Pieter Peeperkorn and Hans Castorp, his humiliated rival, and the strange Clavdia Chauchat, with the almond eyes, were very far away, in a Europe of another age.

Gaşpar had to be looked for in today's America. Gora prepared himself for the adventure, he had before him the guide with photographs and text: *A Day in the Life of America.* At any page you open, you find the America where the runaway is holing up.

On the chair, faded jeans. In front of the chair, on the sandy carpet, the bag made of purple plastic, the large, round watch, black dial with golden digits. In the back, the wooden bed, the white hat of the lampshade. In the foreground, a white shoe made of perforated leather, a brown one, with a cord, the great Webster's Dictionary, *from A to Z. To the left of the image, bare, tanned legs the color of honey. The juvenile foot presses into the carpeting. The face and shoulders and bust are missing from the image. But the legs are here, from bottom to top. Nails painted with pink polish, delicate skin, from the pink heel to the ankle.*

This morning Tara had become Sandra, from the middle school in Lakeview, Michigan, in the massive album called 200 *of the World's Leading Photojournalists.*

The album open, on the table, in front of the computer.

Sandra isn't disciplined like Tara, she's incapable of establishing priorities; the chaos of the room reflects the panic with which she is studying for her end of year exams. Her classmates are all the same. Different times, Professor, another geography and another history from the one you escaped.

The time is 8 A.M. *Deste is getting ready for the ritual. The Prabhupada Palace at the top of Mount Moundsville in West Virginia. Prabhupada, the founder of the Hare Krishna movement, watches over the six hundred followers. Native Americans, the pride of the International Society of Krishna Consciousness. Deste from now on is known as Veena Dasi, in the classic Indian Bhataratanyam dance. Symmetrical barrettes made of gold in her hair. From the center of her tiara, a golden chain, pearl diadem, golden rosette, a greenish jade stone in the middle. On her forehead, Veena Dasi has drawings made with gold filigree. Between her brows, which are blackened with Indian ink, the red dot, of blood. Over her green silk shirt, from her shoulders to her waist, the sari, with a yellow veil.*

The adolescent Veena Dasi, her real name Renee Walker, doesn't look at all like Deste. Deste would sooner resemble the instructor Jatila Devi. On the lustrous page of the album, Jatila arranges the tiara on the crown of Renee's head; Renee becomes Veena.

The mouth slightly open, the lips anticipating. A little mother-of-pearl clover piercing her nostril. The diadem in arabesques. Red, green, golden jewelry. The velvety lobe of the ear, a tress of black hair, black eyes. Lashes and brows of a nocturnal butterfly. A model escaped from a serai in Sarajevo.

In the Prabhupada Palace in West Virginia, United States of America, Deste became Jatila Devi! Professor Gora thinks about her melancholically, waiting for the runaway Peter to appear from one moment to the next.

The time is 9 in the morning. The Cholos Quartet is there in front of the obituarist's unmade bed. The young woman in panties and tank top, a towel tied like a turban on her head, the other girl seen from the back, also in panties and a tank, with curlers in her hair, the hairy man in jeans, with the bandaged head and the little boy Joe, a mere child. On the bed, the brush, the comb, the pants, a roll of toilet paper. Arturo, Lisa, Rosaria, "Cholos," members of a band from a Mexican border town, born in America, in conflict with their Spanish tradition and their Anglo-Saxon civilization. Each one has a nickname, says the album.

Arturo's name is "Chango," Lisa is "Bad Girl," the woman Rosaria is "Smiley." They live together in the district of White Fence, a barrio in East Los Angeles, they move around in the same old car. None of them has a job. They take turns watching over little Joe, "El Boo Boo," Rosaria's child. She's the one with the towel on her head like a turban. Little Joe is the only one among them who is not deaf and mute.

Gaşpar was preoccupied with deaf-mutes, he probably knows about the Cholos Quartet.

At 9:30 Gora was looking for Peter Gaşpar inside the store that dated back to 1921, belonging to the Ciemniak family, on Joseph Campau Street, in Hamtramck, Michigan. Peter the gourmand . . . is undoubtedly admiring through a window some of the Ciemniak kielbasa that was so renowned in the Detroit area.

At 10:30 Gora meets Eileen Slocum, from Newport, Rhode Island, descended from the clan of Roger Williams, who founded the state in 1636. Red dress suit, closed at the neck. Sharp features, freckles; blond, wiry hair. Her wrinkled hand looks like the hand of a sixty- to seventy-year-old. Eileen and her husband, John, a retired diplomat, boast eleven great-grandchildren and an imposing family manor. The short, dark-haired butler carries the tray and silverware and silver cup for breakfast. Carlo Juarez had worked at the Argentine embassy in Washington until 1982, when the ambassador was recalled as a result of the war in the Falklands. No, the fat Peter Gaşpar wasn't there.

At 11:00, the convoy arrives in Nevada, in Golden Valley. Gina Monteverdi, the aunt that Tara had promised to Professor Peter Gaşpar, was there on the side of the road to welcome him. She held in her arms Sofia the cat and the greenish teapot that held the aphrodisiac. Rosy, dimpled cheeks. Rich, thick, black hair, with some white strands. Pink flannel robe that reached the ground. Gina had just stepped out of the house to wait for the guest, at the intersection that bore the name of her adored feline Sofia. Black cat with long, white whiskers. The Sofia Crossroads. On the street sign, an orange rhombus, the figure of a cat and the warning: *Cat. Slow Crossing.* Step on the brakes, Professor; this is how the pilgrims who've landed in the Nirvana of Nevada do things. That crazy Sofia deserves this homage, as well as the siblings, Marta, Rita, and Lucia. Tara hadn't divulged the Italian origins of the aunt from Nirvana, nor the fact that Gina had borne four charmed felines.

Nor had Tara let slip a single word about Anthony, the messenger of God, nearby resident of Reno, Nevada, page 124 in the album.

Black suit, red shirt, white cowboy hat. A crucifix hanging at his neck, on a thick chain. Also a string of pearls that ends with a white cross made of bone. Thick lips, white teeth, large nose, strong. White, shingled house. In the orange minivan there are some busy placards: prochoice murders—unborn babies with no choice—abortion crucifies babies. *On the Archangel Anthony's T-shirt, in large red letters:* PROCHOICE KILLS BABIES. *"People say I'm crazy. Yes, crazy about life," murmurs Anthony, pensively. He arrives at the church at 7:30 in the morning and initiates the crusade on the streets of Reno. "I served in the Army for twenty years, but I've never fought so hard. It's World War III. The massacre of the unborn."*

Gora closes opens closes opens the album. He sips again, thoughtfully, from the tall cup. He closes his eyes, suspended in no place. It's good to be in no place. Peter invokes the time of exile, the PRESENT. Gora glorifies the nomad's geography, "Better to be nowhere than anywhere." He lets fall a daily tear of joy and anguish for the good fortune of being nowhere.

Smitty's in Orleans, Mississippi. The Hardstone brothers, John and Jimmy.

Twin bachelors, the old men dress the same and mimic each other's gestures and words. They sit at the wooden table. J and J gaze toward the door through which Gora is entering. The topographic twins drink their coffee and Coca-Cola here every afternoon, abandoning their eighty-seven-year-old mother, together with whom they've always lived. The French photographer come to capture them sitting at Smitty's in Orleans, Mississippi, for the collection *A Day in America* is no Monsieur Pierre Gashpar. No, no, it's not he.

Gora looks at his watch, to find out what hour the exile Peter is killing and in what time zone. Suddenly, he's tempted by the old phantoms. There wasn't more than a step from Peter to Lu. He looks for Gaşpar but keeps running into Lu. "I didn't know her; I knew her," confessed Gora, at one point. "She'd existed for a long time inside of me. An undreamed of rediscovery, too often imagined in dreams."

The retrospective exercise had captured him again. His wife watched over his straying; he'd have invented her if she didn't exist. Then, as now, he was searching for the torment of Lu.

■

The attraction between cousins, if that's what it was, flouted convention differently from a marriage outside the ethnic community. Lu often protected herself through conventions, but she didn't lack deviations from the norm. When everyone around her dreamed of emigrating, Lu refused to. Afterward, to everyone's stupefaction, she appeared in the New World with a cousin who was younger than the suitors who had most likely stormed her. Her evasions couldn't be found in the obituary that Gora had prepared for Peter Gaşpar.

A thin evening. The castanets of heels on the asphalt, the melancholy of the twilight. Augustin Gora was contemplating the unknown woman. As if the matter at hand weren't the enchantment of beauty, but about other incidental gifts. All beauty did was to heighten those gifts, but it could also diminish them. He didn't want to admit that coincidence that had sent him a stand-in.

"I wasn't discovering her as much as revisiting her," he'd said at one point. "She'd been inside me for a long time." He wouldn't have admitted, however, that "recognition" could blind him, impeding his discovery of what was beyond the momentary revelation. He watched, furtively, the shoe with the heel and the strap. The strap at the back left the ankle free, the stalk of her leg began at her delicate ankle and rose toward her bare knee, and the rest was lightheadedness.

Rendezvous, walks, exercises in intoxication. The world was departing. Fumbling, games, insomnia. The first night. He'd heard her murmuring, "I want it differently." Removed from the stranger's body, Gora remained stretched on his back, as if he hadn't heard.

Eventually he got up. Lu was balled up and curled. Resumed panting, rhythm and exhaustion.

Lu didn't talk about the past. Not because she was withholding scandalous mysteries, but because she refused access to the intimacy that she considered simple, natural, but intangible.

Is that how it all was? There seemed to be too many detours. The unknown frightened her; it took some time before she grew accustomed to Gora. The unknown inside her, however, frightened her even more, and she was unable to touch that unknown in the presence of another, no matter how close he might be.

In Peter she found a relative; was that the prerequisite of the familiar? Was the familiar repetitive and boring, but safe; was newness aggressive and illusory?

"I wasn't discovering her as much as revisiting her. She'd been inside me, she was waiting there," said the husband, bereft.

What could possibly explain Lu's steadfast refusal to follow her beloved husband? Had it been resignation . . . and not rebellion? Lu despised the theatrics of rebellions. Had she carefully weighed the alternatives before deciding that the safest solution was precisely the most unusual and risky, to stay put? The known, no matter how rotten, of one's familiar surroundings? Wasn't conjugal life also a known, familiar stability?

Did the night of the return from the train station, decades ago, portend the future alliance with Peter? Had she discovered herself then, unexpectedly? An obscure, ancestral predisposition, in the troubled depths of the past, of which he knew too little. Hosted suddenly by the chasm that had taken hold? Finding Peter again after Gora's departure had perhaps rekindled the memory of that night. A confirmation. She related to him because they were already related to each other through a past about which neither of them knew enough, a past that didn't even belong to Peter, though he was the product of its malformations. A past with which Lu communicated obscurely, primarily in moments of panic. Was that it?

As usual Gora was nurturing masochistic questions. For many hours he would aim right at the vulnerable place, the bleeding wound.

"You didn't become an alien enemy, not even after your adored wife left you! That's something, really something. Not in our little, idyllic country and not in more honorable places," the phantom Peter taunted in nocturnal visits.

Some decades past, Peter's appearance changed not only Lu's perception of herself and the world around her, but also his own. In the caution with which he'd been surrounded in the house of relatives he was meeting for the first time, he'd felt something mysterious and bizarre. Once he'd gotten back home, he subjected his mother to interrogations. He discovered, gradually, what had been hidden from him. However, for him the effect was not in the least inhibiting, as it had been for his beautiful cousin, about whom he knew nothing except what was contained in his wet dreams. The tragedy that Eva related in too great a detail had, in fact, liberated him. Still absorbed by basketball and parties and mountain hikes among his happy circle of friends, he cared very little about his education, or his career, or his rejection from the architecture university on account of the former Party prosecutor David Gașpar's anti-Party records. He graduated easily from the architecture high school, was satisfied with sports, parties, women, and books. Yes, books appeared, too, among his preoccupations.

"Laughter, Professor. That's the solution when there's none other. Mynheer Peeperkorn is the solution, Comrade."

Gora didn't remember anything except for the title of the story by which Peter had conquered his socialist audience. Was it a deaf-mute Mynheer? That would be something!

"Laughter, that's the solution. Not just during the day, but also at night. At night when the unwelcome visitors appear."

Gora waved off the ghost with a bothered gesture. He hadn't heard anything about the fugitive in a long time and he didn't look for him anymore, except within himself.

"I can't find him within myself, no matter how much I look for him."

Was Peter's interminable obituary his own lament, scored on a foreign manuscript?

The dawn was brightening. Exhausted, Gora was caressing the yellow gloves on the desk. The yellow folder slept.

■

After Peter Gaşpar disappeared in the great American void, the obituary consumed most of Gora's time, putting a healthy distance between his immediate reality and the fictive—and even more immediate—reality. He defied the bureaucratic, biographical limits, accustomed to naming the strict facts of the life lived. After all, any biography was just an obituary; every history has an end and an obituarist.

After Peter disappeared, the Obituary RA 0298 had gained not only legitimacy but also urgency. Who could prove that Peter's disappearance wasn't definitive? Only Peter himself, who was in no hurry to produce the proof. Whom to ask and where to look for him? In the presumptions and potentialities it omitted from the bureaucratic biography.

Gora stopped short, with the red pencil suspended in the air. Shouldn't he address Lu, finally?

The actor and the trapeze artist know what stage fright is; Gora also knew the spell in which every moment can produce a disaster. No matter how well he managed the manuscript . . . his hand trembled, his voice trembled, his temples were wet, as well as his hands, and snakes were ransacking his insides.

The telephone was just a step away, but, gratefully, Lu remained, inaccessible. Happiness was there, in the past that shouldn't be disturbed. He murmured, "I don't want the present; I don't want to let go of happiness."

The pencil in the air, his gaze on the screen with the day's obituaries. Diurnal and nocturnal encounters and reencounters, accelerating his pulse and his mind.

The moment's screen connects you instantly anywhere and transcribes your speaking or your silence. He could manage simple operations at the computer, and when he failed—that is, often—the rules went under. He couldn't recuperate them; he'd lose the point of departure. It was the same with the driving; he'd be fine until the first mistake. Then the bewilderment would cancel his memory and instincts, and he became useless. He'd renounced the wheel but didn't renounce shaving every morning, terrified that he might forget the routine, never to recover it again; it was the same with the tie, the terror, every time, that he'd forgotten how to tie the knot.

As usual, he'd awoken very early in the morning. The superb light of September. Bitter coffee, the abbreviated movements of coming back to life. Afterwards, he'd read Peter's wanderings toward the Italian Gina Monteverdi, Tara's aunt, and the felines that she'd borne.

He watched, stupefied, the gloves at the end of the table. He'd turned his face to the screen. Smoke, fire, panic. Horrified faces. The floors were crumbling. Apocalypse. The sky had become a giant cloud of smoke and flames, chasing the fire trucks and ambulances on the ground. Screams, blood, flames, the sky was on fire, while the sky outside Professor Gora's window remained torpid, blue and free of scars.

Gora was at the window. Nothing was happening, the sky as undisturbed as at the beginning of the world, despite the world on the screen, which exploded with burning meteors. A cosmic alarm.

He hurried to the phone. Quickly, quickly, in just a few minutes contact with the earthlings will become impossible. His hands trembled, the receiver trembled.

"Yes, this is Dr. Koch. Ah, it's you, Gusti. Yes, I'm answering, as you can see. Poor Dora fainted. Yes, I know, I heard, I'm watching everything on TV, just like you, just like the whole world. Yes, we're okay. For now. Of course, for now. There's nothing except for now. Yes, Lu's fine, as well. Nearby, in her office. Alarmed, just like all of us. No, no more than that."

The voice had ceased, and he had no one else to call. He sat back down and rearranged the sheets of paper.

The Obituary of the Planet. You no longer write with a pencil or a pen or with the cumbersome old typewriter, but on the screen of the world in flames. Fingers on the keyboard, letters on the screen, you're alone, but connected to the world that—voila!—rushes into your sheltered place and, with a single thrust, dissipates all of your evasions, and solitude.

The terrorists had tired of the virtues and vices and garbage and splendor of this poor, passing world! Boredom, yes, pure and simple boredom. They just couldn't stand the sins and pleasures of the world any longer. Determined to hurry Redemption, to accelerate the speed toward Paradise. Love! It was love they wanted, isn't it? Absolute, perpetual, blind! The bent cross and the sickle and hammer and the bleeding half-moon defied human love, which was imperfect and ephemeral. Perpetual, blind and blinding love, this is what they promised. Perfection, magic, utopia. The meanness of the quotidian, the grunts of engorgement and sex, the haughtiness of wealth and disbelief needs to be destroyed! Haunting images: bending cross, sickle and hammer, star, half-moon, the golden calf and the mangy goat, the sacred and disabled infant, the rock of philosophy and the deaf-mute oracle, thrashing and adoring unto death and beyond it.

Immense steel wings in the burning sky. The September Bird coasts, golden sovereign and ferocious, above the hysterical anthill. In the steel belly, the captives.

The Monster smashed the Tower of Babel. Flames and smoke and spattered bodies in the black ether, over the cliff and waves of Babylon.

The wired news anchor repeated the details of the invasion, adding the latest breaking sound bites. Through the air were flying hands and heads, hats and wheelchairs, the red card of the watchmaker David Gaşpar, the briefcase of Officer Patrick, Dima's encyclopedias, Avakian's glasses, Detective Lonrot's revolver, the brassiere of the siren Beatrice Artwein and the blind cat Gattino and the melancholic elephant Oliver; the yellow sheets from the yellow folder on Professor Gora's desk flew, turning through the air, like some extraterrestrial kites. The funereal whirlwind unified and dissipated everything, nothing counted any longer, just the OBITUARY.

The alchemists and wise men were right when they spoke of maladies and not just magic. The syndrome of the detour is love, my little one, that's all and *basta*. Fin-ished! Vitality and melancholy to the delirious end. De-li-ri-ous, my child. Nothing else in the charts except for remembrance. Remembrance of love, the final flash, my dear Lu. That's all that remains. Your husband, unable to reach his arms out to the lover who had been his wife, thinks only of you. "It was good for me in your aura; happiness hurt," is what you wrote on the corner of a crumpled sheet of paper, after our first night. You disappeared so that the dawn could give us back the world. Those words are in me, letter by letter, the whirling script of the void.

"It was good for me in your aura; we'll pay together." Husband and wife know the danger of boredom; husband and lover know the spell and curse of the lure. We were all stammering, the blundering words of desire, its delirious powerlessness. In my cell of papyrus, the past is present and the present is an echo of the past.

The September Bird carries the message of love turned into hatred. Transfigured by love and hatred and blinded by piety, the pilots offer a gift of horror.

After Koch's voice faded, Gora found himself alone again; Dima was far away, as well as Palade and Gaşpar and Larry One-Two-Three-Nine. He would have walked out into the street, to be among his kind, to receive the Apocalypse along with them, but he withdraws into his shell instead, away from people, away from the apocalypse.

The second coming of the Savior, Armageddon, the appearance of the Antichrist, the exit of the planet from its orbit, the return of the Imam, the First and Last, nuclear war. The asteroid of Damnation had hit, the meteor, the Cathedral of Planetary Transactions, where mystics, usurers and alchemists murmur, on their knees, every four minutes and fifty-three seconds, their eyes on the monetary diagrams, the same laconic and lewd prayer: MONEY-MONEY-MONEY-MONEY.

The professor sits down again in front of the flaming screen, takes out the immaculate, white folder. On the cover, large letters in blood: THE OBITUARY OF THE PLANET.

8:45 A.M.:   *Flight controllers in Boston intercept a voice in the cabin of Flight 11. "We have plans," the voice announces in an uncertain but intelligible English. "Remain calm and you'll be okay." The plane turns and changes course for the Devil's Metropolis.*

8:46 A.M.:   *An unidentified plane, with ninety-two passengers on board, slams into the grandiose edifice of globalization, the World Trade Center. The floors burn and the gasworks of the heating system explodes. Smoke fills the sky and covers the ground; the ants run, dazed, along the streets below.*

9:05 A.M.:   *The FBI is alerted. A second plane, with sixty-four passengers on board, slams into the World Trade Center, exploding on impact.*

9:37 A.M.:   *A Boeing 757 (American Airlines 77) penetrates three of the five concentric circles of the Pentagon, the Fortress of Power. The offices of the Martian God are in flames.*

10:00 A.M.:   *The North Tower of Babel collapses. One hundred ten floors.*

10:10 A.M.:   *The airports of the New World close. The Democratic Front for the Liberation of Palestine denies its implication in the Massacre of the Infidels.*

10:12 A.M.:   *A new explosion at the Pentagon, the most secure building in the world.*

10:15 A.M.:   *The evacuation of the White House.*

10:24 A.M.:   *The South Tower of Babel collapses.*

10:25 A.M.:   *In Lebanon, Palestinians celebrate their victory over the Yankees.*

10:35 A.M.:   *Air Force One, carrying the president of the Satanic Superpower, makes a course for the presidential bunker, escorted by fifty fighter jets.*

Five hours since Professor Gora had begun the first day of the rest of his life. He stared at the bookshelves, the white gloves on the table, the thick, red lips of the newscaster. Channels CNN, CBS, NBC, PBS, MSNBC, the cartoon networks, the sports channels, music and porn stations all transmit the same spectacle of the band Herostratus. *The anthem of Purification, with lyrics by Yussuma-Osama Ben Laden.*

The Babel Tower of Transaction, the Fortress of the Pentagon, the White House for the White Clown . . . is that all? And the Library?

Gora felt insulted. The planetary explosion in which he'd had the privilege of participating insulted him: he couldn't stand being associated with the symbols of Money and Power. The band of nineteen daggers, the Herostratus Band, wasn't worthy of the Great Ending! The knifemen didn't know the Qur'an, and the fanatics didn't speak the magnificent language of the Library.

Illiterates! The Library holds everything. The memories and projects of the world, the genius and madness of the loyal and the infidels, the Bible of the Jewish prophets and the Qur'an of your own Prophet, and the Testament of the crucified prophet, and *Mein Kampf* of the fool prophet and the *Manifesto* of the Marxist prophet. The decrees of the Inquisition and the Proclamation of the Rights of Man, the games of the child Mozart, and of the earless Van Gogh, Homer and Krishna and Confucius, Madame Bovary and Karenina and Mother Teresa, Cassius Clay and the Bucharest phone book of 1936. Everything, everything, even a volume of verses written by the adored Ben Laden, translated into the language of the adored William Shakespeare, the verses of Iosif Visarionovich Djugasvili and his rival Mao Zedong.

Everything comes from the Library, not from the Transnational Commerce Brothel, nor from the Citadel of Missiles or the Presidential Ranch.

Irritated, Gora shut off communication with the Apocalypse.

The planet's necrologist needed Mynheer. He pulled from a drawer the sheets of paper where he'd jotted down notes about Peter's meeting with Officer Murphy.

"Dima maintained that we live in a desanctified world," Gaşpar answered. The potbellied Patrick jumped out of his seat. "Oh, world where nothing is sacred, but the sacred hides in the profane," continued Gaşpar. "The world is full of churches, mosques, and synagogues. And I go to church," the policeman murmured. "The religious state wants us all. There's the rub. The rub becomes a bomb. The bomb will scatter us and make us sacred."

He'd found the connection! He had to relate it urgently to the young ladies on the TV screen: the END. He waited with his red pencil in hand, he'd grabbed it again, to write in the margins of the page: Too simple, Peter! Old Man Dima was referring to transcendence, not just to God.

The band of sacred knives jubilated in the gong of the crime. Herostratus was the name of the unforgettable destroyer of the Temple of Artemis in Ephesus, the name of whose builder no one remembers! No one. Only the name of the destroyer lingers for centuries in the smeared memory of mortals. The Herostratus Band learned to pilot and destroy the plane, but they wouldn't have known how to build it. Destruction, yes, is intoxication and exaltation and the great anthem sung by the troubadours of The End.

Gora noted, conscientiously, for posterity, the Chronology of The End.

10:43 A.M.: *A plane crashes in the industrial park near Pittsburgh, Pennsylvania.*

10:56 A.M.: *Yasser Arafat declares that his organization bears no responsibility in the disastrous events of this historic day.*

11:14 A.M.: *The United Nations building is evacuated, and the Statue of Liberty hides in the smoke of explosions.*

11:30 A.M.: *General Wesley Clark announces that the criminal action had been planned by the poet Ben Laden.*

11:48 A.M.: *The Centers for Disease Control take precautionary measures in anticipation of a biological attack.*

11:57 A.M.:	An anonymous phone call to the American consulate in Porto, threatening the explosion of the entire planet.
12:17 P.M.:	Disneyland closes its gates.
12:20 P.M.:	An unidentified individual claims responsibility, in the name of the Japanese Red Army, for the aerial attacks, revenge on the part of the victims of Hiroshima and Nagasaki. At the same time, on the phone line of the nationalist weekly Al Wahdej, a voice claims—in Arabic, with a Russian accent—the attack on the Twin Towers in New York.
12:25 P.M.:	The price of oil rises by two dollars per barrel on the world market.
12:26 P.M.:	Over the telephone, Mark Whening, the spokesman for the American embassy in Bucharest, thanks the Romanian authorities and citizens for their solidarity and excuses himself for not appearing in front of reporters, fearing an attempt on his life.

Professor Gora interrupts his transcription of the news at 12:27 P.M. He pours himself a glass of milk and, with the renewed thirst of the survivor, contemplates the white and refreshing liquid of genesis.

12:48 P.M.:	Ahmed Mitawakil, the Taliban Afghan minister of external affairs, rebuffs insinuations that the poet Yussuma Ben Laden instigated the massacre.
1:04 P.M.:	The political analyst Jonathan Eyal qualifies the event of the day as "the best-planned action of its kind in all of history."
2:32 P.M.:	Two aircraft carriers appear in New York Harbor to preempt imminent attacks.
3:27 P.M.:	A possible attack on NATO headquarters in Brussels is announced.
3:35 P.M.:	The military base in Aviano, Italy, declares itself ready for battle.

Air Force One directs its course toward Offutt, Nebraska, to the headquarters of Strategic Air Command. The White House announces that the First Lady of the United States and the two First Daughters are, thank God, sheltered safely.

Professor Gora feels suddenly overwhelmed by the presidential news and interrupts contact with the planet once more, exhausted. He lies down. He sleeps deeply, lost at sea, twisted in his sheets, unable to release himself from the conversation with Eva Gaşpar. From the first moment of the assault, Eva Kirschner-Gaşpar was in hysterics. She hadn't heard from Peter in a long time. The wanderer had grown more and more distant, though there was no longer a distance that was distant enough; disaster finds you everywhere you go. Conceived at Auschwitz, Peter had plunged into the socialist den, then into the free madness of the free world. Now where would he close the circle?

Difficult to calm Eva down. Even more difficult to leave her without an answer. Professor Gora felt responsible. He'd been the only person with whom Eva had maintained contact since Peter had arrived in the New World. No, Peter wasn't among the victims, dear Mrs. Gaşpar; after the madness of these days passes we'll get some news from that fool Peter. All, yes all of us—his parents from the Carpathian paradise, Dr. Koch and his assistant Ludmila Serafim, her ex-husband Augustin Gora, Beatrice Artwein, and the Soviet man Boltanski—will have news from our good boy Peter.

True, he had a meeting that morning precisely at the World Trade Center. Unfortunately, precisely on that morning and precisely in that cursed building, Peter was to meet a lawyer who specialized in immigration, paid for by Professor Gora. The meeting had been scheduled many months in advance, before Peter's disappearance. The meeting was with a famous and expensive lawyer.

However, this is not a fatal certainty, not at all. No one knows whether Peter went to the meeting. No one knows whether he even remembered, in his wanderings, the day and place, or whether he even cared about this bureaucratic disaster. Still, if he'd intended to keep the appointment, it couldn't have been the first hour of the day. It was hard for Peter to wake up in the morning, as you well know, the Hotel Esplanade was far away from the grandiose World Trade Center, the meeting would have been around lunchtime.

There was a favorable new premise, as well. Half an hour ago it was announced, via trustworthy sources, that the sons and daughters of the *Chosen People* had been forewarned the night before not to find themselves in or around the Babel Towers on the morning of the great manipulation. Naturally, a manipulation: the demonstration we all watched is, in fact, a staging of considerable proportions. Those nineteen actors are, in reality, agents of CIA special forces, trained in the Arab language and the Islamic tradition. *Herostratus*, the code name of the operation, was chosen by a star Harvard graduate, Samuel Knish, the leader of the project. His parents had been assassinated when he and his twin sister were five years old. They'd lived in an isolated village on the Lebanese border. Samuel was now a historian of Antiquity, obsessed with the relationship between Athens and Jerusalem, which was why he'd christened the band of knifemen *Herostratus*, the name of the infamous Greek arsonist.

Well, okay, so not one of 2,974 victims of the massacre comes from among the Chosen People. Not one! You're right. The Almighty repaid those who recognized him first and those with whom he closed the Sacred Covenant. If there were still a few sacrifices among them, it was merely due to negligence . . . yes, there were some.

Professor Gora sees, in his sleep, the planetary screen, as he describes to Eva the figures from his electronic mail: 246 victims in the hijacked planes that exploded; 2,603 in New York, in the World Trade Center and on the ground; 125 in the Pentagon of Power. At 8:45 A.M. there were 7,400 civilians in the Towers of Babel; other sources say 14,154. Those who were under the area of impact were promptly evacuated, others died under the ruins, some ran toward the roof, but access was blocked and they threw themselves into the emptiness. Hundreds of firemen also died, in the heroic rescue operation. None of those sacrificed, I repeat, not one was among the coreligionists of Peter! You're right, it's not just the hand of the Almighty looking for redemption after Auschwitz but also the solidarity of those who've learned that they need to rely on themselves, as you say.

Peter and his coreligionists are alive and unscathed in the City on the Moon, as he used to call the metropolis of exiles. It was because of him, I'm sure, that Tara, Deste, Mrs. Monteverdi, and her adorable cats also escaped. When they decided to accompany him, he warned them, I'm sure of it. Peter is a frivolous and unreliable scatterbrain with a generous soul, warm like bread fresh out of the oven.

Of course, there will be unpleasant consequences for Peter, as well as those young ladies, but it won't be death. Peter called the witch with the scythe "The Nymphomaniac," and he played hide-and-seek with her. He said often that here, in America, he will dominate the game. He led the cannibal astray this time as well, you can be sure of it.

What happened today marks the beginning of the new millennium of suspicion and guilt. Inevitably, the infantile college prank that Deste allowed herself to make will become, unfortunately, more suspect than it was already. There will be investigations, important personalities will be summoned, such as Atatürk and Borges, but also the college president Avakian and Professor Anteos and Ms. Tang and the student Tara Nelson. Even more likely, Deste Onal and her husband who was now in Austria, the family exiled in Germany, relatives in Sarajevo and the former Ottoman Empire, and even Peter, yes, Peter Gaşpar and his cousin Lu, Dr. Koch, the Soviet Boltanski, the Italian Beatrice Artwein, and I wouldn't be surprised, not at all surprised if even Professor Gora were to be included in the parade of suspects.

The day had grown long, and he couldn't sleep. Gora tossed and turned, moaning until, at last, he woke up. His absence would not be tolerated in this nonstop staging of the apocalypse. The news of the assault repeated itself and multiplied on that fatal day, and the day that followed, and after, a single and often prolonged day, grandiose and endless.

In the superb twilight, the city was speechless, silent. Long convoys of pedestrians were heading home. Stiffened subways. The sadness and discipline syndrome, solidarity and horror, unified the city dwellers who'd been so hurried and disparate the day before. How was it possible not to suspect everyone? And how could no one anticipate the disaster that a suspect hunt will lead to?

Professor Gora had an ever-increasing need for an interlocutor. The room had shrunken; the tenant had shrunken.

The meeting with Eva Gaşpar had been long. He spoke to her at length, she listened like a deaf-mute, barely out of the crematorium. He wasn't at all sure that he'd diminished her panic. Nor would it have been normal for him to succeed in doing so. He was glad to return to his routine interlocutors.

Books, yes, that's my refuge, dear Eva. Do you remember when Peter gradually began to prefer books over basketball? David, his father, was still a valid and lucid man then, not an invalid in an asylum, desperate and frantic over Peter's metamorphosis. And with good reason. He was ever more bizarre, isolated, hungry for books. Peter wasn't the same; no one remains the same after such an astral initiation.

Who'd heard of a death threat through a quotation from a book? What kind of person beats his brains to find out the code, and only after that, welds something together, ever to be haunted by inescapable phantoms? A code of the sect . . . The sect of readers sent our friend the encrypted missive, through a girl who also reads a few books herself. Sign of recognition and esteem and alarm. A quotation, find it and awaken it and unravel it, if you can! The threat didn't come from the Nymphomaniac but from the cult, unless the Nymphomaniac is actually the cult's deity. Peter had suffered not just from fear and loneliness but because he also belonged to the cult. He wanted, at any price, to decode the message. It was a matter of honor and pride.

We're like dogs, dear Eva. We sniff each other and we instantly recognize each other in the language of citations and charades. Poor Peter couldn't identify the source of the quotation! You could laugh yourself to death thinking about death's invitation to an idle chat. The literary reference was within him, but in the language of his youth. He couldn't transfer or locate it in the vocabulary of his new age. Youth was forever reminding him that it was never returning, no matter what he did.

In the end, I helped him, not only because you asked me in weekly letters to keep you posted on his progress after the breakup with Lu but because, at some point, that quotation became a mark on my calendar. I wasn't a know-it-all, as Peter said, but I had lived that quotation, not only memorized it. I used to frequent a group of students for whom literature and readings had become the supreme drug. We looked endlessly for hidden meanings in the texts. Tyranny stimulates the necessity for hiding and esoteric dialogue. In the dubious loft of the dubious readers, the books that were discussed were hard to procure, old, and new, filled with codes and mysterious symbolisms. It was there that I first encountered the story *Death and the Compass*, from which, decades later, the enchanting student from Sarajevo would extract her citation death threat.

A coincidence spanning countries and seas and meridians! Who could have imagined it, outside of the devotees themselves?

Here on free turf, the sect is somewhat reduced, naturally, lacking the necessary nerve to spy and pry, but even here, exiles and sleepers in search of the North Star wade to their navels in the subterranean and supercelestial black holes of the esoteric. Palade and his great schoolmaster Dima and even Augustin Gora wrote about this enigmatic and overevaluated story that drove the playful Deste to distraction.

I knew the quotation by heart. Translated in all the languages of the world. That's the truth, always simpler than we suppose.

I pulled Peter out of one labyrinth and threw him into a deeper one. "I know what the Greeks didn't know," declared the blind man from Buenos Aires. Uncertainty. I made the mistake to relate these words to Peter. After I indicated the source of the citation, the uncertainty grew. Peter made the connection with Palade's assassination and Dima's obscure past, in which the esoteric had played a fatal role. It was as if he were again living in the captivity of socialism or the terror of the swastika-branded archangels, haunted by ubiquitous shadows with impeccable eyes and ears and weapons. It was fortunate that the hell he'd entered had lasted only little while. Soon enough, the mystery was deflated. The death threat had been the game of a child! But the farce had hurt Peter deeply and had sent him into the great American emptiness.

Yes, there will be consequences, acts of vengeance and arrests and sieges. Maybe that's why Peter's reappearance is so late in coming; he's waiting for things to settle. Either way, he is alive. And whatever unpleasant repercussions he may have to confront, they can't compete with today's massacre.

Today, today, today, repeated Gora in front of the screen that day and the days that followed, unified in the same, long and exhausting day.

So, dear Mrs. Kirschner, our dearest Peter had entered the game initiated by the pretty Bosnian, along with Tara and Avakian and Anteos. They will be investigated, naturally, like so many others, Muslims or Greeks or Armenians or Russians or refugees of all kinds—and, believe me, also Americans.

Days and nights pass quickly, months and years and also we mortals, but the attack of the September Bird continues, a bizarre astronomical paradox. Weeks and months and seasons in a single, dilated, and damned day.

Maybe you've heard, dear Eva, of the formidable Margarete, also known as Margot. American, not Iraqi or Iranian. Margot H. survived the disaster and found out that her fiancé, David, had lost his life in the explosion. Traumatized, she decided not to let herself be defeated, but instead to put her American energy in service to the Cause. She arrives at the front of the Association of the Babel Towers Survivors, asks for and receives support from senators and bankers, from television networks and from philanthropic organizations. Her story reaches the anguished souls of the mourners, soothing their unsoothable pain. She'd lived through horrific scenes among corpses, had smelled burned skin, had seen human bits flying through the air. In the last moments she was thinking, naturally, about her fiancé, David, about her wedding dress and their wedding vows. A fireman brought me out in his arms, the unhappy widow Margot would explain, recovered from the other world. He handed me over to someone else, who started to carry me toward the ambulance. We didn't make it that far. We crouched under a truck, he covered me with his large, benevolent body, explained the faustian Margarete of the softened planet. The air was burning, we couldn't see anything, I breathed through his gas mask, until help arrived. America and the world listened to her, petrified and tearing and drawing courage from her courageous words. She wouldn't admit defeat, she fought with herself and destiny, to win and to help her kind win.

Only the words were strange, dear Eva. Heard so often and in various circumstances. Tired old clichés, in contrast to a circumstance so acute, personal, and extreme. Language, however, is everything, in the end! Style makes the man, as we've learned. Suspicion wasn't too far behind, however, and it was discovered that the brave Margarete, with a burn extended over her entire left arm, wasn't in New York on September 11, but in Spain, where she was studying at a Catalan university.

She conceived her narrative, with great care, about a year after Black September. David had, indeed, perished, even though he was among the chosen people. He'd been overlooked by the team conducting the secret rescue mission the night before. David's poor family, however, had been warned through a special channel, though they declared to the cameras of justice and postcards that they knew of no such rescue conspiracy, and that they'd never heard of the famous Margarete. The first affirmation might make us doubt the second, had there not existed irrefutable evidence of the fantasy readily exploited by the impostor, and not for the first time.

This is the garden of the One and Only God. Full of the many and the varied. Multiple world, multiplying itself in the air and on the ground, as our friend Palade used to say. Multiple worlds in the garden of our Unique and Singular Master.

In the days and nights and months that followed, the anchorite Gora was in dire need of an interlocutor. There were so many things left to debate and discuss, and he grew weary of discussing them only with himself. And Eva's silence depressed him.

On the table, the immense album *A Day in the Life of America* had been replaced with a pile of books about the rabbi Paul of Tars, the exile who sowed discord everywhere he went, like the rebel prophets before and after him. Propaganda and agitation for the unification of the world under a single banner! All will be admitted equally, the converts of the new, singularly valid religion. Let them accept that singular religion, let them form a column in the army of that singular religion. Jesus addressed only his own place and tribe, without ambitions to convert anyone; he was candid and holy, like the legendary idiot Mishkin and like Alyosha Karamazov and their brothers from other legends. Globalized modernity redeems itself from Paul.

The infidels are left behind and, heaven have mercy on them, they teach us about Lenin and Mao Zedong and all the ayatollahs and Fascist fervor. Was the poet Yussuma-Osama the new Saint Paul who decrees who is chosen and who is damned? The terrorists, the deaf-mutes follow his instruction, as if under hypnosis: tear down the sinful world to establish the Absolute and to shorten the road to Paradise.

Lost fools! Sin doesn't lie hidden in the Pentagon or in the World Trade Center but in the Library! The poems of Yussuma rest alongside the immodest Beats and the Qur'an of the Ayatollah and the Epistles of Paul, neighbors to Einstein, Karl Marx's *Manifesto*, *Mein Kampf*, and Dante. Imperial cookbooks are near the manuals for decoding dreams in 888 languages and dialects of the world. War and commerce are nothing but games, in the labyrinth of games that animates the apathy of our kind.

This is what I'm up to, dear Eva, I'm conversing with the solitary

Yussuma and with Paul the exile, while waiting for a telephone call from our dear Peter. Peter Gaşpar, not the Apostle Peter.

I spent the last few nights in useless controversies with the Apostle Peter and Saint Tara and the Apostle Paul from Cilicia, from the Greek Diaspora. I wanted to find out what would have happened if Peter from Galilee had won the dispute instead of Paul the Greek Jew.

What if is another game we use to kill time and boredom, the disease that spares no one, not even the Almighty, and which catapulted the nineteen knifemen in the belly of the September Bird. *What if* is the code of the sect that raises and devours libraries. The shelves are full of bibles and war manuals, legends of ants and dragons, maps of the sky, philatelic classifications, and the dialects of the world.

Eva Gaşpar rested during Gora's long, afternoon naps. Now he was awake and protected again in the fortress of his books.

The groggy professor was thinking about libraries and books. And words. Saramago's scribe was rewriting Portugal's history with a single word; Shakespeare's kings reign in the mind of the playwright; Dante exiled the pope of his time to the Inferno, like a merchant of spiritual goods; Napoleon becomes an understudy in a musical comedy, in the reviews of Tolstoy; Roth sits the Hitler-phile Lindbergh in Roosevelt's presidential armchair; the sacred verses become satanic in the games of the infidel Rushdie; the atomic button ignites the word Start. Mynheer was born in *The Magic Mountain* of a book; Paul and Peter live the pages of the Evangelicals; the prophet Yussuma resides in the Qur'an and in the half-moon of the Holy War. Our dear Peter's misfortune also started with books; I plunged him into the complicated biography and bibliography of the Old Man, an addict intoxicated by books, rattled by the library in flames, watching books and ages dissolve into the ether. I couldn't forget this when I was summoned to unmask the erudite Dima for the sins that deserved to be unmasked, but I also never forgot the millions of Jesus Christs burnt in crematoriums, together with the books they carried in their souls, nor the rabbi Yehoshua of

Nazareth, who carried in himself a book and provoked the writing of a thousand others.

I'm convinced that Peter Gaşpar is alive, but I don't ignore his mother's unease. She asks me, weekly, if I know anything about the fate of her disappeared son. Lu spoke to me often about Eva Kirschner-Gaşpar at the time when we ourselves were discussing the possibility of having a son. Even while irradiated by amorous affection, I didn't avoid hard questions. Peter Gaşpar embodied a revival after death for the couple Eva and David Gaşpar; why shouldn't our own progenitor be the seal of the enlightenment that had been given to us?

The nickname "Mynheer" came from a book and from a parody he himself imagined; the death threat named an author who had proclaimed himself the high priest of the library. Today's and yesterday's and tomorrow's terrorists follow the words in books that they imagine were written by the Great Anonymous One. What are those poor offices of commercial transaction compared to the Temple of the Word? Nothing but vulgar and childish diversions! The grand adventures are all produced in the great, silent halls where Love invents codes of refuge, in science and lyricism and navigation, gastronomy and astronomy. Traces of ether and blood stain the pages of manuals and epistles gathered over the millennia; the recent invention of the little screen of offers and laconic dialogue also had its origins in the Library.

The days and nights that followed the days and nights after September 11, 2001, found Gora captivated by the same dialogue with the void.

There was day and night and the second day and the days and weeks and following seasons, the endless day and night of uncertainty.

The evening was darkening, and the light vibrated through the peaceful landscape in the window. The earth continued to turn on its axis and around the sun that was setting, melancholy; Lu's gloves and the books on the shelf were in their places, alive, as ever.

Professor Gora waited, every day, for the assault on the Library.

His library and all the libraries of the world. A simultaneous, decisive assault on all libraries, the likes of which would make the assault on the Towers of Transactions and Rockets seem like poor improvisations. A historic day, engraved in red and black.

◾

The phone wasn't working or the subscriber wasn't answering on the historic day and the historic night, or any others. Once, at 11 o'clock in the evening, I managed to reach him.

"I'm all right," the professor said softly.

He wasn't expecting me to call, although he'd called me so many times with regard to Gaşpar and Marga Stern. He'd told me about Eva Gaşpar's letters and about the hourly succession on September 11, 2001, hours he knew by heart, about Saint Paul and Saint Peter and Yussuma Ben Laden and about the target that all the stupid and illiterate terrorists had missed: the Library.

I had prepared a piquant history about Lu and Michael Stolz. I had to postpone it, I was taking advantage of Gora's unexpected loquacity.

"It just so happens that farce precedes tragedy and not the other way around, as Marx thought. I'm thinking about the letter Peter received and about Borges' story."

I let him summarize the chain of events once again. I promised him I'd call him soon, so we could try a normal conversation, on a more normal day.

The following conversation opened, as I'd planned, with information about Stolz and Lu. It seemed like my only chance to draw him out of the solitude that followed the shock. I began abruptly. He was listening, quietly, without reaction, as if it were an anecdote about people unknown to him. He didn't ask how I'd come across all of those details. He then allowed himself some predictable questions.

"A party?"

"An anniversary. A pretext. In Long Island, at the house of a couple who ran a banker's club. The man, a former pilot, had deserted to the Occident. First Belgium, then America. He'd managed, through political pressure, to bring his wife, who was a gym trainer. Repurposed in America as a fashion designer. They ran the club together, and they used it when it was empty. The party took place on a day like that. During the period after the great assault. During and after natural disaster instincts intensify. Sometimes, to the point of hysterics. Lu had been a high school classmate of Raluca's, the gym trainer, and Stolz had come with a superb, young African woman who captivated all the gazes in the room. Lu arrived late, with Dr. Wu, a colleague at Koch's office. The atmosphere was already heightened, but no one suspected that it would come to a swingers' party."

Gora was listening, but he wasn't asking for details.

"The flirting intensified, three of the couples exchanged partners, in the end. When she left with Stolz, Lu gave the young Dr. Wu, dazed by Raluca, a short wave."

Professor Gora wasn't asking for details.

Professor Gora didn't seem impressed by the excess of the insinuations.

If he wasn't just faking, if he'd actually become indifferent with regard to Lu's present, Gora had given me good news.

■

The great city had pastoral suburbs. A solemn petrifaction. Ashen squirrels, the red cat. The crows, pompous procession of wild turkeys. The deer among the brush.

The forest had overrun the previous night, white, snowbound, and it was advancing even now, from all sides. The branches were shaking, the white powder fell furiously from the tall trees, stuck into the ground that was also advancing closer and closer, then retreating.

The forest was far away, along the horizon, then again it grew near, approaching, white, frozen. Just as in a silent movie. There was no rustling, nothing. The branches were prostrating themselves, agitated, ready to snap, the wind was whipping the flake powder, but no sound could be heard. A morbid silence, then movement. The bizarre came and couldn't come to an end.

Now, in the first hours of the morning, the trees were solemn, unmoving. The crows were landing and taking off among the restless squirrels. That was all, nothing more, beyond the window of the mute house, not a sound, not even the slightest rustling. Nothing could be heard, not the cars that passed on the road, nothing.

Professor Gora wasn't and had never been a part of the landscape. That was what he'd felt in his former country, all the more so in the new terrain, a lost intruder in unconscious nature.

He was looking around differently from the year before. More attentively to what exists and what will continue to exist after the viewer will disappear, along with the generation of squirrels and crows and supple, stupid deer that populate the meadow. The forest will still be here, just like the river that has flowed through the valley for ages. He'd have been a perishable embodiment in the forests of his former country, as well, the guinea pig of an implacable moment. The traces of his terrestrial trajectory will diminish until they disappear completely. He hadn't left behind any children or grandchildren. Even if he'd wanted to, posterity wouldn't have modified its flows and cycles. He'd detected the code of limits.

Banal melancholy! Instanced by a telephone message, that was it!

"The Nuclear Magnetic Resonance results say that the arteries are blocked. Sixty to seventy percent. It wouldn't be bad, at your age. I, however, am skeptical. It could be worse than that. Let's check. The age of the patient requires precaution."

"Any age," Dr. Bar-El added immediately. Age, again! Koch had said the same thing. His old friend from school. He'd asked him if he'd ever had a cardiac exam.

"No, not recently. The last one was about eight years ago. Then I exchanged the doctor with the dyed hair for a taciturn female doctor. She said it wasn't necessary."

"At your age, it's a good thing to do. I'll send you to a good cardiologist," Koch had decided. "He has naturally colored hair. And he's not taciturn. He's Israeli, however."

"These guys are obligated to think fast."

"At your age you need fast doctors. I'm not much of one. For us in the old country, there wasn't much of a hurry."

And that was how the comedy of old age began.

Youth and the places of long ago truly had a different rhythm. Many years had passed since Isidor Koch listened to the confession of his benchmate Augustin Gora. Not in the room where they did their homework together, but in the large basement, full of wine bottles and old leather armchairs belonging to the Koch family. Izy, as people called Isidor, opened his eyes wide, stupefied.

"What? You want to love the Chosen People? Have you lost your senses? It's the Disease of Puberty . . . Are you in love with the people who crucified Jesus? Isn't that what you say? We crucified him and will pay for the sin, in time everlasting, they say. You want to trade one legend for another?"

"If it's a legend, I can trade it however I want. I thought we'd decided never to use 'you,' 'us,' 'them,' anymore . . . Jesus, yes, loved his people. The Romans had an interest in his execution . . . maybe the Jews, too, though I don't think so. They didn't accept him as the Messiah, they preferred to keep waiting. They chose an incomplete, open thought. Idolatry is a fixed idea; this is idolatry. But you don't understand what I'm saying."

"I don't understand, and it's better that way," Izy had said.

"You don't know anything, you haven't read anything. I'm for Peter, not for Paul."

Izy was silent, stone still, as if he were hearing Chinese.

"Peter said that you can't be Christian if you were never a Jew."

"Okay, you can get circumcised. A slashed prick . . . wait, I'll show you."

Izy made a gesture as if he were about to open his fly. Gusti pushed him, disgusted, sending the little Izy staggering.

"The Apostle Paul was an activist. He wanted to spread the movement, to internationalize it. Workers of the world, unite! I'm with Peter."

"You're an idiot, that's what you are. You trade one fable for another, you've admitted. You'll get over it, your lordship. You've had other fits like this. You wanted to be Oblomov, Don Quixote. That Dutchman, Peeperkorn."

"Who am I, Izy? I'm nobody."

"You're an outstanding student. The best in the whole school."

"Nonsense! A cliché. The obedient boy who always does his homework on time."

"You don't even do it all the time. You want something special? You're my friend, that's something special. You, the outstanding student, are friends with the lazy, fat kid in the house. Izy, the accordionist."

"Your kind is different, Izy."

"You said we're going to avoid saying 'you,' 'they,' 'we.'"

"You've suffered. I'm obsessed with the mystique of suffering."

"Ah . . . you want me to crucify you? I'll train, I promise you, I'll become the most valiant kid in class, in the whole school, I'll get to work, I'll prepare the cross, the nails, the crown of thorns."

"You're the incurable idiot, not me. A real ox, that's what you are, Izy. That's it, we'll talk when you've evolved a bit more and can vote."

Thousands of years had passed, Dr. Koch has been able to vote for a long time, the joke was long forgotten. The patient still remembered it right before the great exam.

"What cardiologist are you sending me to? What's his name? El-Al?"

"No, it's not an airline company. Bar-El. Rhymes with El-Al. Bar-El."

Dr. Bernard Bar-El was a tall, brown-haired man. Elegant, efficient. He was quick on his feet, immediately scheduled an appointment for the exam. The Russian technician was also elegant and polite. He measured Gora's tension, his pulse attentively, performed the electrocardiogram, injected the colorful substance into his vein. After a half an hour, treadmill. Berni Bar-El was holding the cardiac patient's hand, watching the monitor.

"Good, good, go on. How's it feel? Can you keep going?"

"Yes, I can."

Just when you think you're giving your soul, and you're all out, the doctor taps you on the shoulder.

"Okay, okay, we'll stop here."

He hadn't given his all, he wasn't expecting the interruption.

"Have you had any chest pain recently? Shortness of breath, sharp pain?"

"No, nothing. Just the stomach. I went to see Dr. Koch."

"Dr. Koch sent me the endoscopy and the colonoscopy results. Your stomach is perfectly normal."

" 'But the patient has one foot in the grave,' we joke in my country. My stomach is killing me. Koch changed the medication several times. In vain. I have a monster in my guts."

"Okay, we'll figure it out. Now, we need an NMR for the heart. Quickly. I don't know if insurance will cover that. Are you prepared to pay for it if necessary?"

"If necessary, if it's urgent . . . "

"Seven to eight hundred dollars. I'll call the hospital right away."

The patient finds himself at the hospital in an hour. The benevolent black receptionist looked down the list, attentively, right away. "Gora, yes, Augustin Gora."

After two days, Bar-El calls. Unsatisfied by the investigation.

"I don't believe the results. I want to double check. The age of the patient requires precaution. Any age, for that matter. I'm going to schedule you for an angiogram. Call me and we'll arrange the appointment."

That was the morning message.

The beautiful winter landscape knew nothing about Bar-El. A photogenic stoniness, grandeur. The professor was watching the woods. Nearby on the couch, the large, heavy album *A Day in the Life of America*, HarperCollins Publishers. Blue cover. A black rider with a black hat, a black horse, and a white half-moon, against the night's blue sky. Underneath, *We are frenzied and happy and hopeful. We are zealots and zanies and high school kids just starting to wonder what the world is all about.* That was how the Yankees described themselves, with humor. The album of his new family.

The symbolic photograph, a blonde girl and a blond boy, dressed in white, dance, holding each other, with their eyes closed, transfigured. *This is May 2, 1986.*

Where was I on May 2, 1986? Lu was in our former country, Peter Peeperkorn on a page in a German novel, the future patient Gora knew nothing about the blocked arteries or about angioplasty.

■

Gusti Gora and Izy Koch remained friends even after the mysterious meeting in the basement. The controversy continued, Izy increasingly more irritated, Gora increasingly more bullheaded about the possibility, which he'd grown bored of justifying.

"Love isn't necessary, Gusti," Koch was saying, "We don't need love, listen to me. In our madness, it's what we're always waiting for. Love. To be loved, imagine that! After ages of hate and disorientation, the world will suddenly love us. Love your neighbor better than yourself? Your neighbor! Yes, I understand . . . but you can't love your neighbor better than you love your own skin. It's a lie. Never more than yourself. It isn't possible. And if it's possible, it's too much. Why should they love us? Because we're better, more beautiful? Impeccable? We're not. So then, let them leave us alone. That's all, that's all! You hear? That's all! Let them stop asking us to be better, more beautiful, impeccable. That's all! We don't need love, Gusti."

Gusti was walling himself into the mountain. Soon after, he'd given up the disputes with Izy, or with anyone else, on the subject. When conflicts appeared on the taboo theme, or jokes about the side curls or the traditional insults, he'd simply leave the room. He'd go through years of school that way, and for a long time afterward, when, an assistant at the university, he frequented an attic where there were heated debates about the most heated questions in the world. Lu was never to discover her husband's juvenile obsession with the Apostle Peter, and Isidor Koch, was, by then, far away.

At the end of high school, Izy signed up for the Institute of Physical Culture and Athletics, no more, no less! Gora was stupefied. Koch had become a champion weight thrower, weightlifter, and rower. Isidor Koch, an athlete?! This wasn't the image by which his people had gained their renown and antipathy. And, as if the exotic choice weren't exotic enough, Izy had chosen Cluj, the capital of Transylvania, as the place where he would pursue his study.

"This program exists here, too. Why would you go so far away?"

"People are more serious there. I'm fed up with the jokes people make about me, as well as the jokes I make myself. And besides, there's the unknown to consider! Anonymity! Just think, a place where no one knows you!"

Gora was smiling. Cluj was much smaller than Bucharest, the anonymity would evaporate fairly quickly. But he didn't contradict the athlete, he just thought about his friend affectionately.

After a year, Izy came back home. Not for his studies, but for his departure. He'd been claimed by a wealthy uncle in Venezuela, he was abandoning the socialist paradise.

"Our Max has become an oil tycoon! Heaps of money. Remember that. When you want to escape, I will buy your freedom. Don't expect a wealth of correspondence, but you will have my address very soon."

The address from Caracas came late, on a spectacular postcard. A few words, "Here's my address and my hello. Yours, as ever, your Holiness!"

Gora would send him regular bits of information about their classmates' evolution, with no allusion to the Homeland or to Venezuela. No answer. After a few years, he received a photograph. Isidor Koch, in medical school, holding a tennis racket, near a group of supple, smiling young women. The address on the back was that of a studio apartment he'd bought in Caracas, near the university. Then, after graduation, a photograph from New York. The wedding: Isidor Koch and Isabel Motola. An elegant synagogue, elegant grooms, elegant attendants. On the back, some brief words about the bride, a doctor as well, American, the daughter of a renowned rheumatologist. "Today at our wedding on Fifth Avenue, my old friend Augustin Gora was also present. His place is here. Write to me."

Gora didn't respond. Correspondence with the outside could diminish his already uncertain chances of obtaining a passport.

He didn't look for Koch immediately when he arrived in New York. He wasn't ready for that meeting, there was too much to recapitulate, many things that couldn't even be recapitulated. Izy would have found Lu's refusal to follow him very irritating. In the letter where he'd described their first meeting, Gora had outlined her beauty, her intelligence, refinement without mentioning her ethnicity. Izy didn't ask any questions. No, he wasn't ready to convince Dr. Koch that the ethnicity hadn't determined his choice, nor had it been the thing that destroyed their marriage . . . or that the separation from her hadn't shaken his convictions.

When Peter Gașpar appeared, Professor Gora intervened, nevertheless, and asked Koch to hire his former wife. Izy responded with a long silence, waiting for details, didn't get them, the silence continued, but he hired Madam Gora.

Gusti kept postponing the meeting with his former classmate and friend, under various pretexts. Koch understood, it seemed, that there were coded dilemmas at work, he didn't insist. They agreed, during one of their rare telephone conversations, never to speak of it again. They'd kept their word until the September Bird invaded. He'd called to find out if Lu was all right, the most important piece of news that day. Then, silence. Then, the monster in his stomach appeared, and he needed a doctor. Had Izy become just like all the doctors in America, good interpreters of computers and statistics but not of patients? Otherwise he'd never have resisted the competition, Gora told himself on his way to the office of his former classmate.

"And where are you from," the cab driver asked.

"From the Balkans. And yourself?"

"From the Soviet Union."

"It's big. The Soviet Union is a big place."

"Well, 'the Balkans' are no village, either. I'm from the Soviet Union."

The driver had been recommended to him by Peter, long before his disappearance. Gaşpar had told him, "He's from our youth."

"Boltanski isn't a Lithuanian or Kyrgyz name."

"I'm a Soviet. That's what I was, that's what I've remained. I understand you're going to the doctor."

"Yes, a former schoolmate."

"From the Balkans?"

"From the Balkans. He's helping me find the specialist I need. And you, what did you do in the Soviet Union?"

"The army. I was in the army. The Red Army."

"With that name?"

"With this name. Israel Lyova Boltanski. In officer training there were two of us. Out of four thousand students. Good marks, they had no choice. I've remained a Soviet. If a friend calls me at two in the morning and needs me, I'm there. No matter how tired, no matter how sick. And I'm sick. Kidneys destroyed. In your wonderful America I worked the first ten years driving a truck. A giant truck. Day and night. I know their doctors. They ask you about your insurance instead of your illness. What insurance do you have? We're just numbers. Digits, statistics. No, sir, we're very sorry, the doctor doesn't accept this form of insurance, we're sorry. Yankee politesse. Business! The salvation of this country."

"How do you mean?"

"The economy! It maintains the rot. Greed and cunning, the wealthy getting wealthier, the lies of the politicians, the gossip on the TV. Democracy is a bigger lie than the hammer and sickle."

"You really think so?"

"I do. You need millions of dollars to become a senator. You beg for those millions from others, and then you return the favors. A single salvation: the economy. The manipulation of human defects! It maintains the rot. Work, business, money. Exploitation to the point of blood. If the boss wants, you're done in two minutes' notice. You lose your medical coverage, then your house, car, everything. So then you are careful not to lose those things. You work like a slave and slavery becomes dear to you. Where I come from, when you say something about the government, you'd say, "the motherfucking government." Here they say *God bless America!* The mania of work. You work like an animal, to the half-hour before they take you to the cemetery."

"So why did you come here?"

"Eh . . . for the children. For the children, as the story goes. A boy and a girl. We do everything for them. They have no idea and they don't care. We work like mad, my wife and I. To give them everything, so they can have everything. A soulless generation, mister . . . My daughter, dear heart. Little Sofia. Sofia Boltanska. Boltanskaia. A college student. Beautiful, intelligent, spoiled, elegant, everything you want. This summer she's going to a seminar at Syracuse University! She found God knows what on the Internet. Summer courses at Syracuse University. 'You're going to leave us now?' I ask her. 'Your mother doesn't know what else to do for you, so that everything's washed, ironed, starched, folded to perfection. And what about me, my little Sofia? How can you be so far away from me for the whole month?' 'A month, Papa?' she says. 'What's a month? We'll talk on the phone, Papa, we'll talk on the phone.' You hear that? The phone! I bet over email, too!"

Dr. Izy Koch had aged, but his memory was intact and he never forgot to let you know.

"You've arrived where you should have arrived a long time ago. I sent you the address, just as I'd promised, didn't I?"

"Yes, you sent it to me."

"And I updated it whenever it changed. Isn't that right?"

"That's right."

"You buckled! The apathy numbed you. Decades. Decades wasted."

Gora was quiet, smiling. He was looking at Dr. Koch's immaculate lab coat, his small gold-rimmed glasses, his white, disheveled hair, his burgundy tie, the blue shirt, large, hairy hands. He looked and smiled and said nothing.

"I hope you kept the secret. Our secret from the basement."

"I kept it."

"You didn't make any public declarations of fidelity to the socialist Utopia and the socialist terror, you didn't betray the multitudes of gaping mouths, you didn't sign any declarations of surrender. You did none of those things, isn't that right?"

"No, I didn't do any of those things."

"And you didn't provide any secret information to the police? Tell me you didn't. I've heard that informants were everywhere, and that it was very difficult not to become one of them. You'll have to recount it all sometime, won't you? Now we're going to go into the office, to see if you have the same body. We'll deal with the soul another time."

In his office Koch was meticulous, turning the patient over on all sides.

"We'll take care of the stomach, but I don't think that's the only thing."

And that was how Gora arrived at Dr. Bar-El. After the stress test and the NMR, he called Izy once again. For the angiogram Bar-El had referred him to Edward Hostal, an Australian doctor.

"Born and raised in Australia. A wanderer just like us. A great, great doctor. You're in very good hands. Small, but good hands. I know him. Not to worry!"

"And . . . just as we discussed. Not a word to her!"

"My dear Gora, how long have we known each other? We know what a secret means."

We know and we rediscover, every day, until death's bludgeon wakes us.

◼

The treadmill is connected to the heart-rate monitor and to the pulse of the soul. Abruptly, the red warning light. Alarm. The gong announces the countdown. Eyes wide open to the vicinity, to see clearly what it is, will soon no longer see anything. The dead squirrel in front of the house, the rotted tree. The wear of the living, the inevitable that annuls everything that was, as if it had never been.

To absorb the joy of the moment, its delusions. He was no longer young, and even if he were young, he still couldn't call for deferment, the hazard asked to be respected.

Books had kept him unaware of the cycles of aging and diminishing. He looked at the shelves where friends rested in between worn covers, friends who'd accompanied him along the exodus before the definitive exodus. Tomorrow he will present himself, anxiously and politely, to the surgeon Dr. Hostal, for the farewell. A nostalgic fraternization, because it was final. Should you extend a hand, as an epilogue, to the one who tried to keep you among the living, what more human ritual can you seek?

When you have no one from whom you are about to separate yourself, your loneliness intensifies in the final moments, but it's also purer, independent of others. Parents disappeared long ago, he'd adjusted with difficulty to being far from them, and with their painful bouts of longing. Oblomov dedicated long odes to laziness, Izy had remained in the basement of youth, and Saint Peter in Galilee, Kira Varlaam was dedicating herself to her autistic son, Dima was stealing away to the void as to an undeserved amnesty, the Cavalier from La Mancha never forgave Dulcinea's infidelity, Palade was dispatched by a bullet, just like his hero Lonrot, Peter Gaşpar made himself invisible, legitimizing, through a broad prank, his renowned Dutch namesake. The little blonde girl in the blue one-horse carriage was still passing in front of the enchanted and chimerical boy, just as she did in childhood. And Lu had survived, in her magic youth, dizzy with aphrodisiacs. After so many years since the separation that never successfully became a parting, any ritual of separation from Lu would have been ridiculous, and, as was obvious, futile.

He was caressing the clean surface of the desk, books all pushed to the side, along with the red gloves of the past. Tomorrow, after the dying man's last shudder, everything will remain in its place, the books and Lu and the obituary of the disappeared, until they disappear as well, sweeping away all traces of the deceased. For some time the retina of Edward Hostal will preserve the face of the patient who, at the end, wanted to assure him not of his gratitude but of the serenity with which he'd accepted the ephemeral. He had resisted serenity often with a candid obstinacy. Enriched, nevertheless, he would tell Hostal that he'd been enriched often by the ephemeral's immaterial intensity and ineffable joy, even while convinced that in the end, the material would conquer all. He'd tell the Australian that these joyful and passing oppositions were not at all negligible.

■

The patient arrived early at the hospital, as he'd been requested to do. He listened attentively to the instructions: if the angiogram shows that there's need for an intervention, an angioplasty will be performed on the spot; at the point where the leg connects to the hip, a small imaging catheter will be introduced into the femoral artery. It will advance toward the artery that needs cleaning, the catheter will expand, compressing the buildup, dilating the artery, and a small metal tube will replace the balloon to maintain the dilation. You will be sedated, not fully anesthetized, the doctor requires the live and conscious reaction of the patient.

Stretched out on the narrow bed, hands and legs restrained, Augustin Gora was looking at the computer screen. Doctor Pontecorvo appeared, a tall, lanky man with black hair. Then Maestro Hostal, the professor. Small, dense. Small hands and small, blue eyes. White, curly hair, cropped short. Solid, dense, he inspires trust.

"No anesthetic, as you know. We need the patient's lucidity. You will receive a calming syrup."

The Chinese woman handed him a glass with a pink liquor, the patient drank it to the bottom. He felt the insertion in the vein of the leg, the trajectory of the camera for making images of his insides, he closed his eyes, the electronic cricket worked intensely, the patient squeezed the metal railing of the bed to which he was restrained. Eyes closed, teeth clenched.

Hostal is once again by the patient's side.

"I have good news and I have bad news. Which do you want first?"

"The good."

"We can intervene."

It meant it was all going to hell, and the devil was going to humiliate the dying.

"The bad news is that your arteries are blocked. Over 90 percent, some even 99 percent. It's that sour cream from Bukovina . . . If you agree, we'll begin the procedure."

"I don't think I have an alternative."

"Not really. The intervention isn't foolproof. There are risks. Heart attack, stroke. It happens rarely, but it isn't impossible."

The Australian was silent, and the patient, as well.

"So then, you agree? We'll operate?"

"Yes, we'll operate."

"Oxygen will be pumped into the blocked artery. It will clean out the buildup. Then, we will fit in the metal lining. It is called a stent. It will keep the artery open so that circulation can normalize."

The doctor had rolled up his sleeves, and shifted over to the computer.

The arrow directly targeted the chest cavity. Deep, deeper. On the screen, the insect was feeling out its trajectory. A vibrating, bedeviled little locust, nibbling away at the waste in the artery. A sharp, persistent pain. Gora closed his eyes and held the bars alongside his bed with both hands.

"Taxus," Hostal orders. "Express Two."

The patient opens his eyes: the nurse was pulling a little cylinder out of a drawer down below. She'd torn the packaging and was now handing the cylinder to the doctor. A minuscule little shell, delicate. A long, poisonous pain right to his liquefied brain. Then, another cylinder. The long, thin arrow. Another sharp pain, moaning, whimpering, the patient closes his eyes, opens his eyes, squeezes the bars, unclenches his hands, then clenches them again. Time no longer exists, it consumes itself.

"An hour and ten minutes," announces the Chinese woman with a slight speech impediment.

"I've fitted you with two stents," Hostal explained. "We've resolved two central arteries. The others, next time. Come back in a month, a month and a half."

He'd remained by the bed, looking at the revived patient, smiling at him.

"We're only plumbers. Fixing pipes."

The doors open, the professor and the assistant exit. The patient is unrestrained at his hands and feet. The male nurse with the moustache pushes the wheelchair to the room on the third floor. He's hooked up to the monitor. The diagram on the screen in front of the bed. The pills and the water glass on the metal cart. Eyes closed in reverie.

The blonde, tall nurse on afternoon duty had entered the room. "You called?"

The pills had triggered some acidity and the stomach pains had returned. He managed to mumble, "Where are you from?"

The beauty smiled, "Polish."

"I'd thought maybe from Hollywood," the patient murmured.

Tall, thin, superb, she should have adapted to the New World in a bar or on a stage, not in the hallways of the hospital poisoned with odors and moans.

Looking a little like the prey of werewolves, Gora was moaning, but smiling at the beautiful Polish woman. "I feel as if I were Gaşpar . . . I miss Mynheer." Burning and pain. She returned with a spoonful of yellowish liquid. She raised his pillow, and then the spoon advanced toward his livid lips. The patient sipped the liquor, dizzy with stabs of pain, and with enchantment. Mollified and drawn into the waters of sleep.

When he awoke, the nurse had widened. Now she wore glasses and looked Mongolian. She was smiling, happy, motherly, an immaculate set of teeth. The thermometer. In his mouth, under his tongue. "Okay, you don't have a temperature and your blood pressure is normal." She'd removed his bedpan, she brings a small plate with five colored pills and glass of water. Soon, it's time for breakfast, then the morning visit, then discharge. The patients stay only one night, that's the rule, time is money, the sick person comes, leaves, the bill remains, the Soviet Boltanski was right. The telephone.

"I'm Doctor Bar-El. How do you feel, Professor? Hostal told me that you had 95-to-99 percent blockage. We caught it in time, I felt the urgency. Everything is okay, I will see you in two weeks."

Hostal appeared, like a chef in white with a chef's bonnet, fresh out of the cookie lab. Small, solid, trustworthy. In his hand, the folder full of clichés.

"Here is the image of what's been done and what is left to be done. Here's the narrowing of the artery, here the other artery, the corner of the curvature, the casing. There were constrictions in three places along one of the arteries. It's the latest kind of stent, treated with a protective substance that impedes future buildup. I hope you are feeling well. The angioplasty must be repeated. We'll repair the other arteries in two months. I know Koch, he told me about you. He also told me how delicious breakfast is in Bukovina, thick sour cream with wild strawberries."

No, Doctor Hostal wasn't Molière's medic, nor was he the bureaucrat of modern times.

"I see that here, too, just like everywhere, there's a gridlock of patients."

"Yes, it is. I get home at eight in the evening, I wake up at five. I would like to spend more time with my family, my children. All I do all day is postpone farewells between people."

Gora tightened his gaze and his ears perked, he wasn't expecting this formula. Truly, it would have been a shame for him to take leave of this stranger, and it wouldn't have been right for him to take leave of himself in front of any other witnesses.

Hostal extended his small hand, the patient squeezed it in his own small hand. The doctor offered him his business card.

"My assistant returns calls promptly. Call anytime."

The patient leans, with some difficulty, to the left. Hostal had something to add still.

"Oh, yes . . . I forgot. Izy told me that there's no one to accompany you out of the hospital. You have no family here in America."

"No, I don't."

"I've arranged with a nurse. She'll call the cab and accompany you home. Her name is Elvira, and she's from your country."

The little grandma with white hair, leaning on a cane, was taking the place of mother and aunt and concerned neighbor. A touching gift: his native language. The familiar, therapy in the wilderness. Doting Elvira protects the patient with jokes and endearments all the way to his door. Ready to put him to bed, to tuck him in and make his tea.

"Thank you, thank you, Elvira. You are very kind. Were you here in America in 1986?" The little grandma watched him, puzzled.

"Yes, of course, I was here."

"In May of 1986? You were here?"

"Yes, of course, I was here. I came in 1969."

"So on May 2, 1986, you were here, then?"

Elvira was wide-eyed, didn't understand what the professor wanted. She didn't figure into his album *A Day in America*, didn't know that *that day* was May 2, 1986. Gora thanked her for the company, opened the door, bent to the left and pushed the door with his shoulder.

■

The big world is actually quite small. Koch knew Larry One, also known as Avakian, who knew Larry Two, who knew Beatrice Artwein.

Gaşpar had brought his entire, own world into Gora's world, and Gora had given him Dima and Palade. The threatening letter Gaşpar received had revived the attic of suspects from long ago.

Now he was entering another phase of solitude. In his recovery bed, the exile tally doesn't soothe him: he'd published exegeses of medieval Spanish and French literature, essays about Latin American prose, research on popular mythology and the folklore of totalitarian states, he'd taught at major universities. It seemed to him that he was perpetuating a simulacrum.

He admired America; its contradictions and fatuousness didn't bother him. He had no hope of setting roots, so he saw it with a serene detachment. The admiration of a child handling his toy, conscious that it's nothing more than an impersonal toy. He'd exchanged the short and amusing obituaries with a more laborious experiment. "More stimulating," as he used to say.

He was no Don Quixote, nor Mr. K, nor Oblomov, nor Hans Castorp, nor a duller Ulrich, nothing close to the many embodiments of his adolescence. President Avakian regretted seeing him leave the small college for a large university, and he sent his regrets through Koch. To Koch, he described him as civilized, erudite, affable. Koch, in turn, hurried to transmit the kind words to Gusti. "Good for the ego," Izy Koch added.

"Yes, I liked your friend, doctor. Even the commotion that he sometimes—very rarely—produced. Certain oddities. I was told about the departmental meeting when two new courses for the fall semester were discussed. The Russian professor had proposed 'Homosexuality in Russian Literature.' Professor Gora couldn't keep his mouth shut. 'In Russian literature? *Nicevo*. Who? Tolstoy, Chekov, Pushkin, Dostoevsky, Babel? Gogol was impotent, made love to a big rubber doll custom-ordered especially for him. It's not French or German or British literature,' said the Eastern European. His colleagues had fallen silent. The young Russian professor had frozen solid, he'd come across someone who knew more than he did."

The pleasure with which Avakian related the mishap represented the pleasure with which he'd heard it himself, the first time and then even a few times afterward.

"The Russian professor mentioned a few minor names, including Tsvetaeva. 'I don't know about Tsvetaeva,' replied Gora, 'I have no idea about her and I don't care. She was married to a man she loved, she had a son and lovers, but that isn't the problem. One name isn't enough for a whole course.' When it was time to vote, there were four abstainers, Professor Gora against, and the rest, for. Madam Van Last, the professor of Victorian theater, huffed out of the room. Outside the door, she shook her finger at the exile. 'You, sir, you're stuck in your curriculums from the East, here we're in a different century.' Was she right, I wonder? She came to me to report Gora, called him a Stalinist straight out. And there were others. I refused to discuss it. He hadn't shipwrecked himself in America just to be censored, and he wasn't a Stalinist and had never been. I knew his life's story well enough. What else did they want? He never came to report that they don't know a thing about Russian literature. That's how it is here, the great democracy full of taboos. People are people, they need fixed props. Thoughts furiously fixed on those props produce cyclical typhoons. Sexual abuse of children, diets, flying saucers, ghosts in the walls, messages from the dead. In the meantime, I myself discovered some interesting novels by homosexual Russian writers. But at that time, no one knew anything about them. Gora never participated in another departmental meeting. I'm sorry to see him go."

"Avakian's rhythm then slowed down a notch," Koch said, pausing for a long time and waiting for Gusti's reaction.

"After that incident he never again participated in another departmental meeting, Avakian told me. At lunchtime, in the dining hall, if you looked for a table with just two chairs and put your briefcase and coat on one of them, it was a sign you wanted to be alone. And you would succeed. The comments weren't very kind. Solitude is suspect in America. It's considered arrogance. But President Avakian was sorry to see you go."

Izy retold the story, waiting for his wisdom and magnanimity.

"Yes, he's missed. Students took to him, nicknamed him 'Pnin,' Nabokov's hero in the novel by the same title. When he transferred, I told him I'd try to keep him at our little college, even if he weren't the erudite that he is. Simply so that students could benefit from his decency and candor, as a point of reference. When we said farewell, I said to him, 'Timofei Pavlich, I would have tried to keep you here at any cost and under any circumstances. I don't know that I would have been able to put up with Nabokov, but you, Timofei Pavlich, yes, for sure.' He laughed, he knew about the nickname, he liked being called Pnin."

Doctor Koch had his own commentary to add.

"The nickname didn't surprise me. Of course it was from a book! *Green horses on the walls,* our people in the Balkans say. Not just green horses, but green horses on the walls. Or in books. Chimeras. You found Saint Peter from a book as well. You should have learned to drive, to wander around this extraordinary country, to travel across the world. To charm actual people, which you could have done, to allow yourself to be enchanted, as you deserved to be. I never forgot your ideas about my people. The chosen people, the people of the book. The Book, of course! Even though you knew no one other than the fat accordionist in the class. I mean, me. No scholar, as you well know. And you knew Jesus and Peter and Judas and Paul and other Christians like them from books, as well. The Sacred Country is the Country of Books, isn't that right? You asked me if I'd heard about 'the man without qualities.' If I'd heard, not if I'd read about him! As if we were talking about a neighbor. You knew I'm not a big reader. You told me, and I will never forget this, 'Your only aristocracy is intellectual, you never got to sit still in one place, to build a social aristocracy.' The book is the only real aristocracy. Produced through misfortune. I was listening with my mouth gaping, same as my eyes and ears. The man without qualities? Now what was that? The man without balls? You laughed, and I hope you'll laugh now, too. But time has passed and keeps on passing. Even for someone hidden in books."

That was Dr. Koch! Now time was passing differently, a different pace, measured differently. One's body can't be the same forever, so then, everything passes, the mind, pride, frustrations. Even uncertainty changes. Laconic thinking . . . nothing from the great words is what it used to be.

"Has anything remained unchanged," the phantom of the evening asked.

"The woman inside of me," murmured Gora. "Invincible, because she is absent."

Thick, black hair in a thick, long plait down her back. Large, smoldering eyes. Deep, intense, infantile melancholy. Matte, white forehead. Arched, Oriental brows. Aquiline nose, drawn with a thin brush. Pronounced lips, vibrating slightly. A young throat. Blue.

Jealousy begins in imagination, but also in memory. There, the lost body holds the lost soul. There, in memory: naked, on her back, her long legs raised to the ceiling or crouched, her back turned. She received the man with a whimper. There, Professor, you can hear the whimpers of pleasure, you can see the one who was with her and is no longer. And you see the one who replaced him. The stiletto bleeds the memory. The pain of the moment advances slowly, slowly.

Love is just moaning, what books call love. The whimpers of the infantilized soul. Peter above the kneeling woman, who whimpers gently, like other times. Pale breasts, the curve of her thighs, the seashell of her sex. Long arms, clutching Gora passionately, clutching Gaşpar passionately. The abrupt movement of the head. Her black mane thrown on her back.

Old Gora was writhing again. Again abandoned. Ulysses cast away, not toward his home, but away from any home, among wanderers who'd lost the chains that had once tied them to the mast. They dreamed, as he did, of the imposture of survival, liberation.

Old Professor Gora felt old. The couple Lu and Peter sent him back to an irretrievable and poisoned time.

The exile before the exile, then wandering, the hope that Lu might reappear. Then, routine, nonstop work, in the country that works nonstop, to forget itself. Long days and short nights and long years and speed always fueled by the consumption of time. The Crusoe calendar: twenty years in the new territory. Dizziness, enchantment, regeneration, and, once again, estrangement. A hospitable, dynamic country, and a screen that separates. The stranger has advantages in the country of exiles, but he wouldn't dare compose the obituary of a native of this mixture of races and languages and beliefs that make up the Kingdom of the Unknown.

On his table he kept open the massive album *A Day in the Life of America*, the wilderness where he looked for Tara and Deste and Peter.

Gora slowly closes the book. He closes his eyes. He's tired, and it isn't the first time. He lowers himself, exhausted, into the armchair. One minute, five, then five hours.

He opens his eyes and discovers the white gloves on the table. "The most beautiful hands in the world," Professor Gora hears. The index, the middle finger, the ring finger with the golden band, the little finger and the thumb, which wasn't very thick at all, but timid, sleepy. The pink tipped fingernails, with white rims. Five troubled little beings, haptic magic. The professor believed in nothing but books, and it was from books that he learned that the ends of the fingers have the densest areas of nerves in the body, the Latin name *manus-manus*, in the corrupt Latin of his country, ties hands to gloves.* He'd have liked to write a poem to those gloves, but he wasn't a poet.

During a suffocating summer, he'd gone to an exposition in London, called The Hands. He'd wandered through the room for a few hours, back and forth, stone still in front of each image then returning, again and again, to the worn hands of the Indian, the childlike hands of the midget-clown, the ivory articulations of the geisha and again in front of the fist of the boxer and the small, pale fingers of the pianist caressing the keys, then again the transfigured courtesan, touching her sex, the soldier with the finger on the trigger, the potato pickers holding their lucky bounty, the cook happily clutching to his chest an immense grayish cabbage resembling the brains of a Neanderthal, the perforated glove of the cyclist and the greenish glove of the surgeon and the silken gloves of the actress who dominates the memory of century.

It was cool in the great, deserted gallery, no one else but a young Irish woman, with red hair and the waistline of a ballerina, who was contemplating her own freckled fingers while sitting in a chair

*In Romanian, glove is *mănușă*, pl. *mănuși* [trans.].

made of coffee-colored leather. He had watched her, as well, from afar, hoping she'd raise her gaze, but no, the girl couldn't separate her gaze from the image she was scrutinizing.

Outside there were crowds and haze, but before long he found the store he'd heard about. Small, elegant, expensive. He knew the number. He bought the first two pairs of gloves for his collection.

Haptic magic couldn't describe that sensation, he knew only that he was setting his blood in motion instantly. The hands, a part of the brain, controlled by the cerebral cortex in greater measure than any other part of the body! That was what his friends said, his books, that is. He'd researched like a madman, he'd scoured the lines in his own hands, like a pilgrim. The unmistakable fingerprint. The line of the heart, the line of a wasted life. The length and form of the palm and the fingers recalled the coded character of the woman who disappeared from his life. He would unclench her long and delicate fingers slowly, blinded by the rounded, mother-of-pearl fingernails tipped with a white line.

He'd tried to replace the gloves with reproductions of Dürer's hands, gathered in a heap on the table. In vain. White and black and red, yellow, blue gloves made of leather and silk, out of the skins of antelope and snake, the most expensive wool and the finest cotton, hunted in the windows of the most expensive boutiques, during sickly pilgrimages.

Nothing could replace the joy of spending considerable sums of money on his cherished inmates. He studied them, he stockpiled them, he brought them out to the light, one pair at a time or all at once, in a moment of fury and ecstasy, such as on this evening.

■

The angioplasty is followed by depression, he'd been warned by Koch and Bar-El. Koch called him daily to remind him that, statistically, depression was a very normal consequence of the procedure, and that it will gradually diminish.

The statistics, of course, can't do without them, Koch had become a real American.

"The calendar becomes a metronome, I know. But you are all right, you will be all right. You've won yourself some time, modern medicine does wonders these days."

After a few weeks, Koch invites him to meet his family. He can't keep refusing, he can't keep postponing.

"You have to go out, you can't keep sitting around among your old papers. They guard you, I know the theory, but sometimes they don't guard you anymore, they suffocate you. My wife is a great hostess, and it has been much too long since you and I spoke for real."

American time is short, good intentions rarely find their appropriate respite, but they both knew that they could count on each other. Yes, yes, that's right, the patient confirmed.

Isabel instantly lit the atmosphere of the spectacular Koch family home on Madison Avenue. The children possessed the natural tendencies of the new generation, but also the residue of an old world upbringing, they listened attentively, they spoke rarely and intelligently.

Instead of the chocolate cake that everyone refused because of their diets, dessert was a discussion on a troubling theme.

"Now I'm convinced that you were right," Izy began, loosening his burgundy tie, which was perfectly matched to his blue silk dress shirt, "you should be open, on the side of the victim."

He felt no need to specify who the victim was.

"I've come to the side of the Chosen People. Exactly because I reject the role of the victim, and not because I take it on."

The family had probably already heard this emphatic discourse many times. It was only Gora who understood the implications. A code established long ago, in the basement of the Koch family house. Antonio and Carla, the family's beautiful twins, as well as Isabel, all saw Izy as the admirable fighter for the cause. They all remembered the manipulated news in the press, the games of the great powers, the displacement of grudges on the left and right.

"It's not exactly displacement," Izy had corrected him. "It's an accumulation."

Gora was watching him attentively, even though he wasn't really paying attention. The pain in his chest persisted, amplifying his unease and timidity. He couldn't concentrate. The doctor didn't notice and it was all for the better.

"You were right back then, about the two apostles. I assume you've expanded your thinking about the matter . . . "

"I haven't."

"I have. Paul was a radical, Peter wasn't. But . . . "

The dinner companions were now having a coffee. "Izy shouldn't have provoked me," the patient was thinking. Neither coffee nor philosophy is good for a cardiac patient. The cardiac patient couldn't focus.

"I wouldn't have thought that you'd be interested in these kinds of discussions."

"I'm not, I just want to make up my mind. The Messiah means finalization. Certainty, conclusion, an end point. A finite thought. You were saying at one point that incomplete, open, anticipatory thinking appealed to you."

"I no longer need occult justifications."

"But you had them."

"Now it's getting late, and the patients must go to bed."

"I thought you'd become a writer. You loved books and fiction."

"Unfortunately, I'm too rational."

"So you've assimilated. Pragmatism is rational."

"It may be, yes, but that's a simplification. A limitation."

The doctor didn't want the patient to leave, he knew that no one was waiting for him at home.

"Let me tell you a story about our friend Gaşpar."

They were in Izy's room, the others had retreated.

"He came to see me, about a month ago. Before he disappeared. He's disappeared, hasn't he? I heard that, but I don't believe it. I think he's just hiding somewhere and will reappear. Before disappearing he came to see me. Not for a consultation. A courtesy visit. To pay me a kindness. He didn't want to see me. He left a tube with a work of art inside, to be given to me."

"A work of art?"

Gora had perked up, was in focus. Izy's schemes had succeeded in getting his body out of his head. The cerebral machine was shaking again, plugged in.

"I'll show it to you if you want."

"Yes, I'd like to see it."

"He gave me an inestimable work of art. A watercolor done by an elephant."

Gora was present, he was focused, his heart beat intensely.

"Watercolor, drawing, I don't know the difference. The master-work of an artist. Elephas Maximus. Elephantus. The revenge of Peter Gaşpar! B.B., the queen of animals, was right. You remember Brigitte Bardot? Raw, naked beauty. Now she's an old crone who loves and defends animals. I would assume that she also has work by Elephantus."

Izy pulled from under his desk a massive blue tube, out of which he extracted the drawing. He unrolled it, turned it over to show the stamp of authenticity. Thai Elephant Conservation Center. In English and Thai. Nearby, handwritten, *Aet/Male, 11 years old.* The trunk holds the brush. Rounded lines of yellow and black.

"The artist Aet is no worse than their bipedal counterparts who get millions for a scribbling. You know the story with Hokusai, I think . . . the king called him, asked him to demonstrate the making of a painting. The painter spread a canvas on the floor and asked for a hen. He put one of the hen's feet in the red color, let her strut all over the canvas. Then he stuck the other foot in the blue color. The hen covered the field quickly. When the king asked the painter what the painting meant, Hokusai answered without hesitation: autumn twilight. I don't know if the king got the joke. I appreciated Gaşpar's revenge. I used to always call him an elephant. Because of his scandalous dimensions. He was just getting fatter and fatter, he didn't care."

Gora searched the yellow and black forms. The yellow ended in black, the black melted, suddenly, into yellow. It wasn't bad at all.

"What's the title?"

"I don't know. Gaşpar didn't mention a title. Let's call it, 'Untitled.' "

"The art of an elephant needs a title. RA0298. That's the title."

"That's not a title. It's a serial number."

"We all become serial numbers. Not engraved on the arm, like in Auschwitz, but on the credit card. Visa Card, MasterCard, Platinum Card. Social Security Card, Insurance Card, MetroCard. Resident Card. Resident Alien Card Number 0298. That's Gaşpar's number. We're all numbers, says the Soviet cabdriver Boltanski. I know him from Gaşpar, too. He's his driver."

"But this isn't Gaşpar's work, it's by the artist Aet, eleven years old. Your friend attached a page with the history of the work and the artist. He insisted that the gift was an extravagance, not an insult. Many scholarly details, to convince me that it's a serious thing, worthy of respect. Have you heard of the great Cambodian chef at Pierre's? A superexpensive restaurant where Kissinger and Sharon Stone and Norman Mailer and Wall Street suits eat. Monsieur Gerard. Gerard Fun, the Cambodian nobleman who studied in Paris while his country was being devastated by the Communists. He became a famous chef in New York, at Pierre's. That was how he met Beatrice."

"Beatrice? What Beatrice? Dante wasn't resurrected, was he?"

"He wasn't and I'm not disappointed."

"Beatrice, Gaşpar's friend. Larry Five, that was what he'd called her. At the start I didn't understand, Gaşpar raves sometimes. Larry Five, Larry Five, until I understood Larry Five is a woman. A wealthy widow. Gaşpar's former colleague in the New York University doctorate program that he never finished."

"Yes, I know about that. And the elephants?"

"Monsieur Gerard introduced Beatrice to two exiled Cambodian painters, poor and talented. She was very impressed, she agreed to back the project, 'Painting Elephants.' An art school for elephants that are becoming less useful. Looking after them costs money, as well as their medical care. I read that each one receives, at birth, a young male caretaker who will look after them until

death. Asian elephants. The African ones are a different story. Gaşpar bought the drawing at a Christie's auction. Beatrice steered him
there. I don't think that your friend will come back for a consultation. He got fed up with my telling him that he's immense, like an
elephant. Maybe he got as far as Thailand."

"Did he suggest something to that effect?"

"No, but he didn't ask after Lu. He entered the office like a
meteor, dropped off the tube and was gone. *Forever.*"

Gora was silent. Koch, too. The show was over.

"You were wonderful, Izy, you were fantastic. I forgot all about
the angioplasty, the stents, the panic."

Izy was looking at him and smiling.

"I'm glad. There's something else, while we're here . . . Gaşpar
left a letter, too. He wanted to inform me that he's not supporting
the Republican Party, and that the prophet Mohammed was born in
the Year of the Elephant. He told me not to forget this! Forty years
before the birth of Islam. And when the Abyssinian king, the tyrant
Abraha, attacked Mecca, he didn't use just one huge new weapon
but many elephants. Gaşpar wanted very badly to improve my education before leaving."

Now Gora smiled, as well, looking at his friend.

"And there's still another strange allusion. He said to ask you if
you have a code name. He's referring to the secret police, isn't he?"

"I assume so. He's asking if I was an informant. There were
many. Stalkers and stalked, that was the game. Sometimes the role
was cumulative."

"I knew what I was doing when I ran. I'd be interested to talk
about this. You and I can talk about anything, right? Nothing will
ever change between us?"

"Of course."

Izy was convinced that a long conversation would follow. Gusti
didn't seem inclined.

"Yes, it's interesting. We'll talk some other time. I'm tired, and it's late. You were wonderful, Izy, fantastic. I forgot about the angioplasty, the stents, the panic."

The two old classmates embraced fraternally, as they used to many years ago.

Izy remained pensive in the doorway. Surprised not by Gora's refusal but by the way in which he interrupted the questions. He'd thanked him with the same words, repeated mechanically, identically, twice. Once home, Gora fell asleep instantly. The following morning he seemed perfectly recovered.

■

Recovered, he rushed to the small screen.

The Thai National Institute for Elephants was giving away extraordinary gifts for lovers of animals and art. Original paintings, executed by elephants with or without the guiding hands and minds of people. There were no forgeries in this extraordinary collection of abstract creativity—that was the name of the collection, Abstract Creativity.

The paper was handmade, especially for the collection, out of 100 percent recycled materials and free of bacteria, according to the needs of the medium, the acrylics were of the highest quality, imported from England and France.

The elephants had succeeded in forgetting their immense bodies, the patient concluded, encouraged. Each one had, from birth till death, his or her own caretaker and instructor, who knew his or her pedigree and history perfectly. The instructors were trained for the Great Project through special courses: how to prepare the brushes and paints, when to give the signal to start, and particularly, to finish. The opportune stopping of the creative exercise was essential. Elephants don't know when to stop, they would keep going forever.

The celebrated Lampang Conservation Center fought against the disappearance of Asian elephants, reduced by half from the hundred thousand that lived in Thailand only ten years before.

The funds obtained by the Lampang Center served for maintenance and for raising public awareness about the dramatic fate of these creatures.

It wasn't a matter only of Thailand or South Africa, but also of Colorado Springs, where the drawings of the celebrated artist Lucky were being sold in a solo exhibition, held at the municipal airport. Born in 1980, Lucky had arrived at the Cheyenne Mountain Zoo in 1981, after she'd been orphaned in Kruger National Park in South Africa. She lives here with her friend Kimba, also from South Africa. In spite of her spectacular dimensions and weight, Lucky adapted to the courses in just a few weeks. Attentive to details, she works only with the brushes that she likes. "Elephants have over a hundred thousand muscles," the computer was telling Professor Gora, who was following the forty-eighth birthday celebration of the African elephant Hydari, in the Philadelphia Zoo. Hydari, nicknamed Dari, was the oldest of his kind. Then Gora found himself in the Toledo Zoo, where little Louie received birthday presents, a festive cake and gifts to his tastes, for his fifth birthday. In the Oakland Zoo, the public observed the diet and caretaking of the elephants, in Los Angeles they were celebrating the one-year anniversary of the enchanting Ruby's retreat, at seven years old, from an acting career in the Performing Welfare Society.

"The image trumps the word! The planetary transmission has no competition in the library!"

Was it Gaşpar's voice? The question had burst victoriously through the fog of his thoughts.

"Is there another more insane and formidable country than this one? Idealistic, pragmatic, cynical, and religious. For-mi-dab-le! And that's final! The online commercial agency Novica represents fifteen academies of elephant art. Elephantine art, is that right? That's right and it's formidable. For-mi-dab-le, that's all."

You hear that? Online! Elephant painting! Fifteen art academies!

Where do you find this stuff? In books? No, on the stupid little screen!

It had been hard for him to get used to the invention, harder than it was for Lucky with the brushes, but it became a necessity, just like all useless things that replace other useless things. In one second you find anything you look for, but one little mistake and you don't know how to get out of the labyrinth. Lost, humiliated, you don't remember the rectifying action to take. Only the Army of Technical and Infantile Aid can help you; three- and eight- and eighteen-year-old children with tiny laptops in their ears and nostrils. All of them conceived and born of the magic instrument, not in the maternal placenta.

In one second, the can of information opens again, just like in fairy tales. No need for a library, school or books, professors, the child presses a button and there it is: Information. Another era, other needs, another speed, other tastes, the charm of Lucky the elephant surpasses the barriers of time, space, and generations.

Lucky, the star of Cheyenne Mountain, prefers painting in tempera, in pink and red. She signed every artwork. While her trunk gracefully handled the brush, the giant quadruped vocalized her ecstasy: a little grumble of satisfaction, as might be heard only in the studios of the great artists. The voices of the plebe annoyed her. She would stop, disgusted at the buzzing of admirers, many minutes would pass before inspiration came back to her. When the instructor gave the final signal, Lucky would sign the piece with an arrogant gesture of her trunk, and her friend Kimba would apply the stamp over the artist's signature, a proper hoof mark.

But what about Aet, the eleven-year-old male artist, the author of the masterpiece RA0298? Gora searches all over for him, among the celebrities, waiting for some telepathic sign from Gaşpar.

All of a sudden, dubious signals in his chest. He doesn't have the courage to measure his blood pressure, he rejects the alarm.

New headlines had appeared on the screen, thank God: on the coast of the Black Sea, near the same Tomis where Ovid was exiled long ago, a certain Victor-nicknamed-The-Elephant walked the streets alongside an elephant dressed in a giant national costume, for his electoral campaign. So, then, Elephantus wasn't active only in Uncle Sam's electoral campaign, but also on the *Pontus Euxinus,* where the persecuted Ovid bemoaned his estrangement.

Gora was increasingly convinced that Peter Gaşpar was in Thailand, at a school for elephant instructors. At some point he'd published a book about the Baroque, the art of elephants would surely justify a new edition for mass distribution.

He pulled from the shelf the book in which Pieter had died, watched by the melancholic, bibliophile Castorp, and by Lady Chauchat. After Mynheer Peeperkorn had given up his burlesque soul, overcome by the tropical fever, the melancholic Castorp disappeared, as well, swallowed by the apocalypse of the war. "Farewell, brave, spoiled child," whispered Hans Castorp's obituary, which closed with the question, "Will love rise out of the burning sky?"

The question lingered beyond the pages on which Pieter Peeperkorn had died, but there was no more time for old questions. Gora needed to call the doctor. An enterprise even more urgent than reading.

■

Busy, busy, tack-tack-tack. The phone was busy. Five, ten minutes. Finally! The voice of salvation.

"Dr. Bar-El, please. I'm his patient. Last name is Gora. It's an emergency."

"Hold, please."

Five, ten minutes. Click, the connection is broken. Gora takes his blood pressure. Raised. He breathes heavily. He tries to remain calm.

"Dr. Bar-El. The connection was interrupted. I'm . . . "

"Yes, yes, Gora, the professor, please hold."

He waits. No one was coming. Yes, the sleepy voice returned.

"The doctor is busy. He will call you in ten minutes."

He closed his eyes. Ten minutes isn't long, no one dies in ten minutes. Ten minutes, twenty, thirty. Thirty! Three times ten, you can die in less than thirty minutes.

"It's Professor Gora again, Dr. Bar-El's patient."

"Ah, yes . . . he didn't call? He really didn't call? Hold, please."

Click, connection to Dr. Bar-El's office.

"Hello, yes. Professor Gora? What happened?"

"Well, today, about an hour ago . . . "

"One moment, one moment. Don't hang up, please wait just one moment . . . "

The receiver to his ear. One moment, two, nine. The patient looks at his watch . . . ten, twelve minutes. He slams the phone.

Tension, heavy chest, restricted respiration. The nape of his neck ached. In the left side of his chest, the villainous neuralgia. The lining in his arteries, he could feel the lining in his brain. In his left arm, above his elbow in his underarm, sharp, shooting pain.

The vials on his nightstand. Plavix, Toprol, Aspirin, Norvasc, Cozar, Vytorine, Xanax. The remedies of old age.

"Now you're young again, just like new," Koch and Bar-El and Hostal had announced after the operation. "You can eat and enjoy what you want. In moderation, of course, but with pleasure. *Joie de vivre*, that's the recipe."

To assure his *joie de vivre*, Bar-El had renewed seven prescriptions.

In his palm, the small green pill. He broke it. Since he didn't talk to the doctor, he takes a half of a Cozar, he will go to sleep early, will sleep profoundly, in the morning will be back to Earth. That's what happened. The fingers on the keys of the computer. "Dear Dr. Bar-El, yesterday I waited over an hour to speak to you on the phone. I would like to be able to reach you when I need to."

No response. A day, two days, nine days.

"How is it possible that he didn't call you? Not even the next day, or the third day? Not even after you wrote to him? To hell with him! You need a doctor who's available," declared Izy.

"He's a good doctor. He made the right diagnosis, despite the confusing test results. But he's not accessible. I'm having some rough days. I can't fully breathe, the volume of my breathing is incomplete. I stop at three-quarters, I can't breathe to the end."

"I know how it is. I'll find you another cardiologist. I'm sorry it didn't work out."

"I don't want to find another. Bar-El saved my life."

"Listen, Gusti, we've known each other a long time. I know that your favorite team is called *The Chosen People*. I did a residency in Tel Aviv, at Hadassah, their big hospital. Good doctors, better than we have here. But rushed, fast. They're trained by alarms, they live on speed, in between wars and bomb attacks. They don't have time, they're in year five thousand seven hundred and God knows what, they don't have time. Think about it, five thousand seven hundred! No discussion, you're going to someone else."

"I'll try again with Bar-El. It's hard for me to leave someone. You know the way I am."

"I know. I know how you are about the homeland, about me . . . about Lu. It's hard for you to connect with new people. Okay, I'll give you another one of theirs. Of ours, that is. Yours, even, I don't want to insult Saint Peter. Dr. Liebling. He treats me, as well. Liebling! Are you happy with that? I will call him. Look, I'll call him right now."

Gora had muted the phone, he wasn't giving up. He wanted to remain in the care of Bar-El. Fresh panic attacks. Sweating, shuddering, heavy nape. He would have balled himself up in bed or he might have called Boltanski to take him, bed and all, to the emergency room. Bar-El had no idea about the excessive loyalty of the patient. He didn't answer the phone, the fax was dead, email blocked.

Today and yesterday, blood pressure 190 over 95. "We're numbers, my man. Listen to the Soviet, we're numbers, that's all. Capitalists don't know anything outside of numbers. Doctors, lawyers, garbage men, senators, policemen. All of them. Anyone, everyone. All they do is count numbers!"

Gora had called the Australian.

"Yes, I remember your name," the receptionist answered sleepily. Dr. Hostal is attending a cardiology conference in Michigan. He will be back in the afternoon. He's already on the plane. When he arrives, I will tell him you called. High blood pressure and strange, sharp pains in your chest, that's the message, I understand. You don't know if it's heartburn or actually heart pains. Shooting pain, weakness, high blood pressure. Panic? Yes, bouts of panic, I've noted. I will relay the message, you can rest assured."

Hostal called him in the late afternoon.

"Okay, please come first thing, the day after tomorrow. We'll perform the second angioplasty. Tomorrow you'll go to have blood drawn. They will prepare the paperwork for your admittance, and we'll operate the day after tomorrow."

Gora swallowed an aspirin and a sedative.

"Of course, there are risks. There are always risks. I told you the first time, as well. Heart failure, stroke. All possible. It happens rarely. We're working with statistics, the risks exist, but they are not great."

Statistics, of course. The Soviet man would grow very fond of that word. Even Hostal didn't ignore the arithmetic of globalization. Capitalism with a human mask had conquered socialism with a human mask. "He will explode as well, he will explode, we will all explode," sang the group Herostratus.

The shadow was widening in his chest. The spider advanced toward the left shoulder and arm, the thorax swelled and waned with the moaning. A low boil, torpor. Breathing down to a pant. A heavy, granite nape. Professor Gora has no one to leave behind, to whom will he leave his memories, his obituaries. He never managed to finish Peter's obituary, and now Izy and Bar-El and the Australian Dr. Hostal were disputing their positions.

The Gora folder was chock full of images of arteries before and after the rejuvenation, the images of the heart, cardiograms, blood and urine and saliva and dandruff tests, tests of stress and endurance, prescriptions and warnings. A technical Obituary, without words, just numbers, appropriate to the new century. Devoid of memory or metaphor. The stents won't rot in the ground where the bones and heart and memories will rot, said the Obituary.

"You're fixed! You're young, good as new. You can do anything you want, eat quite anything you want," said the god in the white lab coat. "The stents are ultradurable. A rare metal, deathless. They will survive in the ground, long after nothing else has survived."

Gora had dozed off, repeating Mephistopheles' message to himself. He was smiling. The devil was a clown who was reversing his age, without asking for his soul in return. Just proof of medical insurance. Not the soul, Comrade Boltanski, just the account number of my medical insurance. A number, yes, that's all, not the soul. Proof of insurance. Blue Cross, Blue Shield, Medicare, Atlantic, AARP.

Professor Gora was smiling, in spite of his exhaustion, his extreme exhaustion and drowsiness. The panic had depleted him.

He awoke looking out the window at the woods. The setting sun, the day being swept away. His head on the table. His exhaustion widening. A body made of wax. A timorous whizzing sound at first, then more insistent, like a cricket. The phone. He'd set the volume of his phone to minimum, he couldn't stand alarms. He extended his hand. The receiver so heavy, he could barely lift it.

He didn't recognize my voice, he was delirious.

"Yes, I am sleepy. A rough day, yes, and a rough night to follow tomorrow. The second angioplasty. The locust will gorge itself on the waste lining my arteries. And I will be able to watch it all on the little screen. The new millennium's *photo-moto-loto*, on the little screen."

Gora had paused.

"I'm raving, like Gaşpar. I keep looking for him, in vain, inside myself and outside myself. Now, since this illness took me out from where I was among my books and hurled me into chaos, I speak just like him. Isn't that true that I'm speaking like him?"

I didn't think so, or, who knows, at the very least, it was a simple imitation.

"Yes, where were we? Of course, there are risks. Rare risks, the statistics say. That is, the doctors say that the statistics say that the risks are rare. You're right. We should believe them, we have no choice but to believe them."

He was listening attentively to my good wishes, as if they were important pieces of news.

"Thank you, thank you. I should have called you more often, as well, we should have spoken more often. After the surgery. Call me after the surgery. Yes, yes, I've made mistakes, too, and not just one or two. I don't know if she's happy. No, I don't know, I'm not Saint Augustin."

After hanging up, I'd wager that Gora was probably muttering to himself, "People are essentially good, people are good." The world is good, also in dreams produced by illness and medication, but if you happen to encounter dreams and books, then you should neither scorn nor abandon the world.

The telephone message had made him happy. The speaker seemed a man of goodwill who wanted to wish the patient a speedy recovery. A well-wisher, he deserved a good obituary.

Gora smiled, a shadow had passed, an infantile and villainous shadow across his tired face.

Part IV

The taxi driver was no longer Boltanski, but a student from Senegal, in love with America and the vacations in his native country; the nurse was no longer the beautiful Polish woman, but an Indian auntie with glasses. Dr. Hostal was the same. Solid, taciturn, trustworthy.

He'd appeared in the great operating room before and after the surgery, escorted by two young residents, taller than he is by a head. He'd been by three of the eight beds segregated with the floral curtains that rolled along the frames attached to the ceiling.

"Today you are no longer the first one, you're the second. We're performing more stent procedures than last time. It will take longer. Otherwise, the procedure is the same."

The patient was silent, naked under the blue crepe paper tunic. The democratizing effect of his nudity restored his childishness.

"You already know the procedure. The little imaging camera enters through a central artery, passes toward the area of the heart, returning images. The catheter will expand in the blocked area, then the cleaning, the application of the casing."

Improvements! *Plumbing!* Thirty daily procedures in this hospital, eight hundred per month, across America. Like auto maintenance.

Hostal was looking at the patient.

"We're using Taxus Express Two. A precious metal with a protective antibuildup sheathing. *Paclitaxel-Eluting Coronary System.* Let's trust it."

The bed on wheels. The elevator, eighteenth floor, room nine, the door wide open. The nurse is Korean. The glass with the pink liquor. The restraining of his hands and legs. The resident, the professor, the computer. Start.

Now the screen was behind him, the patient could no longer see the insect nibbling away at the waste along the artery. He could see the nurse, the doctor, the resident. Sharply, the needle prick. On the left, in the cavity of his chest, toward the left. Again and again. A fine tentacle, deep needles. Pain. Burning. Thin, elongated. The oxygen balloon dilates the walls of the artery. The insertion of the cylinder. The patient closes his eyes, trying to separate mind from body.

Sleep, Professor Gora, the end will find you the green waters of dreams, an old child, blessed with numbness. For the time being, pain is merely the prologue to numbness.

"Taxus," said the voice of the Australian. "Express Two."

A final, hostile claw. The patient clenches his teeth. The experiment of the previous month seemed a gentle trap, to cheat his vigilance, this was now truly the end of him.

"Taxus. Express Two."

The nurse leaned down to the open drawer, pulled another package out, opened it, extended the tube.

Time slowed, long seconds, stretched out. The tenacious pain was cutting the captive's respiration. Terminal torture.

"Taxus. Express Two."

He gnashed his teeth, his eyes closed. He was no Buddhist, the tortured body could not separate itself from the tortured mind. He was counting the slowly solidifying seconds in his stabbed chest.

"How is it going?"

Whom was the doctor addressing, God, Death? The magic of computerized rejuvenation had its own rules and lexicon.

"How is it going, Professor? How is it going?"

"Ah, so. So, so."

"There isn't much more to go. Ten minutes, maybe twenty."

So, then, an hour, two hours. The stabbing sensation advanced, long razors, his chest weighted down by a granite tombstone. His leather-cuffed hands and legs. The ceiling was sliding down, a giant granite press on top of his chest. An air vacuum, suffocation.

"Express Two."

Maybe he ought to yell, though! Americans respect the ability to grin and bear one's suffering, but also to express it. A jungle yell: please, stop! STOP! This is the patient's entitlement to stop his own torture! Death, that old whore, is enjoying herself, she knows that the rebellion of the dying is pure futility.

"Express Two. There's only a little farther to go, Professor Gora. I know it's hard . . . just a little further."

An hour, two hours, nine, it no longer mattered, the sacred ten minutes are still an eternity. He could no longer yell, he was exhausted, he'd missed his chance to cancel the deal with Mephistopheles, he'd lost his final strength, he couldn't stand another moment, not another moment here.

"All right, we're finished."

Ten minutes, that was all, ten minutes. No, not quite, another second, two, five, eight seconds, done.

"I know it was hard. Five stents! Difficult positions. It was no fun for me, either."

The doctor took off his sweaty scrubs and threw them in the corner of the room. Naked and solid from the waist up, he left the room just like that, naked and shameless.

The scrawny little mustached man wheeled the bed toward the elevator, then toward door 568. A bright room, separated into two by a curtain. In each half, an empty bed. The metal nightstand, the television, the screen that registers his blood pressure, the window toward the courtyard.

"I heard it took a long time. Two and a half hours. A long time! Five stents. You first had two, now there are seven. A major overhaul."

He recognized the voice. The deep, Polish timbre. Just back from the other world, he had too low a tolerance for the dish of the day.

The major overhaul doesn't remove the body from the head. He's connected to the sphygmomanometer and the pulse monitor, the bedpan, the needle in his vein.

"Try to sleep. The bandaged spot will be painful. It's called an Angio-Seal Vascular Closure Device. The wound will gradually heal, the plug will be absorbed by the body in ninety days. If you end up needing another procedure . . . but that won't happen. Anyway, the puncture would be made at least a centimeter from where it is now. Take the pills, sleep. The bell is by the nightstand, call if you need anything."

Eyes closed. He couldn't move, he didn't even want to move. All he wanted was to sleep. The flushing of energy, dizziness, dozing off, intangible sleep. Anesthetized, delirious. Eternity.

The noise from the neighboring bed sounded like a crisis. The patient, the wife, the daughter, the son-in-law. They interfered one at a time, or together.

"I'm Bill McKelly. Kelly & Kelly Corporation, New Jersey. Well known, I realize. A month ago we had proceedings in New Jersey. We need to redo it. That's why I came here. I'm friends with Dr. Chase. John Chase, the dermatologist. The head medic of dermatology. Everyone knows him, I'm sure. As I've said, I want my wife to remain here tonight, with me. I know, I know the rules, there are also exceptions. The armchair, yes, she'll sleep in the armchair. Okay, I'll call Chase."

Irritated, Bill explains to his wife that John had promised to arrange everything, he just needs to keep his word. A heated discussion with Johnny followed, two brave lads appeared, carrying a cot. The commotion continued. There was talk of a wedding in Minnesota in two weeks. Plane tickets, gifts, clothing.

The Polish woman brought new pills, the antacid tea. And a large, thick book.

"You forgot your picture album. In the morning. In the preoperative room. Maybe you can use it, if you can't sleep. Along with the sedatives, it should do the trick."

Halina smiled, revealing teeth as white as Polish snow.

"Would you like me to turn on the TV? Would that entertain you?"

No, it wouldn't. Mr. McKelly's daughter and the son-in-law had left. The wife was quiet, the husband was snoring. Gora groped for the sedatives.

He awoke in the middle of the night. He ought to have opened his eyes, but he couldn't. He could sense a streak of light coming from the street, through the window, he would have liked to open his eyes, but his lids were too heavy.

On the screen, a chessboard, a glass half-full. A black liquor with big bubbles. Nearby, a metal can. A Coca-Cola. The game of the century! Peter had become a celebrity, the New World loves celebrities. The patient doesn't open his eyes, his lids are as heavy as a tombstone. Noise, agitation, someone had overturned the chessboard. The king, the queen, the bishops tumbling mercilessly on the floor, toward the phosphorescent corner of the room.

"A little bit more, a little bit more, to the left. Just a little more. You must wake up."

He awoke groggily, recognizing Halina's cooing voice.

"A little bit, just a little bit, and you should wake up."

She'd fluffed his pillow higher, was raising him up slowly from the waist. He saw her, he was finally opening his old lids.

"Your blood pressure is high. Your pressure went up."

"How do you know?"

"We're watching the monitor. The general monitor connected to the monitor in the room."

On the screen, Peter is no longer playing chess with Mephistopheles. Green diagrams and digits appeared instead. The whirlpools of panic, difficult breathing. In the left part of his chest, a hostile armor. His pressure had risen: two hundred over ninety-nine. The doctor on call, a Chinese resident, and a tall, red-haired assistant had arrived. "Yes, we'll try an injection." The syringe, another two syringes, for the blood test.

"What medication do you take for your high blood pressure?"

Someone murmured, "Fifty milligrams of Cozar. The blue pill, one hundred milligrams of Cozar."

"Rest now, we'll return in an hour."

Halina gestured toward the bell by the bedside.

The diagrams varied. He closed his eyes, he opened his eyes. One hundred ninety-one over 92, 194 over 93.

Halina leaned down attentively to give him the glass of water.

"The control enzyme is too high. You're going to stay another day."

Was that how tests were done, instantly? Who had made the decision to keep the patient an extra day in the hospital against the rules of economy? The situation must be serious, otherwise they wouldn't be spending more money. "We are just numbers, accounts, nothing more," the Soviet man had warned.

Halina leaned over again, took his blood, raised his pillow.

"Everything will be all right. The pressure will drop, it will be okay."

"Yes, I can see that, 189 over 90. Is this a drop or an error?"

Halina was smiling, without responding. The patient smiled, as well, he would have liked to ask her to tell the story of her arrival in America, the ESL classes, minuscule Mexicans and little Chinese crones and busty Brazilians, her first job, a cook at a Portuguese restaurant, the first-aid night classes, the affair with the naval officer, her first trip to Texas, the arrival of her brother from Lodz.

The patient was smiling, exhausted, senile, powerless to ask or listen to anything, grateful for the Polish woman's smile.

Four in the morning. At 6 the commotion would start, they would take the temperature of the dying, they would check every room, they would bring breakfast, morning visitors would arrive, including the magician Hostal.

"The level of the enzymes has improved. We're still going to hold you another day. There's no need to worry. Today you're going to receive instructions for the months and year to come. The medication, the states of emergency, diet, exercise program, the periodic checkups."

Instructions for his resurrection, alongside other similarly privileged individuals.

"Everything will be okay," Doctor Hostal assures him. You've been rejuvenated, but this youth is no joke. Diet, exercise, medication."

The patient was watching him, but he couldn't manage a response. He wanted to be accepted as the Australian's neighbor, wherever Edward Hostal lived, he would promise to be a discreet neighbor, he understood the irritations and the exhaustion of the wizard who passed daily, ten, a hundred times a day, from one suffering heart to another, unabated and precise and smiling, he wouldn't bother him, he wouldn't ask for anything but for a protective proximity to this god of cardiologists. That was all he wanted, that was it, it would be enough, it would diminish his panic and loneliness, yes, why shouldn't he say it, even his loneliness. He would move anywhere just to be close to Hostal, a silent, invisible neighbor, a younger and wiser brother, a man who had succeeded in being much more useful than he, Augustin Gora, would ever be.

"I would like to thank you for . . . "

"No, no, don't worry. Yesterday, Elvira would have accompanied you home just like last time. Today she can't. I spoke with the porter to call you a cab. He'll take you to the cab, he'll speak to the driver and ask him to help you to the entrance of your apartment. You have my number. Call me anytime."

Home, in his solitary bed! He was satisfied, he'd located Peter at the chess table, on the screen of the planetary night, he'd managed to speak to him calmly, whispering as if to a dear and addle-brained cousin, he'd managed to surprise him and move him, Peter had interrupted his game and responded to him in his turn, timidly, submissively, as if he were speaking to an older and wiser cousin.

From wherever he may have been coming, from Nevada near Gina Monteverdi, Tara's cheerful aunt, or from the polygamous refuge with the nine wives of the Mormon Alexander Joseph, from the Long Haul Estate near Big Water, Utah, or from the drama classes from the Methodist Church in Winston-Salem, North Carolina, or from the *Sea Hawk* among the Coast Guard of Key West, Florida, the ship that had intercepted twenty-five million pounds of marijuana and ten thousand pounds of cocaine, from any page of the *American Album*—wherever it was, Peter had in the end arrived, of course, in New York, on the evening of September 9, 2001.

He hadn't forgotten that many months ago, his cousin, Professor Augustin Gora, had reserved for him a room at the Hotel Esplanade, on the corner of 48th Street and Eighth Avenue. On Tuesday, September 11, he was to meet with the lawyer whom Gora had hired, to obtain his miraculous green card. He would enter the ranks of new people in the New World, he'd no longer need to hide in the wilderness. No one knew about the meeting at the World Trade Center, he hadn't told anyone, the secret remained between the two of them, to deter any of the dubious astral alignments that might provoke a crime such as the one that had befallen Palade.

Suddenly at 8:46 in the morning, the formation *Herostratus*, the nineteen knifemen in the Show of the Century. All the televisions in the world watch the planes full of passengers and nineteen angels of death flying toward Salvation.

Peter tries to exit the subway, in the area of chaos. Crowded subway. The world stunned, the deaf-mutes and the cynical jokers, you could barely breathe. Allah-Yussuma-Osama's messengers called for the saintly and eternal paradise, on the television screens across the entire planet. The metro halted. The cars closed tight. No, no suspects have been identified. Captive bodies, stuck to one another, incapable of holding each other up. Among them, David and Eva Gaşpar.

Ten, fifteen, twenty, thirty minutes, David and Eva remained pasted, next to each other, at the end of the train car. Minutes are hours, forty minutes seem like an eternity. A stroke can occur even faster.

A few minutes before the metro starts up again.

■

Cautious movements. The bandage protects the incision, the wound is green, bruised, his skin would regain its usual pallor.

"Short, slow walks at the start. After two weeks, easy exercises.

Gradually, routine exercise. Half an hour per day. Or longer, forty-minute walks. Measure your tension at various hours. Keep track of the figures in a notebook. We will reevaluate in a month."

The walk was short. Bouts of panic, sharp stabs in his temples, the chest loaded with toxins. The body estranged. Confused signals. It was difficult to block the brain's sensor, the body was disoriented. The first warnings, often false, fueled his unease. His mind under alarm, lubricous, can't find the remedy. Quickly, quickly, the ambulance. Neighbor Hostal wasn't his neighbor, and he considered himself merely a *plumber*, a modest repairman of florid pipes. The cardiac patient needed to be connected to the global panel of the ambulance, instant and perfect response.

These aren't just the exaggerations of loneliness, as Izy thinks, they are the digits of the blood pressure monitor. Figures, in the era of figures and numbers, Comrade Boltanski teaches us.

He won't call Bar-El. He's going to clip his fingernails, that's what he's going to do. Eyes goggling the monitor that is going haywire.

Who's going to clip your nails, Professor? Try as you might to concentrate on this minor drudgery, in the end you still can't prevent the unfortunate moment; you've pushed the nail scissors in too deep, the nail and the finger and the cuff of your shirt are covered in blood. Thin and frenetic blood, difficult to stop.

"Try to avoid bleeding. The drugs will thin your blood and you may not be able to stop bleeding, you may get an infection. An infection would be a very serious thing, if it reaches your heart. There have been fatal cases."

Neosporin against cuts and infections! You can't find the ointment, nor the Band-Aids, you never put things back in their place, always playing hide-and-seek. Madam Neosporin and Sir Band-Aid are having a laugh at the blunderings of the blunderer. Where have you hidden, you saboteurs? Hocus-pocus, now you see them, now you don't, just like us mortals, here today, gone tomorrow. Ha, there you are in between the towels. I feel like the fat and playful Gaşpar, his silly games.

The monitor reads 189 over 94. Pressure on his nape, the body returned to the brain. Alarm in the kidneys and intestines, in the urinary tract and circulatory and respiratory systems. Gasps, spasms, you don't know where the next attack will be. You want to sleep, to die in your sleep, forgotten by the Great Dispatcher.

Indigestion, cramps, burning. Will the body's new age be spent on the toilet? A defective spark plug here, another defective connection there, tired suspension, a corroded carburetor, a worn pump and worn-out brakes and worn-down frame. The danger didn't originate in the heart. The passages had been cleaned, the soldered joints reinforced, the engine restored. The spirit was working, the armatures of Faust had enlarged the arteries, the blood was pumping.

The unexpected is the great advantage of the cardiac patient, the great danger and the great privilege. All of a sudden, it's over, you're granted rest.

Gora had paused on the way to the couch. The desire for sleep and the fear of sleep. One hesitation overcame the contrary hesitation. All he had to do was walk agitatedly the length and width and diagonal of the room, until he arrived at the democratic throne of the water closet. There he explored old age and the cowardly tendencies that old age spurred. It was day, another day, then night, then the next day, just as in the Bible. The tension monitor had become cordial, same as with the dialogue between the soul, the stomach, and the brain. The patient was waiting for the multiplying warnings. Day tension, night tension, numbers, numbers, Comrade Boltanski, columns of numbers measure the daily cardiograms.

Gora repeated to himself: there is no fear. No, there's no fear, only the humiliation of uncertainty, the sadism of postponement. I am enslaved to a body on which I can no longer depend. It has betrayed me, it's gone off and moved into my brain, and I can't draw it out of there, it's pointless for Izy to ask me to do it, I can't budge it from here. That's it, I'm going to start the obituary, *Gora's Obituary*. The relating of yet another meaningless death will induce calm, and calm pacifies tension and unease.

A serene afternoon. He sat at his desk, in front of the computer. The blue screen, the first letters. White, clear, clean, familiar, as ever.

In the window, the bulb of the sun where eternity lives. The sun up high in the clear sky, and here, close by in the square of the window and on the red flooring.

Impatient to animate the letters and commas and questions, one born out of another, however, he didn't touch the keys.

The keyboard frightened him. He'd pulled out the large, thick *American Album* from the left of his desk. One last time, Peter chatted with the Mormon and his wives. Then with the Coast Guard lieutenant who had captured the contraband bandits. Then, after a while: the first angioplasty of the obituarist, the second angioplasty. Peter had arrived inside the hullabaloo of old television sets in Backer's store in Phoenix, Arizona. Mr. Backer, naked down to the waist, in shorts and three-quarter socks, old, torn sneakers without laces, large hands blackened by oil and dust. In Colorado, he'd scoured the immense airplane cemetery maintained for forty years by the J. W. Duff Aircraft Company, then Alaska's North Slope Borough, eighty thousand square meters of ice and tundra, surrounding the town of Barrow and seven smaller towns, 20 percent of America's daily petrol production. The Eskimo mayor, like 80 percent of the people he managed, talked about the seasonal whale hunts. Had Mynheer Gaşpar truly arrived there, among the Eskimos, or was he nowhere at all?

Gora put a hand on the album. The blue gloves at the edge of the table. Abruptly, his breathing stops short. He tries to inhale and exhale normally, as he'd been instructed to do. His brow and temples were sweating. Shivers. Tremors. In the bedroom, the monitor. The small, short sound: 196 over 102. Bar-El or Lu or Hostal or Peter or the investigator Murphy or the defunct Dima, someone needed to come to aid the dying man!

It was late, even the poet Yussuma Ben Laden was sleeping, there was no one to call. Izy!

"Call the ambulance, my boy. You can't stay wound up with that tension all night. Nine, one, one. You have the number. The boys come quickly, they take you in, they treat you even along the way, before you get to the destination. After they see you at the hospital, you tell them to call me. When they get word from a doctor, they'll do it. Not out of some collegiate spirit, but out of fear. Yes, yes, have them call me. It's not serious, but don't wait. You waited enough in your life. Now caution means urgency."

The patient on a stretcher, the monitor connected to his left arm. He threw down the sweet liquor, then the aspirin, the EMT was massaging his wise forehead, assuring him that everything will be all right.

The halls of the emergency room. Traffic, many patients begging for the postponement of death. Two resident doctors. One blonde, freckled, thickset, and chatty and another supple and quiet Thai woman with little glasses no bigger than a thimble on her minuscule, childlike nose. Questions and answers, the sick heart's history, tension rising. The patient didn't have a fever, despite the sweating and shivering, which had ruffled him up in the ambulance as well as now. Small, continuous trepidations.

They took his blood, took him to radiology, gave him the first two pink pills and a glass of water. The freckled Irish woman was in a rush to get his case over with.

"Nothing unusual. As you can see, your tension has gone down. One forty over eighty-five. The tests look normal, same with the radiogram, the cardiogram. You're free to go. Taxis come constantly, you'll find one quickly. You're lucky, you get to spend tonight at home."

"What was the cause of the attack?"

The thickset woman had no time for commentary. She raised her short hands to the ceiling.

"We don't know. We don't know."

Her Thai colleague hands him the release forms.

"It just happens sometimes . . . at a certain age, irregularities start to appear. Your test results are clear, the radiogram, the cardiogram, just as Rebecca told you."

Aha, Rebecca, is it? The Irish take their names from the Bible.

Ah, so we're back talking about age! Age is fishing for attention, it compels you, it compels you to . . .

"In fact, at any age," the young woman added.

The incident was repeated two weeks later. The dream of Lu. A white, silken blouse. She was meticulously cleaning the vegetables, preparing the raspberries, the cherries, the wine. The slow joy of the living, concentration and sensuality. Thin, loose-fitting pants made of green silk. A sleeveless and transparent linen blouse over the pants. Sandals with a single strap on an otherwise bare foot. A supple, elastic body. A narrow, Andalusian head. The body vibrated at the first touch. She threw off her sandals, her pants, her minuscule underwear, a rusted leaf. The lips of her sex, the puff of her curly hair. The lashes trembling, as well as her voice. The electric fingers chaining her captive. A faraway look in her eyes, somewhere in the green of the great trees, whisper and whimper, calling the prisoner's name.

Suddenly the heaviness in the chest. He breathed with difficulty, sweat covered his forehead and temples, the cold invaded his feet, hands, shoulders. He was shivering. The back of his neck ached, the anguish was rising. His moist neck and hands. Cold. He was trembling.

The monitor frowned: 201 over 110. The telephone: 911. The EMTs, the hospital, consultations, tests. Benign results. After a couple of hours, his blood pressure goes down: 143 over 90.

From time's lottery machine I pulled out the winning numbers, Comrade Boltanski: the temperature, the white and red hemoglobin count, the glycemic index, cholesterol, even these have been tempered. We can't ask for anything more than that. These are the high marks of good behavior.

On the event of the following crisis, he didn't call the ambulance anymore, he just took a pill for his hypertension and a sedative.

He needed a psychiatrist, Izy told him. He'd never seen one before nor did he aspire to that indifference called equilibrium. His high school classmate assured him that he wouldn't be prodded with indiscreet questions or harsh treatments, nor would he be reincarnated into God knows what hyperactive persona.

Dr. Stephen Kelly was tall, all skin-and-bones, gray-haired, taciturn. The patient informed him that he wasn't prone to confessions, that all he wants is the pill that will make him functional again, that was it.

The psychiatrist smiled. It seemed like an approving smile.

"What is the problem? What happened?"

The professor admitted that he'd gone through a calendar crisis. He wasn't asked to explain what he'd meant by that. He added himself, "Two angioplasties. A slow and uncertain recovery with moments of panic," the patient added. Raised levels of artery tension, cold sweats, panting, shortness of breath.

Stephen Kelly's silence continued. Ah, yes, the patient wanted to add that he would prefer a minimal dose. Even less.

The doctor smiled, he seemed to approve of everything he was hearing. He prescribed a medication with a pleasant-sounding name.

"From the Prozac family."

"Prozac? I've heard horror stories about this miracle drug called Prozac. A student of mine was taking Prozac, and her depression was transformed into a continuous smile. Rictus. Sneering grin. It would have frightened even the president's bodyguards."

"The minimal dose is fifty milligrams. We'll start with a quarter of a minimal dose. We'll try it gradually and see what happens. Is that okay?"

It was okay. On the following visit, the dose went up to twenty-five milligrams. The taciturn visit cost three hundred dollars. Unlike Bar-El, Dr. Kelly responded promptly to any and all telephone calls.

The dosage kept increasing until it reached the minimal dose. Then, panic attacks, anguish. Pain at the back of his neck, tremors, sweating. Kelly recommended reducing the dosage, then trying a different medication.

The patient received a new prescription. He contemplated it for a long time, he never did go to the pharmacy, nor did he ever go back to Dr. Kelly.

Exercise will replace the pills. Dr. Bar-El had steered him toward some three-month regime. Physical therapy. Ten minutes of warm-ups, then ten minutes on three different machines, then ten minutes of cooling-down exercises. The bus ride to the periphery of York Avenue and back. The effort becomes more intense, his exhaustion diminishes, the day arranges itself around the diversion. Revitalization, fuel for self-esteem.

The experiment concluded at the end of August. At the closing ceremony each contestant promised to continue training thirty minutes per day or to walk for an hour at a brisk pace.

Back to deserted hours, specters. The transparent linen blouse. The sandals, the otherwise bare foot. The supple body under the rays of the moon. The Andalusian head, the intense gaze. She threw off her sandals, her pants, the leaf of her underwear, taking the patient's palm in her own long, delicate, and narrow hand, making it into a fist. Her lashes trembled, just like her voice, her fingers trembled, electrified.

"Tell me about your childhood . . . " she said. She listened attentively, avid and already distant, somewhere in the green of the great trees. A fraction, enough to start you awake. And she's back here. A burned look, her fingers touch the torrid center.

After a month Gora returned to the psychiatrist. A new office, four secretaries, elevators, bathrooms. The gray-haired Dr. Kelly inspires trust. Another pill. Small, preliminary doses. The normal dose has a positive effect. He increased the dosage by another quarter-pill. The patient seemed to have found his pill and his dosage. He slept well, didn't feel tired. He took up his reading again, and his Obituary.

He accepted the status of a cardiac patient: a cocktail of six pills in the morning, two for dessert in the evening.

Thirsty for life, he considered its offers. Books and trees, faces and foods, the river, Lu's gloves, the chair, the computer, the bathtub, the wintry forest, the album *A Day in the Life of America*, the cat on the verandah, the telephone, the blue towel, the ridiculous shoes. He'd lost the energy for revolt, the absurd had become comic. The path had been short, short, silly blind groping through the property called biography. He was ready for the retrospective.

He pushed the yellow folder with his hand and pulled the gloves toward himself. He set them down in front of himself, separate, the left glove to the left, the right glove to the right. He placed his palms on each. His hands were shorter than Lu's, but wider. Even if he could manage to slip them inside, he still wouldn't have been able to feel the navel of her long, delicate fingers.

He pressed the palms of each of the two gloves, his left hand on the left glove, his right hand on the right glove. The skin vibrated. Magnetic field, copulation. He looked out at the forest through the window. His hands on the two instruments of reanimation.

Dr. Hostal had given him the chance to feel that magic touch again.

■

The lottery offered a deferment. Brought back from the other world and abandoned on the border between that place and life, Gora was learning calm, serenity, and an ashen indifference.

There were new games: the morning exercises, the evening walk. Controlling the blood pressure, medication, visits to Dr. Morse, who had replaced Bar-El. Elvira visited him twice a week to clean his apartment and to keep him away from restaurants, to which he went anyway on the weekends.

After the second angioplasty, a telephonic interlocutor reappeared.

"And how are you feeling? Any better?"

I insisted that he tell me about the whole intervention in great detail, about why he'd been hospitalized an additional night, about the erratic variations in his blood pressure.

He seemed overwhelmed by the shock he'd endured. I had to try to divert his attention away from his illness.

"Do you remember the revolution at the college?"

"Yes, of course," Gora mumbled.

"I had just arrived then. To you it had seemed like an apt initiation. You explained to me the mechanics of these litigious epidemics. You said they were cyclical, that people need the illusion of morality. Speeches from the balconies, blocked access to the administration, picketing, impassioned slogans. For someone who had just escaped the paradise of Communism, it was a grotesque parody."

I found out that Gora no longer saw anyone, outside of Elvira. He'd become very timid, he said; he wasn't sure of his own body. I was trying something, to distract him; I was happy that he'd agreed to play my game.

"I kept all the clippings from the papers. The scandal of the rape that wasn't a rape. The revolution. The trial. The settlement with the student."

The salad days in the desert of liberty. We'd each discovered that we were looking for our own captive oases. Religion. Rhetoric. Charity. Servility to bosses and bank accounts. Frustration. You can understand the extraordinary experiment only gradually.

"And what about that tall, brown-haired student Tim? The one who'd come to talk to you on Tereza's behalf. Tim and Tereza. And then, the buck . . ."

"The buck? What buck?"

"Tim had hunted a buck. He had a rifle, and a license for it. It was hunting season. So it was all legal. The scandal came after the flaying. He'd brought the shot buck back to the college, and he'd flayed it in his room, together with other students. When he was called to the president's office, Tim excused himself, but he also called for clear and severe measures against the person who might have, at some point, raped Tereza."

"Tim is now the head of some organization that advocates the rights of immigrants in Santa Fe; Tereza is married with three children, and the assailant is a lawyer on Wall Street. You asked me to explain to you every aspect of the incident, so that you could understand your new home."

"Yes, yes, and now I have a question for you. Could Palade have been an informant?"

I imagined that Gora raised his eyebrows to the sky.

"You should be able to find out if he was. Or if he could have been, since we're hypothesizing. Many who could never have been actually were. So does that mean that they could have been, if they actually were? Even if no one, not even they, suspected? We can't ignore the when, the why, and the how they became what they couldn't have been."

"Forgive me, maybe this isn't the best time for this kind of conversation."

"Oh, sure it is."

"I think about it often, that's all. It's my fault that I haven't let go of the old toxins. We should be talking about America."

"Yes, it would be more interesting. Our stories seem interesting only because they are bizarre."

"Okay. I promise I'll call with happier occasions for conversation."

"That would make me happy. No one calls me."

It wasn't at all clear whether it would actually make him happy or not, but I no longer felt guilty for what I'd insinuated.

■

The old hag jerks him around, tightening her grip around his neck. Dressed in a thin, transparent blouse made of white satin. She strangles him scrupulously, with grave attention, with glee. A diaphanous, satin death. But just when you think you've escaped your earthly sins, she lets go, slowly, delicately, with infinite care. You shake out of your nightmare, you wake up in front of the Folder.

On the cover, the date of birth. In a different time, that was the age of the wise; now it's the age of Viagra. The old von Aschenbach, who was embarrassed even by the makeup with which his barber rejuvenated him, could never have imagined what wonders would have been waiting for him in the next century. A time of infinite possibility and infinite substitutions. Substitutions of kidneys and livers, of new noses and lips and new eyebrows, new eye color and gender, all at the client's behest. Pills for your head and your feet, for narcolepsy and insomnia, for insanity, colds, and for cancer, for impotence and for envy, baldness and rheumatism, heart transplants and hair transplants and retina transplants, hearing and seeing and walking aids. Nothing is lost, everything is transformed and can be replaced. The dead have finally found their proper utility; last will and testaments foresee the transference not just of assets but also of organs, the spleen, the liver, the kidneys, and the soul, all ready to serve a new body and to become new themselves.

How did all this time go by?

The exile had accepted this new place and time; he'd assimilated to the fax and the Internet and the cellular telephone, the bank account and flying saucers, religious and erotic sects, education through the Bible and pornography; however, he'd remained in a past named Lu.

Why would Mynheer Pieter Peeperkorn have fascinated him so, when he was the total opposite of everything Peeperkorn was or could ever have been; why would he have reanimated Peter Gaşpar? And why had he never forgotten that conversation with the pudgy Izy, thousands of years ago, in the dark and dank basement, when he divulged his admiration for Jesus' chosen people, even though he himself would always remain religiously indifferent? What was he missing and what would explain his ever-unresolved need to become someone else? Someone less cautious, someone less remarkable. More rebellious, and not just in his thoughts, freer, and not just in his dreams, more versatile and hypocritical, more mysterious, more culpable and haunted by hostility. Someone more worthy of hate and compassion and the admiration of the masked people who surrounded him.

On top of the new earthy-gray folder on which destiny had written in large, red letters, GORA, there was a blue sheet of paper with Dr. Hostal's signature.

It seems that the coronary artery disease and the epigastric discomfort were unrelated. The angioplasty results show that there was a combination of a focalized and a diffused illness, which may have triggered a metabolic syndrome from the past, a state of hypercoagulation. Considering the risk factors of cardiovascular disease, the patient's arterial hypertension is borderline; borderline hypercholesteremia (and low HDL) is at a normal level; and borderline blood sugar.

Borderline! The Citizen of the Borderland Archipelago! The character might be read in the code of Borderland. On the line, on the borderline, nowhere! *Borderline!*

The Citizen of the Borderline had pulled the curtains. *Go to the zoo!* He was talking to himself. In the zoo of the street, he would meet others like himself. Instead, he stays at home, like a vehicle forgotten in the garage.

The coffee, the cereal bowl, the pills. On the TV screen, the mischief of his species, chess players competing with destiny.

Exercises, shower. The day begins. He'd won another day, nothing could compare with that performance, his fellow citizens in the New World would have him believe. They were right. A new day. The farce of being, the wonder of existence.

■

He was watching the screen, the table where the ponderous Peter was playing chess, with the glass of Coca-Cola nearby. It was late.

It was late, but I'd defied the hour.

"Did you read the piece about the angioplasty?"

"Where would I have read it?"

"Today, in the *New York Times*. Front page news."

"I don't get the papers anymore. I would only read old newspapers, if I could, starting with the year of my birth. From seven decades ago."

"That could be amusing. But you would miss all the new medical discoveries."

"Such as?"

"Such as these, what do they call them . . . stents."

"I've heard that word before."

"They came up with a new model a few years ago, coated with some kind of substance that impedes further buildup in the arteries. But now they are saying the old ones were better."

"They gave me the new ones, the ones impregnated by the saliva of Mephistopheles. I had insisted on whatever was newest, most efficient. Dr. Hostal agreed. He's a trustworthy man."

"Eh, don't get melodramatic. In two months they'll discover that the new ones are actually better."

"The most important thing, however, is that, after you rot, those little amulets will still survive. The archeologists will be able to identify you."

"How many did they give you?"

"Seven. A magic number."

I was lucky. Gora was in a mood to talk.

"You know, Palade was your student. They refused his passport but gave it to him after a year, on the second try. In response to pressure from the Americans. They gave it to him begrudgingly. That seems strange."

"What's so strange about it? I know what you're insinuating."

"I'm not insinuating anything; I'm asking. I'm trying to cure myself of the illness with which we all left that place: suspicion."

"That would have made me an informant, too, no? They gave me a passport, as well."

"You were a different case. Ludmila's relations could have intervened. Maybe they were the ones who made the deal."

"And you . . . you came here with a passport, too."

"They wanted to get rid of me. The secret police files have proof of that. I had uncovered informants among neighbors and friends and relations. I was naïve; now I'm suspicious."

"I remember when you first came. Palade had told me you'd arrived and that he gave you my phone number. But you didn't call for about six months. When I asked how you were, you said you were jet-lagged. I appreciated your humor, but you seemed disoriented and lost."

"I was. I'd lost my ability to speak. When I was leaving, at the airport."

"I remember, you were saying that when they stamped your passport with the exit visa, they also cut out your tongue. We all went through that."

"Not all of us. Palade came here as a young man, and Professor Gora already knew the language."

"I sent you to my friend Koch. Izy Koch."

"You were right about him; he wouldn't take my money. But I can see this conversation isn't very interesting; you're getting bored."

"It's interesting, but yes, it's boring me. I'm happy for this country's nonsense and goodwill. I suspect that you're also satisfied with it."

"I am. I thought I might amuse you with my question about Palade. I don't know if I ever told you that we were high school classmates. We went on to different things."

"You never told me."

"Or that I met with him once, after he returned from his visit back to the Homeland, not long before he was assassinated?"

"Not that, either."

"He told me that he'd seen Lu, I don't know if he told you about it."

This was the final bait. Gora hesitates, deciding whether to lie or not.

"He never told me."

"At the theater. *The Master and Margarita*."

"Did he tell you what she was wearing?"

If that was an ironic question, then it meant he was mocking me and that I'd lost my last chance to challenge him.

"Was it a black, low-cut dress? Or something casual? Did she have her hair up in a bun?"

I didn't answer. There was a stony silence. Then, abruptly, Gora flared up again.

"A great doctor, the Australian. He fixed me; I'm all brand new! I can just take it all from the top and repeat all the same nonsense. Are you still there, or have you gotten tired?"

He'd taken on the role of the senile, old man. He was probably enjoying himself, taking notes.

"I'm here. You're right, I'm not so young, either. The invisible hag is waiting in the corner, with gifts of all kinds. Cancer, heart attack, Alzheimer's, epidemics. Fires, terrorism. At your disposal."

"Yes, it's a huge offer. It comes when you least expect it. At night, when the forest darkens. It darkens, but it doesn't sleep. Even here in the city, I still see woods outside my windows. Monkhood. Willy-nilly apparitions."

A long pause. It gave me courage.

"And you really weren't in touch?"

"We weren't. I wrote to Lu when I arrived. She never wrote back. I wrote again. She never answered the phone, either. I didn't insist. And I never really looked for my fellow countrymen. Even now, I avoid them, as you well know."

"Because of this?"

"Not only."

"And you've known nothing about Lu since you left?"

"I recapitulated, going over the past; I didn't find much. Small trivialities, oddities, ambiguities, brief discrepancies. Trivialities. There were things to ponder, to be sure. Nothing important or drastic, however."

"And then?"

"I was surprised by her arrival, but I didn't see her. There was no point. We see each other in the past. The Iron Curtain was a good curtain, sparing us of a lot of things. You worry about what you left behind; you receive no news. You can't simply board a plane and land in the locus of all that mystery, to see with your own eyes everything that's being hidden from you. But it's better this way, isn't it? You're spared all blame, aren't you? What do you say to that? You're an expert in fortunate and unfortunate and nonexistent faults; what do you think?"

This time he was attacking directly; he was asking questions and didn't wait for answers. There were only questions boiling with his fury.

"In any case, now I understand. I'm armed; I'm renewed. With the circulation to my heart and brain so much improved, I can understand. These stents were a magical bargain! They restored the circulation to all of my organs, the major and minor ones; they gave me a second chance."

He was speaking quickly, with fury and speed.

He was the winner alongside his pale Andalusian, under her young gaze, touching those gloves and her young hands. One moment was enough to bring you back; the skin shrivels, the body is dry, the arms livid. Long, old arms and legs. Fragile bones that powder at the first touch. The dust of the skeleton that had been your youth. But I wouldn't have been able to break Gora's spell, no matter what I might have said.

"I was turned back from the gates of heaven! It was a postponement. I returned to find out what was left to find out. After this, I'll bet they'll take me in. And now, I have to go. Excuse me but Boltanski is waiting for me."

"The Russian?"

"The Ukrainian. The Soviet. You know him?"

"Yes, I know him. The chauffeur of all the Eastern European exiles. Where are you going?"

"He's taking me to Penn Station."

"But where are you going?"

"I'm going to meet Avakian. I've finally secured a meeting with Bedros Avakian. Always busy, always worried, that one, but he finally agreed to this one favor. I have some questions about Peter and Tara. And about Deste. Supposedly she's started a fashion house in Sarajevo. I heard that or dreamed it, I don't know anymore; I'm getting old. Senility. The interrupted story. Interesting, isn't it?"

"You could say that."

"As you can see, the New World is a great concern of mine."

I remained on the line for some time, heard his voice again; he was speaking normally, as if everything else that had been said until then had simply been swept away, or just wasn't important.

All that was left was for me to ask him what he was reading.

"What book am I reading? I'm not reading anything. I can't concentrate."

"There's not a single book on your table? I don't believe it."

"The news, some papers, folders. No books."

"And on the nightstand?"

"What nightstand?"

"How should I know, the nightstand near your bed."

"Ah, yes. Rilke. The readers' sect is diminishing, but not dead. Thank God."

"Rilke? Poetry? You still read poetry?"

"Not really. It's a collection of selected works. Short essays, some verse. About love. The protection of one's own solitude, and the protection of the other's solitude! If you try to possess the other's solitude, or try to give your own away, it all goes to hell. That's the idea. You remember? A good marriage is one where each partner is the protector of the other's solitude. Something like that."

"But that's referring to marriage, not to love."

"Some say that love is an error of allocation; the poet is attempting to instruct the reader on how to maintain a contractual love. To watch over the other person's solitude, to protect it, rather, or to leave the other person at the gate of his or her own solitude. A solitude dressed festively, one that comes out of the vast darkness. Not at all badly put. He was young, the old poet."

He seemed to have reread the text recently, unsatisfied with what he'd found.

He was a winner; he had Lu and his friends on his shelves, who kept vigil over his aristocratic solitude, its civilized hypocrisies.

"Coupling means empowering the surrounding loneliness. When someone gives himself with complete abandon to someone else, it's over; nothing remains, there's nothing. Rilke was young then."

He'd stopped speaking for the moment; he had probably also picked up one of the many colored folders, bringing it near, the way you might bring your ear to the ground, to listen for the oncoming train; he listened for a second to the nocturne of the lunatics, then leisurely put the folder back in its place, reconnecting with the wanton world.

"When two people give themselves entirely to one another, when they no longer belong to themselves . . . "

I realized that now he was reading, either from a book, or some notebook of his own.

"When the two give themselves entirely, in order to belong entirely to each other, their feet leave the ground. And living together becomes a continuous failure. A continuous failure, what do you think of that?"

He was reading only because he'd been asked about his reading, and, as usual, he was addressing himself to someone absent. His voice was calm, normal.

■

The following weeks and months, I spoke at length with Augustin Gora about old age.

The subject didn't strike him as somber, not even after the confirmation, albeit in dubious circumstances, of the death of our younger friend, Peter Gaşpar. He didn't respond, either, when I confessed to him my suspicion that, after this recent and belated news, he would write his own obituary, who knows how true to his actual biography. It would have been presumptuous to assume, I added, that after our increasingly frequent conversations following Peter's death, I myself would have become the hero of a similar composition. He didn't answer; he returned to the subject of old age.

"Until the shock with the angioplasty, I never felt my age coming on. Without children, I ignored the speed of the calendar. Forty- and fifty-year anniversaries were registered and forgotten. The meeting with the doctors, with their machines and their hospital rooms, brought me to my senses. What followed was a tough year, a really tough year. The Nymphomaniac, as the departed called it, kept taunting me; I was living in constant tension. I felt, then, that the disease was a warning. That's what old age is, isn't it? Ever more acute awareness of fragility. Initiation in exhaustion, initiation in dying. Alert and hurried time pushing us every day and night closer to that beyond that horrifies us. As if all of life didn't come down to just that. Every new morning is a threshold to an unknown that could be anything, including the end."

He was right; illness prepares one for extinction. Without such preparations, you think you can prolong the ambiguity for as long as you want.

"Melancholy and the abyss? You look into the distance into which you'll splinter just as if you'd never been here at all, but routine is stronger. It returns you to the here and now. Your instincts are still alive and intact. You reenter the chaos that consumes time imperceptibly and ruthlessly."

"Just when the verdict is clearly pronounced, perception changes. The end of your journey is announced to you. Expiration. Just like with any product. The term of expiration, twenty-three years, thirty-four years, sixty-one years and three months and two weeks and five days. The tumor is incurable; you have six months to live. The last postponement. Today's doctors don't have the liberty to lie to you about the prognosis."

"Yes, and every day becomes a gift, ignored up to that point. You become aware of every moment, every leaf, every breeze, every page. You'd like to sip them, to hold them like this, endlessly, inside you. Were you scared? Are you still scared? Of the void, of the nothing that you become?"

"Then, yes. The surprise found me unprepared, it ravaged my insides. Now, less so. A little less. I'm calm."

"Bitterness helps, in the end? Fury, disillusionment, exhaustion, contempt for everything, not least of which for disgusting death?"

"Maybe. But fury is vital; it's not acceptance."

"And kindness? Serenity and gratitude. Resignation, surrender to destiny."

"Like an enlightenment? Candor, abandon? Like faith?"

"Faith promises hope. Unverifiable hope. Maybe we'll get to a point when we can verify hope."

"Palade wasn't a man of faith, but he believed in the transmigration of souls. Successive reincarnations."

"He's not alone. He claimed that he received coded signs. Those who don't receive them can't contradict him," said Gora, quietly.

I asked Gora to tell me what he saw out the window. He announced, first, what time it was: eight past four in the afternoon.

"We can't ignore the hour. We're talking about old age, death, and so, about time. The time of expiration."

After a pause, he added: "July. July 19."

I was waiting for him to announce the year, but he didn't. What did the nineteenth of July look like out his window, when so many people are born while others die, just like any other day?

He described a garden to me, then a green valley. A vital, vigorous green. And then further, a tall, verdant forest. In the garden facing the window, a family of wild turkeys. A mother and nine chicks, the father absent, at the library. Squirrels. Two young and timid deer. A fat, lazy cat.

"Paradise! Paradise, right?"

"Yes, but I'm not getting bored. I have my books on the shelf and my words inside me."

"They'll disappear."

"They'll no longer be my books? Or I will no longer be among them? Is that what you mean?"

"Do you envy those you'll leave behind? Are you sorry to leave?"

"Envy? Those who remain aren't immortal. They remain provisionally. When they disappear, they'll also be mentioned for a while. By relatives and friends, in books and photographs. Until the last trace is gone. It doesn't matter when. Yes, it makes you lightheaded to think about your loved ones. Even if you haven't seen them for a long time. You know that they are still here, somewhere. Our tiring sun will also disappear, won't it? Terrible, right?"

"Is there someone over there that you'd like to see again?"

"Oh, yes. My parents. From time to time. And others . . . in the same way, from time to time. If we keep them in mind, it's enough and it's more certain. Without depressing changes."

I asked him how he imagines the final moment. Extended to infinity, or brief, brief, like a spasm.

I believed myself resigned, calm, biologically calm, the way an interlocutor from the faraway land used to say, but it so happens that the thought of the final hour overwhelms me. Impotence, regret, the insurmountable, drained my vital energy instantly. Like in a sensual and doomed atonement, with no way out.

"I don't know, I haven't thought about the moment; it's an unbearable thought," Gora said, unconvinced.

We weren't talking about old age, actually, but about life. Old age was life slowed down, but still life. Enfeebled, diminished, but life nonetheless. Death doesn't exist without life.

"Material death? The perishable, the organic. What about transcendence? The prayers, the books, the manuscripts, the scores, the drawings that attempt to defy matter, even while they represent it. Mozart and Venice and Borges. All in vain?"

"Intensity. Not more futile than other futilities. Our privileged intensity. Our gift and our dedication."

"Like love?"

The question irritated him, I realized, hearing the angry shuffling of papers and eyeglasses hitting the table.

I retreated from the necrology with a kind of childhood sadness.

Even during the conversation with Gora, I bore inside me a ten-year-old boy, or maybe a slightly older adolescent, although I remembered perfectly the hesitations and the exaltations and the failures from eighteen, from twenty-five years old and those that came later, much, much later. The boy, or adolescent, persisted, even if in another body that was the same, with another mind, which was also the same. It was as if everything had happened yesterday. When did it all come apart? Has it all really come apart, with no possibility of prolonging what was there?

When Lu asked me a week ago if I want to allow, through a testament, the pulling of the plug from the machines that maintain artificial life, the way that she intended to do, I answered no, no matter what. She won't be able to disconnect her last victim from the sinister torture-preservation machines; my testament will deny this redemption. Not because I would hope for a miracle that would block extinction through some new miraculous medicine, or through who knows what incredible natural redress of the organism, but because the disease, even in its extreme form, an unconscious state, still seemed to me to be life. Who could specify with all certainty how absolute is the apparently total amnesia of a dying man? Palade would say I was right, he actually believed in a codified world, in mysterious formulas, in open, unresolved transitions, in magical and unpredictable metamorphoses. Izy Koch would also say I was right; he often said that nothing existed except life and that was all; this was the belief of the elders; this motivates our neuroses, our restlessness, those of us who are denied second chances, exiled unavoidably and without recourse into a predictable direction.

Lu appeared troubled by my insistence, but categorical about her own disappearance, when and how it will come. We accepted each other's every wish, formulated in legal terms and with notarized signatures.

That following morning, I showed her the imprint that our heads left in the pillow during the night, and I suggested that she imagine the pillow with the imprint of the one who suddenly died and was removed from the room. The one with whom she'd shared her bed and her time. All at once time is deserted; the room is deserted, and only the pillow preserves the trace that cannot be preserved.

"Can you imagine it?"

"I can, but I don't want to. It was too great a detour until we found each other."

Her look confirmed that the latecomer had no escape. No, I had no escape and didn't want any.

She'd remained receptive to the ambiguous warnings and to the dark foreboding, but she lived a juvenile regeneration. She came out of the illness and the first ailments of the exile as if emerging from convalescence; that's how she described it. Her beautiful hands were waiting for the novice that I was.

Liberated from the Baroque anguish of maladjustment to the real, she became more real, in her fortifying ardor, more beautiful in her acuity, now free of tension.

Time was patient with our detours and now slyly slowed its pace. We each ignored the loneliness of the other and found ourselves in the solitude that bound us and vitalized us. The longed-for danger felt after that first and last visit to the suspects' attic.

The ephemeral didn't scare me. I looked at the imprint left on the pillow, after the night that had died. Lu was showing me our shadows alongside each other on the white wall, both of us happy for the daylight that would scatter them. We beat the disheveled pillow, to make the trace disappear.

We didn't want imprints and memories. Lu had accepted the captive's decision to defend herself against herself, and himself against himself, even if in vain.